HEART OF DESIRE

A HOCKEY ROMANCE NOVEL

THE HEART SERIES
BOOK ONE

LIANA TIAMZON

EDITED BY
ASHLEY TE

COVER DESIGN BY
AUBREY TE

LT

This is a work of fiction. Names, characters, places, and incidents either are the product of the author's imagination or are used fictitiously.

HEART OF DESIRE – A HOCKEY ROMANCE NOVEL

Copyright © 2023 by Liana Tiamzon

Resemblance to actual persons and things living or dead, locales, or events is entirely coincidental.

Editor: Ashley Te

Cover Designer: Aubrey Te

ISBN: 979-8-9886898-0-5

CONTENT WARNING

DEDICATION

For the people who are just born to fight.

To my friends, Angie, Gabi, and Addi who gave me support and listened to my plot twists and gave me encouragement.

To my cousin, Ryanne who kept me writing.

To my editor, Ashley and cover designer, Aubrey that are the best team I could've ever asked for I love you, thank you for the patience and hard work.

To my parents, if you are reading this, please close the book and throw it away. This will scar you for eternity.

-Liana

UPCOMING BOOKS BY LIANA TIAMZON

THE HEART SERIES

THE HEART OF REDEMPTION
MARGO & LIAM

THE HEART OF ABANDON
VERINA & CHRIS

THE HEART OF MERIT
JULIETTE & NEIL

TABLE OF CONTENTS

22. ADRIANNA
23. ADRIANNA
24. ADRIANNA
25. GRAYSON
26. ADRIANNA
27. GRAYSON
28. GRAYSON
29. ADRIANNA
30. GRAYSON
31. ADRIANNA
30. GRAYSON
31. ADRIANNA
32. GRAYSON
33. ADRIANNA
34. GRAYSON
35. GRAYSON
36. GRAYSON
37. ADRIANNA
38. GRAYSON
39. ADRIANNA
40. ADRIANNA
41. GRAYSON
42. ADRIANNA
43. GRAYSON
44. GRAYSON
45. GRAYSON
46. GRAYSON
47. ADRIANNA
48. GRAYSON
49. GRAYSON
50. ADRIANNA

PLAYLIST

Feeling Whitney- Post Malone
Love on the Brain – Rihanna
Die for You- The Weeknd
Salted Wound- Sia
I Wanna Be Yours- Arctic Monkeys
God's Favorite- Nessa Barrett
Talk to Myself- Nessa Barrett
The Heart Wants What It Wants- Selena Gomez
You Don't Own Me- Lesley Gore
I Wish You Would- Taylor Swift
Where do we go now? - Gracie Abrams
Daddy Issues- The Neighbourhood
Only Love Can Hurt Like This- Paloma Faith
Chasing Pavements- Adele
You're Losing me (From the Vault)- Taylor Swift
Happier- Olivia Rodrigo
Family Line- Conan Gray
Million Dollar Man- Lana Del Rey
Don't Blame Me- Taylor Swift
Forever & Always (Taylor's Version)- Taylor Swift
Opposite- Sabrina Carpenter

Electric Touch (From the Vault) - Taylor Swift
Meddle About - Chase Atlantic
Nobody Gets Me- SZA
You're On Your Own, Kid- Taylor Swift
Sober- Selena Gomez
Same Old Love- Selena Gomez
right where you left me- Taylor Swift
mirrorball- Taylor Swift
Love in the Dark- Adele
Heaven- Julia Michaels
I Don't Wanna Live Forever- ZAYN & Taylor Swift
lie- Nessa Barret
dying on the inside- Nessa Barrett
Call Out My Name- The Weeknd

CHAPTER 1

ADRIANNA

I am perfect. So perfect that I can't even look at myself in the mirror and think there is a single tiny flaw, if I even dared to sneak a glance.

I was born perfect. I was raised to be perfect. I've known nothing but perfection. I'm sagacious as I've been taught, I'm as gentle and as calm as I would like them to think.

Everyone had known of my perfection, and I have never dared to even question my birthright.

"Adrianna..." I had heard banging from my front door as I jolted to take a breath.

Clockwork.

It was Saturday night, and just like clockwork, he would show up. I get up taking slow steps to my front door, my eyes shutting for a brief moment. Before opening the door, his eyes gleamed, and his mouth stretched into a smile.

"Brooks!" I let my grin reach my ears. I threw my arms around his neck with fake enthusiasm as he hugged me back.

He kisses the top of my head, "I've missed you, *my love.*"

I let go of his body as he grins, "Are you sure no one can find us here?" He asks as I laugh, my eyes looking down at the floor.

"Well, I would hope so, I bought this place just for us."

In the past year, I had bought a house in New Crest for Brooks and me to sneak off to every weekend. There was really no limit to my father's AmEx. And as my secret boyfriend for almost nine months, he had wanted it to be somewhere special and private.

I could practically feel his eyes burning on me. "My love, I doubt your father would even see that dent you put in his credit card." He tried to reassure me.

I frown, *he barely notices whether I'm home.* I thought to myself.

He would kiss me at any moment.

Clockwork.

He leans down and kisses me, his mouth traveling down my neck as I pull away.

"Is... anything wrong?" He probed as I looked up at him finally asking after dealing with my deflections for so long.

"Are you ashamed of me?" I ask while also, rubbing my hands together.

I take a seat on the edge of the window seat.

"What?" He laughs. "Why would I ever be ashamed of you?"

Brooks grins, "I love you." Kissing the corners of my lips and my ear, I pull away again.

"You're being ridiculous, Adrianna... I've been waiting for you since eighth grade, why the fuck do you think I would be ashamed of you?" He stands up as I frown.

He's right, I was being stupid... of course.

"You're right. I'm sorry." I took a breath as he smiled, kneeling down to place a kiss on my lips again.

"You promised me a night I would remember, didn't you?" He beams as I swallow my nerves.

My heart beats faster than ever. His hand creeps around my inner thigh as I jolt, slightly pulling away.

"Come on baby... I've been waiting my whole life for this moment." He almost growled gripping my thigh tighter, I wince at his actions.

I let out a painful sound as he forced his hand up my thigh again. "Brooks, enough." I protested as he smiled wickedly, his hand traveling up my shirt. "Brooks. No!" I pushed him away, his black hair swaying in front of his unsatisfied eyes.

I felt like I'd been violated in every way.

He stands up, his gaze accusatory, "What the hell, Adrianna! You said you promised me a good ass night!" He yelled.

I pull further away while covering myself up with a jacket.

"Yes!" I yell with a rasp, "By finally telling you that I love you! Not to have sex with you!" I picked my bag up from behind the door.

Irritation flooded his eyes, "So, you brought me all the way to fucking New Crest for this?!" He slams his fist on the door.

I jolt at his sudden outburst, never really seeing this side of him, "You made me fucking wait, for you to tell me that you love me?" He laughs harshly.

God, I feel like a damn fool.

"What? So, you just wanted sex?" I let my voice break as he suddenly went silent at the realization of what he had just said.

"You just wanted sex from me, so you drove two hours here every Saturday night, for *sex?!?*" I say it with a pained expression.

I practically felt like I had been slapped, Brooks and I were in a relationship, yes but it never left like it, I never thought of it as genuine or even real.

He breathed out, "Adrianna, that's not what I meant at all. You want to tell me you love me?" He tried smiling warmly.

Dick bag.

"Go ahead." He swallowed, "I'm listening."

I smile, putting my Chanel stilettos on, "Okay Brooks, listen to this, I don't ever want to talk to you or fucking see you ever again." I pause, pulling my phone out of my bag, "If you ever come by my house, I'll tell Steve and Carl to personally hang you and feed you to the canines."

I open the door letting the cold breeze freshen my face. I feel him take a step closer, "Adrianna, at least let me take you home...

it's freezing out there." He offers as I step outside, hearing his point. I flinch.

It was atrocious weather.

I come back inside crossing my arms together, "You should leave. This is my house. You can see yourself out, while I fetch my driver to get me." I asserted as he looked up at me almost seeing if I would take the bone to bring it back to him like a good dog.

He stares at me for a moment, like he was wishing for something as I gave him a nasty look.

A moment of silence passed, "Get out." I urged sternly once more as he opened the door hurrying out, got into one of his many sports cars, and left.

T
t was only about three more minutes until I got to my house in Hawthorne. I sat in the back of the small black car that I hoped would not catch any attention. "Oh James, I can't thank you enough for giving me a ride home." I swallowed as he nodded cooly.

"You won't tell father, will you?" I took a breath.

He laughed, "Adrianna, you can't sneak off like this, your father could be worried sick."

He drove slowly as we reached the front of my house. "You act like he cares, James." I assert gently as he smiled lightly while opening the door. I jumped out of the car, before he drove off. The lights were dimmed in the streets. It looked like everyone in the neighborhood was sleeping.

Though I doubt it because all the parents that lived here are workaholics. Everything was perfect, the silence, the stars, and my easy way in my house. But of course, there was always a flaw in my plan, and it was always *him*.

Grayson Nicholas Prince.

Hawthorne University's silver star.

Is there a direct correlation between douchebags and athletes? Case in point, Grayson Prince is the bane of my existence.

He walked. Sorry, no. Strutted, that's the word.

He struts the halls of Hawthorne University like his classes wouldn't even dare to start without him there.

Entitled.

All men wanted to be him; most women wanted him... exception of me. If I dated a talking hockey stick, I think dating Grayson Prince would be the equivalence.

Although he was only really tolerable in his natural habit of the hockey arena, where I don't hear the banging noise of his voice cracking my skull open.

I ignore him, lifting the potted plant where the spare key would usually lie, my heart stopped as a voice interrupted my thoughts.

"Pretty late to be out, Dove."

Dove. I hated that nickname, ever since we could talk, I hated it.

I hated him.

"And it's pretty late for me to deal with your bullshit, Prince," I say swiftly as he lets out a light chuckle.

I turn around slowly to be greeted by his smug face, his blonde sweaty hair, and his... *his*... oh my God, his abs.

Snap out of it.

He settles to a smirk that's been haunting my head for years. As my luck would have it, all I was told was that I was intelligent, charming, and beautiful. A piece of art.

Until I was told I wasn't.

"Prince, how about you give us both a break, hand over my keys, and let me go home in peace just this once." I glared as he looked at me, his dark eyes examining.

He was waiting for me to break eye contact.

"I'm desperate, Prince, come on." I try to steal the keys from him, but he only comes closer to me, I look up as he holds a superior height.

Looking down at me as if he owned me.

He licks his lips placing his hand on the nape of my neck.

I should mind this, but I don't.

He smirks, "Oh, but I love it when you get into trouble, princess. It's so out of fucking character for you to be caught in a slip-up."

My eyes narrow at his, "If I throw a stick would you leave me alone?" Grayson's face was only filled with amusement.

A challenge.

His gaze dropped down to my body, and I felt a shiver run down my back, I felt the hairs on the nape of my neck stand up.

Ignoring my words, he forms a scowl "Showing your father that you aren't his perfect little angel?"

I swallowed, he read me like a billboard. Like I was a flashing sign on the highway. "Oh, but my father will believe his little angel... much more than you and your family."

He laughs, backing off.

"Right."

I fold my arms, "My family is honorable, unlike yours, we don't do dirty business." I snapped back as he leaned on the stone wall.

"Dirty business makes us what we are." He smiles wickedly.

"And what exactly is that?" I calmly turned around to face him again, "Dirty?" I smirk as he clenches his jaw, walking towards me.

"Rich."

He puts the keys in his pocket, "We are richer than anyone in the state... putting you in *second*. Always a *second* step behind. Those words should be familiar to you."

He smiles brightly, "Maybe that's why your little boyfriend Brooks always had you for seconds, after his full course fuck session with Maya... He drives two hours to a cute little house in New Crest for his cute little virgin dessert."

My heart stung like a million shards of glass just stabbed me. I felt like dying at that very moment. But I was trained to never show weakness and I'll be damned if I ever showed weakness to Grayson Prince.

"But I see you still have your ring." He smirks as I roll my eyes, pulling my hand away from his viewpoint.

"You're cruel. And evil. You're a monster!" I smiled, "Is that what you want me to tell you?" My smile dies slowly to a conniving expression.

"I've been using Brooks since the moment I let him in between my legs." I snapped. I shouldn't need to lie to win, but all is fair in hatred and competition.

So honorable Adrianna.

His jaw clenched as his eyes turned a little darker, and his abs flexed a bit more, "Is it so bad that I want him inside of me every Saturday night?" I whispered coolly, near his ear.

I smirked, "It shouldn't bother you that he makes me feel so good." I reach down to lightly touch his bare chest with my delicate fingers, lighting touching his figure so rigid and sculpted. Like a God, he was the perfect combination of heaven and hell. He tensed under my touch.

My fingers ran down to his abs as he tightened his core, his eyes never leaving mine. He was cold, it was freezing outside, and yet he was sweating and wearing no shirt.

I noticed a scar on the side of his torso, my fingers pausing.

"I like Brooks' hands on me and especially his lips on every part of my body," I muttered as he closed his eyes for a moment. I finally dragged my hand down to his pocket to retrieve my keys, a corner of my lips curved up.

Before pulling away he gripped my wrist, tightly and smirked, "You would think that being so rich you could afford a better hiding spot for your keys, *Dove.*" He sneered as he let go of my wrist.

I swallowed. My pulse hammered as my hand burned at his touch. My legs felt like jelly and the insides of my thighs were fresh with a sudden warmth.

He leaned down to whisper in my ear, "I doubt Brooks was

that good... girls that have fucked him before told me that he had a shrimp for a dick, while they were moaning my name." He glowers.

My mouth watered and my underwear soaked at his hot breath that made me shiver. I smelled nothing but his minty breath, and his natural musk smell, it was like oxygen filling my brain.

I would never let him know that.

Never let Grayson get under my skin.

I would never admit to him the way he made me feel but I couldn't deny that he affected me. My fingers itched at the thought to touch him once more.

He pulls away, his breath missing from my neck, and he starts to walk back across the street to his house. I felt my stomach turn as I quickly walk to unlock my front door, turning back to sneak a peek at him one last time.

He picks up his basketball and dribbles for a bit before making a shot. I never knew he was good at other sports, though it would make sense since he was the description of a try-hard athlete.

He puts on a sweatshirt.

What a shame.

Fuck. Get a grip, Adrianna.

He leans on a wall, almost as if he was waiting for someone... but no one ever came.

Instead, he went inside his house, only to come back out with his keys and an angry expression.

I couldn't sleep, overthinking my night away.

As I tossed and turned in the dark, my mind was in endless whirlpools of thoughts, and I could hardly sleep. It felt like a wall was closing in on me, and I caught my breath. I just couldn't shake off the vulnerable yet surprisingly cool image of Grayson. It was a contradiction I had never seen in him before. Was arguing with family a regular occurrence?

But why?

How?

They were the crown jewel of the damn state. Always known to never be anything but extraordinary.

But in a way, I always knew there was something more to the family than what they let on.

From an early age, my parents always warned me about the shady deals that fueled the Prince family, their nefarious professions, and their empire. Despite the family's graceful appearance, their reputation was not admirable. Despite our daily interactions, I had never once seen a genuine smile on Grayson's face. There was always an unspoken rivalry between us, and a relentless game of outsmarting the other seemed to define our relationship. I mean... it could always be that he wasn't fond of seeing me, since it had always been a competition between us.

Who got the highest grades?

Who was better at sports?

Who got under whose skin first?

Any tears that fell in front of the other's eyes was an act of weakness and it was failure dripped into a cup of a sense of accomplishment for the other to hold and brag.

The pain in my heart was like a million shards of glass piercing me, each weighing more than I could bear. This was a moment of despair, and the call of oblivion seemed seductively approaching. But my training instilled in me an indomitable spirit, creating a rigged surface that masked the chaos underneath. And I vowed never, under any circumstances, to reveal even the slightest bit of weakness to Prince Grayson."

I had never cried in front of him. I had never cried in front of anyone.

A perfect person doesn't cry.

And I was an example set at Hawthorne, society watched us kids like hawks, judging our every move and our every decision made by our family. Our legacy is written, and we don't get a say in what we do.

Our future is written for us.

I get up to turn on my lights, walking out to hear rusting in the downstairs office. I put on my glasses and walked down the stairs, only to find my father with his desk light on and him going through paperwork like it was the middle of the day.

"Father!" I turned on the lights, and he looked utterly annoyed, as he continued to then type on his computer, it was obvious he ignored me.

I walk closer, but of course I attempt to knock down one of his books that was set on a small coffee table.

"Yes, sunshine." He looks up for a moment, finally acknowledging me.

"It's three in the morning. Why are you still working?" I let myself fall sideways on one of the chairs next to the fireplace.

"Everyone is doing everything wrong, and I just need to make sure that everything is perfect." He stressed as I looked through the rest of the books flipping through the pages mindlessly.

"I'm sure you're just stressed and that everything is fine." I encouraged him as he sent me an all-knowing scowl.

He takes out his glasses, and places them on the table, taking a sip of his coffee. "Why are you awake, Adrianna?" He watched me with calculating eyes.

I lick my lips looking around, "I couldn't sleep with all the noise you're making, Captain." I stood up.

He frowned, interlocking his fingers infant of him, the look he famously gave to all of his employees, "Staying up late is not good for your condition." I knew he was going to bring it up, he always did, he knew I didn't like talking about my health problems.

It made me feel fragile.

"I'll be okay." I probe as he nods his head.

"I just want you in bed at a reasonable time." He says plainly with no emotion.

"I can't sleep," I say once again with a bit of attitude in my voice.

He lets his gaze fall out on the window, across the road to

the Prince's Estate, "You are sure it has nothing to do with…" By the look on his face, I had an inkling at who is he was alluding to.

What?

My eyes widen at his assumption.

"The help likes to talk Adrianna, and the topic happened to be about my daughter and Grayson Prince being spotted outside of my house getting pretty close." He verbalized as I stood there absolutely lost for words.

Oh God no!

"It's not what you think!" I defended myself.

He frowns, "Perhaps not." He analyzes.

"Father, you have nothing to worry about, he is foul! You have always told me that his whole family are roaches!" I look out the window of his house.

Why should I doubt my own father?

"Good." He says sternly as I stiffen within his disapproving gaze.

"If I even hear one word that you were conversing with that boy after and outside of college hours—" He began to rage.

What if I did?

"—I won't!" I hear my heart beating fast.

Silence rushed through the room as I grabbed the doorknob. "I'm going to bed." I swallowed as he relaxed.

"Adrianna Elaine." He muttered as I turned back to look at him.

"I don't want you near them." He says in a low, warning tone that sent shivers down my spine.

A flash of the phone camera assaults my eyes as Juliette snaps a picture of Verina.

"I definitely think that suits you better than the black one." Verina nods at Juliette as she frowns at the mirror, my eyes locked on the floor as they talk.

"What do you think, Anna?" Verina's voice jumps an octave higher to grab my attention. I realized that I had zoned out the majority of the conversation, once I took a look at Verina who looked at me in a way that questioned her whole decision.

I didn't remember what we were talking about, so I spew off an acceptable answer that would usually be brushed upon.

"Yeah, the heels look good," I mutter as they both spin to look at me.

"We were talking about the dress, Anna," Verina said with graceful simplicity as I finally stood up.

"Okay, I'm sorry. I've just been so... distracted." I swing my arms around them as they pull me in for a hug.

"It's fine. We all have days where our minds are just scattered." Juliette chides.

Verina moves past the situation quickly, like always her mind was running faster than she did.

"Can any of you go to that charity benefit that my parents are hosting tonight?" She trailed off, giving a smile before continuing.

By the looks of her needy face, I could tell she wanted company.

"I don't want to go alone and answer questions like 'How is college going?' or if 'I have a plan' when they know I am not interested in medicine at all." She voices as I gave an apologetic look.

Verina Antionette Du Pont.

The daughter of Florian and Alicia Du Pont. Her mother pushes the idea of Verina becoming a surgeon as she herself is the most well-known surgeon in New York, especially Hawthorne.

It's hard to make any of Hawthorne society's parents proud

when all of them have completed every milestone in existence.

"Why don't you ask Xavier to spend time with you?" I ask as she scowls.

"Oh yes, ask my brother to spend time with me at a charity benefit where he is probably flirting with the male nurse population." She mused.

"Is your father going?" Juliette questions while taking a seat in the cushioned chair provided by the large dressing room.

"Of course! God forbid my father would miss a great opportunity to showcase his perfect family by going to support a charity with his upcoming election." She broadcasted with her hands up in the air, twirling around until she sat on the other cushion, gently pulling off the straps of her heels.

A frown forms on her face right after, "I would die to go to the fashion showcase in Glendale. I would much rather show off the pieces I've worked on."

I smile at her as she twirls around, "Exhibit A." She shows off her outfit.

She wore a pastel pink skirt made of silk, remnants of jewels that cost more than most people's mortgage. It connected to her stitched, white, tubed top with accents of diamonds, to finish off the look she wore beautiful Chanel heels with a matching purse.

Juliette's mouth drops, "No way you made that."

Verina's smile widens, "Just imagine us in Paris, drinking champagne while you all sit in the front row at my fashion show!" She thundered, with the twinkle in her eyes that were always there.

Her frown comes back within a minute at the realization that her parents would never approve of that future.

She looks toward Juliette silently questioning again, who shakes her head, "Sorry V, I have soccer practice."

Verina whines, "You *always* have soccer practice."

When all of us were in the third grade, Juliette told us that her father forced her to take up soccer to help her relieve stress during test weeks.

Only when the test was over, her father also told her she didn't have to continue, but she continued to play due to stress about midterms.

Then finals rolled around, she was practically juggling any type of sphere-like figure. She grew to love it as a hobby, and even played for Hawthorne University.

She doesn't take any game lightly, as an Ivy League college we were always *almost* under control.

Juliette and I look at each other before laughing, "Thank God for it because the team needs all the help it could get. Their conditioning sucks and they spend no out of campus time on drills, they probably get wasted every weekend."

Whenever our sports teams beat Harvard or Yale, the whole campus grows team spirit, of course, Juliette not only shows that she can be ruthless on the soccer field but on the whiteboards whenever there is an academic decathlon.

I never expected Juliette to excel in soccer. Sure, she excelled in many things but her passion for soccer was not in my bingo card.

Juliette never talked about her achievements on the soccer field, even when I knew she worships players like Lionel Messi, she never shows more than her book at hand. Unlike Verina who would rather be caught dead than be at any type of athletic venture.

Juliette Belle Livingston.

The daughter of Brian Livingston. Now Juliette was a hard nut to crack. We never really knew what we would get when it came to her.

She never liked getting involved with anyone other than her close friends. She kept to herself and only talked where she saw fit to include information derived from her highly observational skills.

Ironically, she would sometimes make it known to anyone who could spot her fiery red hair from a mile away that she was ready to party.

The days that her freckles would sparkle under the disco ball.

That's when we knew it was time to approach her about a party or a study session or even wish her good luck on her very needed soccer games.

"Why can't you just like relax and bring them to a spa, even pay for their facial?" Verina adds as I roll my eyes at the two conversing.

Juliette doesn't even bother to answer as she reaches in her bag for a book.

"There you go again, reading." Verina folds her arms together at the copy of *The Bell Jar.*

"Doesn't your head ever hurt?" Verina turns to look at the mirror, her eyes on Juliette in the reflection. Juliette doesn't bother to lift her head to look at Verina.

"Your nose always snuggled up in a book or under your sleeve." She continues.

It was true, Juliette always avoided conversations by whipping out a book and never fails to get lost in her own world of literature.

I enjoyed reading too don't get me wrong, but Juliette tends to live through the characters' lives, and she never likes talking about it, but her father is very overbearing.

"Nothing is wrong with that; I quite enjoy the company of words on a page," Juliette says with ease as Verina yawns.

"Is your dad coming to the event?" I ask Juliette as she shrugs, "I think the team has practice tonight as well. So highly unlikely he will be attending the event."

"Great, my dad won't have anyone to talk to." Verina jokes.

Juliette's father, Brian Livingston, is the private university's beloved hockey coach. How he could handle teaching about forty men how to do twirls around the ice and hit a puck into a net is beyond me.

"Why are you so out of it today?" Verina questions while taking a seat next to me. I realize that I barely have spoken.

"Is this about Brooky?" Juliette teased.

I laughed slyly, "No, I'm afraid that ship has been sunk by an iceberg." Both the girl's eyes dawned and widened.

"And you didn't think to tell us?!" They both scream in unison as I shush them.

"I told Margo and Margo tells you guys everything!" I defended myself as they nodded in agreement, "Speaking of which, why the hell isn't she here yet?"

Juliette's eyes shot up with a curve on her lips, "There's a rumor going around that Margo probably slept with Liam last night." Juliette calmly said as Verina and I almost dropped to the floor.

"What?" We asked once more as Juliette's face turned bright red.

"I said *probably!*" She defends herself, her eyes crawling their way back to the ink on paper.

"Liam who?" I questioned fearfully.

Juliette laughs, "Which other Liam is hot enough that lives in Hawthorne that can bag the one, the only Margo Hamilton."

My face fumed with hues of red.

The Elite Four.

The only thing worse than the man *Grayson Prince* is his henchmen themselves.

Christopher Florence.

Neil Vanderbilt.

And. His best friend, William Brookshire.

"No, she didn't. She wouldn't." I reasoned. "She's smarter than that... and how do you even know that's true?" I stressed.

Before Verina joins in with my mild panic, "And besides she knows William is a player." I trail off.

"You also know that Margo is also a player, right?" Juliette implies. Defeating my positive thoughts about Margo's possible hookup.

"What a match made in heaven." I joked as Verina stood up frantically searching for her bag.

Verina picks up her phone, reading some type of text, "Liam and her were caught in a debacle, fighting in a room." She wondered while scrolling through the pictures that were sent to the class group chats.

Margo Raine Hamilton. The only daughter of Robert and Caroline Hamilton, in which owns an abundance of clubs and banks from around the world. She was treated with nothing but respect by the oldest and richest in the world.

She has been my best friend since we were in Chanel diapers. You can catch her *VIP* at any event as well as the college's fundamental parties. With her perfectly dirty blonde hair and blue eyes, she traps any guy she sets her eyes on, some would even think she was a siren.

"Get Margo on the phone. *Now.*" I calmly suggested to the girls as Verina called her and put her on speakerphone.

Margo's voice started as I interrupt, "Hey V—"

"—Margo, are you out of your *mind!*" Everyone stayed silent as I yelled.

"Well, good morning to you too, Anna!" She sounded happy.

I rolled my eyes, "Margo." I calmly addressed.

"Adrianna..." She asked slowly as I took a breath.

"Please tell me you did not conspire with the enemy and share a bed with that sleaze-ball, Brookshire." I doubted she was going to tell me the truth without me pulling on the string.

Margo walks into the private dressing room, hanging up the phone, and laughing.

At least she made it here.

She starts to laugh incredulously, "Me? With Liam?" She laughs hysterically again, "Over my Christian Louboutin collection I would jump in a bed with that dick." She turns to Juliette who gives an awkward stare. No one was buying her bullshit.

"Don't lie to me, Margo Raine Hamilton." I step up.

She folds, her eyes squinting, "It was once! It was last night, and we were fooling around at Maya's party!"

Maya's party.

I shake my head, "Wait was Brooks there last night?" I had

asked, my hands shake a bit as well as my heart dropped to my stomach.

"Yeah, he was." Margo yawned as I folded my arms together in front of my body.

My eyes burned, like I couldn't afford to have another thing go wrong, "Listen." I take a calming breath. "This year will be nothing but perfection, do you all understand?" I had crept to them as they sat next to each other on a couch.

"I can't afford for my father to think I'm falling behind... in anything." I note. I walk back and forth, practically pacing.

"I need Prince off the radar at all times!" I specified as they looked like they had just buried themselves in the cushions.

"I want Hawthorne University at my feet this year. I want new recruits. I want a year where Grayson and I aren't even on the same level!"

"Anna... you already have the school by your fist, what else—" Verina starts as I interrupt.

"—I'm running for the Student Council Presidency spot." I walk around more.

"You already have class president—" Margo stands up as I walk closer to her, she begins to sit back on the chair slowly.

"You know that Grayson is running for that spot, and you have an equal rule, Adrianna... it's how it's always been." Verina reminds me as I sent out a scowl.

"Not when he doesn't deserve it! He doesn't take anything seriously, he is a cheat, a loser, a dirty... *dirty*—" I leveled my eyes with theirs, "He's a *Prince!*"

"You don't even know him, Anna!" Juliette chimed in.

"I know everything that I need to know about the man!" I defend myself.

Verina finds a counterargument to my statement with her love-struck eyes, "He's in my business class you know, he sits across from me. He's always so nice and dreamy..." She giggles as I cocked an eyebrow at her.

I felt my stomach turn at her words. Prince was far from nice, he's a liar and an entitled dick. But why did picturing Verina and Grayson being intimately close make me feel so disgusted, almost like my stomach got stabbed by a dagger?

I ignore her fantasies, "He's off-limits. So is the rest of his posse." I instructed as they all looked at each other, shrugging in agreement.

I hated the man passionately; It was almost like a fucking addiction to how much we compete and somehow end up in the same spot.

Head-to-head.

Chapter 2

Grayson

Earlier Today.

What a coward. I sit by her as I attempt to clean up the shards of the whiskey bottle, she smashed on the floor.

A woman that I am supposed to look up to. She used to hit me, we fought about anything and everything. Until I was finally old enough to fight back.

"Son..." She says in a husky voice as I stand up, pulling away from her grasp, "Be a friend and grab me some vodka, will you?" She grins as I walk over to the cabinet, taking out a full bottle and smashing it on the floor.

My mother stood up, rather tipsy her eyes fumed with hatred.

She was supposed to quit drinking. She was supposed to quit gambling and this fucking irresponsible act.

"How dare you get rid of that! It was good vodka!" She yelled, jittery, she slammed her hands on the cabinet, ravishing the alcohol that was left.

I couldn't help but feel my tears start to pool. I couldn't look at her, I let her stay in a large house filled with smashed vases, bottles, plates, and picture frames of a broken family. My father wouldn't support her, which I wouldn't blame him for doing.

But unlike him.

I loved my mother.

She might have hit me, and I took them and fought back, but I can still see the woman that used... to care.

I close my eyes, "Mother, I'm leaving."

I mutter as she pauses to look at me, "Where are you going?" She drops the bottle on the floor.

The floor of a house that I fucking paid for her to live in. I provided for her. It should have been the other way around and yet it wasn't.

Speaking of which, I may have to start fighting again to earn more money to help her out.

Yes. I know.

I shouldn't keep hiding her away, not when she's supposed to be in jail for tax fraud, embezzlement, and taking money from her clients' accounts.

And yet I helped her. I hid her and I fed her.

"I'm spending the night at dads." I pick up my jacket and walk over to the front door she rushes over to me, pulling my arm.

"No! Son, please don't leave me." She pleads as I avoid her eyes. "Come on let's play a game of billiards," She laughs as I pull away, opening the door before she even attempts to follow me all the way to Liam's Estate.

I lean on the door for a moment to retain a good composure, the last thing I need is for my best friend to see me in this much of a wreck. I cough out a cold breath, my eyes still blurry. I walk towards my car, pull out of the driveway, then drive to my father's house first, greet my family, and play some basketball outside on the court before I drive to Liam's house.

And I did.

But still, I felt guilty.

I pulled my shirt off because it smelled like shit from my mother.

Still, I can smell alcohol all over me. It makes me sick to my fucking stomach. I feel winded as I drive faster, trying to run away from this miserable town. But I know I could never really leave.

I can't bear the smell of alcohol.

After a regular session of pissing off the perfect Adrianna Cassian, I set off to Liam's house.

Staying at my father's house for more than thirty minutes does my head in. Every time I'm fucking there, he pisses me off or someone else fucking does.

The only thing that calmed me down was catching Adrianna in the act of sneaking back into her house.

I wonder if darling princess Adrianna ever had nights where she just wants to disappear. I doubt it. She thinks the world is her runway. She's probably never had a fucking problem in her life.

I can't stand her. I can't stand the way she talks or even how her hair falls to her back so perfectly.

She tries too much.

I hate her smart-ass mouth, how stubborn she is, and those fuck me eyes she has. I can help teach her how to be obedient, with just a few punishments.

Oh, how I would love to tie her fucking—

"Yo Gray!" A loud bang on my window as Liam came into view. My eyes flash into reality and my angered thoughts leave my head, "You going to stay there forever, or are you going to get out of the car?" He sarcastically knocks on my car door.

"Yeah." I open my side door and take a step out locking my car.

Liam furrows his eyebrows with a knowing look, "You can stay here for as long as you need." I nod as he smiles.

"I think I'll just be here for a day or two. I don't want to leave my mom all alone in the house for that long." I look up as his smile falters.

I've known Liam my whole life, he was practically my brother. Neil and Chris as well. All of them are. I could always escape with them. But I knew their thoughts about me and my relationship with my father. Sometimes to make myself feel better I think it's tough love. Which it is. It makes me more substantial so why fucking change it?

"You spend the day with Emma?" He walks into the house as I follow.

"Why would I spend the whole day with Emma?" I sneered as he sighed.

"Right... I forget you're a fuck boy."

I pause, "Says you." I threw my keys at him to hang by the coat hanger.

"You know maybe I thought you were going to settle. She seems really into you." He laughs as I take a bottle of water from his stocked-up fridge.

"A lot of girls are into me." I scoff, "What makes this one any different?"

I look up at him. "No one is the same as August."

"Has she reached out?"

He puts his arms up in surrender as I narrow my eyes, "No."

"But have you...?" His smile leaves his face abandoned.

"I'm going to tomorrow after the game, I'm going to win her back." I smile. "I'll do whatever I can to get her back." Liam nods, "I know you guys never really liked her..."

"We don't like her. She leaches onto you because of your money, and she just ended everything for no fucking reason. You ended up in the dump because of that." Liam gave me a narrow look.

"She was there for me with my whole family situation." I let out.

August was there for me throughout all of it, until I pushed her away.

I knew what I wanted, and I wanted her back.

"I know what I want and I'm going to get her back." I swallowed as he looked away, "But enough talk about me, let's talk about you."

"What about me?" He's nervous.

"Been hanging out with Margo, haven't you?" I smirked as he suppressed a laugh.

"Don't think I haven't heard." I assert.

Liam's eyes held a type of warning, "Keep me and her out of your stupid need for rivalry with Adrianna." He gives me the deadliest stare I've ever seen on his face. "I'm serious." He turned away.

"Wait, you don't actually like her, do you?" I mock, walking over to him as he throws a pillow at me.

He smirks, "Maybe I do."

I threw the pillow back at him, "You know you can do whatever you want." I sit on the chair across from him, "Or whoever you want... but Adrianna will make Margo end whatever it is you two are doing." I stick a toothpick in my mouth.

"I know what you're doing and it's not going to work."

"I don't know what you're talking about." I smile, as he gives me a concerned look.

"Listen." Liam narrows his eyes at me, "Margo made my fucking summer in Europe unforgettable." He walks closer, "We were together the whole fucking time, and it almost felt like maybe we could work as a couple here too. So, you and Adrianna are not messing this up."

I pat my friend's back with a smirk, "You're joking right?"

He smiles, "Of course." He trails off, "Besides, you know I hate clingy girls. She was basically, up my ass the whole fucking time it pissed me off." I leaned back listening to him, putting a cigarette in my mouth.

"She's been blowing up my phone like crazy. I think I'll just get a fucking new one." He continues.

I smile, "There's my boy. For a moment there, I thought you were tamed."

Liam picks the cigarette from my mouth, placing it in between his lips.

"I think I just stuck around because she's honestly a good lay. Fucking rocking body. She can take it well." Liam blew out a cloud of smoke.

It seemed typical enough that Liam was like this with a girl. He was always the worst one out of all of us when it came to women.

He was smooth with the ladies. He could have anything he wanted at the snap of his fingers. But I knew him better than myself.

"You're a dick." I voice as he sends me a glare, "And you're any better?"

I acknowledge the comment, "Yes. Yes, I am actually."

He had been my best friend forever, and I knew he was trying to convince himself that he didn't like Margo.

Bullshit.

"You ever think about fucking Adrianna?" He asks as I look up at him, my eyes pierced.

What?

"No."

I scoff, "Why do you ask?"

"You don't think it would be so good?" He stands, picking up his hockey stick to twirl it, "The built-up tension. The hate."

Fuck, maybe.

"No, I would end up suffocating her."

Maybe she likes to be choked.

He laughs, "You're right." He sets a puck down and flips it with his stick, "You two would be so wrong for each other. It would be so fucking terrible."

He pauses to look at me, "You couldn't pull her."

The fuck I can.

"Who said I can't?" I stood up, taking the other hockey stick out of the bin, his house was large enough, he had a hockey ice rink downstairs, but he rarely uses it for actual hockey.

Liam laughs again, he squints his eyes, "Deal with it, Prince... she's the *untouchable princess* in New York." He swings the hockey stick hitting the puck in the net.

"Whoever gets inside of her for her first time... Fuck, you know it's heaven."

I threw my hockey stick at him, "Enough. You're making me fucking sick, she's not even that fucking pretty let alone beautiful."

I slouch on the chair once more, "She's repulsive. She's the type of girl to be a fucking fly on the wall you can't get to leave your house."

Liam pushes me, "Or the type you wouldn't want to leave your house."

I shake my head, "Knock it off, it doesn't fucking matter whether she is mediocrely good looking, she is a fucking Cassian."

Liam only drops his jaw at my comment, looking at me in disbelief, "And you're a Prince."

He looked sarcastically shaken as I took a deep breath out.

"Look, man. As much as you want to prove me wrong, and that I'm an asshole for even challenging you to get with her, I know that I've won this bet already."

He pats my back firmly.

"You hate her?" He smiled looking like he was making a compare and contrast diagram.

"Great. She hates you more." He walks in front of me, "Bottom line. There is too much indifference."

"Fuck, imagine you two get with each other, your family would go fucking ballistic. And you don't let your hate for each other just affect the two of you. Your families both hate each other, and friends can't stand each other."

I laugh, "And yet you slept with Margo?" I turn to look at him, "Her best friend since she was born?"

He defensively sat up straight, "Yo, come on Gray if you flip this from Margo's point of view, she technically slept with

Grayson's best friend since birth, and thoroughly enjoyed every bit of it."

I scowl, "Okay, so what you are saying is that... you're both traitors."

"It wasn't even that bad. You're overreacting." He coughs out as I roll my eyes.

"Was she that good?" I ask, more curious if the sex was worth it to my best friend. "Because it looks like she's knocked your fucking screws off your robot brain."

He grins, almost fucking giddy, like a fucking child who got more than needed presents on Christmas, "It was a good fuck over the summer." He kicks his feet up on the table as I push his feet off.

"Over the summer... meaning..." I asked with a low volume as his eyes sent alarms, "Are you actually dumping her?"

"I thought you said you guys hooked up, last night after Maya's party."

"And it was good." He nods to himself as I listen to his words genuinely not giving a fuck.

I then patted his back, "Will." I sigh, making it sound as though I was going to ask a question.

"Gray." He replies.

"I know how you get." I smile nicely as he nods his head.

"Well, of course you do, you're my best friend... but I'm lost on what you mean by that."

Before he continues his sentence, I hit the back of his head causing him to curse out, "When you dump her, dump her for good. Margo is good looking, any guy would fucking love being in your shoes, so if you dump her, don't flip the fuck out if she moves on with someone else."

"We were never really labeled as anything." He goes on a tangent, "I'm sure she doesn't think just because we spent the whole summer together that I fucking love her."

I slap his forehead this time as he attempts to think about why I am smacking the shit out of him.

But nothing, lights out I swear he has no fucking brain.

"I'm going to fucking bed. We have the first day of college tomorrow as sophomores and you're already frying my brain." I walk away as he continues to look at me with confusion.

A moment of silence as he speaks.

"Holy fuck."

I don't even bother to turn around to see his disbelieving face. I smack the door shut. Taking off my shirt, only to fall gracefully on the bed that was made by the Gods.

My vision blurred, and the sign for me to sleep came on, as I shut my eyes.

I hear the front door open slightly, making me jolt back up, with no energy to check, I fall back down to the bed.

CHAPTER 3

ADRIANNA

My head pulses. My alarm makes the most terrible noise known to man as I lift my head up. My eyes blur before I take the glasses off my nightstand and put them on.

I yawn once more, not ready for this day. I opened my walk-in closet door, noticing that Helen had prepared my uniform.

Walking into the bathroom, I take a short shower, then brush my teeth, before doing my make-up and hair.

Everyone at college was informed that the uniform was mandatory, which it was. But to the students, it means to find your version of it. You can use the fabrics of the uniforms and make them your own.

I enjoyed my style, always chic, classy, and of course expensive designer.

Our university practically ran on its student's wealth. The professors were strict and intelligent, but the students were creative and very smart on their own.

But by having money, many lacked responsibilities or empathy for others.

I walk downstairs, to my house being empty. I should've figured it out. My father was probably working. No.

He is working.

I walk over to the counter to some freshly bought grapes, I pop one in my mouth, take a bottle of water, and leave for college.

My driver always dropped me off, the university was already full of first-year students who don't know how to make a simple left or right turn.

It was a short drive, but we made it. I looked out, seeing my friends rally at the front, sitting at the reserved tables.

I smiled at Julius thanking him for the ride before he let me out of the car. I took a deep breath. My eyes fall on my short skirt and my designer stockings, I hide my left thigh bruise, that Brooks left for me before opening the door to walk closer to them.

"Well, there you are!" A voice from the abyss caught my attention as my head turned to my friends, sitting profoundly and comfortably in their reserved lounge outside of the university.

I turned my head back, looking around, seeing the limo had left.

"Well, here I am." I gave a soft smile as I sashayed my way to my group of friends.

Verina sat, with her legs crossed, her eyes set on me walking closer, while Juliette sat with a smile, her eyes scanning the words that filled books and books of many. Is Margo getting her shoes cleaned by one of the first-year students?

They followed us around like tamed dogs, followed every order, and command, and they wanted nothing more than to be us.

Of course, no one would blame them, *we* are great, and there was no doubt about it.

We've shared the rule, but of course, it doesn't take a fool to understand that I was in charge, and to be honest, they didn't mind because I knew how to rule a monarchy, I was fit to *rule*, to *lead*, and no one second-guessed it.

"Amara, what the hell are you wearing?" I glared at her as she stood up, wiping the chair for me to sit on. Her eyes held over me as I smirked.

Her body stammered as she only backed away, and my eyes narrowed as she finally spoke.

"Boots, Anna." She had no courage to look into my darkened eyes, even for a second, she sews her mouth shut. I sat up, crossing my legs as the girl looked at her heels.

The girl was practically shaking, God forbid.

If she couldn't stand up to the queen of Hawthorne, then she is nothing but a joke.

I know I seem morbid.

But I take everything in academics seriously. I can't afford to be less than what I was known for. I know I sound cruel, but I didn't care because they let it happen.

The moment that they stand up to me is the moment I respect them.

My jaw clenched as Verina placed her hand on top of mine.

She smiled as I look away, "Come on A, loosen up, the girl got here on a scholarship. It's explanatory why she chose what she chose." Verina had said nonchalantly, yawning.

No one was here to tell you that my group was the nicest. We were *pretentious, spoiled,* and, of course, *intelligent.*

They envied the power, and all the attention made us the way we were. Though we were feared, people *loved* to hate us. The people *loved* to be *ruled.* The people *loved to follow us.*

I was *domineering, manipulative,* and *loyal.* I was born to have it all, yet I thrive even more. I am an obsessive overachiever with a tenuous moral character, and I go to significant measures to *take* what I deserve.

"I—apologize, Anna... It won't happen again." God, she might as well pee in front of me.

I only turned my head; my eyes left the girl's as she gave a forced smile of exhaustion. The whole section was quiet as I tilted my head, twirled my hair, in between my fingers then crossed my arms.

"Only my friends call me Anna. Take your hideous shoes and get out of my sight. "

That wasn't a question.

The girl *ran.*

Sprinted.

I turned to roll my eyes as everyone finally let go of the breath, they were keeping in during the duration of the confrontation.

Verina's eyes staggered as Juliette finally closed her book shut, making a noise as everyone shuddered. The tension rose as I looked over at her. Her glare was enough to know what she wanted to say.

"Come on J, don't give me that look." I leaned back.

She turned her figure, facing my body, I released a breath, "I get the shoes were ugly, but don't you think that *that* was a bit excessive?"

I turned over to Verina giving the same face, "Even for you, Anna. She'll never show her face here, after that again."

Margo stood up, placing her hands on Verina and Juliette's shoulders, breathing out loudly as I take an irritated sigh.

"You too Margo?" I scoffed.

"Well, it's not like I can turn back time." I defend my own actions.

Verina and Juliette smiled at each other as Margo took a step back, glazing her light eyes to mine as I shrugged my shoulders, "You know, you guys should turn over a new leaf this year."

Margo quickly ran over next to my side, her eyes shooting out to them as I laughed.

"You guys?" Margo questioned as the two girls in front of them stood by their comments.

Margo crossed her arms together as I leaned in closer. The sun rained down on them as Juliette smirked.

She leaned back, almost satisfied with herself.

"I am *a lot* nicer than *Mrs. Flawless* over here." Margo snarled as my mouth dropped, sarcastically, though I did feel as though my whole heart was annoyed.

"I'm nice."

The girls went silent as I tossed my shoulders back and let my hair fall nicely. The air was tight as everyone laughed.

"No, but apparently you're funny."

I reached out, snatching my beverage from the sanitized surface, as my cold eyes never left theirs. I brought the lip of the cup to my full lips, taking a sip so naturally and beautifully, then lowered the cup.

My lips formed a smirk, while my eyes conveyed a twinkle, "I'm nice to you guys."

"On a good day." Verina smiled as I gave a nonchalant eye roll.

My eyes narrowed as my brow furrowed, "The luck you have considering I actually love you is astounding." I made sure my sentence was acknowledged by my peers as I stood tall, letting my skirt ride down my thigh.

Juliette and Verina followed as Margo threw her belongings to three ladies that followed our group around.

My eyes snapped on the building as she walked gracefully, my eyes scanning the crowd as I caught *hers*.

"Don't look, Anna." I heard Verina whisper into her ear as her hands formed tight fists.

"Margo, you went to her party, right?" I stood taller, setting my gaze on my enemy as I continued her journey.

I made sure my stride was powerful, that it didn't falter, and that I hadn't let my eyes fall away, "Yes." One girl that carried Verina's books answered for her as I threw a look of ignorance.

"Did any of you spot Maya with Brooks last night?" I asked politely as they all died down in volume.

"I thought you said the ship had sailed?" Juliette asked as I practically felt my body jolt.

I had left my love life confidential to my friends, or family, it was the one thing I wasn't envious of sharing. It made me seem like a prude, of course, everyone in the city knew that I was a virgin, and it was branded on me.

Not that it branded me a loser, but the worst is that it made me a target to any alpha male in the fucking state.

"I just wanted to know." I scowled as she wrinkled her eyebrows.

"I've just heard from a source that he was seeing Maya." I stammer, hitting something big and muscular.

I turned to see blonde hair, his grey eyes, and his jaw so tight it could cut me.

"Keeping us a secret from your band, *Dove*?" He flashed his famous godly smirk as I swallowed my annoyance down. His whole posse was behind him, Liam, Neil, Chris, and a couple of his other friends.

I could feel the hate boiling inside of me as he ran his hand through his hair. God, he was repulsive, but my body seemed to disagree as his head tilted, almost in a mocking way.

My heart stopped.

"The only secret that I would keep about you is that you haven't gotten laid in over three months," I smirked as he rolled his tongue in his mouth.

"Can't get a girl Prince?"

"I like to call it being selective in my choice of woman I like on my bed, Cassian. Maybe against the wall? On the counter?" He winked, turning to Neil as they all pushed him around smiling.

They thought they were so cool.

"Selective?" I smiled.

His eyes narrowed, "Where's the hidden gold cross on your neck, Cassian? Thought you never leave your house without it on you?" He leaned his weight on the lockers as I let my lips curve into a smile.

"Wouldn't you like to know?"

"I thought you liked to listen to what your parents tell you. Like a good little girl." He stood taller.

"Care to test that theory?"

He laughs softly, and I pull away, "Mhmm."

"Hey, Liam..." Margo pulls me away before smiling at him. "I've been texting you like crazy."

"I'm sorry, who are you?" Liam smiles.

I glared up at him, Margo's hands tightened as I looked back at Grayson.

"Asshole." Verina snapped back as Liam only faked being hurt.

"I'm wounded." He exaggerated placing his hand on top of his chest like he was heartbroken by the insult, I only looked at Margo to see her eyes turn away.

Oh hell no.

Never in my life have I seen Margo be upset because of a male. I watched her as her eyes closed for a moment, her hand letting go of mine, I felt a sting in my heart just to watch her heartbreak.

Because of Liam Brookshire, a guy she slept with one night?

"Good one." Chris smiled, patting Liam's back as his eyes found mine, it scanned Margo's whose eyes were directed to the floor.

His smile falters, it disappears when Margo's expression dies. Almost as if he cared about her. The smile on his mouth morphed into a frown, Margo couldn't sneak a lookup without making it obvious that she affected her. So, her gaze stayed down.

Verina scowls, "Come on, Anna." They started to pull at me as I turned, "Come on Margo."

While we began to leave, a group of freshmen practically drooled over us, some of the football players checked us out as I turned to see Jackson Gollum walk up to us, his face bruised with red cheeks.

"Hey, Margo..." He eases as she looks up, her eyes seeking Liam's.

Why Liam?

"Hey, Jack." She says with no emotion.

"I was wondering if you wanted to go out with me sometime." He asked so nicely as Margo turned to look at me, then her eyes glanced at Liam.

"Really?" She let out a smile, as I turned my eyes away knowing she only did it to make Liam Brookshire jealous.

"Yes, of course..." Jackson sounded giddy; I do feel bad. Of course, she was about to play him, just because of Liam. But I was never one to interfere in my friends' love lives.

"Hey Cassian," He smiles.

"Congrats last night with Brooks. He said you were going out tonight as well." Jackson winked as all the girls behind me practically set off like a spaceship.

They all squealed loudly, and my ears rang.

Congrats on what.

And I'm going where?

All I could think of saying was, "Yeah. Thanks."

I turned to Grayson whose face seemed sour with hate and annoyance, Liam's face plastered with jealousy as Margo smiled at Jackson.

My gaze fell on Brooks who was strutting the hallways the way he always did, walking towards me.

He fucked Maya.

Wait, why am I choosing to believe Grayson?

"Hey, babe." He attempts to kiss me. I smiled, hesitated to kiss him back, and turned my face as his lips landed on my cheek.

"And suddenly it reeks of shit." We both turn to Grayson who held a sneering face.

Grayson was at least five inches taller than Brooks; he held a particular godly figure that the rest of the boys in college didn't have.

"Prince." Brooks takes out his hand for a shake as Grayson only scoffs at his face.

He never learned to make new friends. Just him and his henchmen.

"Come on Gollum, we have class." He pulled Jackson away behind kissing my forehead, "I'll see you tonight?"

He rushes off.

The fuck? Did he experience a whole different night than me on Saturday?

I catch Grayson's gaze before it leaves, "And apparently you aren't picky with your men," He sneers, and before I could answer he and his friends were gone.

CHAPTER 4

ADRIANNA

"You really need a new hobby, J." Verina yawns, placing her hands all around her hair in front of my mirror. I turn around my eyes landing on Juliette who looks up from her book.

"Let her be, Verina." I roll my eyes.

Verina grins back at Juliette, "You ever thought about getting a boyfriend?"

"Not interested V." Juliette mustered, "Besides, unlike Adrianna, I actually get laid." Juliette shoots out as I flip her off,

"Fine! I'll get off your back." Verina smiles again, knowing far and well this conversation wasn't over.

"I'm here!" Margo saunters into my room, her hand full of shopping bags.

"Late as always." Juliette grins, closing her book and standing up from my bed.

She walks over to Margo who was placing the bags on the floor, with curious eyes she hands a bag to Juliette.

"What's this?" Juliette laughs as she takes the bag opening it.

Margo lets a smirk journey to her face, "I think you would look marvelous in that."

Juliette laughs, pulling out pink lingerie, her eyes shutting slightly at the fabric. "Yeah, that is not happening." She throws the fabric on the bed before folding her arms together.

I laugh, "Margo, did you really think that Juliette would wear that?" Juliette looks at my face telling me that she agreed.

"It's not like I'm asking her to strip with it!" Margo picks up the other lingerie.

"Here." She throws the other lingerie at each of us. "We can wear them tonight, under the jerseys." She winks.

"What jerseys?" I questioned, my eyes catching the said jerseys.

I hold the lingerie out, in front of me. "White?" I smiled at her; her eyes held a twinkle.

"For our Virgin queen." She smiles as I throw a pillow at her.

Verina laughs while looking at me, "You can wear it for Brooks."

"Brooks and I won't be doing any of that." I stuck out my tongue at my best friends.

They all pause, "Trouble in paradise?" They asked as I shook my head.

I was nevertheless completely embarrassed at what went down at New Crest, and not really sure if I wanted to revisit anything.

I was more prone to leave things in the past and just ignore them.

"I don't know, I just don't see him that way anymore." I sounded defensive, they certainly saw the signals of me not wanting to speak much of Brooks.

So, they quickly change the subject.

"I never got to ask you about the tension I sensed between you and Prince." Verina smacked her lips together.

I sat up, ignoring their lingering gazes, "What tension?" turned to look in the mirror.

"Oh, you know... how he got irritated when Brooks approached you." Margo let herself fall on the bed next to Juliette.

I definitely didn't sense anything the way they apparently did, but of course, maybe they were overreacting like usual.

"So, what, you act like he's the first guy to ever be mad that he can't have me." I looked back at them with a smile.

Verina walked behind me, placing her chin on my shoulder, "You act like you're the first girl to try and resist him."

"Try?" I smile, "Just being near him makes me revolt."

She turns me around, "You don't have to lie to us, Adrianna." She holds up the white lingerie. "You should wear this little number under the jersey tonight and see where it goes." She smirks, "Unless... you're telling me that you are into the enemy."

"That's funny. I'm not going to that game."

I let my lips curve, "He's vile." I let out. And I was serious, the mere idea of Grayson and I being something more than what we have been to each other our whole life was not possible.

"He's also fucking hot." Verina smiles, throwing me a wink. I let my gaze fall to the floor, and my hand stiffened.

"And just because you hate him doesn't mean you can disagree."

The tone of Verina's voice made my skin crawl. I know, of course, she would never go for him. He wouldn't like her. Yes, of course, she was gorgeous. But he wouldn't actually think about going for her, would he?

"Yes, I can. And I will."

From all the years I have known him, Grayson never liked light brown-haired girls... he liked hair that was so dark you could mirror it to the night sky. I knew he liked plumped lips, just like how he would stare at mine. And as for eyes, he loved dark brown eyes, they would always capture his dark ocean-blue ones.

But how would I even know anything about what he wanted when I was everything he loathed?

He hated me, he hated my family.

"Why do we have to go to this game again?" I look to Margo who frowns.

"I just want to show Liam what he's missing." I rolled my

eyes; Liam didn't deserve someone like Margo. She was far better than whatever he stuck his dick in.

"It was one hook-up, Margo. You usually would be over this by now." Juliette rested her elbows to lift her head towards us.

"This is different. He humiliated me, I was a fool for thinking that it would go further. I just want to see the look on Liam's face when he sees me on the hockey boards, cheering for the other team."

"If he cares." Verina laughs as Margo flips her off.

"That would be a great plan... if the hockey team shows interest." Juliette tilts her head at Margo who looked point-blank confused.

"They always do."

"The boys have a game tonight... against Maxwell University." Juliette rolls over so she faces the ceiling.

"Just thought you would love to know before... you experiment with that glorious plan of yours."

Meaning that they would take this game seriously. The players would stop at nothing to get the win over the university's top rival.

I looked up at Margo, who sent a knowing look, "Oh hell no, Margo." I walked away as she pulled me back into an embrace.

"Come on Anna!" She pleaded as I sighed with frustration. She walks in front of me, placing her hands on my shoulders making sure my attention is all hers, "You would do it if you loved me."

I roll my eyes at her silly request, her eyes still not leaving mine, her eyes piercing into my soul, I flinch away.

"No, Margo I will not."

She shakes my entire body, "Adrianna. Please." It was a full plea. "Come on Anna, you won't even talk to Grayson."

That was a complete lie, and I could feel it. I can already hear the throwing insults back and forth. It was a terrible idea.

I sigh, looking into her bright, blue eyes.

I look at Verina and Juliette who had smirks plastered on their faces.

"You're lucky I like you." I relented, snatching the lingerie from the bed, and walking into the bathroom.

All their faces lit up with happiness. We would do anything for each other, we all knew that.

Juliette stifles a groan as Margo practically rips her away from the bed and stuffs the lingerie into her hands to get changed.

"Wait." I peek out of the door, and they all pause to look at me.

"What jersey am I supposed to wear?" I tilted my head at Margo who had a wide grin, reached into her other shopping bag, and pulled out four different hockey jerseys.

She really thought this through, didn't she?

She throws me a jersey before winking, I pull the jersey up to give it a glance noticing the name *Sawyer* I lift my eyes to Margo's who held a knowing grin.

"Why am I wearing Darius's jersey?"

Margo props her hand on her hips with a smile, "Because we both know you want to get on Grayson's nerves, and wearing his rival's jersey seems so enticing, doesn't it?"

She then folds her arms together as I walk out of the bathroom, the pure white lingerie hugging my curves and my waist.

Verina's eyes lingered on the swell of my breasts.

"Jesus." Juliette's mouth drops as I laugh, slipping the jersey on my body with a tennis skirt.

This must be what fish feel like when everyone watches them in the aquarium.

"Get over it and go change you idiots." I smile walking in front of my vanity to retouch my make-up, my hands shaking as I hold my mascara wand up near my eye.

Margo came up from behind me placing her hand on my shoulder, she was wearing Colton's jersey also from the opposing team.

I let my eyes look at her which reflected in the mirror, placing my hand on top of hers, "Hey, Liam's a dick for not wanting you."

She let out a shaky breath, "What makes you think that it means that much to me?" gun hot Her eyes avoided mine.

I smile, "Because you have never made this much of an effort because of a guy that you only slept with once."

She laughs, "I don't know... I just thought he was—"

I let my eyes narrow to hers, "—Different?" I finished her sentence as I turned around to face her, "Liam learns from Prince. They all do. You shouldn't trust them. They handle their lives like they were raised to, which is being fucking filthy."

I raised my eyebrows, "You want him to fawn over you and that's what you're doing... but what happens if he does?" I ask.

My eyes probing to hers held an uncertain look.

"When he falls for me... I'll walk away as he did to me." She smiles.

I cup her cheeks, "You know your father would not allow you to date him. None of our parents would want us to date Grayson, Chris, Neil, or Liam."

She pulls away, "I know." She sighs, "This is purely just because I want revenge, Anna."

I smile at her, "Okay."

GRAYSON

As I walk into the hockey locker room, my adrenaline pumps heavier, spotting Chris there. He was always early with a book in his hand. He usually comes and gets here first so he has time to study. His eyes shut closed as he leaned against the wall, his small snores were audible.

I drop my bags next to him, and his body jolts, waking him up from his sleep, I smile, "You alive Florence?" I shook him as he glowered at me.

"Glaring at your team captain now too?" I sat next to him, "First, you're asleep on the job and now you're giving attitude. I just don't know what to do with you now dude." I laughed, patting his back as he closed his book.

"You're such an asshole." He insults me as I chuckle.

"You have such a way with words, Chris, really." I place my hand over my heart, "I'm touched."

I opened up his geometry book. I haven't studied geometry since eighth grade. His eyes looked over at me, "Is this your homework?"

I turn to him as he yawns, "No, it's Finn's... he needs help with his math, so I've been brushing up on it again to help him. You know my mom, she's barely there to help." He forces a smile on his face as I frown.

"Hey, if you ever need a break—"

Before I could finish the sentence, he interrupted me, "The team needs me, Gray. I know it and you know it. It's nothing I can't handle. I can play and I can still provide for myself and my brother." I let my frown disappear.

I always understood that the founding families of Hawthorne were wealthy and most of their children would most likely take over their family's legacy or business. Your future is written out for you once you are born, that was always the case. But Chris never had that type of upbringing.

His mother was constantly in and out. She wasn't rich and she didn't pay for the house and the bills. Chris was forced to grow up quicker than the rest of us. His mother never paid for the essentials. He had to pay for the food and the upbringing of his brother Finn.

He would buy the things he needed for school and, of course, buy his brother things that a child would desire. He was struggling but never once did he ask for help because he was too prideful.

I've always loved him like a brother, and as a brother, I knew he was getting overworked.

He would work as a waiter at a lowkey bar that Liam, Neil, and I would go to just to visit him. He lets Finn stay at Liam's house sometimes when we have a game or he's really busy with work.

But the best way that he made money was through the underground fights we would have with others, yes it was illegal, and it was unsafe, but it was good money that he would get.

We all fought, but of course, he did it because he needed the money desperately.

Neil, Liam, and I did it to blow off some steam.

We were good fighters.

Chris took it more seriously than we did. It was his lifestyle; he loved his brother more than himself. He has a good heart and would do anything for Finn.

"I mean, if you ever need help with teaching your brother, I got you, I could hire a tutor—"

He laughed while putting on his uniform as I slipped out of my shirt to also put mine on as well. "I don't want money, Grayson."

I roll my eyes, "Sure you don't want it." I go into my bag pulling out some cash, "But you need it more than I do right now."

I pressed the cash on his chest as he looked down with a frown. As much as he wanted to decline, I wouldn't let him. He pushes my hand back, "You know I won't accept it; I'm making money."

I hold his gaze, "Not enough,"

He breathes out with a huff, "Come on Chris, Finn's birthday is coming up, I know the kid wants a party, a new toy maybe?"

He turns away avoiding me.

"I love Finn as a brother, all the guys do, we all practically raised him."

"I would want him to have a good nine-year-old party." I wink as he rakes his fingers through his hair.

"He's already going through a tough time with chemo."

We both frown, Chris shakes his head, knowing he has to accept the money.

"Fine, I'll take it." He takes the cash from my hands as he frowns again. "But that's all I'm accepting, Gray."

I wink again, "He's a good kid." I patted his back, "All the boys would love to help you guys if you gave us the chance."

He glares at me, "You know that, and I love you guys but I just... I want Finn to know that I'm trying on my own. Our mother is barely in our lives. We're comfortable, and he doesn't need the brand-new video games."

I stalk away to put on my skates, "Maybe. But he needs new clothes, I know that he's growing up and you can't just give him yours."

His face held trouble. I knew that he would never ask for help, but I also knew he needed it without saying anything.

He looks up.

"Can I borrow your rink throughout the week?" He muttered as I paused to look at him.

"Finn wants to join the hockey team and I don't really have the cash right now to buy something new, I have groceries to pay for..."

I held my gaze, "Nonsense you're staying at my house, I'll have Linda cook for us and Finn can pick from the many hockey sticks I have. He can practice in the indoor or outdoor rink, and he can bring his friends."

He groans.

"I'm not taking no for an answer, Chris." I assert.

He frowns, "I know."

"But I can't make it to dinner, I have a shift after the game, and I promised my boss I wouldn't take off again." He opens up his bag to the fighting clothes, "And I also have a fight."

I nodded hoping he would take off to spend time with us, but I knew he wouldn't.

"Fine, just tell me what time I could pick up Finn from school, I know you are working after practices."

He hesitantly says, "He gets off at three."

I smile, "Perfect."

"We'll be at the fight."

He smiles, "Thanks, man."

I throw a puck, and he dodges it, "No problem, just give me your best out there on the ice tonight."

"Don't I always?" He winks.

He always did. So did everyone on the team, I was confident that they would work hard.

"You do. But I'm not planning on losing against Maxwell University just because someone slacks off." I narrowed my eyes, "As your captain, I intend to keep the undefeated streak going."

He nods, throwing the puck back at me, I catch it instead of dodging it.

"Got it, captain."

I smile to myself as Chris gives me a weird look, "What?" He asks as I laugh to myself.

"Finn can pick any sport and he picks hockey?" I shake my head, "Was he not the one making fun of us for being burnt out in high school?"

Chris chuckles, "He said that he wants to be just like his role models, it's all he's ever seen us do. He watches Liam skate like a damn princes, he sees Neil ram someone in the boards, he sees me with my nasty cellys, and of course he sees you and your killer slap shots... which kid wouldn't want to be like us?" He shrugs as I take a moment to think.

"You know... he already does curse like a hockey player." I acknowledge as he points at me, "He got that shit from you."

The doors burst open, and more of our teammates flooded the room, rummaging through their bags as well as lockers.

The coach walks into the room, all eyes on him as I smile

walking up in front of him on behalf of the team. "Want a clean game coach?" I form a smirk as he laughs.

"Against Maxwell?" Coach Livingston looks around, "In your dreams."

The game was heated, ironic, for it being on the ice. But Darius Sawyer hasn't let me off the hook since last year's season when I broke his arm. He's been giving me trouble, don't get me wrong. But he also doesn't know that I love trouble more than anything.

"You miss me?" He skated towards me before the game was almost finished. He didn't approach me with words, only with aggressiveness that shocked me.

"Oh yeah, I did always miss the bickering we had," I smirk as his eyes flared with red.

He looked furious. I wouldn't let it bother me. Not when I know that if I lose my temper, which wasn't hard for me to do, I will injure him again and I don't intend to lose my spot on the team.

His eyes lingered over to the stands, and mine followed.

And there she sat.

Adrianna looked so ardently beautiful since the last time I saw her. She sat with her normal group of friends, her eyes on mine, God, I practically owned her.

Except.

"I didn't know your girls were such big fans of me." My eyes crowded over to Adrianna's once more.

Her body looked tense.

Why the fuck was she even here?

Why the fuck was she wearing Sawyer's jersey?

My hand gripped hard on my hockey stick, maneuvering so I could land a good slap shot.

I was the fastest on the team, I had the best stats, and I was the most committed. All the boys in my family have always played hockey. They were always good.

Father always warned us never to fail the team. I would never fail in front of my team. No matter what.

Sawyer was on my fucking tail, never leaving me alone, of course, I knew how to avoid him, but he rammed into me, smacking me against the boards.

I looked in front of me and it was Adrianna who handed me a concerned look. I turned back around to Darius. His known smile flashed red lights in my fucking view.

"I saw her walk around your campus last time we were here. Her and her cute little ass, I thought she was yours. But hey, she's wearing my jersey, landing her a spot to sit on my mouth." He licked his lips.

"Don't fucking talk about her."

"Why? She probably gives the best head, does she?" He laughs, "To have the *Grayson Prince* defend her?"

"Is she really that good in bed? If so..., why don't I have a try?"

My eyes saw bloodshed as he talked about her.

My body jerks, ramming him as hard as I can against the boards, the glass shatters from above us, shards fall to the ice and the crowd, without even a second thought, taking the puck from his possession, skating as fast as I can across, and passing the puck to Liam, he passes back to me successfully while Neil and Chris defend and make sure the other guys are guarded.

Before the referee comprehends what has happened, I was face to face with their goalie, I gave it my all, slapping the puck and hitting the back of net.

I turn around, Sawyer gets up, and he takes off his helmet, his face looking utterly defeated. The shattered glass surrounding his body, with all its failure. He just ended their season, because before his eyes met mine.

The buzzer went off.

Hawthorne 3. Maxwell 2.

Our team won.

I skate off the rink, my eyes red with fury. If I even saw a glimpse of Adrianna walking up to Sawyer, I would pound my fucking fist in his face.

Making sure he lost all of his teeth before I stopped.

The whole team was screaming with joy, they ran into the locker room to take showers and get dressed as I stayed out a little longer.

Of course, was happy with the win, but not when Anna was fucking cheering for the opposing team. Let alone fucking Darius Sawyer.

Minutes later Sawyer approached Adrianna.

Liam and Neil came from behind me patting my back, "Holy shit, you just broke the damn glass." They looked excited as I shook my head, I probably had to pay for the damages, hoping that no one got hurt in the audience.

"Told you we got that win, Gray." Chris comes later.

I smiled, "I never doubted us."

My eyes wandered over to the girls, they were standing in front of the entrance, Margo was standing near Colton while Adrianna was still in a conversation with Sawyer.

Juliette spoke to Xander while Verina talked to a group of the other hockey players.

Without even thinking about it, Liam saunters over to the girls, I couldn't react in time to even fucking stop him.

He squares up to Colton who Liam managed to pick about eight fights last season. Chris and Neil ran over him before he thought about throwing the first punch.

I walk over quickly, my eyes alarming Anna as she stiffens.

"Any chance why you aren't on your side of the arena, Colton?" Liam seethed as Margo took a step back.

"Yeah, I came because Margo called me over, she and I have some unfinished business." He sauntered over to Margo who held a disgusted gaze.

But, of course, Liam didn't see.

I knew for a fact that Margo did this to get a rise out of Liam, it was working.

I walk in between them, "That's enough." I yell as they both separate.

I look over to Anna. Her gaze locked on Sawyer's I could practically feel my fucking fists forming.

What does she see in that fucking idiot? Did she really come to see him play?

Fuck. Why did I care?

Just like a regular fucking puck bunny she would go for him. Of course.

"Liam, why do you care?" Colton laughs. Liam's eyes are molten to Margo's.

She looked at him so willingly, she was hoping for the answer that any fucking girl Liam had sex with, it wasn't going to happen.

"I don't." He turned away, not able to catch Margo's hurt expression.

"Great, I can take her out." Colton winks at Margo.

"We are having a party tonight at a bar. You guys can come." Colton's smile widened as I winced.

He looks at me and the guys, "Your hockey team can come too, I would love to end this feud."

"Fuck you." Liam lets out.

Colton smiles, "Unless you guys are too whipped by your captain that he won't let you party."

The team looks at me, my eyes fucking feral.

No way in hell are they going to that party. We have practice tomorrow.

I look back at Anna and fucktard, Darius Sawyer, he looked stupid, not a damn shard of glass had sliced through his skin.

He leans down to her ear whispering something that caused her to fucking laugh.

Laugh?

I kept my eyes on them as he pulled away, she let his lips land a kiss on her cheek.

I start to walk toward them, I felt a strong grip on my arm, making me stop, and I look to my side, "Don't be fucking stupid, Gray. Especially not because of Cassian." Neil grits out.

I pull away, calming myself, as Sawyer makes his way back to his team's side of the arena. My eyes held on to Adrianna's.

Why did she look so fucking happy?

"So, Prince, you going to let the team go to the party?" Margo asks mischievously.

I let my eyes worm their way to Colton's.

"No way in hell you guys are partying tonight." I point at each and every one of my team members.

I turn back to Adrianna and Sawyer, only to be fucking annoyed with what I see.

I suddenly felt pain rush to my head, I placed my hand on the spot next to my temple and pulled my hand away, I saw red.

I had been bleeding and I hadn't known. It wasn't severe of course but it was there.

"I'm heading home, I need to take care of this." I looked at my friends as they narrowed their eyes.

"What?"

Chris stops to look at me with an idiotic look on his face, "You aren't fucking driving home."

"Why the fuck not." I snapped as he rolled his eyes, "You got fucking body-slammed to the boards, hard enough that you're bleeding, and I know you have bruises you might even have a concussion."

I laugh.

"Fucking forget it. I'm going home." I walked towards the locker room and starting to take off my helmet I felt dizzy.

I was sure it was just a fucking mild concussion.

I turn back around looking at the clock, "Practice tomorrow from 5 to 6 A.M."

"Grayson come on, let us have a day off." A teammate of mine, Jacob whined as I narrowed my gaze.

"Double session, 6 to 7 P.M." I pierced my gaze into their eyes, "Jacob just earned you a double session, Coach will be there."

"Fucking complain again." I turned, and Adrianna's golden-brown eyes softened when they met mine.

"Let them have a break." She smirked as I clenched my jaw.

"Why should I listen to you?" I challenge her.

She straightens her body. "Well, if you really believe that you guys are the best and can beat anyone... you wouldn't mind a day off." She winks.

I turned to look at all the boys, their pleading baby eyes. I look back at Adrianna, her smile wicked and her eyes challenged.

"Fine." I say blankly, "You guys can go. But we still have practice tomorrow." I looked back at Adrianna's honey-brown eyes.

Those same eyes that I hated. Yet made me fucking feral.

Those same fucking eyes were on Darius Sawyer the whole game.

I always thought she was fucking dense and naive but now knowing that she was giving him the time of day.

She confirmed my thoughts.

CHAPTER 5

ADRIANNA

I make my way back to the girls, I pass Grayson, his eyes looking dazed and fueled with anger. I kept my eyes on him as he disappeared into the locker room.

"Hey... ready to go?" I smile at my friends who were gathered with the opposing team.

They all formed a gaze that held trouble.

"What is it...?" I walked up slowly with caution.

"We are all hanging out at the clubhouse tonight to celebrate the win." Verina throws me a coy look as I groan.

"Margo, you promised me that we were in and out." I fold my arms together.

"Yes... of course but you wouldn't mind." She probed as I darkened my gaze. I look at the hockey team with uncertainty.

"They're going?" I ask.

Verina smiles back, "Maybe."

"I'm sorry guys but I'm going home. I'm tired." I start to walk away as Margo's hand shoots out to grip my arm.

"Anna, come on, please come." She whispers as I turn to look back at the boys, with nervous gazes.

"Have fun with us." She asks so nicely I felt my body heat reach an unhealthy temperature.

"I have to catch my father before he leaves for Fiji." I let out.

She sighs, "It was your plan to let the boys party, and this is the perfect way to get back at Liam."

Did Liam mean this much to her?

"Fine." I seethed out painfully as she hugged me tightly.

"But I'm only doing this for you."

"I love you." Margo starts to lead everyone to her car, and the boys start to get into their sports cars, driving away before Grayson could come out.

Everyone left and I had been sitting outside, waiting for a phone call that never happened, so I took it upon myself to call him.

It went straight to voicemail, so I leave a message.

"Hey Dad, I'm just calling to see if you are going to be here at all for the following week, I could even fly out to you if you want." I let out a tear but wiped it immediately. "I just don't want to spend my birthday alone this Thursday," I mumbled.

I ended the call, my heart thumping. I delete the message. He out of all people didn't need to know that I was being pathetic without him.

But I was.

I heard the door slam open, I jolted up, making eye contact with Grayson as he stopped to keep his steady gaze on mine.

"Great." I let out exasperated as he shook his head at me annoyed.

He started to walk away from me as I moved to block his way, and he let out an annoying huff.

"Cassian, get the fuck out of my way I just want to go home." He tries to avoid me as I walk closer, his eyes roaming down my body, I let out a shiver.

"Oh, Mr. Prince, are you upset with me?!" Mine and Grayson's eyes meet, almost as if he challenged me.

"I suppose. You are the reason why my team isn't getting the rest they need."

"You could've said no." I fold my arms.

Grayson and I had been bickering since we were young, nothing I ever did satisfied him.

One time for Halloween I dressed up as this really pretty princess that had a beautiful pink dress, he *accidentally* poured black paint on it from his gooey costume.

So, I wanted to get back at him.

For Christmas when we were eight, all the founding families of Hawthorne had to attend the Christmas party that the James family hosted, Margo and I made fake treasure maps that Liam and he followed to the lake, where we pushed them in.

He was practically a popsicle when he came back inside.

Or in middle school science, our class had a contest on which person could grow the most flowers, I was for sure going to win.

But the next morning, someone mysteriously cut off all my flowers with safety scissors.

Then I got back at him by telling his crush, Sophie Jackson that he practiced kissing a snail.

And before I thought to myself that I was evil and to say sorry, he would always come back with another plan to antagonize me.

And I couldn't help myself. It was a hobby.

He rolls his eyes, my lips curving.

"Don't look so tough, Cassian. I can still see the mascara stains you have, about God knows what." He advances on me, tilting his head, I start to walk backward, my body hitting the wall.

He almost looked feral; his eyes gleaming darker blue.

Hunger.

He lets his hand travel to my waist still hesitating on *actually* touching me, preventing my full body from hitting the remainder of the wall.

"And you're so tough?"

"Yes, actually." He smirks, "I am."

His hand felt nice on me, he squeezed as I let out a breath, his eyes resting on my lips.

Kiss me.

"Is that what you tell yourself every day?"

I swallow, getting the smell of his cologne.

"You should really get to the party. You wouldn't want to keep your boyfriend waiting."

I shiver, "Aren't you going?"

He forms a smirk, pulling his hands away from me. Now looking at the clear pathway that he made for himself by moving me. "Thanks for getting out of my way, Dove."

Grayson starts to walk away, I couldn't resist myself, letting my hand grip his, "No!"

He turns back to me, his smirk never leaving his face, "Are you concerned for me or something?"

I let go of him, his skin felt like fire on hold.

"Dove, I can handle myself."

He huffs out as I smile, "Why did you walk out of your house in a rush yesterday? You looked pissed."

His eyes grew dark, my heart stopped for a moment.

Sore subject.

"Looks like I'm not the only one with family issues." I teased.

He shifted his body towards me, muscle and all its glory he walked me back towards the wall, "Don't talk about my family like you know them."

I attempt to push him back, "Then don't talk about my father like you know him either."

He turns around, "Except, I know what I'm talking about, and your little phone call is the evidence I need, you have nothing on me." He laughs, pulling out a cigarette, lighting it, and putting it in between his lips.

I felt foolish and embarrassed. I stalked in front of him. His eyes lingered on mine as I took the cigarette from his lips, threw it on the ground, and stepped on it.

Before pointing at the "No smoking" sign on the wall, "You should really stop smoking those cancer sticks, it's not good for you."

"And you should really stop messing with things that are bad influences on you." He leans down.

I roll my eyes, "If you are talking about yourself, trust me. You are no temptation, Prince." I leaned closer, I was practically drugged.

"Why aren't you going to the party?" I asked as he pulled his hockey bag over his shoulder.

"I have shit to do." He mutters.

"Like what?"

"Mind your own fucking business." He pulls away as his bag unzips, and a bouquet of flowers falls on the cement floor. His face looked furious. His face was tainted with disdain as the roses fell to the ground, now unpresentable. "Fucking hell."

I let myself fall to the ground, picking up the flowers and handing them over to him, "I'm so sorry…"

"I don't need your apologies." I swallow, pulling away.

"I didn't know you—"

"—You don't know anything about me, Adrianna. So, stop acting like you fucking do." He pulled his hockey bag over himself.

He starts to walk away to his car before I finish my sentence, "I'm sorry."

"That. Stop fucking saying sorry. Stop feeling sorry for everything too. It pisses me off. Maybe feel sorry for yourself. Go home instead of trying to figure out my life." Grayson yells.

"Don't tell me what to do."

"Let me tell you this, Dove." His voice sounded thick with hate.

"You have lived in a fucking cage all your life, everything bad that's going to happen to you." He smirks, "You fucking deserve every bit of it."

"The heartbreaks." He continues, "The loss." He meets my face, but the burn on my eyes made me resist meeting his.

"You're nothing without your money, your parents, and your fucking appearance." He laughs, "If you ask me... that would be the only reason I would be able to stand being with you for more than five minutes."

I laughed, feeling the tears forming but there was no way in hell I would let them fall.

"You are such an ass, Prince." I lick my lips to suppress my anger. "You think everything revolves around you."

He leaned back just to listen to me.

"You are a selfish arrogant asshole that has nothing better to do with his life other than try to make my life miserable." I smile.

"Your previous comments about me just proved once again that you might be the stone-cold heartthrob. You put up this front that you are the worst and that your family is the best, but you will never grow up."

"You really think someone would love you when you are so repulsive that no one can stand even staying before you end up dumping them in a corner anyway!"

I yell back as he turns around shutting his car door.

The fucking nerve.

GRAYSON

 er mother fucking nerve.

First, she ruins my mood by being at the game. Second, she ruins the fucking flowers I bought for

August. Third, of course, she insults me and tramples all over my boundaries.

She never knows when to stop, when to fucking begin. She's just an expert on how to ruin my fucking day.

I grip the steering wheel, pull out of the parking lot, and turn my head over to the side mirror, she stood out, rummaging through her purse. Probably her keys, before running over to her car.

I sped out of the parking lot, hoping that I caught August before she left her job.

She'd always leave last, she helps clean up, and never accepts help from anyone. I grew to admire her in that way. She always cared for others more than herself.

I turn over to the cafe down the street from the movie theater, the lights dimmed down as she emerges out the front door with her keys.

I jumped out of my car, the ruined bouquet in hand, her eyes met mine, she hurried to her car, but I reached it before her.

"Grayson. Please." She mumbles.

I swallow, "August, please just give me a chance. I'm sorry for pushing you away and I'm sorry I didn't tell you I love you." I handed her the flowers. "I do love you."

She looks up at me, "I'm sorry Grayson, now is just not a good time..."

"I didn't see you on campus today." I interrupt her as she frowns.

"I couldn't make it. I had work."

I hold her hand, "If you need the money, I have the money August."

She pulls away, "Will you knock it off, Grayson!" She throws the flowers on the floor, "This is over. Do you understand me?" She huffs out as I feel my chest break and constrict.

"I'm going to win you back. Is that possible?" I ask with a plea.

"Is it possible to win you back?" I say with my heart on the line.

She looks up at me, "Not right now." I felt my heart burn as she looked away. But she stopped and stood back up to face me.

"Grayson." She whispers, her hand on my cheek, "I love you so much."

I felt my heart lift, "So then what's the problem?"

"I want you to take care of yourself and your family issues first... Once they take you seriously and your relationship with them is rebuilt, I know you can handle a relationship. I will take you seriously." She smiles at me. The smile that I love so much.

She kisses my right cheek, holding my heart on her sleeve.

Then she got back into her car. Closing the door, turned it on and drove away.

Leaving me with a shred of hope, a shred of *maybe* there was a way to get her back.

CHAPTER 6

ADRIANNA

I should stop but I can't, I know. Addiction is bad. I know. I've heard every reason to stop whether, from a doctor, the internet, or the school education, and it pains me.

I start to sweat, and fidget like I was back at square one, where I cared about nothing else unless I got drugs in my system, *anything*.

But as I sit in my car, rummaging through my belongings, searching for any that I have left.

Xanax.

Valium.

Buspar.

Celexa.

Klonopin.

And my personal favorite, *Ativan.*

God, Grayson was right. I should start thinking about what the actual fuck is wrong with me. The reason why my father doesn't feel the need to care for me anymore, or why he's so fucking ashamed of me. I have never been able to escape that night.

I still get nightmares from it.

I still break down and relapse, and I hate myself for it. I *hate* myself for ever going back to drugs, but I promised myself that I wouldn't let it go as bad as it was.

I won't let it get that far.

Ever again.

I would never ever let it get that far.

I take a deep breath. My hands shook my throat feeling as if it was constricting. I turn on the light in my car, only to see my forehead sweating and my face turning red.

You'll be fine.

You'll be okay.

I rummage through my glove box, seeing a bottle of pills, my heart calms down as I pop the bottle open, place two pills into my mouth, and drink my water. My body slows down; my heart stops racing.

The tears that streamed down my eyes have dried, and my shaking hands have calmed as I place the pills back down in the glove box, hoping and wishing to God that I never have to use them again.

But then again that's the first part of relapse... feeling bad about it.

Feeling so bad that it consumes you from the inside out.

You act like it never happened. And that you can always try again, but in reality, you say the same thing next week.

I drove over to the club, my body feeling at ease as I walked in with the whole place buzzing with sound and dancing.

I first spotted Margo; she sat alone in a corner. My eyes were looking for Liam who had two brunettes by his side, paying no attention to Margo.

I walk over, "Hey..." I mutter as her frown quickly disappears into a gleaming fake smile.

But I knew my best friend.

"Hey! You're finally here." She stands up hugging me.

"Babe, are you okay?" I ask as she swallows. Her eyes sought the ground before enveloping me in a hug.

"Oh, it's awful Anna." She stresses. "I'm here making a fool of myself in front of a guy that shows no interest in me. I tried one last time and he's made it clear it was just a hookup and he used me."

I felt tears hit my shoulder as she shivers, "My dad wants me to date Ben."

I pulled away.

No freedom.

No choice.

She hugged me again. "I don't know how you keep it together all of the time. You are always so perfect and put together." She pulls away with a trembling smile.

"I do try." I laugh as I seek out Grayson, "Did your father give you a reason why he wants you and Ben together?"

Margo's face calmed, "Ben's parents are really close to mine. They have been pushing for a great match since freshman year now, he's a great guy, I might as well give him a fair shot."

I hugged her again, "I know it's not easy but maybe Ben is just what you need."

"Yes," Margo mutters. I knew full well that her eyes were on her prize, but she didn't have the energy to go for it yet.

I couldn't blame her. It's hard to make a real connection here. When people are basically out for your money or image. Who you are involved with in Hawthorne is your clique and you stick with it.

Once I pull away from her, I could see her face was still hurt, like she didn't want to let go, "I think for you to really move on you need to talk to Liam, as much as I hate him for what he did to you."

Margo nods, "Yes, thank you."

I place my hand on the corner of her mouth, "Now, show off your dimples!" I laugh as her smile grows bigger.

"Come on! You're finally here and don't even bother to dance?" Verina yells over as Juliette whines.

"I really have to go. My dad would go ballistic if I'm late for my curfew," Juliette yells as we frown.

"Fine, fine." We all beam, "Go on and get home safely please!" We hug her before she blows us kisses, turning away to leave.

"Don't you think the guys played well tonight?" Verina made conversation as I nodded.

"Did you see where Prince went?" Margo asked as I rolled my eyes.

"How am I supposed to know? I don't track down his every move."

The girls smiled, "You got a bit defensive over there." Verina mentions as I take a shot.

"I fucking hate the kid. He misplaces his anger on anyone he's around. Like I don't even mean to pry in his life, but I just can't help it when I do." I scream over the music. "He always has a bad fucking attitude with his inhumane temper that makes me insane I swear." I swallowed more alcohol than intended.

My face is already feeling red and hot.

We hear the doors open to Grayson Prince walking in.

He said he wasn't going to the party and yet here he is.

A liar.

A great amount has passed of me dancing, singing, and it all resulted in me panting, "Great." I groaned as Margo and Verina laughed.

Grayson's dead eyes settle on mine as I scowl.

"This is what my night needed, more of his fucking face and his lectures about how I deserve anything bad happening to me." I scowl over the private bar, grabbing a full bottle of tequila.

I pop open the lid, dosing in the liquid as my body feels more at ease than ever.

Verina pulls the bottle away from me, "Babe, that's enough you barely ate anything."

"No, I did eat," I mutter as Verina sets me upright.

Margo's hands are on my arms, to keep me from just fainting.

"Has she ever drank this much before?" Verina asks as Margo questions herself, "I've never seen her drink more than one sip of wine."

"Oh, how wonderful." Verina smiles.

I get up, "I don't need help, I'm fine." I shudder as they both gave me the "really" look.

"I'm serious, I can take more than one drink, guys." I point it out.

They look back at me, "We don't want to leave you alone."

I roll my eyes, "I was leaving anyways, I don't have any business here, it's not like I'm going to sleep with anyone or have a hot make-out session." I yawn, "Besides, I'm quite tired."

They look back with an eerie expression, "Are you sure?"

I smile, "Margo, talk to Ben." I look over to Verina, "V, go and pick a lucky boy." I mutter.

Verina bends down to kiss my cheek, "Okay, please call your driver to drive you home."

Margo comes back, "Don't you *dare* get in the driver's seat tonight."

"I won't!" I laughed as they both walked back to the dance floor.

I take a turn to leave before slamming into a tall figure, with muscles and all its glory.

"Can you watch it?" His voice was loud and banging in my head, looking up, it was Sawyer.

"Oh, sorry."

He mutters as I smile, "No, I'm sorry I didn't mean to." I take a step back, hitting someone else. I cringe at my clumsiness.

"Fuck." I whisper to myself.

Sawyer laughs, "By all means, you are welcome to bump into me at anytime and anywhere, sweetheart." He winks as I smile.

"I like your jersey." He points out as I look down to see that I was wearing his name on my back and chest.

"Yes, of course. But sorry to say, my team is better."

"Oh, you think so?" He asks, as I smile.

"Well, we did win." I make a point.

Darius Sawyer's head shakes with a smile, almost accepting his defeat with a great attitude, "I swear I'm good. You can see for yourself at my other games." He flashes a smile as I grow weak in the knees.

"Are you... hitting on me?" I question.

He laughs, putting his hands up in the air, "You caught me."

"Oh, I guess I did."

Darius was charming, easy on the eyes, and had a great attitude. Unlike others.

"So, what's a beautiful girl like you doing alone at this party? I would think that many guys would be over the fucking moon with you here, especially if you're single?" He asks with interest as he leans on the wall.

I felt my face turn red from the flattery. "Well, most of the guys here have already tried it and I'm sad to say I have rejected most of them." I grin with my attention on him.

He sends a questioning look, "What about Prince?" He mutters as I shiver at the name.

"Excuse me?" I gave a small laugh as his brows furrowed.

"I don't know, he kind of made it seem like you were *off limits*." Sawyer let out as I felt my body temperature drop.

"That's not possible." I counterargue as he nods.

"So, he wouldn't mind it if..." Sawyer moves closer, his mouth so close to mine.

"If..." I whisper, close to his lips before they touch.

Before someone touches my arm and gets a good grip, pulling me away. Grayson was in front of me, his eyes fired red on Sawyer.

"Don't touch her." Grayson sternly let out.

"She's not even yours," Sawyer mutters as Grayson lifts his fist.

Grayson walked closer to Sawyer, his face radiating evil and anger, as his fist clenched even harder, "Women don't have to be *mine* for me to punch a man that takes advantage of them." He seethes.

Sawyer backs off, "We were just having fun, Prince." He snickers, "Didn't know you were a prince charming." He practically spits at Grayson's face.

"You don't touch our girls. Do you understand?" Grayson pushes Sawyer back.

"If I fucking find out you continue to push yourself on to anyone that's under the influence of any kind, or point blank put your hands on them without consent..." Grayson pulls Sawyer in by his collar, slowly choking him out.

Sawyer taps Grayson's arm, in an attempt for freedom, but Grayson pulls tighter as Darius began to frantically fidget.

"I will cut off your dick." Grayson scowls, as Sawyer turns a hue of white from the lack of oxygen.

"Grayson!" I alarm for him to let go, but scowls at Sawyer then, letting him go. We watch Sawyer relieved that his airway still worked.

He huffed and puffed, looking at Grayson with hatred, before Grayson turns to me with a look of utter relief and annoyance, "And you're going home." He grits out before pulling me out of the club.

We got out of the club, in an empty street. My anger just reaches the top as he looks at me, "What the fuck is wrong with you?!" I pull my arm away from his grasp, though almost completely falling forgetting that I'm a little tipsy myself.

"You ask for me to leave you alone and then pull me away from a great conversation?" I yell as he sighs heavily walking away from me to the parking lot.

"Don't walk away from me!" I follow him as he turns around with his eyes dark.

"You're fucking drunk, Adrianna." He yells as I jolt. "You're drunk, and you were about to fall into Sawyer's trap." He growls, "You should be fucking glad I saved you from him."

"I don't need to be saved," I scream back.

He leans his head back in frustration, "Then don't put yourself in situations where you do need to be saved, you fucking lunatic."

"How do you know Sawyer's a jerk you don't even know him?" I say matter-of-factly as he looks away from me.

"I just know."

"You don't make sense, Prince."

He laughs thickly, "Neither do you, Princess." He whips around, his eyes daggers at mine, "Sawyer has probably gotten away with so many sex allegations because of his rich parents that pay off any girl's family he's assaulted." He yells as I jolt.

"You're making that up." I muttered, embarrassed that I probably was the next victim, I didn't want to admit to Grayson that he might've been right.

Grayson sends me a look of despair, "I don't know what I would've done if something happened like that to you." He said it so quickly that I might've missed it.

But I didn't.

His face contorts into a look of regret for saying it, "I don't know what I would've done if something happened like that to anyone." He corrects.

I send him a scowl that I understood that he tried fixing his abrupt sense of protection towards me as he walks closer, "Want to wipe that ugly look you have on your face for me, Dove?"

"Stop calling me that." I fire back as he takes another step closer.

"Not even in your dreams."

I smile, "Well, actually my dreams don't have any recollection of you at all. Almost like I dreamed that you never existed on this planet!" I say with ease, "Doesn't that sound fantastic?"

"Oh very." He leans forward closer again, "You want to hear about my dreams?" He turns me around, bending me over the hood of his car, his hand squeezing my waist, *"It actually has you star as the leading actress."*

I let my eyes close as his hands ran up, pulling me back up. "You're *touching* me," I mutter with a calm shock.

Grayson was touching me, and it burnt ecstasy. "I know." He winked as I turned around and my face flushed.

"Now get in the car." He commands as I roll my eyes.

"No, I'm actually driving myself home."

He looked at me like I had two heads, "The fuck you are."

I reach down his pockets, pull out a set of keys, and stuff them down my bra. I walk in front of him, "Without your keys, you can't drive, so you either let me drive myself home... or you won't be able to."

I felt goosebumps cover me all around.

"You think I won't get them back?" He walks next to me, and opens the door of his car, "Get in."

"You really think I won't resist you."

His eyes held a twinkle, "Yes."

I didn't understand why Grayson would care if I left by myself or not. He was the last person to think twice about letting me drive home by myself.

Obviously, I wasn't looking too good to drive myself, but he always did. Which was a perfect ploy that he could make up a miraculous event that sent to me disappear.

I was ready to stand there for an hour until he would've just left but by the challenging look in his eyes, I knew that it was a long shot to get him to leave.

Then it dawned on me that I promised Margo that I wouldn't drive myself home.

My father would *kill* me if I called Julius to take me home, even if he's done it before, I hate asking my servants or drivers to do things for me.

Which is ironic of course but, they were my family, it was late and I'm sure they needed the sleep more than I did.

I held my eyes on Grayson's marbled expression.

Yup. He was never going to let me go.

I watch him lick his lips.

"I hate you." I sneer.

I open the other door to his luxurious car to set my items on the back seat, fucking black interior, and exterior of course.

I walked over to the passenger seat to get in the car, he looked at me with an annoyed expression, he wasn't even going to hide his relentless smirk.

He slams the passenger door closed as I jolt.

"I'm quite capable of getting in the passenger seat, by myself." I seethed as he placed his hockey stick and duffle bag in the trunk. He walks over to the driver's side, capable of getting in on his own.

"Listen. I'm having a fucking terrible day so can you just shut the hell up and sit in the damn car in silence."

I roll my eyes looking defeated, he starts the car up and backs out of the parking lot.

My head rests on the window next to me as his hand gets stiff on the steering wheel.

"Nice game today." I swallow.

He laughs, "Oh right, sorry that your boyfriend didn't win." He turns his head to look at me.

"Sawyer did fine." I let out.

It wasn't his business to know if Darius was my boyfriend so why tell him? He probably thinks I like to mess around due to the fact that I was supposed to hang out with Brooks tonight but didn't.

But let us not act as if he didn't just go ahead and sleep with Maya anyway.

"Sawyer only wants you for your ass." He muttered as I held a straight face. "He had a dare to bag the hottest girl in Hawthorne and he was doing exactly that before I pulled you out."

Was he trying to piss me off?

"You don't know that."

"Yes, I do. He told me."

"He is a good person. I talked to him." I defended Sawyer as he turned back to look out the window.

"You fucking knew him for five minutes." He scoffed, "I've known him since our first hockey game. He is not a nice person, and if you do think so you don't have a good judge of character."

"Oh? And is your love life better? Who were the flowers for?"

He looks behind, before slamming on the brakes, causing me to lunge forward, banging my head on the dashboard of the car.

"What the fuck, Prince!"

He forms a smirk, "Sorry, I thought there was a squirrel on the road."

"Yeah right."

He scowls again, "We don't talk about her."

"Why does it matter to you if he only likes me because of my ass? It doesn't concern you at all, so I suggest you stay away from me and my love life."

He huffs out, "No, you're right, you should have a go at him if you really think he's a good person." I let my eyes roam his.

He was acting weird, maybe I actually hit my head pretty hard. "If you were so eager to lose your fucking virginity then so be it, but I just wanted to give you a heads up, most of the girls I've slept with are puck bunnies, they always come running back to me when Sawyer didn't satisfy their needs."

"Right." I mutter while twisting my purity ring around my ring finger, which felt like it was swollen.

My short answers bothered him, which I was happy about, his input on how I manage my love life was very unneeded and irritating.

"But that wouldn't matter, would it?" He smiled.

"Once a guy breaks your heart for the first time, you'll come running to daddy and cry to him about how the world is such a terrible place." He said with such ease, mocking me.

"And Mr. Cassian would be petting your fucking hair telling you that he would find whoever hurt you and make them pay because his little angel didn't deserve what happened." I felt my hands tremble as he kept talking.

My dad wouldn't give a damn to even check up on my fucking whereabouts, or how my day went.

He didn't know anything about me.

My eyes stayed on the road, "We've been at this for a long time. The bickering, the fighting, the insults." He played with the rings on his fingers.

"You hate me, and I hate you." He presses on the brakes lightly as we arrive at the front of my house, "As much as I want the fighting to end. All the words I had said to you that I couldn't take back... it's who we are, and we will never mean more to each other than that."

"It's always been a game." I smirk, "And your moves have been starting to get very predictable, Prince. "

He smiles, turning back to me, his eyes find my lips once more.

Kiss me.

"And I love how you're finally starting to fight back."

My stomach heated, and my cheeks flushed red as he stared at me, I couldn't help but maybe break the rules of our little game and kiss him. His lips look so good, as well as him as a whole.

"It's late, you should probably go." He whispers as I jolt.

"No!" I panic.

My eyes widen, grabbing my belongings and walking out of the car I drop my keys to the ground as he sighs.

I grip my keys and jump up to look at his confused face.

"No?" He laughs as I close my eyes in embarrassment.

Shit. I didn't mean that.

"Nothing." I let out as he tilted his head with confusion.

"Nothing." He says, as I smile falsely.

"Get in the car." He demands when I make the bold decision to walk further away from him.

I shiver, pulling myself in front of the gate. "What?"

"You are not going home by yourself." He lets out in an agitated voice.

"What are you, crazy?" I laugh, "Where do you expect me to stay?"

He turns around over to his house as I laugh, "Oh, you're fucked in the head." I laugh off, but then as his expression didn't change, he was actually serious.

He emphasizes as I take a breath, "I don't need that. Really." I smiled, hoping he would get the message.

He wrinkles his eyebrow. "Oh... well, I'm not really giving you much of a choice."

I grow agitated, "I'll be fine." I say defensively.

"Get in the car, Dove." He commands sternly.

"Prince..." I mutter as he pulls back.

"Get your ass in the car before I carry you and place you in there myself." He runs his hands through his hair as I huff out.

"Besides, you're drunk as fuck." He gives another valid point, "I know how to get rid of a hangover well."

My birthday was tomorrow and the mere idea of having to spend it alone, with an empty house was sickening.

More sickening than spending it with Grayson Prince. I wanted to help myself, and I knew that if I stepped inside my house by myself, I would take the pills.

What better way to resist that temptation than spending the rest of my night with Grayson Prince?

That will certainly keep my mind off of pain relievers.

I smile, slowly rolling my eyes to show I was still hesitant about the idea, "I need to go home early or earlier in the morning."

He laughs, "I know how a one-night stand rolls, Dove."

My eyes widen, fear built up in my throat, "What?!" I let my voice grow higher.

He sends a condescending face, "I was joking."

Oh.

I took a breath, letting my horrific expression disappear as he shook his head.

I jump to the passenger's side, "You know I could've technically just walked over to the other side of the street right." I smile as he turns over to look at me with a twinkle in his eye.

One that was very rare to be seen. I'd never seen him with light in his eyes, and yet they were beautiful. A beautiful blue ocean that I want to swim in.

He coughs, his smile disappearing in a millisecond. I turn my head back in front view as he drives his car to his garage, the doors opening.

He takes a breath, "We have to go the back way." I roll my eyes.

"Well, this is going to be great." I counter-showing him that I was capable of sarcasm.

He smiles, "No, I'll quite enjoy this."

"Did I ever tell you I hate you?" I get out of the car with a huff as he winks at me.

I start to walk towards the gate before stumbling into his arms. I hold myself up.

He was cold.

No. Not even cold, he was freezing.

"Dove." He calmly helped me stand up as the dried blood from his head made its way to my palm.

His face changed quickly from utter satisfaction to worry, which I never thought I would see in the man himself.

"Dove," He repeated as he held my gaze again, "You're burning up, you have a fever."

I pulled away, "I'm fine."

He gripped my arm, his face turning back towards me again, "No, you are not."

He looked at his house and then back at me.

Your house was supposed to be a place you felt safe in, the place your family can love each other. But with the look on Grayson's face, I can tell that love from his parents was nonexistent.

I swallowed, "Your father would lose his shit." He places his hand on my shoulders to steady me.

"My father isn't home." He let out as I squinted my eyes, "Come on, you would just love it if my father saw." He smirks as I roll my eyes yet again.

He pulls me by his arms, halting as he unlocks the gates.

We walked over to the back side of the house, "Which floor?" I ask.

He laughs, "The third one," He looks over at me as I scowl at him.

"No." I breathed out as he tilts his head, "Prince, are you mind fucking me right now?"

I bit my tongue to hold in a laugh, "Yes... but I can't have you caught on the cameras."

I look up to the window, "You're going to ask me to climb to your window, aren't you?"

I slouch as he taps his foot with impatience.

"How perfectly cliche." I mock with a smile, "No. You actually have to climb up to my balcony."

"I'll meet you up there now, and I'll help you by pulling up." He didn't wait for a protest as he zoomed inside his house, running to the room upstairs and staring down at me who was attempting to climb up already.

GRAYSON

I hear a crack, a branch falls as she shook, "Fuck." She curses to herself.

I laugh watching her. "Prince, you better not be laughing, or I'll throw a fucking pebble from this fountain to your head." I paused and watched her struggle. It was adorable.

Adorable?

God, am I fucked in the head?

She makes it up to arm's reach, I pull her up as she swings her legs over the edge, and she lands effortlessly, her dark hair was a mess, and she had dirt on her cheek, without thinking I let my hand wipe it away.

"Can I take a shower?" She coughs, pulling away as I hesitantly pull my hand away from her burning face.

"Yeah, uhm... I have a bathroom, it's the door next to my couch."

She walks in with confused eyes, "Which couch?"

I pointed to the black-colored couch, she faltered, making a stop, and turning back at me.

"This is your room." She mutters as I take a seat on my bed.

"Yes."

She laughs at my answer, what was so funny?

She ends up walking over to me with a smirk which later dies when I got up.

"You know, you shouldn't really trust me to be in a room with you." I stalked toward her, my eyes set on her small frame, the jersey she had on was loose, and the neckline fell to her shoulder.

There it was again, her honey eyes.

Hunger.

I eyed up her jersey which still had Sawyer's last name, I wanted to rip it apart.

Adrianna's eyes held promise, at the same time it could've been because she was drunk, but before I could stop her, her fingers curled on the jersey's seem, pulling it up.

My eyes wander straight to her white lingerie, which I couldn't help but admire, my eyes widening at her beautiful curves, every nook and cranny of her body I wanted to explore.

She shivers, her eyes holding contact with mine as I look away with a worried expression, "I'll go down and get you something for the head, or stomach or, uhm... I'll be right back."

My heart paused as I closed the door from behind me, what the fuck was my exact plan in all of this?

I didn't have one. I only had one goal and that was to get August back. So why did I have another girl in my room?

CHAPTER 7

GRAYSON

My fucking head pounded, and my whole body felt sore. I was sure it wasn't because of the practice. I've been through the worst. I walk around my room. The shower shuts off as I pick up a towel to hand over to her.

I entered my room, no sign of her at all. I didn't care all that much, only knowing that she couldn't have gotten far.

I laid her one of my shirts and a pair of my sister's shorts that I pulled out of her drawer in the bathroom.

Having Adrianna in my room was practically every guy's wet fucking dream, I won't lie and say I hadn't dreamt of her tied up to her bed and naked waiting for me to take her.

I was practically fucking hoping she would strip in front of me when I looked at her sitting so tasteful on my bed.

So fucking innocent.

Untouched.

Except that was just it. She was on my bed and that was it. There was no tension like I sensed. She most certainly does not feel anything for me.

Thoughts about her roamed around my brain once more like when she backed away, shaken up, the jersey she was wearing was oversized, and the neckline once again fell down to her shoulder, God her skin looked so delicate and soft I wanted to explore it.

When I looked down at her legs, her skirt inched up, and her creamy-tanned model legs buried into the back of my brain.

I imagined her legs around my waist, her soft hands gripping my back as I fuck her up the wall.

Her hot breath on my neck, moaning my name.

Fuck. I look down, my dick twitching at the thought of Adrianna just sitting there, her *innocent* brown eyes set on mine.

She was everything I hated and despised.

Why did she have to be so perfect?

Fucking hell her lips.

Lumped and full, the lips that had talked back to me every single day.

How would she fucking love it if her lips were around my shaft, sucking me as I fuck her mouth, gripping her hair tightly, pushing myself to the back of her throat?

Would she be able to?

Innocent.

I would release in the back of her throat, make her gag and swallow, gripping her chin to meet my eyes, I wouldn't hesitate to kiss her beautiful lips.

My imagination was wildly going off and I couldn't bring myself to stop until she opens the door from my closet, snapping me back to reality, I take a good look at her.

Adrianna with her hair up, my fucking eyes must've deceived me because I watch her bend down to pick up a hair tie, she was wearing nothing but the clothes I had laid out for her.

My fucking dick sprang back to life.

My eyes linger on her. Fuck, this *is* my wet dream.

The jersey she was wearing was on the floor discarded, and the skirt she had on was set neatly in the hamper near the door.

She lets her hair down, "Thanks for the clothes." Her eyes landed on my chest.

What a great day to have an eight-pack.

She coughs, throwing me a scowl, "I'll give it back tomorrow." Her eyes flow down to my scars, her face contouring in a concerned expression, then soon disappears as she spots my v-line, and her face flushes bright red.

"You can keep it."

Her face grew redder, fuck why was she so hard to find ugly?

"Listen, put on a shirt!" She breathes out while turning around.

I smile, "I don't wear a shirt to bed, Dove." Her face grew even more flushed, before turning around.

"Do you feel better?" I ask as she sneers, walking over to my bed and sitting.

I hesitantly walked over to her, taking a wet rag, and squeezing it so the water wouldn't leak. I bring it over to her forehead.

"You can lay on the bed," I instructed. I wasn't in the mood to fight her, not when my head was pounding, and my body felt weak. She lay next to me, propping her elbow up so I can continue to brush her forehead with the rag.

I look into her eyes, caramel and soft as honey.

She smelled like flowers and sweet honey.

"What is it?" She roll her eyes.

"Are you uncomfortable?" I asked slowly.

Me on the other hand, I was feeling a lot of things, and uncomfortable was not one of them.

"No, I feel relaxed," She muttered. "I can't remember the last time I felt relaxed," She admitted. Her eyes were soft again, almost as if she was happy.

She wouldn't let her eyes leave mine. I swallowed; it was like time stopped for a moment before her face pulls away from mine.

"Prince, I'm afraid that you are going to have to take me home." She mutters.

I laugh, "Like that's going to fucking happen."

"Oh no. I'm serious." She sat up as I grew curious.

"I will be doing no such thing." I insist as she rolls her eyes.

"No. I can't sleep."

I stand up, "You can, and you will."

She folds her two arms together, "No, I can't sleep without *Shovel.*" She speaks.

I tilt my head in question, "Who the flying fuck is *Shovel*?"

Adrianna frowned, "I've had him since I was a baby, okay? I can't sleep without him, it's my favorite stuffed animal. So sadly, I will not be able to sleep here without getting nightmares." I roll my eyes at her stupid command.

"Then I'll chase them away," I smirk as she pinched her lips in disgust.

I couldn't help but feel amused at my comment, even if she looked annoyed, I had to give myself props for the quick thinking.

But a fucking stuffed dog? The hell?

I walk closer to her as she leans back, burying herself down the bed, "Too bad, Dove. Sleep tight." I seethe as she breathes out in a huff.

I turn the lights off as she settles on the bed, I walk myself over to the couch, set my blanket up, and stare off to the front of Adrianna's house.

Her room was always across from mine, I could see the shadows of what she did, and it always fascinated me. Except, in my view, I saw the fucking stuffed dog she was talking about.

As I turned around trying to go back to sleep, I felt the stuffed dog's eyes burning through the back of my skull as she tossed and turned.

Her white, stuffed husky that she would carry everywhere in the playground.

I looked over to Adrianna who was asleep and yet she tossed and turned all around for thirty minutes.

I got sick and tired of her whines, so I got up.

If I planned on improving my stats the next game, I needed to be well-rested and, her rustling, turning, and whining were not helping me.

I walked out of my room, stalking out of the front doors, across the street in front of Adrianna's house. It seemed deadlier than alive. I climbed over the gate, to the back of her house, then climbed up the tree that led to her room's balcony. I hoped for the best that her balcony door was unlocked and thank God that it was.

I walk around Adrianna's room. I expected everything to be much more girly, all the hot cheetah print.

I wasn't stereotyping, but it just seemed that I was wrong about what her bedroom would look like. I had lived across from her for years and I didn't know the slightest thing about her.

I thought I did.

Instead, for a room that I thought was going to be, pink, purple, and fucking bright. I walked into a neutral, brown, beige, white, and gold. Her vanity wasn't the tacky ones I would see in the rooms of the girls I would sleep with.

Adrianna's room held an appeal of elegance.

Just her.

Her room held an abundance of books, she had a fireplace, a white couch, and a couple of comfortable chairs.

Picture frames hung on the mantle of her family and her friends, and even her help.

I had seen the guy that helped her blow out her candles, he was the one that took her to school every day. The lady beside her, kissing her cheek was the one that would take out the trash every Sunday.

But her formerly known father had a sit-down picture, she was maybe about thirteen, and her face was stone cold and held no emotion.

No love.

How is it that she looked far happier with her help rather than with her own parents? Had I been wrong again, assuming that she was her little daddy's girl?

I shook the thoughts out of my head as I looked at her bed, the stuffed white, dog lying on top practically missing its owner.

Who am I kidding? It was a stuffed dog; it didn't have feelings. If I had said that sentence aloud to Adrianna, I would surely hear a mouth full of it. I walked out of the balcony, closed the door, jumped down to the tree, and attempted to get down without hurting myself, which was the last thing I needed.

I quickly ran over to my house, finally no more parkour to get up to my room. I opened the door, she was hyperventilating, sweating, and shaking. I ran over to her.

I ran my hand through her hair, handing over *Shovel*.

She quieted, not gripping onto her stuffed animal, but instead, she gripped onto my arm.

Great. After I went through all that fucking trouble.

But she stilled, her breathing evened out, and she was at peace. I bent down to feel her forehead. She was still warm, but it calmed my freezing hand, and she groaned.

I let my head sink to her level, and I let my body sink into the empty bed space. She snuggled up closer to me, as I breathed out relief.

She cushioned her head on my chest, her hand on my body, hugging me, I looked at her calm face. Without thinking, I bent down to kiss her forehead.

Pulling away I froze.

I had finally tasted a little bit of her, she was sweet, so fucking delicious. Why had I let myself go there?

This was so wrong. It was forbidden. Not allowed. Me and her in a bed together, no one knew. But now I knew how she felt in my arms, and fucking loved it.

I wasn't sure if I could quit.

I wasn't sure if I was willing to even try.

CHAPTER 8

ADRIANNA

I wake up, turning my head over to the grand clock.

12:43 P.M.

My eyes widen at the clock. I shoot out of bed as my heart drops to my stomach, looking down at Grayson who was sound asleep next to me. Next to him, my stuffed dog lay.

Had he gone to my house to get it?

Holy shit.

I gathered my belongings as I threw a pillow at Grayson, "Prince!" I yell as he lazily opens his eyes.

"What the fuck is the issue, Dove? Get back to bed, it's too early." He mumbled before closing his eyes again I run over to his side, slapping him,

"It's past noon." I urged as his eyes shot across the sky.

"Fuck!" He yells, getting up and running over to the bathroom.

"I thought you said you knew how this works and that I would get out of here earliest or early enough," I huff as he stomps out of the bathroom in a rush.

"Shut up, we don't need your complaining today." He glowers.

I laugh, "You hate admitting you're wrong, don't you?" I fold my arms as he forms a devilish smirk.

"I'm never wrong, this was just a very unfortunate mistake."

I roll my eyes, turning around, "I have no clothes."

Grayson walks back in with an annoyed look, "We'll go to your house to get you your clothes, okay give me a damn second." He shoots out as I fold my arms together, tapping my foot on the floor.

"Can you please stop yelling; we just woke up," I mutter as he looks down at me.

"Why? It's what we always do, anyway, isn't it?" He smiles as he gives a smart-ass comment.

He basically threw every piece of clothing article he owned on the floor of his room.

"I'll go to my house myself; I don't need you fucking yelling at me." I saunter downstairs as he runs after me.

"You think that you can just walk away from me like that?" He yells back as he catches up fast.

"You should be thankful, without me you would probably be in a dump somewhere dead, or worst being raped by fucked up people!"

I turn around, my eyes scorching, "I didn't ask for your help!" We reached his living room. "Don't expect me to thank you when I didn't ask you for anything."

Grayson's face looked about done with me, I could see smoke practically coming from his ears.

His eyes were dark, and my face was red from yelling.

"My bad for being a good person for once—"

"Ahem."

We both turn around urgently, my soul left my fucking body, because the view of his entire family in the living room, was nothing pleasant.

Oh fuck.

Grayson stiffened behind me, as I remember that I was only wearing his shirt and his sister's shorts, he was eyeing me down.

Oh, this really wasn't good.

I began to shake as he interlocked my hand with his, my anxiety going down in an instant.

"Grayson." His father stood up, his mother's gaze on us as I swallowed.

"Father..." He utters without emotion.

His siblings were right behind his parents.

"Hello, dear my name is Sara." His mother's hand shoots up to shake mine before Mr. Prince walks in front of her.

"Dove, this is my mother, Sara." Grayson adds as Sara frowns slightly.

Grayson's father looked at me like I was the absolute scum of the Earth, like I wasn't allowed to even be near him.

"Grayson. May I please have a word with you in private?" He seethes like a snake; goosebumps surround my body.

I swallow as Grayson looks at me, almost like he wants to tell me he didn't want to leave me all alone but didn't. He just looks straight into his father's eyes, following him over to a large room that looked like his office.

Sara follows them.

I couldn't help but walk the rest of the way down, standing over by the entrance, my hands also couldn't help but shake without Grayson being next to me.

I didn't want to eavesdrop but, the voice of Grayson's father practically echoed through the entirety of the mansion.

"Would you like to explain why you have a Cassian in our home, let alone in *your room?*" He said it with venom.

"Are you serious, Grayson? Being seen with the enemy?!" I can infer that it was his brother, Easton shouting.

I swallow down, I never really predicted that they hated me this much, I get they had problems with my father, but I have never had interactions with any of them.

It was a two-way street, I guess.

"You could've picked any girl to settle down with, but you

pick a motherfucking Cassian!?!" His father seethes as I jolt at my last name.

Excuse me?

Grayson hasn't said much in the conversation which worried me, to the fact that he couldn't keep his mouth closed when he had argued... which was every day.

"This better not be one of your fucking games Grayson-"

"I don't want to fucking talk about this with you." I hear the door slam as I straighten, I turn around as Grayson's dead eyes stare into mine.

Although his father and the rest of his family ran out with Grayson.

As he reached the corner, his eyes looked like mischief and trouble mixed together, I was scared of what he was about to say, "This isn't a game. *She's, my girlfriend.*"

WHAT.

THE.

FUCK.

My eyes widened, complete fear folded within my face, absolute atrocity.

My eyes directly over to his father, his face already to explode before his wife pulled him in for a sidebar chat.

I look up at Grayson who almost can't believe he said it too.

Utter terror.

"What are you doing Prince?" I whisper harshly as he grips my hand harder.

"I'm not sure." He replies fast and quietly, his face holding the promise of uncertainty. It wasn't a common expression Grayson would have since he was a know it all and an ass wipe.

His siblings looked like they had all swallowed a lemon and saw a monster.

I wonder how I looked right now. I'm pretty sure I look utterly terrified, like a pale ghost.

I couldn't even bring myself to say anything. Grayson had a

plan in his head somewhere and if I ruined it for him, I wouldn't hear the end of it.

Which I didn't even care about... So why am I staying quiet?

Safe to say... I panicked.

His father walks back up, his eyes serene.

Before he walks away completely, his wife coughs, as if she was forcing him to do something.

I swallow, feeling my hands curl into fists.

"I would like to have you for dinner maybe on Friday?" He mutters as I almost choke on my own saliva.

Grayson's face looked gob smacked.

"I'm sure she's busy—" Grayson starts.

His mother pauses, "Well, I was very excited to see her have dinner with us—" She probes as I smile thinly.

Grayson's face died, almost like he was upset that he was once again disappointing his father if I had said no.

And it was not going to be on my watch, I let Grayson's face fall.

I smiled. "Of course, I would love to have dinner." I voiced as he changed his face to a stern look, his eyes back to his son's.

I wasn't sure myself why I said yes to the invitation, my heart was practically exploding.

Grayson tensed, but I rubbed my thumb on his palm, easing stress, almost like it was an instinct.

"This is really the first time I've seen you serious about something, and as the man who will be inheriting my business, I want to trust that you can be serious about certain matters." His father fixes his suit.

"Whether it is something I disapprove of." He coughs out.

I flinch, my heart rate is basically up to fucking Mount Rushmore. "I am proud of you."

It was almost fucking painful to hear his father say it.

Grayson swallowed; I could feel him shake like his whole persona was getting broken.

It was odd to see him this way. I had never seen him so off guard. So terrified, so down.

So not himself.

Did his father not know how serious Grayson was on a regular basis? It was almost like he never showed any emotion at school or even at hockey. During games, he would get run over and yet he still came out on the top.

I had only really seen him... *serious.*

"Will your father be attending the dinner?" Shock waves send fireworks through my body as I look at Grayson.

My face was alarmed. "I'm not sure, sir... he is pretty busy." I let out as his face was stricken.

"You can call me, Silas." He says sternly as I nod.

"I'm sure your workaholic father can take an evening off for his only daughter." He smiled, but I could tell it was a fake grin.

"I would love to have a chat with an old friend." He winks.

They were far from friends.

"I might even have my people contact him!" Grayson's father smiled as I felt my heart drop.

"That's great!" I coughed as Grayson gave me a look of utter disbelief.

He was going to hear a fucking earful.

"Oh, Grayson! I am so happy for you!" His mother smiled, walking over to us with open arms, and hugging us together. I send him a "fuck you" look.

She lets go, "We actually have to, get to our morning classes... and I'm taking her out for lunch... It's her birthday." Grayson mentions as I turn over to him.

"We are?!" I mistakenly let out as his eyes widened with mine.

"Well, it was supposed to be a surprise, Dove."

I laugh, "Oh!"

His little sister runs over to me, "Does this mean I have a sister now?!" She smiles with flying colors. I let her hug me.

"Well, of course." I smile back.

"Rhylee." Grayson coughs out, "We really have to go." He

probes as I start to make my way over to the front door, Grayson following.

"I'll see you on Friday." I grin over, waving, "Thank you so much for having me over." Grayson pushes me out of the door, slamming it closed.

I don't even look behind me as I feel my anger build from inside me, I speed walk over to my house before he catches up to me. I turn around.

"I cannot fucking believe you right now, Prince." I seethe out as he lets go of my arm.

"Look, I am so sorry," He lets out as I look at him with irritation.

"Your 'sorry' isn't giving me satisfaction right now!" I fold my arms in front of me as he sighs.

"You said your parents weren't going to be home."

"They weren't!" He answers.

"And your siblings too?!?!" I yell as he flinches, "Well..."

"Un-fucking-believable!" I scream at him as he knits his eyebrows as well as his eyes.

"What the fuck do you want me to do then, Cassian!" He threw his hands up, as I gave him a blank look.

"Go back in there and tell them you were lying!" I argue as he laughs.

"Over my dead body."

I run my hand over my hair, "Why?" I fume as he covers his face with his hands in frustration.

"I need your help okay!" He screams out as I shut my mouth.

"Why?" I sigh.

Grayson looked defeated like he was embarrassed.

"Because this is a great opportunity to show my father that I can be serious, that I can get my ex back, showing her that I can handle another relationship." He lets out with a shaky voice.

"You are lying to them!" I mused.

"I want to prove it to myself too, Dove." He admitted as I bit my lip.

"Prince, you are nothing but serious," I assured him as he shook his head, disagreeing.

"That's not enough." He dictated.

I felt my heart tighten.

I hated Grayson. I hated him and I loathed him. But the way he looked at me now was full of vulnerability.

He was serious.

"What do I need to do?" I closed my eyes, not believing the fact that I had just agreed to this.

CHAPTER 9

GRAYSON

"So, we are actually dating?" She asks as she sat across from me, with a paper in hand and in a pen in the other.

I roll my eyes, "*Fake dating.*"

She impatiently muttered, "How are we going to play this?" She rolled her tongue in her mouth as I knocked my head back.

"Hey, don't give me this attitude. This is your doing; we are in this predicament in the first place because of you." She said with conviction.

"This should be really easy." I huff out.

She scowls, "How are we going to tell our friends?"

I fidget with my rings, "We tell them the truth and they help us with the lie."

Adrianna's eyebrows furrow as she looks down at her checklist.

"Is this all necessary?" I lean forward, folding my hands together.

"I like being prepared." I sneered as she let out an effortless smile.

"You will not be running for president this year." She folds her arms together with a wide smile.

I lift myself up with urgency, "The fuck I will."

Adrianna places the pen's tip in her mouth, "Do you want my help, Prince?" She says in a friendly fashion.

I deemed aggravation as she winked, "Your relationship with me will give me great publicity as well as make Brooks jealous." She went on.

"You actually like that dickhead?" I laugh harshly as she glares.

"I don't like him, I just want him to regret his decision to cheat on me with Maya, which is another candidate I'm running against."

I nod.

It was rare to see Adrianna bothered by anyone else other than me really, and the way she talked about Brooks made it really look like she was betrayed.

"So, revenge, more like?" I yawn as she nods.

"And besides, not to make your head any bigger but, you are the hottest guy known around here, so..." I smile at her as she looks away quickly.

"Did you just... compliment me?" I let my grin advance as she snaps her mouth closed at the sudden shock of realization.

"No, I'm just repeating the latest gossip."

I lean closer again, looking into her honey eyes, "It's not gossip if it's real, Dove."

"I hate you." Adrianna huffed as she scribbled with her pen.

"Why? I'm quite lovely." I flash a smirk that she so famously hated.

"So, when is our anniversary?" She asks as I just looked at her blankly.

"Today," I say, irritated.

"Great." She rolls her eyes, writing down on the piece of paper, "If you want this to look believable, you need to actually put the effort in."

I look at her, "I don't even understand why you're willing to help me, you have never done anything else than argue with me."

She looks up, her smile thinning, "I'm feeling generous."

She places her pen down, "I have a question."

I lean back, "Okay..."

"...Will you be seeing other people?" She asks, "Like... will you sleep with other people?"

I haven't really thought about this aspect of the fake relationship. It was known that I slept with many women, I was of course safe and clean. But being in a relationship with August, I had never slept with anyone but her.

So, it wouldn't be different from this would it?

"Will you?" I question as she smiles.

"No." She said it rather quickly.

I flash a smile, "Why?"

Adrianna had looked at me like I had seen a ghost, but her face calmed down, "I know what you're doing." She urged.

"I don't know what you're speaking of." I roll my eyes as she grips the collar of my shirt.

"I'm trying to have a serious conversation with you!" She probes as I form a smirk, "And I'm trying to subtly avoid it!"

Adrianna's eyes turn a dark hue of brown, not like the honey she would have, "Well, fucking stop. Can you please work with me here?"

"I know how to be in a relationship, Dove. I'm not a rookie, I know my *boyfriend* duties." I simply smile as she frowns.

"Well, I need to know the basics of your so-called *duties*." She puts it in quotation marks.

Until I finally figured it out, she was nervous this whole time because...

"Dove." I flash a look of curiosity as she looks up, her lips trembling.

So kissable.

"Prince." She answers while giving me her full attention.

I tilt my head, "Have you... ever been in a relationship?"

Adrianna's eyes widen, as her face flushes in a light hue of pink and red.

I smile, her expression embarrassed. "What?"

"You haven't!"

She caves herself with her hands, "You make it seem like it's a bad thing!"

I keep my eyes on her red cheeks, "It's not! I think it's cute!"

She reaches over, slapping my arm, "Hey! You are not allowed to think that I am cute!"

Adrianna covers her face up as I quickly swipe the paper and pen from her reach.

"Prince!"

I sent her a playful scowl, "I want to see what you wrote down!"

"You do realize that we have to spend time together and enjoy it." I yawn as she nods.

"In classes, out of classes, at home." She listens as I take the pen, scribbling down on her paper.

"Hey, what are you writing down?" She looked unsettled.

"I'm not going to ruin it," I mused.

"No, it's not that. I like my things organized; I need it all in my handwriting." She went on as I held the pen out.

Before she took it, I pulled it away, "This is a relationship, right?"

"Sadly." She mocked.

"And it takes two to tango, Dove." I take a look at the pen, then back at her, "This list or contract of yours should have a little piece of both of us, shouldn't it?"

Adrianna bit her lip, rolling her eyes, "Fine, but tell me what you wrote."

I tap on the written words, "You must come to all my hockey games and show me, your *boyfriend*, support." Adrianna gives me some type of dirty look that could kill.

She was very un-enthused.

"Great! I just love hockey."

I coughed, "Well, because of that attitude of yours." I wrote down one more thing, "I wouldn't mind a handmade poster."

"Sure!" Adrianna smiles, "I'll give it to you after I shove one of the million hockey sticks you own up your ass."

Adrianna looked at me with demise on her mind as I laughed, I hadn't really seen this side of her. We barely even had any conversation since the time I knew her we were always taught to stay away from each other.

"Hey, if it makes you feel better, I'll tell our parents that I said that I liked you first."

Adrianna nods with her shining smile in view again.

"But we have a problem." She makes a notice.

I yawn again, "Which is?"

"Obviously, it's known and very well captured by our peers that we hate each other." She points out, "But even our friends hate each other."

"You mean, Liam and Margo." She nodded.

"If we want this to work out, we need to convince everyone around us that we are dating."

"Isn't that the whole point of this?" I stress.

She continues, "You know, you're going to have to work really hard not to fall in love with me after all of this."

She smirks as I rub it off. Over my fucking dead body.

"I would rather sell my whole car collection than ever actually catch feelings."

Adrianna's smile grows, "Here, how about you try flirting with me?" I laugh, rolling my eyes as she settles back in her chair.

"Pretend we are at dinner with our parents?"

I shot her a blank look, "You look like a Picasso painting."

Her face morphed into an offended expression.

"Do you know how Picasso painted people?" She exclaimed.

I laughed, "Indeed, I do."

"I can't stand you." She slaps my arm again.

"In my defense, I never really passed art."

"I knew it!" She shakes, "What is it?"

"I knew you couldn't be genuine, even if you tried."

She starts to pack her things up, "I can be genuine!" I defensively stated as she laughed, "I'm serious."

"You flirt like how you play hockey." She looks me dead in the eyes, "Without effort."

She continues, "You think everyone just wants to be with you because you are the *great* Grayson Prince!" She mocks, "Everyone throws themselves at you, I bet your friends aren't even really your friends. They only stick with you because you might sue them if they abandon you."

Adrianna's well-composed self was out of the window, and with my stubbornness and her pride. We bickered but we were well into arguing.

"God, of course, how foolish could I be to think we can have a solid conversation without fucking screaming at each other?"

I certainly felt my blood pressure rise, "As opposed to you, who lives in a princess world where maids make your bed, and you spend about five hours on your make-up because you need to be perfect for others' approval."

Adrianna's eyes boiled with bitterness.

"You are so arrogant about everything, including people's feelings, maybe that's why your ex dumped you in the first place. She didn't feel compassion, instead, you looked at her and paraded her around like a prize." She grew out of breath, "It's what all you men know how to do."

"And you think you aren't arrogant as well, Dove?" I laugh in frustration, "You think you can just run that pretty little mouth of yours whenever you want?"

I stood up, "You take pride in other people's insecurities, you shame others for the way they dress at school, you don't do favors, because there has to be something for you to get in return, and you have all these great ambitions and yet you haven't achieved anything in your life that's worth something your father can be proud of."

Adrianna sat back down slowly, her eyes staring off.

"We both aren't perfect." She starts as I look down at her,

"You need this fake relationship to work because you want your parents to take you seriously and to prove to your ex that you can handle a serious relationship." I swallow.

"And you need this fake relationship to work because you want to win the election. It boosts your image, and you want Brooks and Maya to kick rocks. And to make him realize he shouldn't have cheated." I repeat to her as she breathes out.

"Look, we know that we both have differences and that we can't stand each other."

"We both don't want to do this, I know. But you have to understand that we need this, more than anything." I continue as she finally looks up at me.

"Everything is temporary, this is very much just temporary." She reassures herself.

I bend down to her, "I promise that I will break your heart at the end of this, *fake girlfriend.*"

Adrianna smiles, standing up and placing her hand out for me to shake.

I take it, "I'm counting on that."

CHAPTER 10

ADRIANNA

G rayson and I arrived at the front of the university, though it wouldn't have mattered because we had practically skipped the whole second day.

"I guess..." He looked at me with hesitation, "We can gather them together at Hawthorne's Cafe." He asks as I nod.

"Don't forget. Do not tell the boys why until you see me and my friends. Right, when Liam finds out that Margo will be there, he will bolt." I felt stressed as he shook his head.

"I think it would be your girl that would bolt, sweetheart." Grayson walks closer, leaning onto me as I scowl.

I smile sarcastically, "Oh right! Because he's the asshole and heartbreaker in this situation?"

His eyes narrowed as I smiled, "Don't start."

Grayson's brows furrow with agitation, his annoyance with me was out of the roof, "You know as my girlfriend you should—"

Without letting him finish, I shut the door quickly in front of his face, flipping up my middle finger as he smirks, winking at me before turning his head to drive away.

Yeah, we would be such a great power couple. I walk into the hallways, as everyone is dismissed. I watch as Verina, Margo, and Juliette spot me.

"There she is." Margo made a point as I walked toward them with a guilty smile.

"Where the hell have you been?" Verina exclaimed, "You missed the lab today and we still have the bake sale tomorrow."

Margo looked upset, "We thought you missed your birthday!"

I smile, hugging my best friends, my ride or die. I know it seems cliche, but I honestly wouldn't know where I would be if I didn't have them.

"I know I'm sorry, but we had an emergency, which I need to bring you all over to now!" I grip all of their arms, pulling them over to the exit.

"We?" Juliette questions.

I let out a nervous laugh, "Oh yes, that's a funny story."

She gave me a concerned look, "How funny?!"

"Margo, unlock your car and drive over to Hawthorne's Cafe."

Margo takes her keys, pressing the unlock button, as I run everyone over to the car.

"What is up with you?" Verina questions.

"I will not be explaining anything until we get there." I make a point as they all glance at each other.

Margo raced through traffic as I caught a glimpse of the destined cafe.

We all unloaded and walked in. The cafe was small, as if it came out of a storybook. The cozy couch looked like it had our names on it.

The cafe was not well known and honestly, it was a perfect hang-out spot.

I took a look around, noticing not a single customer was in sight. Unbelievable, he was unpunctual as well.

The girls looked at me like I had lost my mind, "Anna." Margo began as she folded her arms together in front of her, Juliette sat down on the cozy couch as Verina paraded around snooping.

"Is there a reason why you are acting so bizarre?" Margo looked behind me, her eyes were a scorching mess.

A fire burned, as the doorbell of the front door rang.

I turn around, sighing in relief at Grayson and his friends looking about as lost as little ducks.

"Grayson." Liam gave an irritated look as I widened my eyes at Liam and Margo's death stares.

"Sit." Grayson had only said one word and his group listened, and there we stood, in front of everyone.

They looked at us with curiosity and with furious faces.

"What was so fucking important?" Liam nudged as Margo crossed her arms.

"They were getting to that part before you opened your fucking mouth."

I looked at Grayson one last time, he had no expression on his face, he was a cold block of ice.

I coughed, "We're dating." Both of our groups looked like they swallowed poison and just discovered it.

Margo's jaw dropped to the floor, as Liam's face lost life.

Verina dropped a plant that she was examining, Juliette had been bothered enough to close her book, fully may I add.

Neil pulled his cigarette away from his lips to form a concerned expression.

And lastly, Chris let himself fall on the couch with ease.

"Excuse me?" Margo laughed at the idea.

I opened my lips to say something before I was easily interrupted by Verina who walked over to us yelling, "I knew this day would happen!"

Juliette rolls her eyes, "I had more faith in you!" She yells at me, whilst passing a one hundred bill over to Verina.

My eyes widen at the trade, my face fuming, "You two made a bet on me?!" I bug out with complete and utter annoyance.

They quieted as my eyes narrowed at the bill.

"It was only a silly bet!" Juliette tucks her face back in her book as I let my face grimace.

"Give me that." I walk over to her as she scowled at me, slowly handing me the hundred-dollar bill, "I cannot believe the both of you."

Margo walks up next to me, with her finger pointed, "This is so upsetting!"

Verina's eyes bulged so much they looked like billiard balls, "You owe a thousand!"

My mouth dropped open, looking at Margo with a condescending face.

Her lips thinned, "Well... I'll just..." She walks away from me slowly, scared that if she moves the wrong way, I might skin her.

"Listen up!" Grayson sternly commanded, causing me to jolt and everyone to quiet.

"We are *fake* dating." He addresses smoothly.

"I was just about to get to that." I said irritated.

"You were taking too long."

"Why?" Chris's eyes shot over to ours.

My smile reached both of my ears, "Oh yes. This is a wonderful story! Tell them, Grayson, *tell them why*." I smirk, folding my arms.

Liam interrupts, "Was this because of August?" My head turns over to Liam, "Let me guess, she wants you to prove to her you can be in a serious relationship, so you fake it to get her back?"

Margo laughs, standing up, "No, this is about Adrianna's campaign. It has to be, or to piss off your dad?"

Juliette hands the money back over to Verina, "It doesn't count if you two aren't actually together."

"A, you have got to be joking, you can't possibly be up for this with a Prince!" Margo shoots out as Neil places the cigar back in his mouth.

"Well, it doesn't really look like they are asking for our approval."

I looked up at Grayson who nodded, "It will only be temporary." I assure them as Liam nods in agreement.

Margo flashes a wicked smile, "Of course, you would agree if it was only *temporary*."

I nervously started to fidget as Grayson's hand crawled behind my lower back, causing me to calm myself.

"We have to make this believable, and of course, you guys are going to help us."

"And what if we don't?" Neil smirks.

Grayson's eyes darkened in a way that held a promise that no one would enjoy, "You want to run sprints, Vanderbilt?" he seethes.

Neil's posture changes quickly, "No, cap."

I roll my eyes at Grayson, "Stop ordering them around like servants, they are your friends!"

He laughs, "I was only joking!"

"Right." I held my arms, holding question to his statement.

Grayson, being insufferable, ignores my expression, his eyes direct over to our group of friends.

"We have to make this relationship really believable. I want August to be really shaken up, I want her to be jealous." He starts.

Grayson takes a look at me for a moment before continuing his plan.

Well, *our* plan.

"Cassian wants Brooks and Maya to get pissed as well, she's also running for president, which I *kindly* backed away from the position."

I slap Grayson's arm, "No, you did not!"

He gives me a dirty look whilst rubbing his arm with a low curse. I think I smiled a little at his pained expression.

Margo shuffled, "What exactly do you need us for?"

Liam interrupts, "They need to make this believable so, obviously they are asking their trustworthy friends to help, sweetheart."

"By how, exactly?" She quickly asks Liam with attitude.

Juliette stands up, "We know them the best, we teach them the other's dislikes and likes."

Margo smiles, "Oh! I'll start." Margo grabs my arm.

She pulls me in, "She dislikes you." She didn't fail to send a horrid look over to Grayson, whose eyebrows furrow at the disrespect.

Liam pulls his best friend in next to him, completely dividing us, "You're no picnic either, sweethearts." Liam spits out as Grayson gives him a playful irritated look.

"Get your fucking hands off of me." Grayson shook Liam off as he walks near me, pulling me in, causing my goosebumps to appear.

Grayson's blue eyes capture mine, softening, then hardening, his hand brushes my face, and my face turns red.

"We can be convincing." His lips curve into a deadly smirk.

I felt my throat dry up, "Yes, of course."

Grayson winks, letting me go, turning over to Liam and Margo.

"Now, I can't believe I have to say this, but you all have to get along. Even if we can't stand each other, you most certainly can try."

Liam and Margo looked at us like we were delusional, "That is rich coming from the both of you! Do you realize that you two have been put against each other since I don't know..." Margo flipped.

"You were born!" They both exclaimed.

I roll my eyes, "Gee thanks for the massive support, you lunatics."

Verina laughs, "This is obviously a satire." She turns to us, "Right?"

"No." Chris stands, "This is sadly not a satire because Grayson would never touch Adrianna like that *just because*."

He looks at both of us, examining our every action like we were lab rats, "Not even within a ten-foot radius." He finishes his sentence.

I look at Grayson with an offended expression, "What, do you think I have lice or something?!"

Grayson shrugs, "Maybe mono."

Neil laughs, "Look, does this mean we have to hang out as a group?"

"Yes." Grayson and I say at the same time.

"Because there is no fucking way in hell, I will be able to stand being around him by myself for maybe an hour give or take."

Margo takes a deep breath, "Okay, we need to make your debut in Hawthorne University tomorrow." She says nervously as I smile thinly.

"Wonderful." Grayson mutters under his breath.

"Why are you complaining? This was your idea."

He laughs, "Yes, but I shouldn't have underestimated how difficult you would make it, can we just fake a date and move on?"

"No, are you dumb?" I address as his jaw clenches, "You said you want your ex jealous. You said you want to prove a point, and you also, might I add said that you can handle it."

"I can handle it, Dove."

I smile, "Are you sure?"

He took a look at his friends, as I took a look at mine.

"Tomorrow morning, I'll drive her to campus, make sure everyone is up at the front, especially August." He looks back at me. "Make sure to look pretty."

"Don't I always?" I smirk.

He bends down, "You sure you want to ask me that?"

I think my hand twitched, my brain sending wild signals for me to take a heavy swing on the six foot five inches of muscle next to me.

Chris frowns, "You guys sure about this?"

Neil walks over to Chris with a playful smirk, "This is going to be fun."

I pull Grayson back, "We have award ceremonies tomorrow, I get presented, I want you there."

Grayson coolly nods.

"I'm serious, this is important to me, and even as my fake boyfriend, I want you there."

Grayson smiles, "I'll be there, Dove. I promise."

He turns over to Margo, "I don't think I need your help to figure out Cassian's favorite things." He says with a smirk.

I told my arms, "Oh yeah?"

The girls walk over to my side, as Grayson sits on the large sofa, next to his best friends, "Give me all you've got. I've spent my years studying up on my enemy."

Juliette's smile widens, "Know thy enemy and know yourself; in a hundred battles, you will never be defeated. When you are ignorant of the enemy but know yourself, your chances of winning or losing are equal—"

"—If ignorant both of your enemy and of yourself, you are sure to be defeated in every battle." Neil interrupts.

"Sun Tzu." Neil finishes.

We all look at them with odd expressions.

Juliette's eyes dawn on Neil's, while tilting her head.

"You read Sun Tzu?" She asks.

Grayson, Chris, and Liam looked about as stunned as the rest of the girls as he was quoting one of Juliette's heavily praised books. Grayson looking lost kind of made me want to laugh.

Liam's jaw had dropped, and I don't even think he knew.

"You *read?*" He says exasperated.

Neil pushes his friend, "Not a lot."

I look over to Juliette whose lips curved into a small smile, her dimples showing. She hadn't smiled in a while since her mother's passing.

Grayson coughs as I snap back into the current situation, which was the fact that he thinks he knows more about me than my friends could teach him.

All I have to say about that is... *good luck.*

I smile, "What's my favorite color?"

Grayson yawns, "Beige."

"It's red." Verina scowls.

"What's my favorite book?" I fold my arms.

Grayson smiles, "The Beautiful and Damned."

Margo flips up her middle finger, "Little Women."

"What's my favorite flower?" I ask.

"Roses. Which girl doesn't like roses?"

Juliette opens up her book, "White tulips."

"Oh, so what?" He muttered, folding his hands together.

"That shit doesn't matter. We just have to put on a show." He said with an irritated face.

Grayson reaches into a bag that Neil held out, pulling out a necklace, "What's that?" I lean over to look.

He smiles, his eyes narrowing at the necklace, "I bought it for you." He throws it at me.

"To make this," he motions to both of us, "more believable, I spoil my girlfriends." He yawns as I walk toward him with a challenging smirk.

"I'm not your *girlfriend*, Prince."

Grayson took a step forward in front of me.

Making me feel like I was helpless around him, "Oh but you are...my love."

I frowned, defeated by his words because he was right. And I hated the fact he was right, nor the day that I would ever admit the fact that he was right.

He smiles, "Now, why don't you flip that frown upside down and put it on."

"Put it on her!" Verina smiled, pulling out her phone.

"Ew no. Don't touch me." I sneered at Grayson who pinched his lips.

"I'll take photos of you guys to make it look like this has been going on for some time, and it makes it more believable. Why would someone want to take a photo if it wasn't memorable?"

I look at Grayson and at the necklace that simply had the letter *G* attached and dangling on it.

"Take it as a birthday present. I never wished you a happy

birthday." Grayson whispers as I felt goosebumps cover my whole body.

He made sure to say it quietly enough that the whole group didn't hear, make it a moment just for us.

I smile, *"G?"* I question as he smirks.

"Of course, I want everyone to know you're mine, Dove." He admitted as I shut my mouth momentarily apparently losing all my ability to speak.

"No one owns me." I finally say as he nods slowly.

"We'll see."

I opened my mouth, kind of hoping I would get a word out again. But nothing left my tongue, no sarcastic comment, no bite-back response, nothing. Instead, I swallowed, handing him the necklace, and turning around for him to lift my hair.

His hand was rough and calloused, strong, and muscular arms. He was close to me, he had to bend down a bit, his breathing ragged and brushing the nape of my neck, causing goosebumps to emerge.

My body shivered and I swear I wanted to slap myself for letting him affect me.

I felt relaxed and my body even hummed, I closed my eyes as my lashes fluttered.

I look down at the necklace as my eyes scan the gold, "How much did you spend on this?" I scowl.

He winks, "Too much."

"You have like seven million dollars around your neck right now." Liam yawns as my eyes widen.

Everyone's mouth practically drops, especially Chris who looked like he wanted to bury himself in a whole and never come out.

"My birthday was yesterday, and he didn't even get me anything!" Liam voices as I laugh, looking at Grayson who rolls his eyes.

"Your friendship with me is your present every year." He advertised while walking over to Liam messing up his hair.

"You did not spend that much on this," I pondered as Grayson walked back towards me.

Grayson looked like he couldn't be bothered, "Well don't you women like that shit?" He turns, "Especially you?"

Suddenly, the goosebumps and relaxation from my veins get replaced with rush and annoyance. "What's that supposed to mean?"

"Don't give me that shit, Dove." He says, shaking his head over to me, "You have never worked a fucking day of your life."

"And you have?" I shot back as he formed a smirk, pulling out his phone which coincidentally rang.

"Hey Shauna, please book Mr. Peterson tomorrow. I have to postpone this meeting, I have plans tonight."

Grayson's eyes sparkled at mine, he turned off his phone, "Bossing people around isn't working. It's called being lazy and privileged."

"Oh, so you're admitting that you are lazy and privileged?" He seethes as I feel my blood boil.

How come I never get to fucking win with him, he always gets the last word in or the better grade. I felt my face turn a hue of red, "Careful, Dove..." He caresses my cheek, "We wouldn't want people to think I could rile you up you?"

I snap his hand away from my cheek, "You do rile me up. Not in a good way. You make me fucking irritated." I sneer as I pick up my bag, looking at the girls as they all stand up.

"Good luck playing with yourself." I wink as I walk out the door.

"I'll pick you up tomorrow!" I hear his voice in the far direction as I slam the door shut, the bell drowns him up.

I take a deep breath out as I look at Margo, Verina, and Juliette.

"I can't believe you went through with this." Verina looked shocked as I walked away.

"I mean, it's Grayson. Grayson, remember?" Juliette probs as I continue to walk.

"The guy that put gum in your hair."

"The guy that pushed you in the pool during gym class."

"The guy that crashed right into your car just because."

"The guy that put a permanent marker all over your favorite pair of Louboutin."

"ENOUGH!"

I pause, turning to look at all of them as they bolted still.

"Margo?" I turn to her as she smirks over to the other two, "How long have you known me?"

"Well enough to know she has something else planned for Mr. Prince."

Juliette looked frazzled, "Will you tell us?"

She walked closer as I smiled, "And ruin the surprise?!"

"Anna." Margo rolls her eyes.

"I'm joking." I laugh, do my friends think I'm a serial killer because damn.

"Do you not have much faith in me to not guess that I will be making sure his relationship with me is hell? I will keep doing my duties to win the election and of course, that means forcing him to do things he wouldn't want to do."

"Like?" Verina asks.

I wasn't quite sure yet.

"I'll get back to you on that."

We all take a breath, "What's the deal with you and Liam?" Juliette yawns, addressing Margo.

"What do you mean?"

"I never really knew that your one-time hook-up was serious, and you just look like you were way more hurt than if it were just any other guy."

"I don't care about what Liam is up to or doing, it's none of my business. Frankly, he's a douchebag and I should've seen it before I slept with him.

"You did know he was a douchebag before sleeping with him." I mutter, "Or do you not remember the years of endless torment from not only Grayson, but Liam too?"

"How is this even going to work?" Verina interrupts.

"What do you mean? We literally just had a meeting about this." Juliette answers.

"I mean." Verina says, "Do we have to... converse with them? And act like we like them and that we can stand them?"

I turn to her, "I'm not even going to answer that because I dread the words."

"But come on, have a little fun with this." I smile at them.

"Margo, this is the best time to start getting to know your new boyfriend that your dad set you up with, and you can compare how great he is compared to... Liam."

Margo smiles.

"Juliette, this is your moment to help the boys with some of their hockey, since you're obsessed with it and complain about their techniques."

She scowls, "They wouldn't listen!" She huffs out.

"Besides, my father would never let me interfere with that shit. That's his hockey team and just because I'm his daughter doesn't mean that I get to make calls."

Verina smiles, "It should."

I looked over at Verina who already had a smirk on her face the moment we left the cafe.

"I'll stick with soccer." She nods, "At least I know that's my playing field."

"V..." Margo says with caution as she pulls her phone away from, her face.

"You're going for Chris, aren't you?" I roll my eyes.

Her eyes gleam, "How did you know?"

I sigh, "Chris is a hard one to crack."

"I like a challenge."

Margo mumbled in disagreement, "I didn't think he would be your type."

Verina thinks to herself, "That's just the problem... he's not my type but yet I can feel myself pushing to get to know him."

"Good luck," Juliette laughs.

"You guys don't think I can get him?"

We all looked at her, "No." saying it plainly might have been harsh, but it was the truth.

Christopher Florence was known to be quiet in the group of boys. He might be hot, but he holds baggage. Don't let their charm fool you. Chris was known to keep his relationship and home life private; everyone respected it, and no one pried. Because if they did, the boys would have his back.

"He's good in bed, I've heard."

Verina's eyes sparkle, "Even better."

"Hey, but I'm serious. Chris is a really hard one to crack."

"These boys are supposed to be players, he gets what he gets."

"I'm sure he knows about your player personality too, V."

Verina rolls her eyes, "Agree to disagree."

CHAPTER 11

ADRIANNA

When I returned home, it was quiet as usual. The housekeepers had been dismissed by tonight and were worn out. I take a breath before entering the kitchen. After I washed my hands, I looked down at them, I was shaking. It's been a couple of days since my drug intake.

I promised myself I wouldn't do it again.

But I did.

I never did well in following what I preach. My phone rings.

Prince.

"Hey Dove." I hear his underlying tone.

I roll my eyes. "What is it that you need, Prince?"

"Do you know if lilies are the go-to for "Hey, please give me a second chance?" He asked.

The smile on my face softens, "Does she like lilies?" I ask.

"I don't know." He breathes out.

I stand, walking around in circles around my kitchen island.

"Roses are a go-to." I sigh before he interrupts.

"Well, last time I gave her flowers she actually threw them on the ground so..." He says with a weary tone.

I take a deep breath, I'm sure he could hear my frustration through the phone, "Fine, if you want to make an impression, make her a bouquet, with all her favorite colors." I say with irritation.

"K." He answers, then hanging up the phone immediately.

I couldn't help but think to myself, Grayson Prince may be in love with a girl.

> Thanks, nice for you to be useful for once.

> > Pleasure to be at your use, Prince!

> You say that like it's a bad thing...

> > Oh no, I'm honored.

> Admit it, you like it when I make fun of you.

> > Bye, Prince.

> No, but really thank you Dove. I appreciate this.

READ 7:09 P.M.

I take a calm breath; I mean he's willing to change for her. Sometimes, I think he would be ready to even sacrifice himself for her.

I didn't know that love like that still exists. Am I that pathetic and clueless?

No, I'm not clueless. I'm just unloved.

I sit down on my big couch, it's very well-kept since no one uses it. I come from sitting to just laying, and I'm not quite sure if I have any energy to sit up.

I felt my heart rate slow down, and my phone rang again.

Father.

I shot out of the couch, running to my phone, "Dad?" I say almost pleading.

"Adrianna." He says but his voice was strict and tight, "I just got off the phone with—" He starts.

I interrupt, "Dad."

"I raised you better than this, or I at least thought I did, but you dating the enemy?"

"If your idea was to get a reaction out of me then you fucking did it. Now, stop this nonsense and get back with Brooks. I don't want you anywhere near those fucking rats." He screamed at me.

I slowly sat back down on the couch.

Laying down once again, but with every word he uttered, my body lost energy, and I felt my voice drown in the silence.

Tears ran down the side of my face, and all I saw was a blur. "You have greatly disappointed me, Anna."

I felt my heart drop as I got up.

"You will never see that boy again; do you understand me? Don't make me come over there."

I swallow, "You can't tell me what to do."

He hangs up the phone as I walk slowly to the kitchen cabinet, my eyes targeting the doctor's prescription pills.

I never really paid attention, but I woke up, on the cold floor of my kitchen, opened pills and capsules lay on the marble floor.

I feel like a certain part of me is healed when I take a painkiller. Not physically, but the deep gaping hole within my heart.

And this time, I felt my heart ache.

I close my eyes and swallow, and the pain is gone.

No one knows about what I struggle with, my eating disorders, my drug problem, my depression, my OCD, and the fact that I had been diagnosed with being on the spectrum but was way too insecure and had grown to hide it pretty well.

I can't say I feel alone because truthfully, I'm not, I have my friends, but inside I feel so dark.

I'm lost.

I feel like I'm standing in a chasm that only gets bigger, and the light grows further and further away.

The only way the light appears closer is when I take the pills.

It sounds terrible but it's true.

I'm fucked up.

T woke up the next day, Prince and I's plans were at work, and I heard a loud engine, his fancy car parked outside my house. My eyes glance through the window at him.

But his eyes looked colder than ever. I had a feeling the flowers weren't a good idea. I shivered as his eyes stayed straight, I looked through my closet and then panicked, my phone started to blow up.

It was Grayson. I couldn't find a good skirt that didn't ride up to my crotch, so I ran downstairs as he honked the horn.

But before I left, I looked at my figure in the mirror, my skirt wasn't leaving much to the imagination.

"What took you so long?" He glances up from his phone, his eyes reach my body and scan, "I think you left half of your skirt at home." He comments with a snort as my face grows red.

"I couldn't find my skirt." I inform him as he looks at me further with examining eyes.

"Don't you have a maid for that shit?"

"Yes, well, I told them to take a day off."

His eyebrows furrow, "Why?"

"Because they needed a day off."

"Liar." He shakes his head as I pull my skirt down again.

"Just shut up." His mouth curves the playful way it does that makes my blood boil. He laughs, taking off his hockey jacket, and offering it to me.

"Fuck off, Prince," I swore as he tilts his head, growing irritated I moved away, before the firm grip of his hand caught my waist, his mouth was close on my ear.

"You're going to come back and put this jacket on so that no man can fucking look at you like you aren't my girlfriend." He grabs my waist even tighter. I felt myself shaking.

"If you don't, I'm going to force it on you." I swallow.

"Stop playing the boyfriend role, no one is around us, asshole."

"Well, I think practice makes perfect and aren't you a perfectionist, Dove?"

I felt my stomach tighten before I turned around his mouth so close to mine, "Yes I am, but you've spent your whole life making sure perfect was unattainable."

He smirks, "Speaking of practice, you can come and practice being a great girlfriend, by coming to one. Luckily for you I have one today, so you can either watch me practice and I take you home after or you go home by yourself."

"I have plans," I say seething as I walk towards his car as he runs after me again.

I finally put on his jacket, not because he told me to but because I had self-dignity.

Grayson walks over, opening the car door for me, I roll my eyes plopping down on his fancy car. "Hey, be careful with Robin." He says as I glare at him.

"You name your cars?"

"And you probably name your bags."

I scowl yet again, "My shoes."

He laughs, "See? That's stupid. You just put shoes on your feet. At least with a car, they can take you anywhere, with style too."

He smirks as I roll my eyes, "Then take me to Paris in a car." I came back.

He shakes his head, "I can take you to one of my islands instead."

"I'm not interested in going to one of your islands."

Grayson looks at me, "Well, better get used to it, if our *relationship* is still going on until spring, you have no choice if my father asks for you to come on vacation with us."

I gave a concerned look, "I think you would win your girlfriend back by then." Grayson's face changes, and he finally starts to drive. It was a silent ride to the university.

"I know you aren't pleased with this deal." He acted like he didn't hear me and rolled his eyes.

"Do you think I want to be with you?" He looked annoyed and I'm sure he was, but at that moment I knew he would never hurt me because then he took a calming breath.

"August is a subject I don't like talking about."

I stayed quiet, "No, but you're right," I sigh, "You are the last person I would want."

Grayson's eyes pierce, "So there is someone?" He probes.

I feel my heart hammer, "No." I swallow.

"It's just me," I say plainly.

Yes. It's just me.

GRAYSON

It was a rough morning on my end, I had to swing by my mother's house and give her medication. I left forgetting that my election posters were forgotten. I drove back to my father's house to pick up the wench.

Well, I need to go back anyways, the pain in the ass girlfriend was waiting for me like a fucking princess. She argued with me the whole time.

First, she left half of her fucking skirt in her house, but I have to say, she looked good.

I might hate her, but I'm still a man. She looked fucking delicious, which made me think if I looked at her like that, even when I'm practically repulsed by her, just imagine all the greedy eyes of others. God forbid she's already the queen of the university.

Everybody already looked at her like that on a daily basis, except... Well, has she always looked this good?

My eyes have never been swayed by her; they have always been for August. But back to the subject, I gave her my jacket after having to threaten her to put it on. She's stubborn that way.

"It's just me," she mutters.

"You can have any guy you want in Hawthorne; you understand that right?" I laugh as she holds an uneven smile.

"None that appeal to me."

I scowl, "So Sawyer wasn't good enough for you?" She squints.

"He was good looking, I suppose."

I smirk, "Well, your boyfriend is far better looking anyways." I smile.

"Right?"

Adrianna falters, "You don't need another person to tell you that you look good." She laughs.

"But I am... is what you're saying?" I could feel my face light up as she tightens her upper lip.

"Well, since I am your girlfriend, I can make you look more presentable, I suppose."

The nerve she has, "Says the one with the preschool skirt and *my* jacket."

"Oh, so you want me to take it off?" She starts to peel off the jacket.

I pierced my eyes into hers, "If you take off that jacket Cassian, so help me god."

She laughs, I look at her, her eyes sparkling. A genuine smile on her face. Her laugh fills the car. I park in my regular parking spot, in front of the university, and everyone's eyes are on us.

"Well, this is it." She lowers her head and shakes.

I felt her body convulse a little. I wasn't sure if this was a regular occurrence.

I wasn't sure how to comfort her so I hesitantly place my hand on her thigh, weirdly enough, she calms down instantly.

I walked out of my car, then opened her door, helping her out.

Everyone's mouths drop with confusion and some with dismay.

Adrianna scowls, "Looks like some of your fangirls are a bit shaken up." She nods over to the many blonds that send sneers over our way.

"You jealous baby?" I smirk as she gives me a look of smugness.

"As if they could ever be me."

I look over to our right as Neil and Liam come out to welcome us to the snake pit.

The snake pit.

The snake pit is the area in the front lawn, tables, and seating for the people who only matter.

In our society. It's the elite of high society.

Wealth.

Bloodline.

And relevance.

Many people wish to enter but can only really be accepted by... Well, Adrianna and me.

The top of the food chain.

"The signal." She whispers as I look down at her.

She licks her lips, her hot breath freeing, as I lean down. I swallow. My heart is beating fast while she lets her hand grip my white polo.

Her lips were so pumped and ready for me.

Her eyes set on mine, a light shade of brown.

She looked golden.

"Look at me." I whisper as she smiles, her hand cupping my jaw pulling me in as my hand wrapped around her waist.

Both of our lips are so close, I almost don't find her revolting.

"You sicken me in every way." She smiles as I grip her waist tighter.

"Yeah?" I smirk.

"Tell me." I continue as she catches her breath.

"Tell you what?" She smiles devilishly.

"Tell me you hate me."

I catch the smell of her perfume, "Why?"

She asked as I leaned closer to her lips, "Because you always do as I tell you, *Dove*."

She bites her lips, almost like she was antagonizing me.

I turned red, frustration filled my face, and I knew it.

I let my thoughts get to me, everyone was fucking staring at us, and I couldn't stop staring at her.

Her scent filled my lungs like a drug.

I pull her in, slamming her lips against mine. My hands grasping the back of her neck. I couldn't help but engulf her, she let a breath of relief out as she kissed me back, tugging me closer. She pulled away a little, and I felt like a fucking thirsty animal that got its water dish taken away.

I groaned against her mouth.

But before I slam her against the stone walls of the main campus building, I pull away.

She bites her bottom lip, placing her finger against it as it looks swollen.

That's right baby. Those lips are mine.

My notorious smirk lingers, "Don't act like you didn't enjoy it, Dove."

"I don't enjoy anything that involves you."

Her lips clamped, and I bit my lip, my eyes on her beautiful face. I bet she wanted to hit me and do some damage to my perfect features. But I could only stare at her angered expression.

My stomach coiled and my breath caught.

"Tell me, Adrianna, when you bite your lip like that. Who do you think of when your cheeks flush scarlet red?" She swallows, her heart racing as I advance on her, "Is it Brooks?"

It looked like her legs almost buckled, and she looked like she was out of words, so I finished it off for her while shaking my head slightly, "I didn't think so."

She opens her mouth to say something, maybe a comeback, but Liam and Neil beat her to it.

"That was a good one!" Liam smiled ear to ear.

"You know I think you guys might actually pull this off." Neil added as Adrianna twirled her finger through her beautiful curls.

"It looked like you guys actually... enjoyed the kiss." Liam suggested as Adrianna pulled away.

"It was just for show." She says with conviction as I smile.

"Well, don't want to ruin your spirit Dove but, you were a pretty mediocre kiss." I say plainly.

She smiles, "Can't hold a girl right." She fires back as I give her a confused expression.

What the hell does she mean? I can't hold a girl, right?

I've held many girls in my lifetime, and I can fucking tell you that my hands are made for handling.

Not in a bad way, might I add.

Some might even say, *Touch of God.*

Well, I wouldn't go that far, but let's just say no woman has ever been unsatisfied after being with me, let alone being touched.

Adrianna just loves to get into my nerves, anytime she fucking can she's knows me like a spider on a web.

I snap back into reality.

She thinks I can't handle her.

Fuck that.

ADRIANNA

Fuck him.

He's so fucking full of himself. Does he really think that he's that irresistible and that every girl wants him?

It doesn't really matter, because everything that we do is fake and there is no evidence that it's real. It can't be real.

"Get a room!" Margo comes rushing in as she hugs me from

behind, "Come on, let's go to the pit and show off the new couple."

I almost physically gagged at the thought.

I look at her awkwardly, "Well, come on Prince, put your arm around the princess." Margo insists.

She smiles while placing Grayson's arm around me.

"I hope you're ready, because it's not even past 7 A.M. and my fucking head is already pulsing."

"Oh, you don't even know." He whispers while leading me over to the rest of our friends.

"Princess, are you coming to practice today?" Liam smiles.

I scowl, "I was told it was mandatory that I attend."

"I want you to attend since you are my girlfriend." Grayson says while setting his bag on the table.

"Do the other player's girlfriends attend too?" I question.

He smiles, "No."

My eyebrows furrow, "So why do I have to go?"

He stands, "Because August sometimes visits the practice, she loves to ice skate on the other rink beside ours, and I need you to look like you're in love with me."

"But that's pretty hard to do." I smile back, twirling my chair to face him, as he walks over to the trunk of his car.

"Well, you might like me a bit more after this." He pops open the trunk, and I see an abundance of posters for my election.

I stand up, caught off guard as he winks, "I told you I would help you win." He probes as I run up to him, stopping frantically, not really sure if we could hug, I mean we just kissed not too long ago.

Grayson takes a look around, hugging me anyways.

I never noticed that he smelled great, like a drug that I can take without repercussions. It was oddly comforting, his height, his arms around me. And I fit perfectly, molded just right.

He pulled away, smiling over in a direction, I made a mistake of following where his eyes were landing and then I met her eyes.

I see August, red hair, a smile that could cure most health

problems. She looked at us, and I couldn't bear to keep looking. She hates me, she hates all of us.

She was the type to be a bystander, whether it would be at school, or at a social event. I could understand why he fell for her. I bet she baked cookies on the weekend and gave them to the less fortunate.

I would like to think and act like I am like that, but I'm not and I know that for a fact. She was one of the good ones.

"Grayson!" She walks over, as he stiffens next to me.

"Hey August," He says, completely forgetting that I was next to him.

"Noticed you look smitten." She smiles over to me,

"Oh yeah, August. This is my girlfriend, Adrianna." I placed my hand out for her to shake.

But instead smiles and rejects it.

My eyes narrow, it looks like she's not as nice as she makes out to be.

I smile back.

"Weird that you're dating someone new when you've made it clear that you wanted me for so long."

And there's her true colors.

"Well, after you made it so clear that you don't want me, I figured that I should just get over it."

He made a point as I stayed quiet.

"Well, I really hope you're happy with your decision." She smiles thickly.

"He is." I smile, her face dropping.

"I wasn't talking to you." She says viciously as I let my eyes hunt hers. "Everyone knows a rebound doesn't stay for long."

"You can't be serious enough to date her."

I somehow felt shocked and a bit disrespected.

"Excuse me?" I walk closer.

"Grayson would never touch you." She makes a point.

I smile, "Oh, he's touched me."

"Places that only a woman can dream." August's eyes narrow.

"You wouldn't be the first one."

I nod leaning closer to whisper, "Maybe not the first, but the last. I'm not dumb enough to dump something that has given me the best orgasms of my life."

August swallows hard, her eyes squinting, I walk closer to Grayson, putting my hands on his chest, "It's a miracle you finally let him go, finally I can have him." I place my cheek against his chest, "It's a shame really."

Grayson pulled away from me, "August, why don't you just..."

"Leave?" She interrupts, "I don't mean any harm or disrespect, but I would just like to point out the obvious that this—" she signals at Grayson and I, "— is not going to work out."

"Why not?" Grayson arches an eyebrow.

"Because I know you two can't stand each other and that it's just a plan to get me back."

Grayson took a breath, "You don't know a damn thing."

"Maybe," She smiles, "But, I do know you Grayson." She says before walking up to her group of friends.

Grayson walks off, and I follow him, why?

Don't fucking ask me because even I don't know what my purpose is right now.

"Grayson!"

I catch up to him as he shoves me off, "Fucking hell." He pulls me into a storage closet.

"What's the matter with you?!" I yell as he gives me a scowl.

"What's the matter with me?!"

I felt my face fire red, "I'm playing the fucking part that you wanted me to, the girlfriend."

He grows infuriated, "Well, you aren't the girlfriend!" I flinch. "You're not even a friend." He calms down.

"Fuck you!" I walk away, "Have fun fake dating yourself."

I didn't know what to expect, it definitely wasn't to be Grayson's best friend. But I mean, what a jerk! He acts like I'm the one who set this whole plan up. I've always known he was selfish, but he has reached such a low.

"You know you're such a dick." I lip off as he smirks.

"You want to say that again?" He challenges.

"You're a dick." Grayson's eyes reached a feral look, his eyes looked hungry.

Grayson's hands landed on my waist, and I couldn't help but almost moan at his actions.

"Don't lip off at me and expect nothing back as punishment." He whispers.

I smile. "I can do what I want."

Grayson's eyes pierce through me, my eyes looking at his lips, like I want to kiss him again.

Stupid move.

I breathe out, my heart began racing and I wasn't up to having an episode at the very moment, it would be my worst nightmare if Grayson out of all people found out how fucked up I am.

"I don't know why I thought that August was going to come running back to me, the day of." He confessed.

Without thinking, I placed my hand on his heart. "August will come around. If she's the right one for you then you guys will always find your way to each other. I know it sounds cliche but it's true." I smiled at him, his eyes examining mine, like it was a trap.

"I don't know why my parents told me to hate you so much, you have nothing but life in your eyes."

My smile dies, it was the first time my heart beat during the whole minute he looked into my eyes. "Stop looking at me like that!"

"Like what?" He laughs off.

I sigh, "Like you want to kiss me." I glared at him, trying to open the door, but it wasn't cooperating.

I push some more only for nothing to move, I knock my head into the door, "Fuck."

Grayson's panics, "Dove, please don't tell me."

"We are stuck." I let out as I slid down to the floor.

"Call Hamilton." He instructs as my phone gets sent straight to voicemail, "Call Brookshire." I ask as it also sent straight to voice mail.

"This is your fault!' I yell.

Grayson's face turned red like he was restraining from just murdering me in this closet and stashing the evidence in a graveyard somewhere.

"My fault?" He whispers.

"You are the one who stormed in here like a baby!" I argue.

He laughs, "You followed me here Dove, so I can't be completely repulsive."

"But you are." I pointed at him.

Grayson's joined me on the floor, we sat across from each other, the room wasn't too tight, and it wasn't too roomy. It was just right.

"You know, I don't understand you." He mutters as I go through my phone trying to get someone to open the door.

I glare at him as he continues to talk, "Your life is so picture perfect. It's kind of sickening."

"Thanks for that input." I smile sardonically.

He leans closer, "No I mean, you are so complex. You should be this beautiful, nice person but you're just not."

"Are you calling me ugly?"

I stopped to look at him, "Not necessarily no." He sighs, "I don't know how to put it."

"Then shut up." I grew annoyed.

"You know what my problem is with you?" He speaks.

I look up, even as we sit, he is still taller, "Enlighten me." I seethe.

"You're selfish." He exclaims, "You never just want to help someone out because of the goodness of your heart. There has to be something in it for you."

Maybe because all my life I was relying on myself.

"I'm already helping you, isn't that enough?" I mutter.

He smirks knowingly, "Well, your kiss was a bit mediocre. Maybe we should practice a bit more for the public."

I laugh, "I recall when we were eight, and I was outside playing hopscotch and you bumped into me accidentally, you vowed never to touch me, and you even signed a paper and hung it on Mrs. Reed's desk."

Grayson smiles, "I also vowed to quit hockey that year because this bigger guy that transferred was better than me and I flipped my shit."

"Didn't you injure him *accidentally* in the game right after?" I ask with my brows raised.

"No, that was just a coincidence."

"You would practice your slap shots until after midnight every single day!" I let my body turn to him.

"You were watching me?" He smirks as I catch myself turning back away from him.

"No, you were so noisy I couldn't paint."

I couldn't concentrate.

Forty-five minutes passed by, and Grayson actually attempted to make good conversation, he was different.

He was tolerable.

And I was starting to think maybe he was *okay.*

"Truth or dare?" He smiles as I look at him exasperated.

"Truth."

He smirks, "Do you want to kiss me?"

I smile, shaking my head, "Dare."

Grayson sits closer, "I dare you to kiss me."

I roll my eyes, but leaned closer, "If I kiss you, I don't think I'll be able to stop." I whisper as he closes his eyes.

"Don't fucking say that to me."

I pull away, before Grayson's hand grips my shirts forward, his lips so close to mine, "Are you teasing me, Miss Cassian?" He whispers huskily.

I pull away, "You do know that my father hates you right?" I laugh.

He places his forehead on my shoulder, "We can make this fake dating thing so believable." He groans.

Suddenly, I'm back in reality.

"We had a decent conversation for about an hour. Are you telling me we can't do that when August is watching?" He makes note as I start to get up.

How could I be fucking stupid? Of course, the basis of each conversation we've had always had an underlying purpose. For a moment, I thought that we understood each other.

"Three months." He mutters. "Three months and if I don't get her back, I promise I won't ever bother you or contact you ever again."

"Three months?" I ask incredulously. "Seriously? Is the sight of my face so repulsive that you can't be with me for three fucking months?"

Three months so I don't have to fucking speak to him again.

"You're my only option." He pleaded.

"Incorrect." I sod off as he shakes his head.

"You're right, but she hates you the most."

I hate you.

I smile, "Three months."

CHAPTER 12

ADRIANNA

"You want me to come with you." Margo groans as she paints her fingernails.

"Yes!" I shoot out of my closet, "Will you please?" I pulled out two different colored beanies.

I hold both of them up as Margo points at the white one instead of the blue.

Juliette walks in with a bowl of cereal plopping down on my bed as Verina puts on mascara.

"I thought you had a date." Juliette says with a muffled mouth.

"I do." Margo yawns.

"Margo!" Juliette turns to face us.

"What?" She says defensively.

"We all know why you want to go to the game and liking hockey is not the reason." Verina twirls the chair.

"I love hockey!" Margo gets up.

"You mean you like hockey boys." I add as she frowns.

"No." Margo gets up rolling her eyes.

"You know that day that I flashed an old couple when I was really drunk on campus?" She mentions as we nod our heads.

"Well, I have to earn community service for the university. So, my dad thought it would be a great idea if I was helping the hockey team with their physical therapy."

I nod my head slowly, "So like if they get injured you would have to tend to their wounds?" I look at Margo as she gags.

"Yes, but also… this is a great way to meet many guys, even from different schools."

"More like she likes guys that won't ever like her back." Verina laughs as Margo throws a glare at her.

"Says the one making it a decided plan to make Christopher Florence fall in love with her." Margo takes a scoop of cereal from Juliette who then swats her hand away.

"Isn't he hot though?" Verina smiles, "Very mysterious!"

We all gave each other a look before laughing, Juliette continued to talk even with her mouth stuffed, "If by mysterious you mean you caught him with your greedy eyes all by his lonesome at the party, then yes."

"Chris is beautiful." Verina falls on my bed besides Juliette.

"Don't get attached to him."

I walk over pulling her back up, "Grayson mentions that Chris is not looking for a girlfriend. He keeps to himself a lot."

Margo runs over to us, "Oh so it's Grayson now?" She sat on the bed next to Juliette.

"I've called him Grayson before," I point out as they all send knowing looks at each other.

"So you were talking to Grayson?" They say in unison with smirks, as I roll my eyes.

"Very mature." I mock, " But yes, well we were locked in the janitor's closet, and forced to talk to each other." I say quickly.

"Oh, I know, I was watching the door as it banged multiple times from you trying to open it." Juliette winks.

My eyes swarmed her.

"I sat on the other end and eavesdropped for my whole study hall period then told Mrs. Benson to let you two out."

I smile, "I know you're joking because Mr. Hoffman was the one who opened the door, but nice try!"

Juliette stood up, placing the bowl down on the table, looking back at us, "You guys are ridiculous, men don't deserve our time and attention," She runs over wrapping both her arms around all of us, "We are all we need."

I sigh, "I couldn't agree more."

Margo pulls away first, "Jules, you know I love you, but one day you're going to fall in love, and you are going to know how it feels to be in love and you will never wish for it to end."

Juliette laughs, "Maybe when I'm dying, I'll wish for love."

"You would fall in love with the unexpected." Verina gets up twirling like a princess.

"Someone quiet and he wears glasses, he would have brown hair, maybe goes to your church on the weekends and volunteers to help orphans!" She continues.

"NO!" Margo gets up to join her, "Juliette will fall in love with a business boy, like the typical type of men that our fathers want us to marry. He would be proper and would know how to play the piano beautifully, like me!"

They sounded ridiculous.

Juliette shouldn't be with a guy if the guy doesn't let her do what she wants.

But if I had to wager a guess…

I shot up next to Margo and Verina staring back at Juliette who looked like she wanted to end us.

"You both are terribly wrong." I yawn, "If both of you know Juliette, she doesn't want a relationship!" I continued, "So this guy would have to be consistent!" I walk around, "He would be everything that Juliette wouldn't expect, he would be a boy written in one of the books that her nose is always in."

Juliette smiles, "He would be tall, I would say a jock. He would be everything that she wants but is too stubborn to admit."

Juliette gets up, "I don't care if he's tall, I don't care if he helps orphans, or even if he plays the piano beautifully." She turns around, "I care if my father thinks he is worthy enough."

"It doesn't matter who I like unless my family accepts them."

"Love doesn't shy away because of your parents."

I walked up to her, "Love is a beautiful thing that should always be embraced."

"Not if I dishonor my family." She laughs off.

Juliette was always a hard person to figure out. Her family is very strict and very religious, I wasn't really sure if she was, I mean she would always follow her family values and decisions, but what does she really want to do?

The doorbell rings as Margo smiles at me, "The Prince has arrived!" She pulls me toward the door as I roll my eyes, mouthing *help* to Verina and Juliette.

Juliette gets up, "I was thinking of going to the bookstore anyways."

Verina groans, "I don't want to go to a bookstore!"

"You don't have to come, you know." Juliette laughs.

Verina follows her anyway, "Yes, but I wouldn't want you to have to force yourself to have any conversation with someone random who isn't me."

Juliette smiles, "Oh, thank you so much for thinking about me!"

Verina blows her a kiss, "And maybe we can find a hot boy for you who is mysteriously reading a book all by himself drinking black coffee."

"Why black coffee?" I ask.

Verina smiles, "Guys who drink black coffee have big dicks."

Juliette stops to analyze the sentence, "Please tell me you don't plan on homeschooling your children."

"Of course not! I'll call you!"

Margo and I approached the car upfront, only that it wasn't one of Grayson's cars. Margo ran back inside to get her lucky lip-gloss while I walked next to the car, knocking.

It was Liam.

He rolls down the window, "Grayson had an emergency to take care of that's urgent, I was told to pick you up." He says while staring off to the front of the car.

Liam was very popular in Hawthorne; I mean he is Grayson's best friend so it would be very understandable. Everyone knew what game he was playing as he was always with a different girl every night and was quite popular with his... abilities.

Margo and he had a one-night stand, but I mean she'll get over it.

"What's the emergency?" I ask, I don't know why, it's not like it's any of my business.

Liam looked uncomfortable answering the question, making us worry, even if I shouldn't.

"He always makes it in time for practice." Liam dodges the question. I simply nod, I can ask Grayson about it maybe later.

Liam smiles, "Well, hop in!" He gets out of his seat, running over to open my door.

"You didn't have to really," I flash a smile as he rolls his eyes,

Liam raises his eyebrows, "I didn't have a choice, Princess. You're Gray's girlfriend. You would get the same treatment from anyone in the damn state, not that you would have different treatment." He looked over at my house, which was a full-blown mansion.

Acting like he wasn't loaded himself.

I couldn't help but itch at the idea of punching him.

"Now let's get going! I wouldn't want to be late,"

I pause, "Wait!" I stop him as he tilts his head, "Margo forgot something in my house, she'll be back down soon."

Liam's face turned red. "Margo?" He almost panicked.

I nod, "Yes, well she's getting her lucky lip gloss," I turn around as Margo runs over, "What took you so long?"

I ask as she smiles, "My bra keeps unclasping, so I switched." She looks over at Liam who seems to be looking anywhere but her.

"Well, let's go." He forces out as she climbs on the seats in the back.

"Why is he taking us?" Margo asks.

I roll my eyes, "Prince couldn't make it."

"What do you expect us to do while you guys are skating around like figure skaters?" Margo groans as I grin.

Liam stares at the road ahead, "Talk like you guys always do." He smirks, "That shouldn't be a problem."

"You can flirt with the players." I turn over to Margo who winks in conspiracy.

"You bet." I turned over to Liam who looked agitated.

"You have no shot against the boys." He laughs.

Margo leans in between the seats, "Why not?"

"They are way too focused on the season."

Margo only smiles, "I sense a challenge."

The tension between Margo and Liam is setting the whole car on fire. I, for one, don't care about what Margo does in her love life.

Margo knows that Liam and the rest of the elites are off limits.

"The arena isn't far from the mall." Liam says.

I look over at him with an annoyed look, "Grayson wants me to watch."

"Grayson also wants a Bugatti, but his father will flip his shit if he buys another car."

Margo snorts, "Like that would create a dent on his card."

"No, but Grayson tends to splurge on things he doesn't need."

"And you don't?" Margo's powerful gaze meet with his on the rear-view mirror.

It was like watching an intense staring contest, I certainly felt like I was breeching some sort of privacy.

"No," he smirks, "I tend to resist the things I want."

"Too bad maybe that thing you want will end up being sold out."

We finally reached the hockey arena, seeing Grayson parking, my eyes found his as he pulled his hockey stick out of his trunk.

"There he is."

I jump out of the car, walking over to Grayson who smiles at me, "Hey Dove, how was your ride?"

"Where were you?" I ignored his question.

"I had something to take care of."

"Which was…" I question.

"You worried about me, Dove?"

I felt my face turn red, "No, I was just asking, nothing to dig too deep in." I snapped, his eyebrows furrow.

"It doesn't matter anyways, I'm here, I just had something to take care of." I nod.

Still wary and curious but, I had no right to know about his whereabouts, it was none of my business, no matter what ever happens between us.

Not that anything was going to happen between us. I had to keep remembering that it was just a plan, and it was just for three months.

"You have something on your lips." His nose scrunches.

I smile, "It's lip gloss."

"It's shiny." He retorts back.

I laugh, "Good, it's doing its job."

Grayson had a cool exterior, that's for sure, but small conversations just simple as this one makes it seem like he's so much more than what I predicted my whole life.

He was still human. I often forgot because I consistently compared him to a rabid animal or even a troll.

"You know you'll be late if you stay out here chit chatting, captain." Liam interrupts as Grayson's eyes glared at him.

"Yes, I know Brookshire." He gives Liam a dismissive hand gesture while leading the way to the rink. The whole team staring as they skate around waiting for their one and only captain.

"You can sit over there." He points at the seat nearest to the benches.

"I don't want to just sit around while waiting for you to finish up." I scowl.

Grayson faces his team then at me, "Dove, can you just listen to me for once in your life." I smiled, almost a smirk, but I did find that I loved that he noticed that my daily mission was always to defy him.

"I want to go to the other rink."

I look over to the other rink as he smirks with confusion written all over his face, "You know how to skate?"

I lift my head up, "You underestimate me."

Grayson's eyes looked cautious, "I don't want you to get hurt or anything." He warns.

I turn back to him, "Careful, Prince you almost sound like you care."

Grayson pulls me closer, his mouth close to my ear, "Got to act the part, right?"

"You get on the rink when I'm with you." He warns, "Don't fucking step foot on the other rink."

Grayson was odd... I did sometimes find myself staring, it wasn't hidden that Grayson Prince was admired at Hawthorne University. He never cared much about relationships. At least that's what I thought. He kept his girlfriend a secret from everyone else.

"Please be careful." I didn't even think about letting the words slip out of my mouth to make sure he was fine.

Grayson turns back around to me, his eyes a bit questionable.

He didn't say anything, instead he quickly put on his helmet and skated away.

I sigh, I felt jittery, like my arms were jelly and my face was pale, it only really took a second for Margo to notice and bring me over to the bathroom.

Tears started streaming down my cheeks as she looked at me, kneeling. "You didn't take your pills?" She said pleadingly as she pulled out the emergency pills from her bag.

I didn't say anything, one look she knew, she's my best friend. She was the only one that really knew anything.

"I thought I could go a day without it." I mutter as she frowns, genuine worry plastered her face.

"I know you think you can beat anemia, but you can't." Margo scolds.

She puts the pills into my mouth, pulling out a water bottle from the fancy fridge in the bathroom.

This was a time I was so glad our parents paid good taxes for this private university.

"I want you to keep taking your pills." She pats my arm as I nod. I know it seems like it's simple, and that I'm like a toddler who doesn't want to eat her broccoli.

"Now let's go, before your boyfriend thinks something is wrong." She pulls me away from the sink.

"He's not my real boyfriend."

Margo pauses, "Will you stop saying that!"

"Margo, it's true."

"I don't think you should completely ignore the clear signs of him flirting with you."

Margo never shied away from telling me the truth, she always explained her thought process whether it was her own life or mine.

We walked out of the bathroom to see two girls sitting at the seats that Grayson told us to sit in. The average puck bunnies have camped out to watch my *boyfriend* skate.

Margo tensed as well, I began to head to the seats, and stand over them they smirked.

"Problem?" One with pink hair had crossed her legs, almost kicking me.

I smile, "It's a closed practice."

"It doesn't say that." She stands up as her blonde friend stays seated.

"No, but I do."

"Listen, you don't own the rink." She tries to vouch for herself.

"Oh, I wouldn't have a problem if you were using the rink, but you're not." I felt eyes on me even Grayson's cold gray eyes.

"I'm watching the practice; I'm not bothering anyone."

You're bothering me by sitting here watching Grayson, I wanted to say.

Margo panics, "How about—"

"—No," I interrupt, "I can buy this damn rink with a call, just so you can be told to move."

"You don't want to fight me." She says her eyes look like she just awoke from the dead, only I felt my blood boil and my eyes narrow. The boys rally from behind me, Grayson's figure came to view as the pink haired girl pulled away.

"Hey Grayson!"

"Daisy, what are you doing here?" He says in a hurried voice.

Daisy.

Of course, Grayson knew her, I sounded stupid now, he's been sleeping with her and now I look like the girlfriend that had been cheated on.

"You have a crazy fan girl." She shrugs over at me as I couldn't look Grayson in the face.

I felt my hands shake from embarrassment.

It was only two days ago we said that we wouldn't be sleeping with anyone else and the thought of him touching her infuriates me.

This whole thing infuriates me, since when did I care who Grayson Prince put his hands on? Maybe it was because of my lack of relationships, he was my first boyfriend. Well, fake boyfriend. I don't know how relationships work.

I've never been in a real one where I was shown off. Brooks always made it a big deal that I would ruin everything for his parents company if he ever went public with me, his father is running for mayor. He's seriously running against Verina's dad, and he said that if he ever were to tell people that he was dating me it was a "conflict of interest."

I could argue that I deserved better than what I had with Brooks. And I can even accept the fact that I was blinded by the attention that was always given by Brooks. He made me feel like shit, but in private he made me feel like I was the most precious girl in the world. Everyone always treated me like that.

Except for Grayson.

Is that why I'm so keen on getting his attention?

I admit it, I care about what he thinks.

"Well, are you going to let her speak to me like that, Grayson?" She yells, she was off the rails, throwing her drink into his face.

I almost laughed.

"I'm his girlfriend." I smiled at her as she brought her hand up and smacked my cheek. I felt warmth and a sting hit me as she pulled back.

Is this the fucking back lash I get for dating this six foot, five inches ripped, blonde hockey player that has always had it out for me?

Joke.

"Did you just slap me?"

Daisy's eyes didn't look at mine, instead they looked at Grayson's. He looked about ready to throw something in the glass window.

I always knew he had a temper, mostly because I was always the fuse.

"Not only are you a slut, but you're also a liar too." She spit back at me as I took a second to look at her eyes.

"She's not fucking lying Daisy. She's, my girlfriend." Grayson growls in frustration, this was embarrassing.

Daisy's eyes then turned from red to just normal, but water started to build up, I almost felt bad.

But a bitch that slapped me, does not deserve my pity.

"I can't believe this; you don't *do* girlfriends."

Grayson laughs, a chuckle, "Then what do I do?"

"Me." She refers to herself like an object. It was sad.

"I've been throwing myself at you, and you slept with me every week, you're telling me that wasn't leading to a relationship?"

Grayson took a deep breath. "No, it was not."

"I'm sorry, really Daisy if I seemed like I led you on, but I'm very happy in my relationship right now. How do you expect a relationship when you slept with Liam on the weekends?" He gave a shrug. Margo tensed next to me, looking over at her certain dark-haired fantasy.

Daisy lifted her bag off my seat, her eyes never leaving mine.

"She won't satisfy you." She looks back at Grayson, "Once you get a taste of her virgin pussy, you'll get bored."

It was all she said before exiting and her friends following without another word.

"I should just put your name on that seat." Grayson mutters as I look down.

It was humiliating, I've never talked about my sex life to anyone and even if the girl Daisy didn't know if I was a virgin, I knew I was.

I always thought about just handing my virginity to someone, so the pressure of when I would finally give it to someone would be gone, or the burden of the thought that a guy is just with me for one thing.

Did Grayson completely just ignore the girl's last sentence or am I the one hearing things?

"No need." I smile thickly.

Grayson's stone-cold exterior was never weakened so he just looked at me with no sympathy, not that I was looking for some.

"I'm going home." I say, my voice a bit shaky.

Grayson runs up in front of me, "Let me take you home." He pleaded, maybe he had forgotten that he still had his uniform and skates on.

But at that moment it seemed that he didn't even care.

"You have practice." I look back at his team skating drills.

"Shit, you're right." He whispers under his breath.

I smiled; a small laugh traveled. Grayson catches a wind of my lips curving upwards.

For the first time ever his face looked warm, not pale. But blush covered the spots that I could see through his helmet.

"I can go home by myself." I start to walk away again as he runs in front of me *again*.

"I don't trust you going home by yourself." He says, I don't even think he realized he said it either.

"Margo's with me—" I smile as we both look over to Margo flirting with one of Grayson's teammates taking a water break. "I'm a big girl, I can handle myself."

Grayson picks me up by the waist, pulling me over his shoulder, and setting me back down on my seat.

"Forty-five minutes until practice ends," He looks at the clock, "I will take you home." He looks over at Margo, "You don't come home with anyone except Margo or me."

I begin to open my mouth, "And Liam was instructed by me to pick you up today, that doesn't count." He smirks.

He knows me too well.

"What if I'm dying?" I inch closer to his face. Grayson uses this moment to take off his helmet, staring at me in the eyes.

"I hope you don't expect anyone else to give you CPR other than me." He licks his lips, my stomach heats, and I feel my core pooling.

I breathed in his musky scent; he smelled like mint and cold weather combined. That doesn't make sense, but it does to me. And that was really all that mattered.

Grayson let his smirk travel, and puts his lips gently on top of mine, I breathed out, opening my mouth more, my hand traveling up to the nape of his neck, wanting to pull him back towards me.

But noticing that we were still in a public setting.

He pulls back, turning to Margo, "Do you mind?"

I smile as Margo rocks her expensive heels against the paved floor, "You guys are so believable that you even need to kiss when August isn't even here!"

I swallow, pulling my hand away from his neck, Grayson coughs, pulling his helmet back up.

We didn't even notice or cared if anyone was watching, the temptation of his lips close to mine was good enough.

"Forty-five minutes." He says returning to his cold tone, I nod. I could feel my cheeks heat, but I was way too stubborn to believe it.

"Forty-five minutes." I breathe out.

CHAPTER 13

GRAYSON

"That was good practice boys." I yell as everyone exits out of the locker rooms.

"You good?" Chris comes up to me.

"Yeah?" I smiled at him, packing all my belongings into my bag.

"Why? Did I do bad today?" I question as Neil comes into the conversation.

"Quite the contrary actually, you multiplied your speed on the ice today even more than your records."

I hadn't noticed. I felt great today, very energized and I wasn't really sure what the cause was. An adrenaline rush, I guess. Liam walked over laying on the couch, "Or it may have to do something with a certain leggy dark-haired vixen that you're supposedly dating."

I laughed. Adrianna was a temptation of course, but I never lost track of my goal, and she was just collateral damage.

"No, Adrianna was not the reason. I'm captain this year. I want to make sure that I am on my A-game and a girl does not change that."

Liam smiles, "I don't know about that..." He looks over at the stats board, "The last time you were on your *'A-game,'* he says while making quotation marks with both of his hands, "was when you were with August." He says matter of factly.

"Do you still really want her?" Neil closes his locker door.

"Yes."

I was sure that I only wanted August ever since she broke up with me, I've wanted nothing more than to get her back.

She's all I've ever wanted.

"Adrianna has made it clear that what we are portraying is fake and that's what it is."

Chris yawns, "Where are you going then?"

I smile, "Back home with Adrianna, my family wants to have dinner."

"I can't believe you lied to your family." Liam points out.

Neither can I.

"This is just a white lie." I looked over at the clock, concerned that Adrianna had bolted out of here already.

"Yes, of course, you faking a relationship to earn your father's trust is a white lie."

His voice was sarcastic and yet I had nothing really to say to him.

"Three months is my fucking limit of spending time with a Cassian." I huff out, I can't stand her.

"Our bad." Chris pulled up his hockey stick, "We thought you might have changed your opinion, she's not bad looking you know."

I have thought about it and found myself thinking about her in ways I shouldn't or ways I wouldn't fucking think about before I let myself convulse in her plump lips.

She's every man's wet dream.

Maybe if I let myself, even *mine*.

Two guys from my team come back into the locker room, "Captain." They addressed me.

I swiftly turned towards them with my bag, "Yes."

"Your girlfriend is getting hit on by the other team that practices on the ice in the late evening."

Something in me boiled.

I ran out of the room, my bag on my shoulder, quickly slammed the door shut behind me, my eyes zoning into a tall red headed guy speaking to Adrianna with full intent of probably getting into her pants.

I stomp over quickly pulling his collar and slamming him on to the rink's dash boards.

"Prince!" I heard Adrianna's yell as I ignored her, and the guy began to struggle.

"You don't fucking talk to her." I instruct as he nods. I took a moment to look at his bag that he was carrying, seeing a full hockey gear.

"If I ever see you fucking talking to her or I hear from someone you even took a step close to her," I pull him up even more so his attention wouldn't wave anywhere else. "So, help me God, I guarantee you will never be able to walk into any fucking ice rink in America."

The guy pushed me off, but I didn't budge, he was a lot smaller than I was.

But I wasn't blind to the fact I knew that he gets girls.

I let the guy go, he took a look at Adrianna whose face was red from anger and picked up his belongings and fled the scene.

"What the fuck is wrong with you!" She screams at me.

I looked around to Liam, Margo, Neil, and Chris watching but looking like they were not interested in the screaming match that Adrianna and I were about to have.

"He was fucking flirting with you." I said with ease as she gave an unbelievable face.

"Many guys flirt with me." She counters back.

My fists clenched, "Then many more guys will either get a broken nose or a busted lip. And since I'm so nice I'll let them pick which one they prefer."

"He was just asking me what I was doing tonight." She defended him like he didn't have bad intentions.

Which was a possibility yes, but I like the thought of me always being right better.

"He wanted to take you home and fuck you, Dove."

She looked at me with wide eyes.

Her cheeks reddened as I licked my lips staring at hers. "He wouldn't have slept with me."

"You're too naive." I laugh, "You sit there all innocent, really thinking that guys that approach you don't want one thing," Her face gloomed blue, "You're smart. How about you think about the odds of you and a guy having a happily ever after in this fucked up power hungry town?"

Adrianna didn't say a word to me, she just stared, and I shut my mouth.

I didn't feel bad. I wasn't a good guy, and I knew that, she knew it too so if she thought that even when we were "dating" that I would change myself she was sadly mistaken.

I wouldn't change for anyone.

I wasn't planning on it.

"Take me home." She said sternly as I grabbed my bag, fetching my keys from the front pocket, "Margo can go home with Liam."

Adrianna turns back without another word she walks off outside to my car, she sits in the passenger side.

The silent treatment.

How mature.

"How is it you can get mad about Daisy, but I can't ram my fist into that guy's mouth?" I asked as she looked at me with her judgmental expression.

"I wasn't mad about Daisy." She defends me as I roll my eyes.

"Don't make her comment about you being a slut and a liar true." I let out as she shifted in her seat.

"I'm not a slut." She lets out.

"You don't need to prove that to me. You can sleep with whoever you want." I raised my voice as she looked tiny.

Kind of embarrassed and I can't really understand why I let that slip.

She turned around to face the window as I turned on the ignition.

Moments of silence made me cringe; she sat still but I felt the fury of her anger reign upon the whole car.

You'll get bored after you get a taste of virgin pussy.

Daisy was delusional if she ever called Adrianna a slut.

I knew that Adrianna was as pure as can be in Hawthorne. She has always been an eye catcher.

Boys stare at her like she's some type of prize to be won, and she's used to it.

I've always made sure to look at her and not bat an eye.

I tried my hardest to never listen to the rumors in Hawthorne but sometimes you can't help but hear it from gossiping peers. Everyone knew she was untouched, *the forbidden diamond.*

Every guy had it out for her, all on a mission.

I've never really understood why she was praised, but then again, I don't even understand how I am praised.

In a world full of wealth and status, you're lucky if your parents haven't married you off yet.

But as I look at her now, her legs crossed together, her lips pouting, and her eyes narrowed. She was a vision that not many men should be able to touch let alone fucking look at.

I sighed, "I'm sorry."

I looked over at her as she turned her head to look at me, "Did you just apologize to me?"

"It won't be often. I know I acted like a fucking dick." Adrianna smiled at my words.

She did it a lot, it would light up a room. I always hated it when I saw her pearly whites but now... it seems that I am a sucker for her smile.

Adrianna started shivering in the corner of my eye, she was way too stubborn to say anything of course.

"Cold?" I asked with a sly smile.

"No." She pulls the sleeves down from my jacket with was obviously oversized on her, to cover her arms.

I take her hand and place it on top of the gear shift, my hand on top of hers.

Her eyes found mine, "You don't have to do that, no one's here."

She was right for once.

"Just some practice before we get to my parents." I say quickly as her smile falls into a frown.

"Oh."

She pulled her hand away; she didn't look at me for the rest of the ride to my house.

I park into my driveway as she shuffles to get her bag that she kept pretty close to her at all times.

I was not at liberty to ask about it. She was so nervous about losing it, and I simply shouldn't care.

The things that Adrianna Cassian does are things that I should not care about.

I got out of the car, opening her door as she stepped out, she looked shaken.

I pulled back to grab my hockey bag, walking to the front of the door, I inserted my key unlocking, and walked into my humble household.

Adrianna had been here already, and it was only because of how drunk and wasted she was.

She's never been here sober, and her face was something that I should've taken a picture of.

She scanned the walls of every generation of the Prince family.

My stepmother walks in with a huge smile, "Grayson, my

love! Great, you're here, your siblings and father are in the living room." She makes note of our arrival as Adrianna smiles.

I walked into the colorful living room, my sister was on the floor, flipping through magazines, makeup was scattered on the floor, looking up at me when her smile flourished at the sight of the both of us.

She runs up to be jumping so I can hug her tightly, "Took you so long to get here!" She laughed.

"Amelia Rhylee Prince." My father voiced as I let her down.

"Don't jump on your brother's bones when we have guests." He looks over at Adrianna whose face turned pale.

Amelia runs over to my father, laughing, "You need to take a chill pill, dad."

Adrianna smiles warmly, "I don't mind. This isn't my home. You can do whatever you please." Her voice shook.

"Where are the others?" I asked my father.

He turned back, gesturing over to the basement, "Your brothers are having a lovely game of hockey downstairs."

I look over at my stepmother, "You can go down too, but don't have too much fun. Dinner will be done in about an hour, tell them to keep it quiet and safe please."

I nodded, holding out my hand to Adrianna who wasn't sure if she should take it.

She did.

I led her downstairs, "Loosen up a bit. You aren't dying, Dove."

She scoffs, "It certainly feels like it."

I stop, "My family isn't what you think they are."

Adrianna licked her lips, her glossy eyes looking up at me, there was nothing more I wanted to do than sink my tongue inside her mouth.

I swallow as she turns back, I catch a whiff of her perfume, "Your father seems fun." She mocks.

I roll my eyes, "He's different."

Adrianna stops, and looks into my eyes, she's never been

scared to tell me about her real feelings. "You and your dad don't have a good relationship."

She said it so nonchalantly, like it was out in the open, I never really heard those words out loud before and yet she was here telling me what I already knew.

"It's complicated." Adrianna nods her head, we enter the basement, cold air slapping both of our faces.

Her eyes widened, "You have rink down here?"

"Being in a family of hockey superstars, we have to have a rink down here, Dove." I wink before walking over to my brothers skating and having fun.

Adrianna looks over to the seats, a pair of skates sat as she looks back up at me.

"Go on, I want to see your supposed skills." I turn over to my brothers as they all look at me.

"How was practice, Captain?" Bentley smiles, out of breath as Elliot and Easton skate behind him.

"Tiring." I mutter as they look over at Adrianna.

"How's the enemy?" Elliot rolls his tongue, his eyes stare over mine.

The worst.

I haven't gone a day without a fucking argument.

"The best." I smile, "Do you guys mind if she plays with us?"

"Nah, besides, I always loved it when she kicked your ass at a lot of things." I flipped Bentley off, Adrianna's smile lingered in my mind as she stood up walking over to me as she stepped on the ice.

She quickly twirled, tilting her head at me as if to say...

Try me.

I laughed, slipping my skates on, skating over to her as she skated away. I had to give it to her, she was fast.

But I was faster.

"Where did you learn how to skate?" I ask as I slowly follow her.

"I took lessons during Christmas." She looked over, stopping at the ledge.

"You know how to play hockey?" I gestured over to my three brothers.

Adrianna looked at the puck, "It shouldn't be that hard, right?"

"Are you flirting or trying to fight me?" I wink.

She smirked, "Maybe both."

I give her a weird look, her eyes looking at mine intently, "What?"

I skate closer, "You seem nicer." I point out.

She laughs, pushing me to the ground, "I'll punch you in the face, if that's what you really want."

She skates away as I lay on the floor, my brothers laugh at me and yet I had to think if I want to ever get up.

But when I got up, we spent about forty-five minutes playing hockey and skating around. I had to hand it to her, she was good.

For never playing in her life, she was really good. I mean I wasn't even trying. Okay, she got two goals on me, but I blame Elliot on being a bad goalie.

Adrianna skates over to me, her face beaming with happiness, I was glad to see it because I'm the cause.

I'd like that to be more consistent.

"I was good. You don't even need to say anything, *babe.*" She pulled my hockey stick.

I let go, "You were okay." I smirked as I let go off the hockey stick, letting her fall to the ice.

I laugh, my brothers watching intently, smiling to themselves.

"Ouch!" She yells out loud, "Grayson you jerk, I tried to not fall for the whole time!"

I laugh at her, her face turning red, fumes coming out of her ears, "I'm sorry." I held out my hands for her to take as a peace treaty.

She takes it, her face turning from annoyance to satisfaction, her lips curved, *smiling.*

Oh fuck.

She pulls me towards her on the floor, yanking me, I fall on top of her, we both burst out laughing.

She laughs making a perfect melody of happiness, it's beginning to be my favorite sound.

"That was hot." She takes her hand, moving my blonde hair out of my eye's way so I got a better look at her.

"What was hot?" I ask.

"The way you fell on your ass."

She looks down at both of us on the floor, I roll my eyes, "You realize that you did fall first right." I laugh.

Adrianna, pushes me gently, "Fuck you."

I look at her glowing eyes.

"You called me *babe*." I wink at her as she settles, her eyes close to mine.

"What do you want me to call you then?" She moves closer.

Mine.

Elliot coughs, both of our attentions getting taken by him, he smiled, more than happy to interrupt us.

"Dinner's ready." He winks at me as I groan.

I wanted to kiss Adrianna.

And this time I don't think it would've been because I had to.

But because I *desired* to.

ADRIANNA

We all sat at a designated place at the table. Grayson and I sat at the nearest head of the table. I couldn't help but zone out, as they talked about the boys' lives as they were planning to take over the business.

I felt Grayson's body tense as they talked about it more.

He kept sneaking me looks, I wanted to return it, but I knew I shouldn't.

Who knew I would've enjoyed playing hockey but not really, I enjoyed the part where Grayson looked like he was fed up with being beat.

Even when I knew he wasn't trying hard for my sake.

I even wanted to kiss him. Worst of all, I wanted him closer than ever.

"Adrianna?" My attention snapped back to place.

"Yes?" I smile awkwardly.

"Your father couldn't make it?"

I frown.

I know, I'm disappointed too.

"He's working really hard nowadays." I make excuses for him, even when he doesn't deserve it.

Grayson's father nods, while fixing his tie. "I'm busy too, but I always come when my children need me."

He looks at me, "I always make time for them."

I smile thickly, "You're a good man."

Grayson's mother looked upset, "Where do you eat dinner?"

I cough, I certainly didn't feel like unleashing my eating disorder on everyone tonight, "My maids usually cook." She deepens her frown.

"Your mother doesn't cook?" She lets her eyebrows furrow as I shuffle in my seat.

I swallow, "My mother is not present." I let out, taking a first bite of my steak.

Everyone went silent, until Grayson looked at me, his stone cold eyes never changing.

"Will you be here every day?" Amelia smiled ear to ear as she looked over at me.

I smile back, "Only if Grayson will let me."

"Nonsense!" His mother praised, "You come here whenever you need to, I insist."

I looked at Mr. Prince who looked exactly like Grayson. Their eyes were so alike you could tell he was his son. Grayson's brothers looked like their mother. Amelia was a good mix of both.

"Thank you." I look back at Amelia, "I get to hang out with you!"

I couldn't help but feel a bit comfortable as the night went on, I was exhausted, but my body had never felt more itself.

"I can't believe Grayson settled." Elliot gave a concerned face.

I looked over at Grayson whose face said it all.

Neither could I.

It was plastered all over his face, and to be quite frank, I couldn't really believe it either.

Grayson's mom smiles widely, "Well, don't hog her. I want to get to know the person who finally got my son to fall in love."

IN LOVE?

Oh, she was crazy, a dreamer if you ask me. There is no way in absolute hell he or I would ever fall in love with each other. There was way too much hate and indifference.

Grayson sits back, his face contorted in disgust, though I've never loved a look more, "Oh yes. He even mentioned how I was the only one for him and his eyes." I beamed, "Like he was going to die if he didn't have me."

"Really now?" His father spoke up with a smirk I knew too well that would usually come from his son.

Grayson smile looked faker than ever. I did find myself enjoying this more than I should have. "Protective." I mutter.

His father tilts his head, "How so?"

"I don't really want to talk about it." Grayson interrupts with a concerned look.

"Grayson threatened a guy's life because he was talking to Adrianna." His brother attempts to say while chewing on his food.

Grayson's eyes narrowed, "How do you know about that?"

"Does it matter?"

Grayson raised his voice slightly, "Yes."

Clear and stern.

"The whole university is talking about it." Easton laughed, "The guy called you *terrifying*." Grayson Prince was terrifying, there was no doubt about it. But everyone in Hawthorne University worshiped the ground he walked on. Every hockey game was full because of him. He was worshiped, feared, and loved.

"I am terrifying." Grayson said with a smirk.

"So are bees." I teased him, his eyes contacted mine, he looked content, like everything he had wanted was in one room.

But...

"Grayson isn't that terrifying, you know."

"And you know what!" Amelia leaned closer to me, she laughed, "Speaking of insects..." She looks warily at Grayson who gave the worst dead stare of all time.

"Don't you do it." He warns, getting up, Amelia bolts away from him.

"Do what?" I whipped my head over to Grayson who had a glorious smile, a genuine smile.

This was so normal. A fun dinner with a family who looked like they enjoyed each other's company instead of the comfort of their business.

Mr. Prince was right, even if he is one of the busiest men in the world, he still manages to take care of his children. I've always thought my father was the best man on earth.

But as the days grew further from the overdose last year, I realized how mistaken I was from the truth.

"Grayson's afraid of butterflies!" She screams as my mouth drops from shock and interest.

Grayson finally catches her, tickling her while she laughs and tries to pull away.

"You're scared of butterflies?" I exaggerated as he looked at Amelia with annoyance.

"I bet you're not attracted to him now." Bentley laughed as his mother told him to quiet down.

I smile at Grayson. He must be out of his mind if he thought I would ever let this go.

This is total black mail, a three pointer in my scoreboard against him.

"They're all liars." He says coolly while walking over to him by the living room chair.

I couldn't help but find Grayson's fear to be hilarious. He looked annoyed. He was trying to keep a brave face that I knew was a bruise in his masculinity.

He looked embarrassed, something I never thought was possible for a man like Grayson Prince. He looked at me with an annoyed expression.

"Don't worry, I still like you." He widens his stance urging me to sit on his lap, patting it.

So, I did.

Grayson 's hand traveled up my shirt, gripping my waist with his calloused hand. I shivered, my heart rose.

"Yeah?"

I swallowed.

I wanted to give in and kiss him again.

"I'm so in love with you." He winks while talking to me.

"You're so full of shit." I whisper back. He stops to smirk back at me. The smirks that make the ladies go weak in the knees.

"Oh sweetheart, but it was so believable."

What is wrong with you Cassian?

Grayson's face showed no sexual interest in me, but being on top of his lap made me sweaty and the smallest type of friction between the both of us made me want to moan.

Except, I've never felt this before. I felt a type of craving, longing for someone, wanting someone to devour me whole, by looking at him.

The worst part is, looking at Grayson now... I knew he could.

And smile at me while doing it.

CHAPTER 14

GRAYSON

I took Adrianna upstairs to my room. It wasn't somewhere she wasn't familiar with.

I want her to be more familiar with my belongings, she is one of them. I know I shouldn't sound so protective of Adrianna, but I am.

She was mine and fuck— I might kill someone who thought any different.

She was in my room, on my bed, under my fucking skin.

"I'm tired." She almost says in a whisper, my scowl warmed down from finally leaving my father's presence.

"Then go to bed," shrugging, "You can make yourself comfortable."

Adrianna just sat on my bed, like an angel she is. She looked untouched and yet she was on my bed, a very sinful place. A place where her golden skin shouldn't be even near.

And yet I was too selfish to push her away from it.

I begin to take off my shirt, her eyes widened, "What are you doing?"

I yawn, "I'm tired too, I'm hopping into the shower, hockey practice took my energy." I look over at her as I pull a towel out of my drawer.

"Why?" I smirk, turning to her, "Want to join?"

She didn't say anything, but she rolled her eyes, I guess that's enough of an answer. Her eyes yet again return to my scars as I turn, so it wasn't in view. It wasn't something I liked flaunting.

I turned to get up, but her comeback stopped me from entering the bathroom, "You're a pig." She scoffs.

"And you're any better, Dove?" I threw her a pillow that I had grabbed on my couch, she caught it but sent me a look.

"Hey, I'm sorry if my parents were a bit judgmental."

She simply looked at me dumb founded. "Are you kidding?" She throws the pillow back at me.

I couldn't help but looked somewhat surprised.

"Your family is a dream."

I might actually believe her with the look on her face. Like she hadn't been surrounded by many families to truly judge for herself.

"They're annoying." I make a point as she grimaces.

"Are they actually annoying if they ask about what's going on in your life?" She folds her hands together.

"I would love it if my father asked about my day, or maybe just care about me for once. You're lucky you have a family who cares."

Adrianna looked like she meant what she was saying, and it made me uneasy. I always thought her father was on her tail about everything. When smallest thing goes wrong for his daughter, he comes running to help his princess. But I couldn't be further from the truth.

I shouldn't care who would ask about her day.

It was surreal for me. A week ago, if someone told me Adrianna Cassian was sitting in my room after having dinner with my family. First, I would've told my cleaners to bleach my entire room, then I would've punched them in the mouth for lying.

But as I stand here and look at her now, a halo of light on her head, she was a vision.

A vision I should never have touched or looked at because I

never saw this before. I've never batted an eye and now, when I really am alone, I'm ashamed that I need to hide the fact that I do think about her.

In ways that I should not.

"So, you think that August will buy this relationship soon?" I smile, inching away from a real conversation with her.

Adrianna's face fell. I shouldn't have noticed but I did.

"Yes, I think so." She turns around to face the head of my bed where her stuffed animal lay.

"Then you can go back to dating your boy toy." I shake my head with a laugh.

"I didn't want to get back together with Brooks when I agreed to help you out."

"What?"

"I wanted to be with him, trust me, spending so much money to just be with him in secret... but the day that we ended things, ironically, was the day I wanted to tell him I loved him." She frowns.

I hated the way she looked vulnerable.

"How is that sad?"

Adrianna's eyes reached mine, "Because he didn't care."

"He kept me like a dark secret that he was ashamed of. I want someone to show me off, like I'm their whole world. I hate being left in the dark, I hate that I let him gaslight me into thinking how he treated me was okay,"

I almost wanted to punch Brooks. Not almost, I wanted to fucking slam his face on the ground make sure his golden boy smile was gone forever.

He didn't deserve her one bit. I sure as hell shouldn't be the one making those calls, but I wanted to make sure that not even his mother could recognize him after I was done with knocking him out.

"And the worst part is, I was going to go back to him, the day that you gave me back my house keys. But then you mentioned

Maya, and I found out that not only am I a pushover, but I'm also a moron too."

"You couldn't have known." I cut her off.

"At least with her, he was getting sex. Which is what he wanted anyways and the moment I said I wasn't ready, he yelled at me."

"I didn't know any of this," I stared at her.

She smiled, "It's okay," rolling her eyes, "Everyone knows Grayson Prince doesn't have a heart, but that was before you told me about your love for your ex."

"I have a heart; I just don't know if it's beating sometimes. Don't expect me to be good and kind. You'll get disappointed, Dove." I walk in the bathroom, trying to avoid the direction of this conversation.

Not really wanting to look back at Adrianna.

She didn't need my fucked-up life to add to the pain she's been having.

Don't expect me to be good and kind. You'll get disappointed, Dove.

I take a deep breath.

God, could I have sounded more emo?

Maybe that sentence will make her remember why she hated me in the first place.

It was for the best.

This was the most selfless thing I've done.

T stiffened, walking out of the room, I swung the door to the bathroom open, stripping off my smelly clothing then turning on the shower, I jumped in, I set my arms on the handle of the shower, gripping tightly.

Adrianna being in my room was practically every guy's wet

fucking dream. I won't lie and say I hadn't dreamt of her tied up to my bed and naked waiting for me to take her.

I was practically fucking hoping she would strip in front of me when I looked at her sitting so tasteful on my bed.

So fucking innocent.

Untouched.

Her sweatshirt was over sized, was that the appeal nowadays? I mean if she really wanted, she could just take some of mine. The neckline of the sweatshirt fell down to her shoulder, God her skin looked so delicate and fucking soft I wanted to explore it.

When I looked down at her legs, her skirt inched up, her creamy tanned model legs buried to the back of my brain.

I imagined her legs around my waist, her soft hands gripping my back as I fuck her up the wall.

Her hot breath on my neck, moaning my name.

Fuck. I look down, my dick twitching at the thought of Adrianna just sitting there, her *innocent* brown eyes set on mine.

I grip my cock tight; I stifle a groan. I had never felt so fucking tense in my life.

I shouldn't be jerking off to the thought of Adrianna. She was everything I fucking hated and despised.

Why did she have to be so fucking perfect?

God, I'm pathetic. I was in the bathroom, soaking in the shower as I pump my fucking cock to the thought of her shoulders and legs.

Fucking hell, her lips.

Plumped and full, the lips that had talked back to me every single day.

How would she fucking love it if her lips were around my dick, sucking me as I fuck her mouth, gripping her hair tightly, pushing myself to the back of her throat?

Would she be able to?

Innocent.

I would release in the back of her throat, make her gag and

swallow, gripping her chin to meet my eyes, I wouldn't hesitate to kiss her beautiful lips.

I felt my stomach tighten with pleasure; I release letting my head knock back in satisfaction.

I lift my head, rinsing off the remaining forms of shampoo from my hair, grabbing a towel, and drying my whole body.

I felt filthy, I shouldn't have done that, and I knew it. I shouldn't have felt the need for her lips on me. But I did.

Did that make me a bad person?

Yes. It does. I had to remember one thing and that one thing was that she and I were only pulling off this fake relationship for one reason and that reason was because of my ex-girlfriend damn it.

I want August. I want her and I don't want Adrianna.

Never again will I give into my temptation for Adrianna, it made me dirty.

Like I was betraying my father. My family loves her, but my father would never forgive her family for what they did to him.

I pulled off a pair of sweatpants, my hair was still a bit wet, but I managed to wash off the sweat from my body. Adrianna was lying on my bed, her outside clothes were still on.

And that bothered me, why the hell was she laying on my bed with her outside clothes?

I pull out one of my many hockey shirts I've gathered through the years of playing the sport.

I look at her, "Put this on and change."

"This is just a shirt, I'll be freezing." She gets off my bed.

"I have a pretty warm body." I spilled out as she gave me a shocked expression.

"Oh."

I cough, "And what the hell are you watching?"

I look over at the TV as a blonde lady cries during an interview, "Duh, it's *Love Island.*"

"*Love Island?*" I felt my eyebrow arch in confusion.

"In my opinion, one of the best reality shows ever made." She smiles happily.

"Yeah, good for you. We need to change it to my hockey tapes to learn plays." I say sternly, plugging in my phone to the TV.

Adrianna pulled up the remote, "It's just one episode, grumpy much?"

Her mouth curved into a smile, "I'm not grumpy, I just want to win the next game."

"You won the last game." She beamed.

I sigh, pulling a dumbbell in front of me, "That's just one step to being the best, and we were sloppy."

"You looked like you were having fun."

"Having fun means nothing if I don't win or get what I want." I huffed out.

The smile left her body, "I think you're wrong."

"Excuse me?"

"You wouldn't be that good at your age if you don't love what you're doing, having fun is the most important thing."

My mouth snapped shut, I hadn't really thought about hockey on a bigger spectrum, and maybe there was some truth to what she was saying. But tonight, wasn't the fucking night I would ponder on it.

"Give me the remote Dove." I got up as she bit her lip.

Oh, she wanted to play.

"I'm serious, sweetheart." I walked toward her on the bed, "I'm giving you one last warning." She lifted her hand with the remote on it, bringing it towards me.

I try to grab it before she pulls it back towards her, I grow frustrated.

She was cute.

I felt a muscle in my jaw twitch, "I'm joking here," she handed it over to me, before pulling it back again, I jumped towards her, her laughter was music.

But now I was straddled on top of her, she clearly hadn't noticed it yet.

But when she did, she quieted, she smelled like me, absolutely fucking mine.

She paled; color flushed all over her face. Her pupils dilated, swallowing.

I felt my heartbeat faster by the minute as she stared at me, nothing to say her lips glistened like a fucking jewel.

"I'm sorry." She blurted, her hands shaking.

"No." I breathed out, fucking consumed by the heat and tension between us, "Don't give me space. That's the last thing I fucking want with you."

She places her hand on my cheek, still shaking.

And even after my fucking pep talk, I stagger, I bend closer to her lips.

And she lets me, pulls me closer even.

Mine.

We were almost there, her lips so close. But I couldn't, so I pulled back the remote on my hand.

She looked at me with her smile fading as she looked at the remote in my hand.

"Are you blushing?!" I smirk, her eyes grow irritated. "Embarrassed because you think I would've actually kissed you?"

"No." She gets up, gathering her things.

"The only thing I'm embarrassed about is your pathetic attempt at trying to seduce me."

I turned around and she was all ready to leave my house, "You've got quite a mouth on you, don't you? Someone should teach you what to do with it." I yawn as she turns around out of my room.

"You're a dick."

"Do you forget that this is supposed to be forced?" I laugh harshly.

"You do understand that I can't actually tolerate you." I get up, my eyes set on nothing but hers.

I grab her stuffed animal out of my bed, handing it to her, "And lastly, you do understand that I would rather stab myself in the eye than touch you, let alone kiss you." She didn't say anything, only stared back at me with an expression I couldn't read.

"Have a nice night, Prince."

And she left.

CHAPTER 15

ADRIANNA

I hated him. I was fucking stupid to think that there was more to him than just the guy that made my life miserable from the day I saw him on the other side of my driveway.

I hated him with every fiber of my being.

I hated his smirk that challenged me every moment of the day.

I hate how he runs his fingers through his hair every time he gets frustrated. The way his arms flex when he gets angry, or the snarky remarks when he enters the room.

I hate it when he says things to me that are too hurtful for others to say. When he says sarcastic things even when he actually means it. When he even addresses me with a disdain in his rough voice. I can't stand him.

But the truth was, he wasn't doing anything wrong. He was just doing what we agreed on. He was being the person I always knew, and I don't know why it upset me so much. It shouldn't have and the bottom line was that he had every right to treat me like shit.

What had really happened between us made me think that maybe there was a change in our hatred for each other. I was crazy, and he was the reason for it.

He drives me crazy. Fucking mad.

But what's more maddening was that it made my decision easier.

I had no emotional attachment to him, and I knew for a fact that he wouldn't either, it was the perfect thing for me and finally letting free.

My logic didn't need to make sense to others but that was what was so great about it. It didn't make sense.

I picked up my phone, clicking on Margo's contact.

Ring, ring... ring.

"Babe?" Margo answered as I let go of my shaking breath, my anxiety took over me as I fidgeted with my rings.

"Margo. Thank God." I got up pacing.

I quieted and I heard rustling from her end of the call, a boy's voice, but I wasn't about to ask about her love life, she would tell me when she was ready.

"Am I interrupting something?" I mutter as she laughs, going on mute for a second.

"No, of course not."

I hear her closing the door, more rustling, "Are you okay?"

"Yes. Actually, Grayson and I got into a screaming match."

"Sounds typical, what's the problem?" From the sound of a thump, I imagine that she finally sets the phone down, more rustling.

"Well, you know how much we hate each other, and I would rather stick a blade into my torso than ever be affectionate with him."

"Your point?" Margo asked.

"Well, I think I'm going to ask him to take my virginity." I look at my purity ring once more.

I hear a big ruckus, envisioning that Margo dropped her phone, a big gasp came from her, "Adrianna."

"Margo."

I couldn't believe I even said it out loud. I did sound crazy, I mean this was my virginity I was talking about, it was special.

"Anna, you can't be serious," She exhales, "You can't possibly want Grayson Prince to take your virginity."

"I don't want him too; I'm giving it up."

I felt my heart constrict, "Margo, I'm not asking you to understand, but I can't take this anymore."

"I have guarded my virginity for my whole life, and this ring on my finger has practically branded me."

I look at my ring once again, "Little miss perfect." I laugh harshly.

"That's what they call me right? They have no right! They don't know me. They don't know the side of me that has overdosed and attempted suicide. They don't know *me.*"

Margo walks closer to the phone, I could hear her voice getting louder, closer to the speaker phone.

"I don't have the perfect life people assume I do. I have days where I can't control myself, and this ring on my finger is my most prized possession that I had never given to anyone."

She didn't say anything, only stood on the other end of the phone silently.

I never expected her to really think about how it was to be in my position and to be waiting to give up something people all my life expected me to keep.

How much I have wanted to let go of something that has eternally branded me? How much I have just wanted to scream at the people who have labeled me, throw away the perfect act, and do something I would never do?

"This isn't because I'm desperate on losing my virginity, Margo." I exclaim.

"This is because I'm desperate to walk onto campus tomorrow without this ring on my finger and not feel that label or brand on my back." I finally closed my eyes like I had been keeping that in for my whole life.

And I did.

She probably thinks I am going crazy.

"Your virginity is very important. You should have someone

that will cherish it with you for your first time, you do understand that Grayson is notorious for...”

“...*being a God and a Devil in bed.*” I sigh. “I know.”

Why does that only make me want it more?

Heaven and hell in one person. How could I resist?

Sure, he was more of hell, but I couldn't help but think that we would be the perfect mixture of both.

All my life I just listened to everyone. I defy him and him only. Why was that?

Because I was trained to please everyone like my father always told me to do, but my father always told me to make the Prince family’s lives hell.

I never understood why he hated his family. They treated me like a human, someone who wasn’t breakable.

I wanted to obey Grayson Prince just *once* in my life, just to see his face with a jaw-dropping look at me because he would have never predicted this. I wanted to be destroyed.

I wanted my perfect streak of innocence to end. Every bit of it is shredded into billions of pieces.

But I wasn’t going to ask for it. No.

The perfect plan to seduce Grayson Prince was genius, because with every fiber in his body, he hates me.

He despises me, and he will fight it. My winning trophy would be him on his knees for me.

“Adrianna?” Margo’s voice interrupts my thoughts.

“Yes, I’m here.”

“Grayson will never agree to your proposition.” She says matter of factly.

“I’m going to act like that did not hurt a little bit.” I jump on top of my counter, crossing my legs.

“You know what I mean.” She groans.

“Yes, I do,” I smile looking towards my window, “I have a plan.”

“Do you?” Margo laughs.

"Yes, and I'm a genius, but I have to go." I jump off the counter, rushing up to my bedroom.

"I know, Einstein." Margo pauses for a moment, and that's how I knew that whatever she was about to say next was serious.

"Just please promise me, you'll think about this virginity thing before actually going through with Grayson being the one to take it."

I close my eyes for a second, taking in a breath and letting it out, "Margo, I really want this large weight of my virginity to leave my shoulders."

"I just don't think Grayson is the right choice." She counters as I smile.

"I know."

I'm pretty sure anyone I would've asked would've said the same exact thing.

"Then let's go to a bar this weekend and find someone for you to lose it to."

I bite my top lip, really thinking about this idea. "Okay, I'll think about it."

"Thank you."

I laugh, "Okay, I really have to go take a shower, I love you!" I send a kissing sound over to her as she does the same.

"I love you too!"

"Oh, and Margo," I smile as I walk into my closet, "Use a condom." I hung up immediately.

Did she somehow think I was an idiot if I didn't know there was a guy either next to her or in her?

And I did take Margo's concerns into consideration. I really did.

But my plan sounded better for now.

One thing I always knew was that Grayson's bedroom balcony was right across from mine, and I had a clear view of him sometimes.

Right now, I saw him. Just how I left him. He was sitting on his bed with a bunch of hockey tapes.

His hair was slightly drier than when I saw him last, I didn't want to make it obvious I was looking because I knew he had a view into my bedroom sometimes.

Instead, my plan was in action.

The Devil in Heaven Plan.

I smiled to myself, that was pretty clever of me, I wasn't going to lie.

I put my long hair up into a clip, a couple of strands still out. I lit a candle to make my room seem more romantic and special. I sneaked a glance over to Grayson who took a second to look over to me quickly, before returning back to his tapes.

I stood in front of my mirror. This was only phase one, Adrianna, damn it. I breathe in pulling my shirt up over my head, leaving me in just a bra. Then I push my skirt down until it hits my ankles. I stepped out of them, bending down making sure my ass was in Grayson's range of view.

I swallow. What if he thought I didn't want him to imagine me? He loathed everything about me already, it would hurt even more if he hated my body like I did.

I take my towel, resisting looking up to Grayson's window, and walk into my bathroom. I take a pretty short shower.

My hands were clammy as I walked out of my bathroom. I checked to see if Grayson was still sitting on his bed. He had multiple books on his side and more tapes on the bed. He looked frustrated.

Ruffled hair, his face was red, and he fidgeting more than normally.

He looked over-worked.

Maybe I could help with that.

Phase Two.

I let go of the towel, my eyes scanned to Grayson's room. His eyes on my image, gawking.

I decided to put on Grayson's jacket with my underwear. He gave it to me to wear, and I lay on my bed.

Grayson's eyes couldn't seem to pull away from me and I couldn't tell if I liked it or not.

Phase Three.

I pull one of the blankets up to my stomach, spreading my legs a bit further apart, my hand creeping down to my pulsing heat.

I had restrained myself from playing with myself in the shower, just for this moment.

Grayson just stared, he looked feral.

He craved it.

I swallowed, as my hand began to rub my slick folds. I was sensitive, my heartbeat racing as I relaxed my head, not even caring if Grayson was watching.

My phone began to ring.

Grayson Prince.

I answer it, "Dove, you—"

"Sorry, call me tomorrow." I looked over my phone making sure it was on speaker, so he could hear me.

So, I let go even more, I played with myself with the thought of some other man doing it for me.

"Fuck me." I groan, wishing someone with large hands would be able to just gather me like a handful and spread me apart.

"Adrianna—" Grayson mutters once more as I interrupt with a sudden moan.

"Yes, just like that." I let out, imagining someone diving in between my legs, eating every bit of me up, even when I tell them to stop, they dive in deeper until I physically can't come any more.

"Fuck, fuck, yes, yes, baby, yes."

I pleaded as Grayson's face looked distraught. He could've hung up by now, except he didn't.

I arch my back, "Please don't stop." I grunt as I reach over to my drawer, pulling out my vibrator, placing it on top of my throbbing clit.

"Yes!" I yell, the more I inch closer to my release, the more I see Grayson, his hands being the ones to hold my body, his strong build, and his beautiful face in between my legs. "Please," I rasp.

"Please, Prince." I sob weakly as I reach my end, shaking. I sneaked a last look at Grayson who was standing on his balcony, no shame in staring at me on my bed, as I moaned out his name to my release.

I swallowed, and Grayson hung up. I, myself, couldn't even believe I moaned his name out loud.

I was too tired to even think about it. I shut my eyes, and everything went black.

I could feel my heart rate slow back down.

CHAPTER 16

ADRIANNA

I haven't spoken to Grayson the whole morning. I saw him at the university, but I couldn't look him in the eyes. And rightfully so, what happened last night was so out of line I wanted to bury my whole body six feet under.

He must think I'm fucking crazy. What's worst is that he's seen me.

I'm embarrassed and I had to take pills just to keep me from going crazy. I approach my locker, taking a deep breath. I unlock it, seeing my pale face in the mirror, touching it up even more with some makeup.

"You don't need that junk on your beautiful face." I jump as Brooks comes up from behind me, his face in view from my mirror so I didn't need to turn around.

Instead, I look at his eyes from the reflection, "I would say good morning to you, but I prayed last night for you to spill coffee on your favorite pants."

Brooks looked at me as if I was a completely different person, he wasn't entirely wrong. I definitely never showed him the side of me he regularly saw when I interacted with others that I wasn't a fan of.

"Ah, Adrianna, always a joy. You were never like that when we dated. You choose now to be interesting."

I scowl at him, kind of embarrassed to act out in public but I was infuriated.

It was like a slap to the face and Brooks was looking for a slap to the face.

"You always brighten my mornings with the sweet nothings you would whisper in my ear." I smile sarcastically.

"Come back to me." He groans, "We both know we miss each other."

We do?

I was seriously contemplating whether I should kick him where the sun doesn't shine but then realized that he would probably cream at the thought of any part of my body touching him there.

I let my head wander for a while before I answered, "I'm with someone new now, Brooks." I pulled away, finally turning to face him, closing my locker.

"Yes, I heard you're dating the one and only Grayson Prince."

I flinch at the words being said.

"Yes, so I think if you know what's good for you," I rip his hand away from my waist and push it to himself, "You should stop gawking at me, touching me, talking to me, or associating with my friends."

Brooks looked at me to ask if I was joking.

He laughs harshly, "You wanted me to be like that during our relationship, remember?" He stresses.

"I thought you wanted the whole world to know you were mine." He adds on as I hold my arms together in front of my body.

"It's too late." I say with a look that would usually send many to the doctor's waiting room.

"I did not lose you to fucking Prince." He seethes in a way that made me jolt, like a damn snake.

Brooks exhales a long breath, he looks frustrated, "He gets

whatever he wants with a blink of his eye. Please don't be one of the things he takes for granted."

I snicker, "Funny. So, it's okay if you do it, but not if he does?"

"You're acting like a damn idiot, I always knew you weren't a damn scholar Anna, but being reused and recycled by a Prince isn't a good look." He snarls.

I didn't want to hit him. I didn't want to hit him.

Oh, fuck it.

I take my hand, heavily swinging as my palm hits his cheek. I could feel the heat rise from his face, hoping that it would create a handprint.

Brooks stiffens.

"I really think you should remember who you're fucking talking to. So, unless you want your dad's business to file for bankruptcy, you will never speak to me again."

I spotted Maya's face in the distance staring, "If you keep staring at me, it's going to earn you a broken nose or a bruised eye."

He places his hand on his cheek, looking raged more than ever but he calms down, his eyes burning onto mine.

"I don't care. I miss you, Anna. Give us another shot." He pleads as I look at Maya's scorned expression.

"Your girlfriend is waiting for you." Brooks nods in defeat.

"She's nothing to me."

"That's what you said during the relationship, and you were having sex with her while telling me you loved me every night."

Brooks silenced with a gulp, "Forgive me. Please. This time will be different."

I didn't want to entertain anymore, but looking at Brooks, he seemed like he really meant it. You don't know how important something is before it's gone.

He grips my wrist, flashbacks of the night we broke up flashed through my brain like a movie montage.

"I'm sorry, I didn't mean to touch you." He jolts back.

"You can't be happy with him," He looks at me with passion, almost as if it was real.

No. I'm not.

"Yes, I am. Now please." I walked away.

He runs in front of me, "Just come to my game tonight, for old times sake."

I sigh, "Okay."

I knew I was making a mistake, but I also believed in second chances. Brooks didn't deserve me, and I knew that. But I thought about how he could still be a part of my life without any romantic relations.

He takes a step closer, his arm snakes behind my back pulling me in for a hug, and I hug him back, looking forward to seeing the whole hockey team staring.

Great. Just fucking great.

If there was one thing I knew, it was that this team had their captains back, and this was surely not going to go unnoticed.

It surely didn't matter to Grayson since it was all fake. He shouldn't care about what I do with my real love life. But still, he had to keep his act going.

I pulled away from Brooks' embrace which made me feel like I needed to take an hour and a half shower.

I flinched as he smiled at me, "I'll play my best for you."

I smile thickly, "You always do."

I begin to walk to class as the bell rings, a tall, muscled body interferes as it pops out of the corridor.

What is up with the universe today? Can it just give me a break from testosterone?

But I knew those arms anywhere, the smell of Dior Sauvage cologne, Grayson Prince was gracing me with his precious presence.

"Glad to know that you can ignore me for a whole morning but have an intimate meeting with Brooks." He says with a large scale of sarcasm.

"I wasn't ignoring you."

I was lying to him, yes, but I didn't care.

"I don't like liars, Dove." He licks his lips, his silver eyes skimming my figure, making my problems with having a pale face disappear.

"I came to pick you up this morning, but it seems that one of your guards said you already left." He pointed out as I looked at him, tilting my head. It was a reminder that I was only five foot five inches.

"I left with Verina." I stood taller, even if it did not help because he was six foot five inches of glory.

Seriously, as much as he was the bane of my existence, God must have taken his time on him. I'm sure there are some muscles on this man's body that haven't even been discovered.

He would be tested in a lab to see if he was supernatural or something.

But then again, I remembered that he cut a huge chunk of my hair in grade school, "Why are you ignoring me?"

I sent him a look that openly said, *are you fucking with me right now?*

"If you don't know why I'm mad at you, you need to take this as a sign to reflect on your actions in the past twenty-four hours."

"Is this really because of our fight last night?"

I'm glad that he skims over the fact that he watched me intently playing with myself while moaning his name.

I ignore him, walking away from him he catches up to me, "Oh, you have to get over that. We bicker all the time." He makes a point as I continue to act as if he wasn't there.

He walks in front of me quickly, like he was frustrated at my act of defiance, "We don't want to blow our cover." He whispers as I felt a bit of my control snap, "Couples fight!"

I walk closer, "This is far more believable than you thinking people will actually believe that we can stand being with each other for more than a fucking minute."

Grayson stares back with an expression I can't quite read again, "You doing something tonight?" He asks with a low voice.

I grow even more agitated than I thought was fucking possible. He was pushing all of my buttons all at once and repeatedly.

I hate how he dismissed everything I say like I'm a pop-up ad that deserves no attention and just gets crossed out.

"No!" I say with a ragged breath, swallowing.

"I'm just asking, Dove." He smirks as I feel my fists forming.

"And I answered your question." I condemned.

Now I wanted to slap him as well, but I knew that would cost more controversy than my mental health could take right now.

Grayson rolls out his tongue inside his mouth, my annoyance has decreased from one action.

"We have a game tonight; I just want to make sure that you'll be there. It's a home game, my family will be there."

He pulls my arm, gently pushing me against a wall. "Especially August, and that means you really need to brighten up your spirits when you see me on the ice sweetheart."

I push him away with a scowl, "I'm not going."

"What?"

"You heard me," I dust off my shirt.

"Where are you going to be?" His eyebrows wrinkled, like he couldn't believe what I was saying.

"None of your business." I snarled at him.

"Considering you are my girlfriend; I have a right to know about your whereabouts." He growled, looking a bit more frustrated than he was prior to my answer.

"I am *not* your girlfriend." I snap back as he obnoxiously shakes his head.

"Oh yeah?"

He challenges, "How about we ask people here if you are?"

I gulp, "Grayson knock it off." I looked at him, visibly seeing his need to prove he was correct, it only made me want to ruin things for him even more.

"I."

"Will."

"Not."

"Be."

"Attending."

"Your."

"Game."

I say with conviction as his jaw clenches. He grabs my waist pushing me into a janitor's closet, the bell ringing.

Wonderful, I'm late to class.

Grayson's large hands made me feel so small, so delicate, he touched me with anger and need. I defied him and he loved it.

I hate that I loved it too.

"You're fucking going to that game." His mouth was close to mine, I wanted to bite his bottom lip and draw some blood.

"You can't make me." I laugh, struggling out of his grip as he tightens his hold even more. Fuck, he was strong.

I wonder how he would feel while fucking me.

I swallow.

"You have a kink for janitor's closets or..." I question him as he slams my body against the door.

"Trust me, Dove." He smirks, his eyes burning into mine in a good way where I felt like he wanted to leave his dominance in my body.

"If you go missing because I tied you up in a janitor's closet, no one will look for you." He beckons as I felt a smile creep onto my lips.

I smile. I shouldn't have but I did.

He looks down to my hand, a glittering diamond caught his eye, he examines it with a devilish smirk.

"Purity ring." He said with a rasping tone.

Something clogged up in my throat that made me inaudible, I nodded.

"Fuck." He whispers in my ear, full of lust I could feel my body tingling.

His voice thick and soft with need.

His hand reaches for the nape of my neck gripping the roots

of my hair for control. He positions my head for my eyes to look into his.

He leans closer, "You're right. You're not my girlfriend."

I grew shocked at the fact that he confessed he was wrong, but my need for his touch has not changed, only intensified.

"You're not my fucking girlfriend," he rasps nearing my ear, "but I'm the first man to watch you come." His lips close down on my lobe, I softly moan, "My name was the first to come out of your lips when you finished... *which makes you mine.*"

I wanted to rip him away from me as much as I wanted him to consume my heated body.

I anticipated for him to touch me in ways that I would never profess to wanting, as my body was slammed against the janitor's closet, the tight space made me only want him more than I should.

My heart rate was erratic, he made my heartbeat so fast. I felt alive. I wanted his lips on mine as well as his hands gripping my hair. I wanted him to rip my clothes away from my wavering body right at this moment.

Would he?

Would he overstep my boundaries?

Grayson pulls away and looks at me with a haze of guilt and anger, he didn't want to touch me like I wanted him to, he liked to play with me.

He toys with me. Like an owner lowering a string to its cat to jump toward.

But I wasn't a cat, nor a damn plaything.

"You will be at that game, Adrianna." He sternly commanded as I looked back at him. I contemplated whether I should be the one to place my hands on his body.

But before I replied, he made a rushed exit outside the closet, leaving me alone with my filthy thoughts.

I was obedient to everyone else, except for him.

Why should that change now?

The fuck I'm going to that game.

CHAPTER 17

GRAYSON

I've been an absolute mess. She drives me absolutely mad, always fucking defying everything I ask of her. For once, can she just go, and do as she's told?

But then I remembered, what's the fun in that? We wouldn't be who we were without the need to agitate each other.

This hockey game tonight was very important for me. We were finally celebrating my collective 400 goals collected throughout my life.

And I was going to reveal which team I was planning on committing to. I wanted everyone to be there, my whole family was coming, not including my mother of course. All of my friends were going, and I knew the whole school was going.

I wanted her there. I shouldn't care, but I do. I want her by my side for all of my life goals. Literally.

"Earth to Grayson?"

I look up with an annoyed scowl, "Can you cool it? My head is fucking pounding." Liam smiles as he scores another goal.

"What's up with you?" Chris skates over to me.

Liam laughs, "Got into another fight with your girl?"

Neil skates over as well leaning on his stick, "You know, a girl shouldn't be clouding your brain this much, it's like she's all you ever think about."

"No, she's not." I skate by them as Liam passes me the puck.

"It doesn't take a genius to figure it out." He urged me to play with the puck.

"Figure out what, exactly?" I muttered I could feel my veins pump as they drill stupid sentences to my head.

"Just put us all out of our misery and admit you are starting to..." Chris smiles, putting out his hand for Neil to grab, twirling him around like a figure skate dancer.

"... I am not! We are not." I exhale, shooting a puck into the net, quickly.

"Don't even say the fucking word." I growled at Chris as he placed both of his hands up to his sides. "She's just a pawn for a plan I've thought of for a while now, and we all know that August can't stand girls like Adrianna."

"Is that really all Adrianna is to you?" Liam probes and I slap another puck into the net, my muscles tighten.

"Yes."

"You haven't fantasized about her in any way?" Neil skates closer as I roll my eyes.

Yes.

"No, of course not." I grumbled, gripping my stick tighter than ever. I could feel my knuckles whiten.

"You're so full of shit." Liam comments as I send him a stare that would've frozen hell.

"Good." Neil looks at me with a calm expression.

I slapped another shot into the goal, it was beautiful.

"Will she be at the game tonight?" Chris joins us, it's been a while since he's had free time, but he made an exception to take a day off for my celebration.

"Yes." I say plainly.

"Odd." Neil threw me a concerned face, "Did she tell you she was going to be there?"

I smile, "No. I told her to be there."

Neil clamps his mouth together skating away from me as I narrow my eyes, my eyebrows furrow and I gather another puck, my knuckles white as fucking snow, "Why?"

"I heard that she was attending the football game to support Brooks." Neil spilled out as I shot the puck so fucking fast it flew straight to the goal, making a hole on the net, everyone froze.

I straighten, "She wouldn't do that." I look at Neil as he nods slowly, Liam grabbing at the hole that burned through the net.

Or would she?

"She will have to be here if she wants to keep this stupid fucking relationship going." I scowl.

They smile knowingly, "Fake relationship." They look over, "You mean fake relationship."

"You know what I mean." I skate over to the net examining it.

Boy, I wish that this net was Brooks face. He has the nerve of asking her to support him when he was all but nice to her during their relationship.

Sure, that makes me hypocritical, but what me and Adrianna had was purely fake and did not overstep boundaries.

"It really seems to me that you kind of need her more than she needs you."

True, but I would never admit that.

"Adrianna is fucking desperate for any chance she gets to get any type of attention from her bastard of a father." I take off to the side.

"We need to head over to the arena." Chris makes note as I nod.

It was basically a ritual for us to cool off before a hard game, and this game was riding on my shoulders. I was nervous, and I never was this nervous when it came to hockey.

But my parents were going there, and my father was my biggest critic. He always had something to say, mostly bad, which only made me want to be better at what I did. I always felt the need to prove him wrong or that I can be a better man than he will ever be.

It was hard to prove myself. I was the oldest of my siblings, I was the one with the burden of being the next Prince, everyone compared me to my father.

I knew from the moment I watched him work I wanted to be the one to take on the job. I wanted to make our company the best it was, but hockey was the reason I was hesitant.

I wanted to go pro. I want to be the best and I want to play for the world, be the best in the world, which I know was a reach, but I like to challenge myself.

My friends knew I was tough on myself, and it was something I never wanted to change. I was hardheaded and I liked being right.

"I really wish for all of the hockey team that Adrianna won't be there." Liam smiles as I look at him with a confused look.

Liam gives me a scorned look, "Are we going to act like you won't slam a puck like that through the net and make a hole if she doesn't show?"

Chris intervenes, "Or ram a guy through the boards?"

Neil skates over, "Or talk mad shit that will make another player get pounded on the ice?" I sent over a look to all three of them that made their laughs die down.

"Knock it off." I mutter as they straighten, "I just want her there because I know August will be there. My girlfriend not being there would raise suspicion not only for her but for my parents too, will it not?"

Chris and Neil look at each other smirking, I want to punch both of them in the face, the fact was if I did, they wouldn't even ask me why I did it.

Liam picks up his skates, pulling me in for a side hug, "You got this, we have your back."

"You always do."

CHAPTER 18

ADRIANNA

" I don't think that's a good idea." Verina gives me a wavering uncertainty of words.

"I know it's not a good idea." I smile at her as Juliette walks over with so much school spirit gear, I'm surprised she can walk straight.

"I'm so ready for tonight's game." She smiles at us.

I walk off to find a sweater, "I'm not going."

"You're joking, right?"

"No." I whip my head over to them, "I'm attending the football game."

"Do you want to die?" Margo laughs.

I roll my eyes, "Grayson would never hurt me." I flinch, "Not physically anyways."

"He does have a way of verbally abusing people, doesn't he?" Margo continues, "Now that I think of it, just you."

I picked up a red cable knit sweater and slipped on a pair of my white platform converse that always raised my height a few inches.

"Why are you even going through these lengths? I thought you and Brooks were over and you weren't going back." Verina walks over, opening my closet and picking out my red scarf.

She looks at me tilting her head, a gesture of whether she can wear it tonight.

I nod as she twirls it around her neck, "I'm not going back."

"Then why are you ditching your boyfriend's game to go to your ex who treated you like shit?" Margo sprays perfume on.

I huff, "Grayson Prince is not my boyfriend, it's fake. Brooks asked me to go, and I see nothing wrong with that."

"We do." Juliette directs at me.

I groan, "Stop it, I just think that it would be nice to enjoy some football once in a while."

"You are such a liar."

I look at them with a smile, "How?"

"You are going just to piss off Grayson!"

"Why should he be pissed off?" I saunter over, their eyes never leaving my body.

I think everyone was making a big deal out of this. I mean come on, it was just another silly hockey game that he wanted me to be at and it was stupid. He's going to have more, and it wasn't important.

"It's a very important game." They gave me an honest look.

At the pit of my stomach, I did see their point and that this was a very important game for Grayson but what was more important was that he should know that I never just do what I'm told.

I wasn't the girl he thought I was. I was done being obedient, I was more than what he thought of me.

Something that I could be proud of, or maybe something my father could grow to be proud of.

Of course, I had to do something that would change the world for my father to be proud of me, but defying Grayson Prince was always one of them.

"All of his games are important. What makes this one more interesting than the others?" I pick up my bag, walking over to the door as they all block the way to the exit.

"Get out of my way." I say sternly with a smile,

"That might work on the girls at school, but you know damn well that won't work on us."

I stood up taller, "No, but I can make it work, so get out of my damn way."

"I think you're making a mistake."

"So are you." I nod over to the heavy wall they made.

Margo looked concerned and I understood immediately that my attitude was not needed.

"If Grayson wanted me there, he would've asked politely."

"When are you two ever polite with each other?" Margo points out as I look at both Verina and Juliette agreeing.

Of course, they would agree.

"That's beside the point. If he really wants me there, then he can come get me. Other than that, I will be attending Brooks' game. One that he politely asked for me to attend, thank you." I passed them, grabbing the keys to my BMW. Over my dead body was someone going to drive me over to a boys football game.

My father would never approve of Brooks, but he most definitely will never approve of Grayson Prince.

I t felt exhilarating being at the football game knowing that Grayson was losing his damn mind that I wasn't with him, though I know nothing much about football. It was a bit messy and there was rarely action. I spotted Brooks.

Maya was there too. She looked at me like I was some type of plague, and I saluted her for holding eye contact with me and not peeing her pants. She was one of a rare bunch in Hawthorne who found it intriguing to stand up to me.

I would love to see her try.

Brooks was on the field a lot, and I would hope so, because if I dated him and I only found out now that he was a benchwarmer. I think I would have to eat Hawaiian pizza for a punishment.

I couldn't really see his face. Reasonable since he is wearing a helmet, I didn't really desire to see his face.

Sure, I only did this out of spite and my only reason for my being here...

...was because of Jack Frost himself. But I would never admit that to anyone, not to a human anyways, I told my stuffed dog before I left.

It was painful to sit here and act like I cared about Brook's accomplishments when I didn't. Maya looked like she could fill my spot in that department.

She had the jersey on, the stripes of red makeup on her cheeks, the big posters just for him, the perfect girlfriend.

I felt sad that he didn't think of her like that, but still upset that he entertained her while being with me.

It was a big slap to the face that I was so clueless.

But as I spent more time at the game, the antsy I became because I wasn't paying attention to Grayson's hockey game. As I checked my phone, I saw that they were losing.

1-2.

I instantly called up Margo, she seemed to be occupied, so I tried Verina's phone. However, she had about two percent left on her cell, so my last resort was to call Juliette, whom I love dearly, but had a hard time with being anywhere near her phone.

If it was up to her, she wouldn't have one, her father forced her to have one just for emergencies. Desperately I tapped on her contact, it rang four times before she answered.

"How's the football game, Anna?" She says, I could hear the smirk in her voice, almost like she knew I was not enjoying myself.

"Fine."

I huff, irritating because I was lying through my pearly white teeth.

"You want to come to the hockey game, don't you?" She lures me in as I look around at the empty bleachers groaning and not wanting to admit they were right.

"No, I don't. I just wanted to ask how the score is doing and..." I falter.

Juliette quiets for a moment before speaking, "The team is losing 1-2, how do you think the team is doing?"

Good point.

If there was one thing I knew about the team, it was that they were competitive beyond words.

Especially Grayson.

"Who made the one goal?" I mutter, I didn't need to ask. I knew the right answer, but something about my body shivered when I did.

"Who do you think?" She says with sarcasm.

I felt a pit in my stomach like it was consuming me, I felt awful... I felt *guilty*.

"Listen, Anna, I think it was a bad decision you didn't come tonight. Grayson could really use the support." She speaks.

I found it stupid how people thought I could've changed the outcome of a game because of my presence, or that I was some type of charm for him to take anywhere he wants for luck.

"Grayson probably doesn't even know I'm not there." I remark as I hear a bunch of yells from her side of the phone.

"Is everything okay over there?" I hear more ruckus as I stand up, my attention on the phone.

"You will not believe what just happened!"

CHAPTER 19

GRAYSON

I slam into the locker room, the second period had just ended, and I managed just one point against Halston Academy, which I thought was a fucking golf school.

They weren't even playing well. I just felt like I wasn't playing my best, even when I knew I was trying.

Everyone huddled inside the locker room, they all looked at me with worried faces. I honestly didn't know what to say, only that I was letting them down.

"We're losing." one of our freshman teammates, Josh says. And by the looks of the whole team, they wanted to sacrifice him to God then and there.

"No shit. Maybe because I've seen better hands on a digital clock than you." Andrew muttered.

Chuck felt the need to add, "Shut up Drew, at least he can skate longer than a fucking period."

I just stood and watched as the team kept up the aggression, and inside me, something sparked.

We were playing well, and that was our first mistake in the game. We had let go of our roots, what made us who we were, and firing this fight up was the best way to continue the game.

Liam looked at me curiously, as he had a drink of water.

Cole Smith was our goalkeeper, and he was the best. I couldn't help but push others to trash tell him a bit more to make sure he saves every puck going into the nets direction, I smile at Chris and Liam, "And what the hell is up with you Smith? I've seen coupons that save more than you!" Chris instantly got what I was doing, while Liam...

...Did not.

"Shut the fuck up, Prince." He growls as I smirk.

"Maybe I'll ask the coach to switch you for Lawrence. At least he doesn't look like the Titanic, only looking good until he hits the ice." I squared up to Cole, he was a nice height. He had to be for a goalkeeper, and I did admire his work.

But I was taller, and I was angrier, I heard him talk under his breath, most likely something we did to piss him off, and it was the perfect ammo.

I grinned devilishly as Liam grew cautious, I grabbed Cole's shoulder, "I'm sorry, what was that?"

I look at him in his visor, "Could you please roll your windows down so I can hear you talk shit?" Cole's eyebrows furrowed as did everyone else's as they grew angrier with each other.

We needed this. We needed this aggression. I needed this.

Everyone was pushing each other and almost about to punch but I made my voice louder than some of the pretty harsh insults, "Everyone hear that?" We heard coaches whistle blow, a warning to start heading out of the lockers.

Everyone looked at me angry and a bit shaken.

"Are you guys angry?" I walk closer to the whole team as Neil smile, he was always a bit fucked up, and loved it when I schemed.

"Of course, we're angry. We just got insulted by each fucking teammate here!" Justin yells.

Liam steps up, "I didn't insult anybody!"

I pushed him down as the team stayed stiff and irritated everyone, "I want you mad." I let out as they looked around concerned,

"I want you to be so fucking mad that you play with that aggression on the ice."

Everyone nods, understanding, "You guys want this win?" I yell.

Everyone yells as I look at Coach Livingston, him nodding with my leadership, "Then let's show them we want this win."

I huffed out a breath as everyone ran out of the locker room and asked to go back to the rink. I took a second to scan the crowd looking for the familiar faces.

Luckily, I found my family, Amelia sat in front of my father and stepmother loud and proud. My father looked generally pessimistic about being here, even when he knew it was an important night for me. He didn't hide his disdain for being here on a work night.

I turn over to the student section, my eyes directly at Margo, Juliette, and Verina. There was still no sign of Adrianna which made me feel uneasy, like my stomach was tight and my body tense.

I wasn't a moron, I knew she was at the football game, and she would find it pleasurable when I got aggravated by her.

As the team gets regulated, I skate over to Margo as she walks towards me, "Where the hell is she?" It wasn't a question.

Margo smiles, "Why do you care?"

I sent a look over to my parents, as my eyes shot directly to August who has a flat and center seat with posters for the school hanging and something about saving polar bears.

Margo nods her head a bit hesitant to answer, "She's at Brooks' game, isn't she?" I scowled as Margo stayed quiet.

She didn't need to say anything, I only skated away from her, with my blood boiling and my hands gripping my stick as tight as ever.

A player from the other team skates over to Liam who I could sense was not looking for a new friend, Liam looked about ready to pound the guy in the face.

And the game began again, the puck was flying everywhere, it was like the other team had completely lost its puck control, just skating with the puck was a challenge to some of the players, they tripped.

I skated right past them, pulling the puck away and fast speed skating over to the other net facing the other goalie, he was testing me.

I love it when I embarrass people, I skated behind him as he continued eye contact with me, "You will never get through me, his eyes squinting, I smirk, the devilish type.

"Pucks already in you, bozo." I skated over to Liam, hugging him as Neil celebrates by hugging Chris who was not affectionate.

2-2.

They finally brought in a player I was familiar with, Alex Twain.

He glides over with his skates, a nice look on his face as he keeps me at guard, "Does your coach know you're out here?"

He approaches me with a pathetic attempt to scare me into thinking he got better since the last game I played against him. I smirk, my eyes stare into his helmet, his brown eyes looking like a deer, "Do your feet know they're on ice?"

He looked like he was in the headlights, that's for sure.

"Daddy out here to watch your important game?" He pouts as I keep my eyes on the puck, Neil slams it out to Liam who was looking at me to see if I was a good option.

I was.

He flings the puck to me, Twain gets on my tail as I skate away, his body stiffens, his eyes stare like daggers at mine like he was out to injure me.

I was out to kill.

I bolted straight to him, I wasn't planning on backing down, "You can just give up now, Prince." He smiles looking over to the crowd, "I think the reserved seating for your girlfriend is empty because she'll be sitting on my dick tonight."

Red.

Blood pumped through my whole body as I gripped so hard, I was surprised my stick hadn't snapped in half. Anger seeped through my bloodstream as I looked at the empty seat.

I ask her one thing that she fucking can't do.

There were alarms that went through my brain as Twain skated towards me, my heart pulsed so fast as every drop of sweat that fell from my body made me stronger, I skated towards him, my fastest capable speed.

He faltered, the puck lost as I slammed his body, causing him to flip over me, he groaned.

There was a small chance I might've heard a minor crack to a bone, but I didn't care. I cared about whether the puck reached Liam's stick.

The other team's players stayed still, too afraid to go after me as they watched their captain on the icy surface, blood leaking and his body limp, tears were a major addition to the show.

I know I sound morbid.

But he talked shit about *my girl*.

Liam scored another goal, a great assist from me, as the game buzzer rang, ending the game, paramedics rushed out to the rink, checking up on Twain's injury.

My arm was a bit sore from him slamming against me, I looked over to Alex who was lying on the stretcher, unable to move. I might've actually paralyzed him.

And the worst part was that I didn't feel bad, not even a fucking bit.

No remorse.

The game felt unfinished, like I could've done more damage, but instead I walked out of the rink, my head beating with my heart as adrenaline pumped through my veins.

"Will he be, okay?" I ask the coach as he nods, "A concussion and broken legs."

I nod, not quite understanding that I might have ended his hockey career, and his ability to walk.

At least he was alive.

Everyone in the crowd was unsure on how to feel, one side had their college winning and celebrating to my 400th goals, on the other hand I was a fucking monster who couldn't control my anger.

I wasn't sure what else to really do to make sure that Twain would still walk.

But he said what he said, and he got what he earned.

He got driven to the hospital by the ambulance, and I took many pictures with the team and my family for my achievement.

My eyes going towards August, she smiles, "You were morbid out there." She comments as I nod.

"Oh right, sorry you have a girlfriend. I can't speak to you."

August walks away before I could get a word out, my stepmother looks at me, "Where's Adrianna?" Even Amelia looked like she needed to see Adrianna.

I smiled thickly, "She couldn't make it." I mutter.

No, she couldn't.

But it made me think.

If she was here during the whole game, all the posters, the screaming and shit, would I have sent someone to the hospital?

I looked at the blood on the ice.

Yes.

Yes, I would have.

CHAPTER 20

ADRIANNA

I couldn't help it, here I was yelling and cursing at myself that I made the stupid decision to go to a damn game I didn't even want to go to.

The football game had ended, and I sat away from everyone, Maya was close to the fence looking for Brooks, and yet he paid no attention to her.

It was sad, really, that he was looking for me. He shows off his bright smile, taking off his helmet running to me as I take a step back, I didn't want it to look like I had forgiven him for everything he had done.

"You enjoy the game?" He smiled wildly as Maya's eyes stared back at us.

"No." I plainly said as his smile disappeared.

"Surprised you didn't bring Margo or your friends." He looked boyishly shy.

I tried to hide the disdain from my voice, "Margo and my friends are at the hockey game."

"Right, well... shouldn't you be there as well?" He started to look away.

Yes, I should be.

"Why?" I asked.

Brooks walked closer, "Prince would want you there, wouldn't he?"

Brooks looked like he just swallowed a big lump of rocks, like he was sick of just talking about my current relationship.

I guess I would understand, but it was different, he was the one who wasn't faithful. He was the one who hid me from everyone.

"Yes, he would." I swallow.

Guilt.

"But you're here." His smile builds up again, I won't be sad to see it go away once again. "This means you want to see me. That you want me back." I back up as he steps closer.

"No." I pull away, "I'm with Grayson." I defensively called out; he looked a bit more feral as I pulled away. And here I was again cursing at myself because I thought he would be a bit more different now.

"You can't be serious Adrianna." He yelled, his face contouring a bit more as I swallowed. God, I wished that I had listened to Prince.

"But I am." I started to grab my belongings.

"Adrianna, he doesn't belong with you. He doesn't fucking deserve you!" He scoffs.

I laugh, "And you do?"

"I'm better." He whines.

He whines like a damn child. He was a fucking three-year-old trapped in an twenty-year-old's body. "Why can't you just stop being so fucking stubborn and come home with me? I can cook your favorite." He blurted trying to catch me from leaving.

While a plate of his famous spaghetti was tempting, I could only think about getting out of here.

"You and Grayson don't make any fucking sense." He places his hands on his head, frustration filling his face as I look back.

"Grayson and I are figuring things out." I state while putting on my jacket.

"We've both known Prince forever and you know damn well there wasn't a day where you wouldn't complain about him!"

True.

"I guess we fell in love." I mutter.

Unlikely. Grayson and I were too powerful to be together, and no, I didn't mean something like we would save the world type shit. I mean we would make the galaxy explode because we're two ticking grenades when we're near each other.

Our hate for each other is very much mutual, hell, hate was an understatement.

"Adrianna, please." He held my sweater, as I pulled away, the fabric tearing he lets go.

"Fucking hell." I sneered as he gripped my wrist, "You better think about what your next move is Brooks." I gestured to his hand gripping my wrist.

"He's not here." He places my hand on his cheek as I flinch, "He doesn't have to know."

I managed to get my hand back as my wrist was sore. A man sucker punched Brooks, making him fall to the ground in a hysterical cry. I couldn't help but smile.

"Are you okay?" the man mutters.

I smile at him, "Yes, thank you!"

He straightens, I pull out my bag, pulling out my wallet, "You must receive some royalties from doing that." I pull out two hundred dollars.

His eyes widen, "Ma'am, you don't need to do that." He insists as I look at him with confusion.

I realized that he wasn't the type to take money from just anyone.

"It's not tampered cash, I assure you." I smiled again looking at his pretty put together outfit, he was wearing a suit. "You can buy..." I pulled out another three hundred dollars as he took a step back. "You can buy a new suit!" Personally, I didn't think the gray suited him well. I was wishing to the Gods he would take the damn money and spend it on a nice Tom Ford suit.

But I couldn't say that.

"Really, I insist." I take his hand, placing the money and pushing his hand back towards his chest.

But then it struck me, Brooks was still on the ground, I pulled out my pepper spray can, "Adrianna, I won't stop until I get you back!" He yells as I pop open the can, letting the spray hit his eyes which were already swollen. I laughed.

So did the guy.

Brooks screams, getting up and running in a random direction, I look back at the middle-aged man.

"What are you even doing here with a suit on, you know it's a private school football game right?" I laughed as his face stayed stone cold.

It's like he had an answer but felt it was inappropriate to say it.

I stood taller, folding my arms tight, "What are you doing here?" I asked once more before looking at his car which appeared right behind him.

Fucking hell.

The front of his car had a crown emblem on the hood. Fucking Grayson.

Suddenly, it was like I was sideswiped on a highway. Here I was thinking he would leave me alone for just a football game.

"God damn, Prince."

I looked at the guy as he gave me a sheepish smile, "Bosses orders, Miss Cassian."

I got in my car, blood rushed up to my face as I felt my anger reach the bottom of my soul, then settling.

"Miss Cassian!" He yells, pulling out in front of me.

"I won't hesitate to fucking run you over!" He pulls out his phone, probably to call Grayson.

"You work for the enemy!" I yelled as he laughed, it was funny, but at this very moment I didn't have the urge to smile a bit.

"For your safety!" He screams as I drive forward.

"And I gave you five hundred dollars!" I said with disgust as he dropped his head in front like he was trying hard not to burst out laughing.

I pull out, "Let's see if you still have a boss after I'm done with him!" I bellow as he gets out of the way, I speed out of the parking lot. I felt my anger wavering under my skin at Grayson.

It was like he was always in my bloodstream, injecting himself into me as it raised my blood pressure.

It was like his pure goal in life was to make sure he pissed me off.

Why couldn't he just accept that I wasn't going to the damn game and to leave me alone? I could've taken care of myself from Brooks.

My worrying over Grayson from earlier had surfaced and calmed down as my anger shot up as a priority.

I guess I would find out if he was okay when I got to his house to give him a piece of my damn mind.

But I thought about it even more, if Grayson hired a damn bodyguard to keep an eye for me at the game, he banked at the thought of me not going.

And that makes my heart squeeze.

Just a little bit.

I didn't know whether to slap Grayson for hiring a damn bodyguard to watch me or kiss him because he knew I wasn't going to be at his game.

I was overthinking this.

All I really knew at this very moment was that I wanted to be near Grayson, whether it was me giving him a mouth full of words or just being with him.

I took a breath as I looked ahead at the road, my pills in the glove box, I swallowed before looking at them. It was tempting to take one.

I was incomprehensible. I didn't even understand my own thoughts when it came to him.

He was the only one who made my whole mind chaos like I was living in a daily hell.

Yet why was he the only one that could manage to calm my thoughts, like my brain wasn't smushed into a burger patty?

I knew there was a lot of mystery to Grayson Prince, but what I didn't know was why he made sense to me. I could read him like my favorite Jane Austen novel and understand every fucking word being said.

Grayson Prince didn't just read me. He listened to me. He could hear my struggles and not treat me any differently, he saw me.

But with that, he absolutely knew how to push my damn buttons.

CHAPTER 21

GRAYSON

I lay on my bed, replaying the whole game in my head before I heard my balcony window being banged on by a lunatic.

So, judging by this depiction of her looking like she wasn't going to shut up for thirty minutes, she found out about Harvey.

I rolled out of my bed slowly walking over to the balcony door, opening it as she stared back at me with her golden, honey eyes.

I tilted my head slightly to the right to take a good look at her remembering I was still irritated that she didn't go to my game.

Then I realized that I was half naked wearing gray sweatpants that hung just above my v-line. She looked at me like I was some type of God.

My hair was still slightly wet with water dripping from my torso to my abs. She looked like she hadn't drank water and had been traveling in the desert for months.

"Like what you see, Cassian?" I couldn't help but smirk.

"I've seen better." She snapped back as I looked at her intently, from the top of her raven black hair to the bottom of her shoes, she shivered. Her eyes snapping right to my covered scars, I wondered when she was ever going to ask me about them.

I laugh, leaving the doorframe and letting her quickly enter the room placing her bag on the top of my table that was set next to the door.

"Someone's not in a good mood tonight." I laugh, "Shouldn't I be the one to give you a hard time tonight?" I gave her a glare as she stayed standing, I sat down so I could see her clearly at eye level.

"I can't fucking believe you!" She starts as I roll my eyes, rubbing my hair and face with a towel, drying myself.

Pure silence sliced us like a knife.

I walked towards her, so close I could smell her perfume and hair. She stood directly in front of my balcony door. She swallowed a hard lump before taking a step back hitting the glass behind her.

I smile, my lips so close to hers, my body wanting to embrace her heat. I brought my hand next to hers, locking the door as her gaze kept on mine.

I examine her face; she was trying hard not to look down to my flexing muscle. I was trying not to throw her on the bed and fuck her.

I was practically drooling over her. What the hell had happened in the last twelve hours that made her so irresistible now?

She took a step closer, her body's heat enveloping mine.

She would never give in. "Could you hand me my sweatshirt, Cassian?" I teased.

Her eyes narrowed, "Get it yourself, I'm not your maid, asswipe."

Still facing the opposite of her, I could feel her body inch closer to mine, her hot breath radiating next to mine.

"When I tell you to do something, I expect results." I say slowly, obviously referring to her not going to my hockey game, her chest heaves.

I smirk as she quickly grabs my sweatshirt from the top of my dresser, placing it against my chest. His soft hands touched against my tense and hard body which softened at her touch.

"Here." She scoffs.

I grabbed her wrist, making her tense a bit more, "Don't give me attitude, Dove." I growled as she looked away.

"You're obnoxious." She snarled while turning to avoid my gaze. She looked about ready to scream at me and for the first time I let her.

She looked at me, "You're being cruel." She said with emotion.

I stood and looked at her breaking expression, "You hate me."

"Does me being here not bother you?" She gets up, "Because it should."

"I came here even when I missed one of your big games just to be yelled at by you," She says with reluctant honesty, "What does that say about me?" Her face was pained, and I was scared that maybe I was giving the same face.

"You stand there like you don't want to rip my clothes off when I know your fingers itch at the idea. Mine do too!" She inches closer, "I come here to get yelled at only because I get to see you."

She rattles off, "I go to a damn football game, yet I can't stop staring at my phone to see if you fucking scored."

"When Brooks talked to me and I met the damn guard you hired, all I wanted to do was kiss you." She was closer to me than she ever preferred to be.

I couldn't even really comprehend what she was saying, yet I understood.

"We aren't even supposed to be friends!" She yells as I stare at her blankly, "But I don't want to admit I like your company even when you rattle on about damn cars or hockey." She started to run out of breath as she sat back down.

"I don't know what to do with my need to be with you." She says in defeat as I couldn't give her the expression, she would find the most endearing.

"You want to be friends? We can be friends, Dove." I whisper close to her as I kneel to look at her confused eyes.

"Okay." She relaxes.

"But you hate me." She frowns.

I smile, "You hate me too."

She looked at me, like she wanted to say something but couldn't. All I could think about was the night she moaned my name.

Her lips were made for my name.

I let my hand travel to her cheek, cupping her face gently, her soft skin made me get goosebumps like I wanted her to melt on me.

My thumb bruising against her bottom lip, I could tell she wanted me to stop teasing her and just lean in closer.

She places her hand on my chest as I shivered at her gentle touch, backing away. It was so silent; she could probably hear my damn heartbeat.

She leaned closer, our mouths were inches apart, the temptation was wild because she knew that it was my turn to reveal the cards in my hand.

She stared at me, her knees growing weak as I leaned closer, I couldn't fucking breathe.

I let my eyes wander to hers, she looked so utterly delicate and beautiful.

Her eyes scanned to my bruised shoulder, her eyebrows furrowed from worry, she tensed, "What happened at the game?"

"Why does it matter?" I grumble.

She sends me a glare, "I don't want you to pass out or something because of the pain." She smirks as I shake my head, smiling.

"You're a bitch." I rolled out as she smirked, there it went again. Us fighting because it was what we were good at.

"But seriously," She looked back into my eyes, with a serious expression.

"It doesn't matter."

"Of course, it does, you could—"

I cut her off, "I already got it checked out, Dove. It's just bruised, nothing major happened."

She shuts her mouth, looking at the bruise on my back.

"How was the football game?" I speak. I didn't mean for it to be a question.

"It doesn't matter," She looked down to her hand, "I wish I went to your game. Your family probably hates me."

"I told them you were sick."

"I was so sick of you telling me what to do." She makes a point as I smile at her, well my lips curved.

"You're going to learn that you love it." I mutter as she swallows. She didn't say anything, instead she placed her head on mine, *"You're mine."*

"Never."

She licks her lips, I felt feral as she stared at mine, I couldn't take it anymore.

I pulled her in, my rough lips enveloped onto hers as I gripped her waist making her moan. She opened her lips, letting my tongue travel inside. I felt the need to explore her, my hand traveled to the back of her neck, feeling her warmth, her breath calming me down.

I pulled away, "We can be friends, that kiss." She says with minimal breath, her hand shaking.

"We can be friends that—" She pulled me in, her lips crashing on to mine, eagerly.

I exhaled as she let her finger roam my hair. "I want you." She groaned as I froze up for a millisecond.

Her eyes sparkled like never before, she looked at me so full of vulnerability and it was like she pushed her walls down.

Her lips were so soft against mine, so addicting, her hands were still shaking, I let my heart race the same speed as hers as we took in each other's lips.

She pulled away, "Don't ruin me."

My eyes looked at hers for a second, I wouldn't let anyone, or anything ruin her. She was perfection, someone that should be in a gallery for everyone to admire. I couldn't think of anything to say.

I push her body back gently, gripping her hair, I pulled her closer. I held her as our lips struck together, her body tightened around me, not one fucking inch of space between us as I let her lips dance with mine.

Adrianna caressed my cheek. I took a breath out, she swallowed, before pulling away to look at me hovering over her.

"We shouldn't be doing this..." She whispers as I smile, running my fingers through her soft hair, pushing a strand behind her ear, "This can't be real."

I didn't say a word, she leaned closer to me, her gentle lips pressed down on my black and blue bruised shoulder, I exhaled a relaxed breath. "This shouldn't be real." I muttered as she kept her lips on my shoulder for five more seconds.

She didn't have to say a word, her eyes presented her thoughts.

And I loved looking at them.

CHAPTER 22

ADRIANNA

I wake up next to Grayson, who looks almost angelic in his state of unconsciousness. I hadn't planned on falling asleep in his bed again, but when I was with Grayson, I hadn't found myself making any sense.

I forget that Grayson Prince was the devil himself in disguise, I pulled away from his cold body, readjusting to my warm one. I stayed to look at his restless face and his bulging body. His face, despite still looking handsome, looked like he needed sleep.

My phone rings, but my bag is still on the table. I pull out his sheets, answering, "Margo." I whisper.

She talks with a raspy voice, "Hey, did you get home okay?"

I sigh, "Yes, I did."

She hums, "So you're on your bed right now?" I smiled when I looked at Grayson who was awake.

"Yes. Of course."

His body weight leaning on the headboard, "That's funny because I'm at your place right now and you are nowhere to be found." She pauses as I hear a door creaking open, "Especially in your bathroom or closet."

Grayson laughs as I place my finger on the top of my lips telling him to shut up. He gets up, looking out the balcony door,

Margo was there alright. He looks at me with a smirk, it's like he wants to get caught.

"Adrianna, why are you lying to me right now?" I froze, I never lied to Margo, just kept her in the dark about a few things.

I groan, "Margo, I just left."

"Yes, well you have your appointment today."

I look at Grayson, frowning, "I'm coming."

Grayson's eyes furrow, concern grew, "What appointment?" I look at him, quite unsure on what to say.

"Margo, I'll be there in five minutes."

She sighs, "If you think you can skip on your appointment just because you sneaked away you are surely mistaken and don't forget your pills."

"I won't." I blurted, hanging up my phone.

Grayson's body was towering mine as he looked down, "What appointment?" He asked as I spewed off something random.

"Nothing."

Grayson runs after me, "I can take you."

I pause, looking back at Grayson, "I mean, isn't that what friends are supposed to do?" He scratches the back of his neck as I narrow my eyes.

He would be right technically, but I wasn't in the mood to let Grayson know that I was a raging druggie.

Or that I go to therapy. Or have body dysmorphia. Or the fact that I overdosed and reached the afterlife for twenty-two seconds.

I gave him a blank look, "No." I muttered as he nodded his head slowly.

"Okay, fine." He reached for a jacket from his closet, chuckling it at me, as I flipped him off.

"Don't act like you didn't love it when you had this on." He leans closer, "Actually, nothing but the jacket on you."

I slap him playfully, "And you're going to act like you weren't invested?"

"Of course, I was invested." I felt my skin prickle, "Why

wouldn't I be?" He pulls me in, placing his lips on my neck, making me groan.

"I have to go. Margo won't shut up." I laugh, looking out the window to see Margo's silhouette.

I halt, pushing Grayson down on his bed.

"Damn." He groans as I remember his bruises.

"I'm so sorry!" I whisper as I hold out a hand.

Yet I seem to forget that he was an asshole, pulling me in, crashing on top of him. I laugh.

I looked down at him, I was straddling his hips and he seemed to have an arousing situation, Grayson moaned, and it was a beautiful sight.

"How long do you have to get back?" He whispers into my ear.

I smile, "Well, now I have three minutes." I place my hands on his chest, running my hands down to his abs, just admiring his entirety.

He leans closer, his mouth kissing my ear, "Ride me and I'll make you come in three." His husky voice on my neck as I close my eyes, swallowing.

"I... don't know how to—" I moan as he grips my hips, rolling me on his erection.

My stomach flutters when he looks at me the way he does, his eyes so warm. I've never seen it this way before.

I don't think that it was possible for me to resist it. I was eager to listen to him, eager to just drown in him.

My heart shook as I swallowed, one of his hands grabbed the nape of my neck, running his fingers through my hair. I had noticed he had a liking for my long, raven lock of hair. I let him bury his face into my neck, grunting as I felt my core wet with arousal.

"You can do it, Dove." He whispers as I rocked my hips forward making him groan, a bit shaken by the electricity that ran through my body. Heat and fire burned through my veins; I wanted him to grip my hips harder.

I leaned closer to him, letting him feel my warm body, pressing my boobs closer. Even as I straddled him, he was bigger than me, his abs were tightening as I shook. I took his hands from my neck, placing them in my hips.

He grips, causing me to jolt, "Fuck, baby." He groans, his lips on my ear, his hands grabbing my ass, slapping it, making me jump again.

"Oh." I moaned, moving back and forth, my breath hitching, and yet it didn't even look like I felt anything.

Grayson's feral eyes loomed over me, "Yes," He groans out.

I rock my hips even harder against his dick, making me shiver, "Oh god." I threw my hair back.

His fingers find their way to my pussy, "So fucking wet for me." He bites my neck as I place my hands on his shoulders, helping with my intense arousal.

"Oh fuck, oh fuck... fuck." I groaned, it was like my brain chose to pause, my whole body at rest as my orgasm took all of me.

But he hadn't stopped, Grayson's fingers worked overtime, it was like they were magic, rubbing and caressing me. I start to pull away, but he grabs my hips keeping me in place.

My head knocks back again, as my hips ride out with his fingers, trying to follow his hard hand, Grayson does the unspeakable.

"Good girl." He groans against my neck as I look at him with a shaken expression. Grayson brings his soaked fingers close to his lips, placing them into his mouth, and sucking on them one by one.

Like he was savoring me like a meal on Thanksgiving dinner. "Holy fuck, baby."

I look at him, as he smiles, "Baby?"

I get up quickly, pushing him away, my heart racing, "I figured that's what I should call you when August is near." I smile, gathering all my belongings. He looked utterly amazed by me, shaking his head like he was in a dream.

Like I was in a dream.

I had just gotten my whole mind blown by Grayson Prince. And I don't feel us stopping in any upcoming time. I felt caught in a spiderweb of complicated feelings. I'm tangled up, unable to save myself.

I mean Grayson Prince was exploring uncharted territory when it came to dating me. We aren't dating so I absolutely wouldn't know how to guess if we were just friends with benefits.

I've never had benefits before. I don't trust it.

And yet here I am.

It was unsafe for me to agree with this. I just had one hit of Grayson, and I was unsure if I was ready to be addicted to another drug.

I felt like if I went through this relationship with him, the rehab would kill me. I walked out of his back door. I knew for a fact that if Margo ever saw this, she would have a panic attack and so I was as careful as one can be.

Only I wasn't that good at it apparently.

I dropped my bag, many of my belongings fell out. Books, lipstick, makeup, my fortunate pepper spray, and condoms.

I know I've never had sex before but having condoms in my purse was a safety regulation. Except, I ran into a familiar face.

"Adrianna Cassian." Liam smirks, bending down to pick up the pack of condoms that had fallen.

Great. Not only am I late to my appointment with Margo, but I think I was already in the afterlife.

I snag them from him, my face heating.

"Has Hawthorne's most precious diamond... been touched?" His smile was shining as I felt like I wanted to spray him with the remainder of the pepper can.

"No, but nice thought." I reply.

He looks up to Grayson's balcony, "You spent the night?"

I nod.

"Is he okay?" He puts his hands in his sweatpants' pocket, looking genuinely concerned.

"What are you talking about?" I shove the pack of condoms into my bag, looking at Liam like he was ridiculous. It looked like he had overstepped, into a conversation that Grayson and I hadn't spoken to each other about.

"Liam, I won't ask you again." I asked sternly as his smile looked forced.

"Grayson sent a guy on the other team to the E.R. last night at the game you didn't attend." He says with a bit of criticism. "And apparently, the topic of the conversation before the fight was you."

I swallow, "Liam—" I sigh.

His mouth thins, "I think you should talk to Grayson about it." He walked around me, opening the door and I stood there shaken.

Chapter 23

Adrianna

I walked into my room, Margo sat on my bed as I entered, groaning, "Adrianna Elaine Cassian." She stands, "Where the hell have you been?" I roll my eyes as she follows me into my bathroom.

"I've been out."

Margo runs up in front of me, "Please take your pills at least."

She hands them to me as I look at her. I take them, swallowing. "Margo, I can go to my appointment by myself."

"Nonsense." She exclaims. "You are out of your damn mind."

"I don't want to take up your day."

She quickly changes as she looks at me, "You are my favorite part of my days."

I couldn'y help but smile, she had the talent of making me feel special when I shouldn't be.

"I love you." She sighs.

I smile back, "I love you too."

"I'm worried about you."

"You shouldn't be, I'm okay."

Was I about to tell Margo that I have intentional cuts on my hips, I've been taking my drugs again, and that I've started to throw up after my meals?

No. It would break her, more than it has broken me.

Margo is my best friend. She is my safe haven.

"I just hope you know what you're doing." She comments as I swallow.

I don't

"I do."

I seem to have forgotten that the idea of Grayson and I being more than what we were was insane. I was doomed and he is meant for another woman.

He was doing this for August, yet I still made the bad decision of being his new conquest.

I wasn't sure that I wanted to stop, but I was prepared to get hurt. I knew I would the moment I saw him.

It was his specialty.

I finished my shower, finding a pair of jeans, my Louis Vuitton heels, and a Chanel crop top. Margo was styling a cute pink Prada dress. "I'll be done soon," I mutter, Margo sighs.

It happens every other Saturday morning. I get up, go to therapy. Go to a doctor that thinks they can fix me, that thinks that what I'm dealing with isn't valid enough to be serious.

They were shitty doctors.

My dad claims he's hired the best of the best, but sometimes the best of the best don't do any work but tend to take credit for healed patients.

It was the new doctors that excelled in the department.

"How are you feeling?" My therapist, Martia, looked amused as I smiled back, trying to contain myself from shaking as Margo held my hand.

"I've been great." I say plainly as she writes things down on her clipboard.

She looks back up, "I'm going to have Margo sit outside for this portion of the appointment."

I look at Margo who grins sheepishly, kissing me on the forehead before leaving, "I'll be in the car."

I nod, my attention returning to my therapist. "Adrianna, have you been self-harming again?" She asked me as I nodded. I couldn't say it out loud.

I pull down my jeans a bit for her to view my cuts, "And what else?" She looks up with a sympathetic face, I couldn't seem to look at her, because if I did, I feel as though I would've spilled everything, and I'd be forced into a mental institution.

The worst part is that it would probably be funded by my father. I didn't want anyone to know what I was going through. If it was up to me, Margo wouldn't know.

But she was the one who found my body when I overdosed.

"I know I'm going to end up doing it when I fight hard not to bleed onto the ground or stick my fingers down my throat." I say plainly.

"And are you proud of that?"

I looked down, "I don't want to die anymore." I smile.

I had mentioned last session that I wanted nothing more than to die.

Maybe this time she won't be up my ass about it, this time around.

She smiles warmly, "I'm so happy to hear that." But then pauses, "Have you been staying away from stressful situations?"

Absolutely not.

"Yes, I have learned it is not good for me."

No one really knew about my stance on mental health or any of my crazy abusive thoughts to myself. They said therapy would help so I had to take it.

Deep down, I didn't really want to get better. I only wanted to do it for my father, but he had barely known about self-harming or my eating disorder.

I know people say, "Do it for yourself."

But I hate myself. I don't plan on saving myself.

It was messed up, but after I was done helping Grayson I was planning to leave for good.

And I wasn't planning on telling anybody about it, especially Margo. No, I'm not being selfish, I think about it in a way that I don't want her to think much about me anymore.

She cares so much, and it would kill her to find out what I still do to myself.

"I've noticed that your phone has been beeping for the past thirty minutes." She looked over, unsure if I was going to answer her.

"Yes, I've been getting involved in a relationship."

I swallow, thinking maybe that I said the wrong thing.

"I don't think that you are in a good state of being in a relationship." Her eyes sank to mine like she was antagonizing me.

"It's not serious." I quickly said while gripping my sweater.

"Adrianna, you have to be honest with yourself... and make sure you are taking care of yourself."

"I am. I think that this relationship is distracting me from all those thoughts. It helps me."

I felt like this conversation was dragging on and I wasn't in the mood for more conversations.

"Whether you believe it or not Adrianna, I want you to be happy. I want you to prosper and live a great life. If I didn't, I wouldn't have sat here for the past year."

I hadn't really cared much for therapy. I didn't think it helped. I believed that she was a money sucking machine, a lot of employees in Hawthorne are, they know that people here are willing to pay so much fucking money for whatever.

"Tell you what, I want you to go out with your friends tonight, with people you find peace with and make you feel you are safe."

I roll my eyes. If she asks me to go shopping, then that is my therapy.

"It must be something that you don't normally do."

Great, I can just go shopping and tell her I knitted or something.

"I already told Margo to fix something up for you guys to enjoy."

I narrowed my eyes, "She told you about my new relationship, didn't she?" I stood up, looking at the clock, it was almost time to go.

"She mentioned it."

I laugh, a bit irritated, "I don't think that it was necessary for you to have gone to Margo. A truthful relationship between a therapist and their patient is important. I suggest you consider that if you want my father to continue paying for these sessions."

I grabbed my bag, walking out of the room, rage filled my body as I looked over to the door to the parking lot. Weirdly, Grayson's mother was outside at the garden, pruning some shrubs or even planting even more.

Before I could hide, she spotted me smiling. I would look like a coward if I didn't walk up to her now, but would she judge me when she sees me walking out of a therapist's office?

Grayson simply could not find out.

"Adrianna, my dear!" She walks up to me, hugging me like I was a teddy bear. I let out a breath as she grins brightly.

The hug felt nice, "What are you doing here?" She mutters looking back to the office.

I frown, "I go to therapy here." There was no way to sugar coat it.

I look at the beautiful garden, "What are you up to?"

I bend down to look at the flowers sprouting in front of the grass. I always loved flowers around me, especially tulips.

Flowers were special, each one had a special meaning, whether bad or good, they were all beautiful in their own way.

"I come here to volunteer and help troubled families on the other side of the building. I'm building this garden because the children love to play here."

I smile down at the garden, "You've done a wonderful job. It looks beautiful."

She places her hand on my shoulder, "You can help out if you want. You must be busy, so you don't have to if you don't want to."

I get up, "Nonsense, I would love to help out. It's never a problem to help out families in need."

I never really thought about the other side of the building. I was ignorant in thinking it would be just more doctors that don't know shit. "I would love to see you here on Tuesdays?" She grins profusely, I had also never imagined Mrs. Prince to be a great woman.

Many framed her to be a stuck-up rich mother like the rest in Hawthorne, but she was more than that, she had a beautiful heart. I had never really wondered about my mother. I knew she left and that was really all the information I needed.

If you can't stay for your child, you don't deserve your child.

But I had pondered my whole life, what had I done to make my mother leave without a trace.

I mean, those were the days that I don't remember but I've seen photographs of my father smiling. It was rare to see. I wish I remembered the life I had before my mother left.

Maybe I would've turned out differently. Maybe she would help me through my fucked-up decisions or yell at me when I wasn't thinking straight. She would sit with me, and I would lay on her lap as she caresses my hair telling me that it wasn't my fault.

But there was a certain age that I stopped thinking about what could've been, I realized it would just make me sadder because it was never real.

She was gone and I had to navigate my own way and grow up by myself. God forbid my father would inconvenience himself to teach me how to use a tampon or pad.

I was nine years old when my father hired someone to teach me.

Unfortunately, he hired a man who would touch me inappropriately. I didn't tell anyone.

I requested to take self-defense classes and earned a black belt in karate, ultimately breaking the man's arm the next time he touched my ass.

Then I told my father, who went off the rails and got the guy arrested. He said he would never forgive himself for letting it happen. And I believed him. I shouldn't have believed him. Because he made broken promises.

It's hard to think good things about my father when we were so disconnected from each other. I was a fool for always making up excuses.

"I'll be here." I smiled at her, "But I have to go, I'll stop by later and drop off food," Grayson's mother looked delighted like she was blessed with a paid nose job. She bends down to pick up a tulip, it was red.

She handed it over to me, "You are extraordinary."

I smile, taking the flower, "Thank you." I look over to the doorway, where Margo had been standing. I turn around to walk to Margo, looking back to see Grayson's mother get back to gardening.

I smile, "How was the session?" Margo probes.

I roll my eyes, "Same as always."

"What's with the flower?"

"Apparently, I'm extraordinary." I take a sniff at the flower, "I think I love the red."

I make a note as Margo pauses, "Red compliments you."

"I think so too." I lick my lips, "Why do you think that is?"

"Red is the color for passion and courage. You are the bravest person I know."

I wasn't brave.

I looked at Margo with admiration. She started the car; I took one closer look at the flower.

Red tulips... beautiful and extraordinary.

Margo frowns at me before driving, she takes the flower and

places it in the crevice of my ear, "You're beautiful Anna. Even if the world was blind, they would still be impressed because you are extraordinary."

Margo was lying. I was a joke. Then, I understood why red suited me better than white.

I was a tainted spirit.

CHAPTER 24

ADRIANNA

I would say my hobbies consist of a lot of things. I love to read, write, paint, go shopping, bake, and even cook. But baking with others was surely not it.

"Oh hell no." I laugh at Margo as she pulls up to the front of my house, "There is no fucking way I am baking with anyone!"

"Too bad, this will be fun!" Margo giggles, pulling out a bunch of groceries from the back, "Guess where I went while you were in therapy?"

"This has got to be a nightmare." I groaned, opening the door to my house, Verina and Juliette lay on the couch like they always do. But disdain filled my face when I saw Grayson, Liam, Chris, and Neil gathered by the pool table looking incredibly pissed at each other.

Remembering the past events this morning my face heats at Grayson who looked better than ever. He sends over a smirk.

I take a breath, "How was the shopping?" Verina yells, running up to me for a hug.

"I didn't buy anything."

Juliette and Verina froze. Damn, that wasn't believable at all. "I just bought a lot of perfume, it didn't count." I save myself as they nod, agreeing with my lie.

Margo walks over to the kitchen, dumping the food over the large island.

"Why are they here?"

I scowl as she looked pleased, "Well, I thought this could be more of a media date. We take cute pictures and videos of you and Grayson to post so it makes it more believable!"

It was smart, but I wasn't fond of the idea.

Grayson leaned on the pool table, his abs flexing as I swallowed, remembering the sensation I felt when I orgasmed. I wanted to crush my lips on top of his. But that would be an obvious no.

"I think it would be a fun idea if we did a bake off!" I knock my head back from distress.

I would lose my mind, and no it wasn't because I was a control freak. Well, I was, but I have OCD and thinking about someone intervening in the creation of what is supposed to be a masterpiece would be the end of me.

"But before that, we can play a board game," Verina smiles while sitting by the fireplace, signaling for everyone to sit, her eyes scanning the room to look at Chris.

"You can be my partner, Chris!"

She urged, gentle as Chris scratched his jaw, unsure on what to say.

This was going to be a long night. I knew that for a fact. With the endless battle of Margo and Liam, the endless flirtation of Verina towards Chris who clearly couldn't have cared less. Juliette clearly couldn't be bothered because she was reading her new book that she spent thousands on while Neil looked as happy as the Scrooge on Christmas morning.

And lastly, Grayson and I's unresolved sexual tension.

He looked like he'd been starving since the last time I saw him. I was almost half naked and he was without a shirt.

I couldn't help but imagine him without the damn sweatshirt he was wearing.

And the worst part is, he knows that I won't stop thinking about it.

"Margo, you can be with me." Liam grins like he was waiting to say it.

"Over my dead body." Margo scoffs as she looks at Juliette who laughs, "If you think I'm going to be partners with you after you threw a wooden stand at me last time we played, then you're clearly delusional."

Juliette walks over, sitting next to Neil who gives a weird look, "No way I'm being partners with you."

Juliette looks back with a challenging smile, "You scared you might be in my shadow?" She winked as he sneered.

Liam reaches for Margo, "Looks like you should be nicer to your friends in the future, sunshine." Liam winks as Margo gags.

I look at Grayson who lets his lips curve into a smirk.

"Fuck that." I laugh, turning to walk up the stairs.

Grayson pulls on my waist, "Oh, you're not going anywhere." He lifts me up to his shoulders as I my body freezes.

His hand caresses my lower back, traveling behind my thighs making me silent.

"Sit down." He places me down as I send an angry expression, "C'mon Dove, I'm not even that bad."

Liam nods, "He's right. He's pretty competitive."

I stayed silent, Grayson's wide eyes settled, "I'll take that as a yes!"

"It was most certainly not a yes." I flip him off as he shakes his head.

"Once you have me as a Scrabble partner, you wouldn't ever ask for another person again."

"Doubtful." I assert as he fidgets with his rings.

"Can we play the game now?" Verina asks politely as she hands the bag of words to Chris eagerly.

Chris picks up seven letters from the bag as did everyone else.

"Does everyone know the rules?" Juliette asks as everyone grew silent.

Liam beams, "Can we get three more letters? Ours suck and three is my favorite number!"

Margo tilts her head, "Okay, my favorite number is thirty, should we have thirty more Scrabble tiles to add?" She voices with attitude as Liam scowl.

Grayson places the tiles on the wooden stand, I rearrange them into alphabetical order. It was making me anxious when it wasn't before.

"OCD much?" He questions as my lips thinned.

He places his hand on top of mine, caressing my hand as I breath out, "I like them in alphabetical order too." He makes notes, earning a smile from me.

Liam mocks Margo before he places the letters "O" and "E" down next to each other, "That is not a word." I acknowledge.

"Of course, it is!" Liam insists as Margo surprisingly backed him up, "It's a suffix."

"It's desperate." I sneered, squinting my eyes at him.

Grayson gives a smug look, "If you put down a different word, I'm going to shove this wooden stand up your ass, Brookshire."

Neil laughs, "He'd probably like it."

I looked over at Liam who was mindlessly staring at me with intense focus, I couldn't help but grow uncomfortable. I fidgeted in a way, letting Grayson know I felt uneasy.

Grayson's face turns into a scowl, "Is something wrong with your face Brookshire?" He addresses Liam, while Neil grins widely.

"You know Prince... If you're fake dating Adrianna, you're technically dating me. I mean come on... the dark hair, the dark eyes, the tanned skin, I'm practically your type! Except you can stand me and we've seen each other naked."

My eyes widen as everyone laughs. Grayson's face was scrunched up like he didn't need to envision Liam and him in a relationship.

"You and Adrianna do not look remotely alike. That's disgusting." He gags.

I burst out a grin, now understanding why Liam was heavily examining me, prior to this wonderful conversation.

I look over at Margo, who was now examining both of us, "Margo, I swear to god if you tell me I look like Liam I will never let you borrow my Birkin."

She pretends as if she wasn't doing anything by putting her hands in the air, with no guilt.

"I didn't even say anything!"

Verina laughs, "You were thinking it."

Juliette shakes her head, "Are we going to skip over the fact that they've seen each other naked?"

Neil nods, "Hockey locker shower room, it's basically dick central in the fog."

Juliette winces, "I didn't need to know that."

"Hey, you asked!" Neil suddenly places his hand in the air.

"Ahem!" Chris coughs loudly, making the whole group quiet down.

"Sorry." We all say in unison.

Silence.

Until Liam explodes into a laughing fit, everyone joins in hysterically laughing.

Chris on the other hand looked miserable as we quieted down.

Chris takes off the two letters from the middle, placing down *"alright"* in the middle using up all of his letters.

He leans back, "How many points is that?" He says in a way that was overly confident.

"Great job, Chris!" Grayson exclaimed as I looked up at his heated face.

"Shut up. This is killing you inside so bad." Chris looks at Verina who couldn't stop looking at him.

She was head over heels.

"It was Verina who put it together." Chris mentions as her face lightens up.

Juliette connects the word, *"ratify"* from the previous work as we all look at her.

"Why can't you pick something normal?" Liam sneers as she cracks a smile.

"It's not my fault you boys don't know your vocabulary."

"We do." Liam fires back.

"Well, maybe enhance it." Juliette opens her book and starts reading. Neil looked at her like she grew three heads.

I couldn't help but smile at the interactions within this new group. But I would never admit that Margo was right.

A couple more rounds went on and a couple more arguments took place. It was pretty clear that everyone was getting frustrated, Grayson had looked like he was ready to strangle Liam.

He stood, running off with the bag of words while Chris and Neil tried to catch him. Everyone was laughing, it was great.

"I think that we might win." I whisper to Grayson as he looks down at me nodding.

"You want any food?"

"No, I'm good." I urged, not really realizing that I placed my head on Grayson's shoulder.

He didn't move. He didn't dare to move. Margo looked at me, but my eyelids were too heavy to lift as she snapped a picture of Grayson looking at me.

"This definitely looks believable." She beams as I straighten, pulling away from Grayson's cold body.

"You have to be kidding me." Verina stands up.

"What is it?"

"Grayson, when were you going to tell us that your father is hosting a gala?" My eyes sparkled at the thought of beautiful gowns and shining chandeliers.

"I didn't know." He simply muttered while placing the word, *"suppose"* making us win the whole game, Neil flipped the board as Juliette groans. They won second place.

"And the winners are the best people ever!" I start twirling around as Grayson lifts me up.

"I still hate you though." He mutters as I look down at him smiling.

Of course, he did.

"Well, I loathe you, so it doesn't matter what you think." I walked away as Margo walked in front of me without saying it, I knew what she was trying to say.

Did I have fun?

Maybe.

CHAPTER 25

GRAYSON

Whatever happened between Adrianna and I this morning, it shouldn't have happened.

Not that I didn't enjoy it or crave it, it simply was a dumb decision. I clearly wasn't thinking straight.

It wasn't fair to use her when my head was all over the place. I didn't come when she orgasmed. And I think it was for the best that I didn't. Whatever was happening was pretty complicated in many different ways.

I wasn't the type of guy she would want to be with.

I wasn't the type to buy her flowers just because.

I wouldn't be the one to go to if she needed chocolates.

I was clearly someone she can just mess around with. She obviously saw it too which is why it happened, but I was still so lost on what was happening,

This situation is different. She's different. She's Adrianna Cassian, damn it. She's the girl that burned my favorite hockey stick.

She's the girl who put a virus on my laptop in 5th grade and told people I had pink eye when I had just gotten a hockey puck to the eye.

For God's sake, I fucking cut a huge chunk of her hair in 8th grade and blamed the kid that ate glue.

She stood across on the other side of the island in her kitchen grabbing the sacred ingredients for the damn cookies that Margo is forcing us to make.

Liam takes a billion pictures of every interaction that Adrianna and I have to post on social media.

I thought it was absurd that people genuinely check their phones just to find out about my love life or my friends. On the bright side, August gets to see how much fun I have without her in my life.

"Get the fuck away from the eggs, Brookshire."

Liam pulled his hands away from the carton while staring at Adrianna in a way that was way too bold.

I was surprised that he didn't get his dick cut.

"You know you might want to be nicer to me, Cassian." Liam whispered as her face turned red.

I would ask her about it later, but it couldn't have been something major as her face contained control.

Juliette read off the recipe for the type of cookies that Adrianna was preparing. Adrianna's hair was up in a messy bun. She also had an apron on, flour on her fingers, and her long eyelashes directed towards me.

I had realized that it had been a while since I had antagonized her. Just because we had a changing relationship doesn't mean I should stop.

I picked up my phone and walked over to her. She was a bit irritated that I was in her baking station, "What are you doing?" She questions as I smile, placing my finger in the flour not used, plopping my fingertip onto the tip of her perfect nose.

She looked shocked before she picked up some frosting, slathering it on my cheek. She laughed like an angel.

I take my phone, snapping a picture of her irritated face, full of amusement on mine as she gives me a look I hadn't figured out.

Liam sat on the floor with Chris. Liam winks at me as I scowl at them, "You need help?" I question Adrianna.

"Not from you." She snaps back.

I look at her ingredients, "You love my help in a lot of things." I lean to her ear whispering as her body tenses, goosebumps gather everywhere.

"Yes, well that was a one-time thing." She pulls away, gathering the pan and placing it in the oven.

"One time?"

"Yes. This should just be strictly business." She makes a point as I scan her body with a smirk, "I'm serious, Prince."

"And I am too. I've been craving to kiss you again."

Her cheeks reddened, and heat traveled to my dick. I truly couldn't control myself around her, could I?

"What did Liam mean when he told you to be nicer to him?" I plop chocolate chips into my mouth as she rolled out the cookie dough.

"He caught me on my escape out of your house this morning." She shakes her head.

"And? He catches girls walking out of my house all the damn time." Adrianna's mouth thinned at my comment, I realized that I shouldn't have said it. She turned to look at the fridge, pulling out an egg, before smashing it on my head.

Everyone's eyes on us as she takes off her apron and walks outside. I look at Margo who gave me a nasty look, her other friends staring unsure of what really happened.

I quickly wash off the yolk from my hair, running off to her direction outside on her back porch. I slowly closed the door behind me, "Thanks for that. Eggs are great for hair."

She turns around to look at me, then turns back around to look out to the abyss.

"Silent treatment." I nod, walking closer, "I didn't mean for that to spill out. I just... I don't know what's going on."

"Nothing important." She looks over, "I shouldn't even care that you think of me as another conquest."

I didn't know what to say to her, something that wouldn't hurt her. "You were my first orgasm without using my hand." She lets out as I swallow.

Sex talk never frightened me, I mean we were all over eighteen years old, "Dove."

"Stop calling me that!" She exclaims.

"It fits."

"Why?"

I pulled her close to me, bringing her body to sit on the ledge.

I stood in the middle of her thighs, "Because it symbolizes innocence, and you haven't been touched by anything dark." I gripped her waist; her skin practically had my fingerprints imprinted on her.

"You're wrong." She remarks, "You've touched me."

I smirk at her, "You don't know what being touch by me even fucking feels like." I tilt my head.

She grins warmly, "Oh right, but the other girls that sneak out of your house do!"

I saw that coming.

"Are you jealous?" I ask with a hidden smirk.

"No." She pulls away from me, "Are you sure you didn't get jealous when I went to Brooks game?"

I quiet down as she looked pleased, "Hiring a guard?" She twirls around, her fingertip running to my shoulder, "Don't think I don't read news articles, Mr. Prince." Her finger stays on my shoulder's bruise.

"What? From hockey?" I defend.

She smirks, "So you didn't break a guy's legs and give him a concussion?"

"He was asking for it."

"I highly doubt that."

"If he didn't want broken bones, then your name should have never escaped his fucking lips."

Adrianna looks at me with a thoughtful look, "I could only

imagine if it was about August," She laughs, "You obviously only did that because you had to keep up the fake boyfriend act."

I nodded, as she breathed out, "I would've sent him to an early grave."

Adrianna's mouth thinned once more, but I refused to think much about it. "Clearly your intentions are just strictly for August. She's lucky."

I stayed quiet, I had no idea how to answer, "Even if this fake relationship goes on, we still are very much incompatible, and you are just a frenemy."

She ran up to me, crashing her lips onto mine. I couldn't help but moan into her mouth. She was fucking addicting.

Her fucking smell all over me, her hair in between my fingers, such a perfect length for me to wrap around my hand to pull while I fuck her senseless.

Just my frenemy, my fucking ass.

Her body always seemed to soften when she touched me, and mine hardened. She was a fucking catalyst to my body, and I didn't know how to react. She gripped my shirt, "Fuck you."

"You're pathetic." I couldn't help but smile against her lips, my hands roaming to her ass, "What do you want from me, Cassian?"

"I hate you." Her hands clash with my hair, pulling and wanting.

I pull away looking at her, "What do you want from me?"

Her throat looked like it was clogged. So, I fixed the issue as I pulled her in, her soft lips envelope on mine, scared to let go because if she did, she might disappear.

"Do you still hate me?"

She gently laughs against my lips, her hands shaking as I look at her, "This." She kisses me, "This makes me feel alive."

"I think the cookies in the oven might burn."

I interrupt as she pulls away, "Grayson." She mutters as I look at her a bit concerned, "Do you not like kissing me?"

The burning question. Of course, I liked kissing her. Fuck that, I love to kiss her. I could kiss her all day if I could.

But I couldn't tell her that.

"I just think that we should cool it." I advised her as her hands pulled away from my body like she got burned.

She stayed silent, "I think you're making a huge mistake in letting me be the one to explore your sexuality with." I defended myself as she looked at me, I wasn't sure what else to really say.

"So, you're saying that I should go find someone at a bar and ask them to take my virginity."

"I didn't say that."

"That's sure what it sounds like."

"I just don't want to betray August more than I already had."

Her face fell. Her face fell all the way to the fucking ground. I wanted to take everything back in a second.

"Right." She wraps her jacket around herself even more like she was freezing.

"Then we should try and keep this completely professional." Adrianna coughs out, a bit nervous for the next words.

I felt something for her, but I wasn't sure what it was. I wasn't even sure if I wanted to dig even deeper into it, but even if I felt something for her, it wouldn't beat my strong feelings for August.

It was the whole reason I started to date Adrianna. Sure, there were reasons like dealing with my father, but this was a line that could not be crossed.

"The cookies are probably burning." She cautioned as I nodded. Clearly, she didn't feel comfortable with being out with me anymore.

I couldn't blame her. I wouldn't want to talk to me either if I just told someone that I wasn't down to fuck her.

And I don't know why it was so hard for me to just scream at her, like we used to.

Her big brown eyes glistened as she turned away to walk back into her house, I knocked my head back to look up to the sky.

"What do you want from me?" I whisper to the abyss.

Liam walks out, "There you are, I was worried she killed you and dug you a grave," He pauses, "Why the glum face?"

I breathe out, "I don't think she deserves this." I muttered to Liam.

He walks closer, "No one deserves it." He laughs, "I know you aren't going soft Prince."

"Of course not."

"This is Adrianna fucking Cassian we are talking about. Her father is the reason your mom is breaking down every night on alcohol and meds."

Did that mean I should take it out on her?

"A father's worst fear is the heartbreak of his daughter," Liam makes a point as I nod, "It's a one and done, Prince. You get August back, you get your dad's trust, and you get the company."

My life was set out for me, wasn't it?

"Now come on and make that fake girlfriend fall in love with you."

I smile at Liam who winks, "You know she dropped a box of condoms outside when I ran into her, you bang her?"

"No." I suppressed a laugh.

"Why not?"

I push Liam as he laughs, "If I'm going to play the diamond of Hawthorne for all she's got, then she can keep the one thing she's been guarding for her whole life."

"Spoken from a true poet himself."

"Fuck you."

Liam walks to the door, "You coming?"

I start to walk over to him before my phone rings, I answer it, "August." I smiled at Liam who took the signal and walked off.

"Prince."

"What do I owe for this pleasure?"

"I realize that I shouldn't have yelled at you at the game."

I smiled, and I couldn't help it.

"You got the flowers?"

"Yes, I did."

"Your girlfriend has a problem with that?" She says in a whisper.

I roll my eyes at her comment, "Adrianna is purely a means to an end, I think you know that."

"Does she?"

No, she didn't, and I wasn't planning on telling her of course, "I think you should stop sending me flowers." August mutters.

I pause, "Why?"

"Well, I've been seeing someone. It just doesn't seem fair."

"Who is it?" I let my voice grow a bit higher as I pace around the porch, "Fucking hell, August." I took a breath, "I know him, don't I?"

She sighs, "Goodnight Grayson, I love you."

"No, don't fucking say that if you don't really mean it,"

"Okay." She pauses, "Goodnight."

I hear her hang up, and I groan.

If she thinks I'm giving up without a fight, she's wrong.

CHAPTER 26

ADRIANNA

I lay on my bed wide awake since twelve A.M. this morning. I had been dreading going to school for the past few hours and was completely horrified to face Grayson.

My housekeepers come up to bring my uniform up as I groan, "Ms. Adrianna, you're going to have to get up."

I sat up taking a blueberry from the plate she held out for me. "Why can't I be homeschooled?"

Ellen smiles while bringing out my Prada bag, "Because you love being in charge in school."

"They are just afraid of me. They don't even like me." I get up from my bed and finally walking into the bathroom to brush my teeth.

I took a shower and made sure to do my whole skin care routine, and applied little make up, I could tell I wasn't going to like today's plans.

"Julius is waiting outside for you, and don't forget your father will be home today."

I roll my eyes, "It doesn't matter, I'll be out of the house tonight."

Ellen interrupts, "Unless, Mr. Prince will be picking you up today?"

"No, he will not be. Make sure he doesn't breach the premises unless I tell you he will be here. Keep an eye on the back door."

I was compelled to absolutely shield myself away from Grayson and his antics. He made it perfectly clear that he didn't want anything real from this fake relationship so it makes sense that he shouldn't be allowed into my house.

"Tell Julius I'm on my way down."

Ellen nods as I take a deep breath, pulling out my phone and calling Margo.

"Hey babe," She greets as I make my way down my staircase.

"You need to help me."

"How about, Hey Margo! I'm so glad you answered! Good morning to you too!" She exclaimed.

"No time for nonsense, I've been feeling like a dumpster the past week and I'm in the mood to be a bitch today."

"And you need my help, why?" She sounded concerned and it only made me smile even more.

"You have my back up phone, right?"

"Well, yes."

"You remember all those guys who asked me out?"

"Do you?" She counters as I walk over to the car, opening the door, greeting Julius before taking a seat.

"No, that's why I'm asking you to tell them all I'm interested."

"Are you?"

"Of course not!" I make a point as she laughs.

Her face settles into a calm expression, "This doesn't seem like a good idea. Some of these guys hate each other, Anna, I mean they are all alphas in their own categories."

I smile at the thought because they all have something in common, other than having spectacular taste in women, they all want to be better than Grayson Prince.

What's a better way to declare you are better than him like taking away his girlfriend? Sorry, *fake* girlfriend.

"Did you see what Brooks posted?" Margo asks.

I roll my eyes, "A football lineup?"

"Says that a psycho punched him in the face and broke his nose,"

I smile again, "He deserved it."

"You did that?"

"For legal reasons, no, I did not."

I spotted Margo on the phone as she waited for me in the front of the university, "Glad to know you wore your Hangisi Pumps, they look beautiful."

"You creep! Out of the car!"

I laugh, thanking Julius for the ride and telling him I won't be needing it for the afternoon, I walk up to Margo who smiles wildly.

I hung up the phone, approaching her, "You finally wear that pair after a month of owning them?"

"Yes, well I forgot I even had them." Margo expresses, while looking around to see everyone, "You never told me how the talk with Grayson went."

I walked up the stairs to the Snake pit, sitting since we all had no classes this particular morning, "There was nothing to say."

"Seriously? Grayson looked pretty pissed when he left."

"Why do you automatically think it was my doing?"

Margo shot me a face that looked like she was being extremely serious. I mean, sure, I tend to piss Grayson off but this time it had nothing to do with me.

I should be the one upset, and I was but I wasn't going to show I genuinely cared.

"Hey, Margo... You feel like going to a bar tonight?" I smiled.

Her eyes shined, "Actually!?"

"I mean why not?"

I prop myself up as Juliette and Verina come over, "Why do you guys look so excited?"

"Margo and I are going to a bar, want to come?"

Verina's eyes widened, "Oh my god! Of course, I have the perfect outfit planned already!"

"Over my dead body!" Juliette yells at us as we give her a contemplative look.

"J, come on."

"We can get in trouble, we're supposed to be studying! Our parents can find out!" Juliette looked stressed and it was the perfect reason we all should go out, but then again, she was always the logical thinker.

"My dad doesn't care," I rolled my eyes as she looked at Margo, "Everyone is stressed, and we all have things to drown our sorrows over."

"Not me! I'm fine!" Juliette sits down angrily.

"Come on glasses, it will be a blast! Besides, we can sit in the VIP section. My father owns all the clubs and bars, I'm sure we will be fine."

"It's a school night! And may I remind you that you have to go to your community service thing after-school?"

Margo rolls her eyes, "It will take me like an hour or two for practice and I'm all yours."

I smile, Margo winks at Verina, "And I have fake IDs just in case."

Juliette looked like she was about to wave a red flag when she turned to her last reasonable option, "Adrianna, you're on my side on this right?"

Now, I normally would be, because I hated going out in public and flaunting myself to strangers, but it seems that it piqued my interest over night. I was ready to lose my virginity.

"Now, I could see why I was your best option, but it was my idea."

"You traitor!"

"Yes, but I love you and we need to have a fun time!"

Liam and Chris walk in together as we all quiet down, "Number one rule is not to let Grayson or any of the others know about this." I whisper while smiling at the boys.

Liam took a seat next to Margo before she moved away from him, "I have an announcement."

She took a deep breath as Grayson and Neil walked in with angry faces. I tried not to look at Grayson as he calmly sat next to me, placing his hand on my thigh. I shrugged him away, "Professional." I coughed as he pulled away.

"Yes, but I meant in private. We still have to keep a good act in front of everyone, especially at the pit." He suggested.

I snatched his hand, "Can you shut up now?"

"I sense that you're still upset with me."

"I'm not upset, I simply don't care."

"You don't look like someone that doesn't care."

I grip his hand a bit tighter, "So you can look like you don't care but I can't?"

"Fuck you."

"That's not something that someone who doesn't care would say."

I felt like arguing with Grayson could lead to an ultimate battle that would take forever and it wouldn't scare us one bit.

But through the mindless sounds or agony of using nagging at each other, "I'm engaged." My body froze for a moment looking at where the statement came from.

And it led straight to Margo who looked like she finally took a breath of fresh air.

I looked over to Liam who looked like he just got shot a billion times, and suddenly everything went back into regular time, and I swallowed, "What?"

"His name is Ben." She smiled at me as I got up.

Everyone's faces were still agape at the news. I couldn't really understand it myself.

"Ben, as in Benjamin."

I approached her, "Yes, Benjamin Grimaldi." Margo looked ecstatic, "He is from a very honorable family that owns a bunch of hospitals and businesses that imports from foreign countries."

"He sounds like a momma's boy who gets whatever he wants to me." Liam grumbles.

Margo shoots him an unbothered smile, "Oh, so like you?"

Liam shoots an irritable look at Margo who looked happy about her current relationship, "Are you happy?"

"Yes, well he can provide, and my family approves of him."

"I'm happy for you!" I hug her, "But if he hurts you, I'll kill him,"

Margo laughs, "Is Liam looking?" She mumbles as I roll my eyes taking a look up to Liam who looked like he was about to break the next thing he sees.

"Yes."

She squeezes me tightly, "Great." She pulls away.

Juliette and Verina come to hug her as well, but "You're engaged, like to be married."

Verina interrupts, "Like 'Will you be my lawfully wedded husband and wife' type of married."

"I feel like it's what I need. I need commitment in my life. A man that knows what he wants." She points out as Liam walks away with a scowl.

"Well, then you can't go to the bar." I whisper.

She sends me a shocked expression, and her eyes widen, "Nonsense, you guys can meet him there!"

Grayson smirks as Chris and Neil look at him.

Knowingly they all smile at each other, "You think your fiancé can meet us at the game tomorrow?" His eyes gleamed.

"Yeah, sure why not?"

"Who are you guys even playing tomorrow?"

"Van Doren." Neil notes, "Tough offense."

"I'm sure no one is better than you, Prince." I look at him as he coughs out.

I lower my eyes to the ground, "Well, everyone knows that the only way you can beat a good offense is a good defense." Chris mutters.

"Wrong. The way you beat them is to have better defense and offense." Grayson adds, "No reason to slack off on offense."

"Your point?" I interrupt.

He rolls his eyes, "If you don't know by now, Hamilton... You seem to be Liam's catalyst."

"What?"

"A catalyst by definition is a person or thing that precipitates an event." Juliette looks up with a coy smile, "Or do you want a biological definition?"

"No, we're good." Neil groans.

"A catalyst for Liam." She restates as I smile, "So you mean if he shows up at the game, he will..."

"Turn into a fucking monster." Grayson eagerly interrupts as Margo looked pleased, "Anything to help our hockey team win a game, right Anna?"

She looks at me as I form a confused face, what's that supposed to mean?

"Oh yeah! Grayson flipping the guy over was fucking crazy." Neil fist bumps Grayson in the shoulder as I look at him without emotion.

"Talk about catalysts." Verina laughs as Grayson stays quiet.

"I bet he would've done it for anyone." August pops up as I look at her.

My bitch radar had gone off the fucking cement roof.

"But he didn't." I smile at her, "He did it for me."

"Yes, but Grayson likes to show everyone that he's tough, but at the end of the day he would've done it for anyone."

I sunk into those words, really thought about them, and she was right. Of course, she was right about Grayson. She knew so much about him compared to me. Grayson looked at her longingly and I felt like a damn fool yet again.

It was easier to hate him than try to be friends with him. And like my father said, I should've stayed away from him a while ago. And it was my fault for thinking I could handle this fake relationship.

I still believed I could. If someone was prepared to handle Grayson Prince, I knew I was still a willing candidate.

CHAPTER 27

GRAYSON

Adrianna had ignored me the whole day and I was glad for it. It was better this way, better to have our old animosity back. As I skated around the rink, my head was like a case full of exploding bombs.

Margo skated up toward me. She took a job to be the physical therapist for the hockey tea. She didn't need an excuse to be on the ice.

She wasn't half bad on the ice.

"Hey, Prince." She smiles.

I rolled my eyes showing that her presence wasn't appreciated at the very moment. She was about to add to my irritation.

"Okay, you have to stop being rude to people." She scowls, folding her arms together.

"I'm not in the mood to talk." I spit out.

"Well, I am."

I look at her, stopping, "You're always in the mood to talk."

She scowls, "I never understood why you seem to hate everything Adrianna is associated with."

"I don't." I skated faster, hoping she didn't catch up with me.

"Why do you hate her?" She asks and I let a nerve snap inside me. I pause looking back at her.

"That's none of your fucking business."

She smiles, but in a devilish way that made me kind of wary. "Okay. Then I'll say this once."

She skates closer to me, "You hate Adrianna purely because you desire her. Because you can't have her."

My head felt like the former bombs had been lit and ready to explode in any minute.

"At least she admitted she wanted you, but you... you will never stop being a coward because even with her right in front of you, you still choose the option that you don't really want."

I stared into her eyes, and she was dead serious, I was taller, and I was sure she was intimidated as she shied back down after her comment.

"Why are you telling me this?"

She looks around, "It's the end of practice and you are out here skating around wasting your damn time while she's in her room getting ready to lose her virginity tonight."

"Why do you think I care?" I laugh, "If I did, you would think I would've just fucked her the moment she walked into my room."

"I think you care because you chose not to fuck her." She says plainly as I quieten down.

"She can do what she wants."

Margo ignores my comment by asking another question.

"Why do you want August?" She folds her arms together.

I turn around to leave, "I'm not about to talk about this with you."

"You will." She yells.

I turn around once more, "She was my first love, it makes sense. I treated her terribly." I sigh, "I want to make it up to her. I can treat her better."

"That's guilt. That's not love." Margo looks over to the locker room, "Just because you want to be with them because you made a mistake doesn't mean you loved them at all, it means you're selfish and you want to make yourself feel better."

I look over to the locker room seeing Liam walk out with his bag, "Are we still talking about me?"

Margo quiets down, "If you really loved August, you wouldn't be kissing Adrianna or thinking about her, you wouldn't be giving her a jacket because you don't want men to look at her."

"The jacket stunt was because everyone would see she was my girlfriend."

"That's bull-fucking-shit and you know it. You hired a body-guard for her, Prince. You sent someone to the fucking emergency room because of her."

I didn't even know what to say. Margo Hamilton left me speechless.

Not that I talked much anyways.

"If you love August then don't give Adrianna an indication that you want to be together, because I will make sure she will never acknowledge you ever again."

I shake my head, "What if I care about Adrianna?"

"If you care about Adrianna, then once I leave here, you will take a shower and change. You will search every bar in Hawthorne, hell, maybe even in New Crest, just to stop her from picking who to lose her virginity to." Margo shows her pearly whites at me as I roll my eyes.

"You've been smoking crack." I laugh, skating away from her, I turn my head to look at Margo who skated out of the rink, beginning to walk out of the rink. I keep skating further away from her so I would be tempted.

Who was she to tell me that I cared about Adrianna? She was full of bullshit, and she was acting like a damn fortune teller. She has no idea why I'm doing the shit I'm doing.

Maybe she should figure out her problems with Liam before trying to fix my fucking life, I didn't need her advice and I surely didn't fucking ask for it.

Adrianna being in my head is simply a fucking joke and what I felt for August was not guilt.

Before I knew it, I was close to the hockey board, nearest to the door.

"Which bar are you guys going to?" I scream as she looks back with a damn smile on her face.

"I'm not sure." She yells back.

I grow irritated, "You mean to tell me you give me that fucking speech and you can't even tell me the bar you guys are going to?"

"Oh, I know which bar it is!" She exclaims.

I bang on the hockey board, "You going to tell me, Hamilton?!" I scream.

Margo's grin widens as I knock my head back, "What's the fun in that?" She winks at me before running out the door.

I look at the clock at the top of the doorway before she runs back in, "Don't tell her I told you, you aren't supposed to know!"

Before I yell at her, she slams the door shut causing me to catch my words. I take a deep breath, walking out of the ice rink, and into the locker room, pulling out my gloves and my phone.

"Prince?" Liam answers as I groan, "We're bar hunting tonight."

I inform him as he laughs, "Okay? You need me to tell Chris and Neil?"

I pause "No, don't bother Chris, he's with Finn and I don't think Chris has had a good night's sleep in forever."

Liam's silence had been an indication of him agreeing.

I sigh, "What is it?" He asks.

"I need to find Adrianna tonight."

"You finally admit that you want her?"

"No." I grumble.

"Right, so you don't need my help?"

"If you hang up on me right now, I will beat the shit out of you." Liam laughed, I was obviously serious, but I also knew that Liam would do anything for me, including finding the girls.

"And Liam?"

"Yeah?"

One thing I knew about being a good captain was that everyone respects, we would do anything for each other. I even helped Smith build an Ikea table for his mother on a Tuesday night.

We were ready to do anything for each other, but I never asked for help from the team, and I had always taken pride in that.

Except now.

"Call the team and ask them to search every fucking bar in Hawthorne, New Crest or even fucking Van Doren." I sigh, "If they don't find Adrianna, they can stay and have a drink, it's on me."

Liam laughs with a pause, "Roger that Cap."

I felt like I was about to spiral. If I had found out that Adrianna had gotten touched by another man, I would rip the guy to shreds and even fix him a new face.

He wouldn't mind getting his balls shoved down his throat, right?

I hope not.

ADRIANNA

Pepper spray? Check. Lip Gloss? Check.

"Do you have condoms?" Margo asks as I roll my eyes, pulling an extra one out of my bag and handing it to her.

"You are a lifesaver." She voices as I look over to Juliette and Verina who already downed two shots of tequila.

Not my type of alcohol to be honest I was more of a champagne or Riesling type of girl. But tonight, was my night to get wasted.

My night to get rid of a burden.

"You guys going to make it until the end of the night?"

Verina gave a bright look at me, "Oh sweetheart, Juliette and I can take it, but can you?"

"Why do you just ask me and not Margo as well?"

Margo laughs, looking at me, "Oh sweetheart, I'm engaged. I can get wasted and I'll just have to send him a text and he's there to my rescue."

"Let's be for real. Since, Liam Brookshire isn't grazing our presence, do you actually like this guy?"

Margo pauses, "He's attractive."

"That wasn't the question." Verina interrupts.

Margo hesitates to answer for a bit, "Of course I like him, I wouldn't have said yes if I didn't."

"It's just you have never mentioned him before." Juliette pops a grape into her mouth, "And you haven't shut up about Liam for the past month."

"My infatuation about Liam was a joke and I only liked him clearly because he's the biggest player in school. I couldn't help myself and I got burned."

"Ben treats me the way I need to be treated. He wants me, he can't keep his hands off of me, and he has beautiful eyes that holds mystery."

"Any skeletons in the back of his closet?" I ask as she pushes me over playfully, "Don't try to distract me with your questions, your wings are getting plucked tonight, Dove."

I flip Margo off, "Don't call me that, it makes me gag."

"Oh sorry, is that only reserved for Mr. Grayson Prince himself?"

The limo comes to a stop as my heartbeat falls to normal levels, "Oh look! We're finally here!"

Juliette and Verina's eyes gleamed as they practically flew out of the limo as I started to walk out before Margo pulled me back down to the seat a bit harshly.

"Ouch!" I scowl at her as she smiles, giving me a thoughtful look, "Please be careful."

"I will, you know me, I won't just pick a random guy and get it over with."

I mean sure it was the plan, but I wasn't going to tell Margo that, "What if you see the dick size and you think it's too small or too big?"

"Margo!"

"I'm serious!" She laughs, putting her hands on mine, "You have to be comfortable, and you have to be careful, don't let him come inside you."

I roll my eyes, "Margo Raine!" I let out a laugh, "I'm not uneducated!"

"No, of course not, I just don't want you to think that boys won't take advantage."

"I have pepper spray." I say nonchalantly as she nods.

"And don't forget the karate we've been learning since second grade."

"Are we done here?" I grew irritated as she smiled at me, pulling me in for a hug.

"I love you." She whispers.

I shake my head, feeling bad that I was irritated at my best friend, "I love you more."

Margo and I jump out of the limo as she tips the driver two hundred dollars, "Keep this quiet to my parents, will you?"

Shaq smiles, "Yes ma'am."

I smile at the driver before he rolls up the window then drives off.

I look to the bar, *"The Ringer?"* I send a condescending look to Margo.

She beams, "It's cool inside."

"Then let's get moving on! You guys take forever to confess your love!" Verina complains as I place my arm around her shoulders.

"Calm down, babe, you will get your shots in." Margo walks over to the bouncer, slipping in her card, all he really had to do was look at her last name before mindlessly letting us in.

She winks at him before flipping her hair, "You have a room ready for us?"

"Of course."

He directed us to the VIP room, while greedy men looked at us like expensive cattle. I tend to look for the guys that don't mind that we were here.

And one certainly caught my attention, he seemed to be blonde which made my heart race thinking about Grayson.

Margo places her bag down on the table as I smile, "I'm off!"

Verina and Juliette had been lost already as I spotted them taking body shots off of a shirtless guy.

"Use the condom!" She screams as I wanted to shove her bag into her mouth, even without a mother, Margo acted like one when it came to my safety.

She was there for me when I overdosed. She was really the only one I told.

Nothing would make me happier than to finally tell Verina and Juliette, but I wouldn't want to worry them like I've worried Margo.

Margo was the type of friend who would take your pain just because she hates seeing you upset. She was my sunlight when I was at a very dark place in my life.

I have always felt like I won the friendship lottery with Margo. She was my priceless jackpot.

If there was one thing, I was thankful for, it was that she was in the same world as me and she was my person.

I approached the guy that made my heart race, I seemed to forget that I had anxiety out of the roof. I popped a couple pills before meeting Margo out front.

She didn't need to know I was using it again.

I tap him on the shoulder. He turns with a scowl before taking a good look at me, "Hey precious." He murmurs as I feel butterflies in my stomach spread.

"Hello." I smirk back looking at his drink, "Can I?"

He brings the drink up to my lips, pouring some in I swallow, wiping the remainder that dripped down the chin.

I take out my hand, "Adrianna." He smiles.

"Anthony." He takes my hand, bringing me by the bar.

"Can I buy you something sweetheart?" He shifts his body weight, also giving me a wink.

"Can you afford me?" I whispered by his ear.

He tightens, "I'd like to find out."

I had barely listened to him before looking at his lips.

That could do.

I pulled him in, kissing him fiercely, not caring about the music or the people around us. I needed to find out if he was the man that I was picking tonight. Anthony kissed me back; he kissed me with passion as I took it in.

He moans as I grip on his collared t-shirt, hearing whistles from strangers as he drives his tongue into my mouth making me groan, but he shoved it so far down my throat I almost gagged.

He grips my waist making me uneasy.

When Grayson would grip my waist, he would do it like I was his salvation and his last breath.

I pictured him. But I shouldn't have. I shouldn't be.

I walked and pulled his arm close to me, directing him into a private room with a bed and a couch, a room that Margo had reserved for me.

I wasn't sure if having sex for the first time was wise at a bar with someone I barely knew. It wasn't smart, but it was my best plan. And it was too late to change my mind.

CHAPTER 28

GRAYSON

My whole fucking hockey team had been scouring each corner of New York's bar and I wasn't about to give up knowing an unworthy man had touched her.

I sat on the driver seat of my car, too riled up to let one of my drivers drive me around the whole New York city area.

Thinking of Adrianna possibly being somewhere alone made me sick. And again, I don't mean to be possessive, but I can't help it. Her golden skin was made for my touch. And that's how I always imagine it.

My phone rang as I swore a bit before picking it up, "Did you find her?!" I came off a bit rude and I took a breath and calmed down.

"Calm down, Prince. She's not dead." Neil answered as I laughed, "Not yet."

"I found her." Neil teased as I let my mouth turn into a devilish smile, "Where?"

I hear a pause as I roll my eyes before they start talking, "Liam and I have decided that we will not be revealing her location unless you tell us you like her."

They cannot be fucking serious, leave it up to Neil and fucking Liam to ruin the rest if my fucking day. "How about you tell me where she is, and I won't make you skate laps all of next practice?" I grew impatient as I walked off of a random bar.

From the five bars and three clubs I have went in and out of looking for Adrianna, three girls asked me if I was into orgies, and I rolled my eyes before slamming the door into their faces.

Still on the phone the two idiots pondered on my proposal.

"We have thought about your proposal and we both are prepared to make that sacrifice."

I laugh to myself, checking my phone to track their locations, "You two are fucking dickheads. You will be running all the time next practice, and I know where she is."

I hung up the phone, only hoping that I had a camera for their priceless reactions.

I was about four minutes away from the bar they were at, "The Ringer." I let my eyes narrow at the glowing sign that became more of a view as I drove closer.

I look at the guard as he shakes his head lightly with a smile, "Are you Grayson Prince?"

I gave a concerned face, "Yeah?"

He nods, "Miss Hamilton said you would be coming."

I rolled my eyes again, of course she would let the bouncer know that I was attending.

I stare at the man long enough for him to be reminded that I could easily reward him a black eye and a matching busted lip.

"VIP section two, table twelve." He whispers as I nod, opening the door to see Liam and Neil looking at me with embarrassed faces.

"I don't even want to fucking hear it from the both of you." I passed them.

They tried to speak, "How did you know?"

"Grayson, we are so sorry!" I hear Liam yell.

I shake my head, "You are still fucking skating."

I approach the tables, spotting Margo and Verina as they take shots, looking hammered. Juliette had been flirting with some random guy that only looked at her boobs.

They were wearing revealing clothing and they looked beautiful, but all I could think about was what the fuck Adrianna was wearing.

My blood pressure rises as I look at Margo, "Where is she?" I say with a strangled breath.

Margo smirks, "She's getting laid."

Margo yawned obviously trying to get me riled up, "Fucking where?" I demanded as I looked around only to see people dancing and drinking.

Margo looked around yawning again, only this time, she had gotten me riled up. "Margo. I swear to God if I get asked by another girl to have an orgy, I'm going to fucking lose it."

Margo laughs, handing me a key, "Room two." But before I snatch it, she pulls it away from me, her face gloomed a darker shade.

"The only reason I'm giving this to you is because I know Adrianna deserves better than to hand off her virginity to a guy that she just met."

I nodded knowingly that Margo was serious, she was always carefree in many things, but her best friend's feelings were never one of them.

I nod as she dangles the keys in front of me.

I grab the keys running to the individual rooms, knocking on the door before entering. I see Adrianna and a blonde six-foot stick grabbing her waist.

Her pale face looks at mine with a terrified expression.

Their clothes were still on, and I've never felt more empowered than ever.

I look at the blonde guy besides her who looked hammered as fuck.

I laugh, shaking my head, "I'm going to give you five fucking seconds to get your ass out of the damn bar before my fist meets your face."

My fist were clenched as well as my jaw, venom in my eyes as I sent the man a cold stare that he knew could only end badly if he didn't obey.

The man grabbed all his belongings running out as Adrianna looked at me with a serious expression. He slammed the door leaving me suffocating in a room with her.

"Take your shit. I'm taking you home." I felt my blood boil and my heart race as she fixed her bra.

"Are you serious, Prince?" She sits on the bed, running her fingers through her hair frustrated.

"Take your damn shit and we're fucking going." I started picking up her heels that were scattered on the floor.

She looked annoyed and upset with me. "Adrianna. Let's fucking go."

She gets up on a huff, running out, running into a random man, who grabbed her by the waist, she flinches as the man then tried kissing her, "Come on baby, stop playing hard to get and fuck me." The man murmurs as I feel fire shoot up my peripheral vision.

I laugh harshly, with a devilish smirk, building my fists, without even processing everything I smash my hard fist into the man's jaw. I'm pretty sure I dislocated and broke it at the same time.

He falls to the ground, cold and out. I shoved everyone off that watched, Margo's face was in view as I took Adrianna's hand who was in shock, pulling her out of the bar.

"Let's go." I command as she listens, "You killed him!"

"I don't give a fuck." I pull her closer to me, "If another man touches you tonight, I will commit murder."

She closes her lips, as I turn to her, "And don't think I don't have the money to cover it up."

I turn around to see Margo, Verina, and Juliette run out waving at Adrianna and I's glamourous departure.

"I'll take care of the dead guy!" Margo takes a sip of her beverage while Adrianna practically flops around outside with no shoes, "Get in the damn car."

My jaw clenches as she scowls at me, "You didn't need to knock him out."

"It's not my fault he can't fight." I counter.

She sneers, "You result to violence every time."

I knew that, but it only really happened when something happened to people, I care about.

I would never tell her that, so I stayed quiet instead.

It was yet another silent ride home as she looked out the window.

I didn't feel like I was up to talking anyway as I pulled into her driveway.

Her body freezes, "I can't go home tonight." She mutters.

I roll my eyes. "Why the fuck not?"

She sighs, "I just don't want to fucking go home. Take me to a damn hotel." She looks at me with fear in her eyes.

I backed out of her driveway, pulling into my house, "You're sleeping in my room."

"Fuck that." She scoffs.

I park my car into the garage, "You can sleep on my bed, I'll take the couch."

She gets out of the car, slamming my door as I groan, knocking my head frontward to the horn.

Why did she have to be so damn difficult?

I walk up to my room quickly, not quite sure if she tore my whole fucking room apart already.

She stood out looking at the balcony door, hearing me set down my keys and she looked at me, rolling her eyes.

"Did you seriously fucking pick him?" I fold my arms as she laughed harshly.

Her eyes sank onto mine, "That was the plan, remember?"

She stands walking over to the door, "The plan was that I pick someone in a bar and let him fuck me mindlessly."

I grit my teeth inside my mouth, "You *don't* pick *him*!"

"Oh, I'm sorry, do I need to run things by you first before making any advancements in my love life?"

"That would be much appreciated."

She looked like she was about to explode, "How *dare* you! You are so inconsiderate, selfish, arrogant, vile and everything I hate all at once."

She shakes her head like she was going crazy.

Frantically trying to convey her feelings, but I knew how she felt, I felt it too.

I was frustrated and upset, but it was her time to rant.

"My love life is none of your business, especially when you made sure of that yourself or do we want to re-run the conversation yesterday."

"You wanted this, remember?!" She accused me.

I knock my head back in frustration, "Throwing your virginity like a damn bouquet of flowers on a wedding day wasn't the ideal idea."

"Screw you!" She screams with conviction as I take a breath.

"Adrianna, you were fucking kissing him." I growl at her, obviously angry and annoyed.

"I was informed that people do that when they have sex, and you should know that when you bang the whole fucking school, but God forbid you can't touch me."

I laugh, "You think I don't want to touch you like he was touching you?"

"You make it seem like I'm a damn virus." Her voice settles.

"You aren't a virus." I walked around, she was panting from the lack of oxygen while we yelled at each other.

"Then what the fuck am I to you?"

"You want to know what you fucking are to me?" I lose my composure as she backs down.

"You are a fucking drug. I can't seem to get enough of you, and I don't want to quit. But if I fucking do, I think I might die."

I walk closer.

"Isn't that how drugs work?!" I look deeper in her eyes. "If so, I'm a drug addict. Hell, I'm fucking addicted to everything about you damn it!"

I walk off I didn't even care if I was rambling, "Ever since the day I saw you at the lake house in the Hamptons when we were kids, I'm pretty sure I was infatuated."

"You were wearing fucking white dress with ruffled roses. You practically had a halo on your head and that's when I knew I saw an angel for the first time."

I run my frustrated fingers through my hair, "I made it my mission to always fucking protect you from anyone." My breath was ragged, "Whether you hated me for it. I have made sure that everyman in Hawthorne knew you were and still are, off fucking limits."

She stood in front of me with wide eyes, her chest heaving as I took a step closer. She didn't back away this time. Instead, she walked closer, water built up in her sockets.

I didn't know what exactly to call what we have been going through, what was happening between us, but I was addicted. She was a type of drug that was lethal if discovered.

"I don't know what you are to me." I swallow.

"But I want you." I lick my lips, "God, I want all of you."

Adrianna's face stayed neutral, but then softens, "I have fucked up parts." She laughed softly.

"I want them too." I mutter as she breaks, her face falling as she runs to me, enveloping her body to mine, tightening her embrace as I place my hand on the back of her head, slowly petting.

She sobs, "I didn't want him to take my virginity."

Adrianna's voice was muffled as she stuffed her face in my chest, crying, "If you hadn't stopped me, I would've been done for." She lets out, "I would've lost the last thing that doesn't make me a burden."

I shush her, calming her down, "You are not a burden, Cassian and don't you ever blame yourself." My hands couldn't help but dig through her vixen hair.

She gulps her sobs, "I always do."

She quiets down as I close my eyes, "You really want to lose your virginity?" I asked her.

Adrianna pulled away, "I don't want you to do it if you don't want to. I don't want to force you or guilt trip you." She says with a racing heart. I look at her, her beautiful self.

I pick her up, her legs wrapping around my waist as I crash my lips into her mouth, "I wouldn't have asked if I didn't want to."

"August would care." She whispers while sending shivers down my spine.

I didn't care about what August wanted. I took one look at Adrianna and August wasn't even in the picture anymore. I didn't want to hurt anybody, but I wanted to be selfish with Adrianna.

Damn, I wanted to take her away and never give her back. She wasn't mine to take, but I knew... if someone did take her away.

I would kill.

She trembled as I swallowed, "August moved on. I wanted to move on too, but I felt too guilty taking what I've really wanted from the start."

Adrianna looked into my eyes, "Don't say that to make me feel better."

I grab her face, letting my lips crash into hers. My heart raced as she held on to me for dear life. This was a need, and I knew it. This was what I needed, and she wanted it too. She pulled me closer, which I didn't think was possible.

She started to rip my clothes off, my shirt being thrown to the ground as she moaned into my mouth.

"I want this to be special."

She pulls away as I tilt my head, "This is special."

"No." She breathes out.

"I want you to destroy me."

She takes a deep breath, walking away, her eyes still set on mine as I take a seat on my chair, my eyes never leaving hers.

She places her hands on the waistband of her skirt, her chest heaving as she bites her lip.

ADRIANNA

"I don't want to disappoint you, Prince." My voice burned through the tension in the room as Grayson slowly placed his gaze on mine.

My heart felt like it was running a marathon.

"Disappoint me?" His voice lowered as his body inched closer to mine. My body shivered as he pushed a loose curl behind my ear, placing his hand to cup my cheek again.

"You let him kiss you?"

His thumb grazed my bottom lip as I breathed out, "Yes."

"These lips... only belong to me." He breathed out as I took a huge gulp of my own words.

Silence.

Grayson and I felt our bodies shake as his cold hands confined my warm body.

I placed my hand hesitantly on his chest as he hesitated to let me rest there. I looked down at his scars on the side of his body, my heart ached.

I almost wanted to cry as I touched them, I hadn't asked them about it before because it was never my place. He would tell me when he was ready.

"And these scars on your body are only to be mended by me..." I mutter, tears falling down the side of my cheeks, my fingers couldn't help but run across them.

His scars weren't fresh, and I knew that, but I could tell it still affected him like a reopened wound.

My eyes glistened as I thought a moment of relief spread across his face, I was unsure if I was hurting him.

But I was mistaken.

He avoided my eyes as he looked away from me, my heart melting as I knew it had no right to... but it did.

"Why would someone do this to you?" I say as my voice breaks.

"*Who* would do this to you?" I ask with pain riding my voice.

"It was a long time ago." His eyes reach mine with tears falling down his cheek. I knew he was talking about his scars.

"Little by little, I don't really remember how it happened." I bit my bottom lip as he took his time to explain. I didn't want to force him.

Grayson lifts my body to the chair as I sit on top of him, he lifts my shirt revealing my mending cuts.

"We match." He says with sorrow behind his words, we matched in the most fucked up way possible. We needed each other in the most screwed up way.

I laugh gently, *"We match."*

He takes a shaky breath, his hand hesitant to roam around me. He touches me so lightly, like feathers, he drew stars around my scars.

My eyes flashed, "No, I can't. It's too fucked up." I muttered as he placed his hand on my cuts, my body jolting as I pulled his hand back.

"Why is it so hard for you to believe someone will stay with you through thick and thin?" I resisted Grayson's touch as I felt him soften.

"Do you honestly think you are that broken that no one is capable of loving you?"

Yes.

Silence.

Grayson pulled me back to his body as my face was glowing with iridescent tears.

His hand squeezing mine as I felt the pain radiate through my body to his.

"Yes, I am broken. I can't let the only good thing in my life be destroyed by me."

I couldn't help but close my eyes.

I shed a small tear as I breathed in and out slowly, Grayson placing his hand on my heart.

"You don't think I'm broken too?" He forced his eyes onto mine as I looked away slowly.

He brings my face back to force his gaze on mine.

I turned away once again, walking away to sit down across from him in his armchair, his eyes still boring into mine.

His eyes sent goosebumps all around my body as he relaxed his touch, still staring into my eyes.

I bite my bottom lip as I slowly walk in front of him, taking a deep breath while gently taking off my coat, dropping it on the ground.

His body shifted as he took the sight in.

I slowly unbutton my long sleeve shirt, showing my black laced bra, my eyes still locked on to his.

"You don't want this," Grayson muttered as he bit his bottom lip, gripping the arm of his chair tightly.

"I do... and I can prove it to you." I breathed out, placing my hand behind me, slowly unzipping my skirt, until it seductively fell down to my ankles.

Grayson sits up, loosening his collar slowly, standing up, walking closer to me as I was only left in my underwear.

He slowly pushes me to sit on the desk while gripping both of my hands behind my back, tying my wrists together. My whole body was on fire, excitement rattled through my body.

He makes himself back in front of me as I hear both of our hearts beating faster by the second. Grayson's hand crept to the back of my scalp, grabbing a fist full of hair, and pulled my head back, so his eyes could meet mine.

"Open your legs." He demanded me with such force that I felt my knees buckle.

Without hesitation, my legs spread wide open as his hand crept itself to my heat, causing me to groan out.

His fingers trailed lightly, like feathers to the inner parts of my thighs. He sucked my jaw, knowing with hesitance, rush, and passion.

I tilt my head to the side and let out soft moans that release from the back of my throat. My hand unable to move he bends down and gets on his knees, making unbreakable feverish eye contact with me the whole time.

He pulls my waist closer to his warm radiating breath as I knock my head back.

His fingers wander up to feel the skin on my lower back as he placed a soft kiss on my throbbing heat, through my laced underwear.

"Wet already?" He looked up with a smirk on his face as I closed my eyes with embarrassment. "Keep your eyes open and look at me at all times." He demands as I swallow.

His eyes met mine again as he gave a subtle smirk. His kisses trailed from my underwear, along to my abdomen... then to my nipples.

His breaths gently brush them, he inches out his tongue, which I feel on the tip of my nipple, I shiver.

I moan out. He takes it as an invitation, shoving his face deep, and biting as much as he could, sucking and rubbing the skin on my chest. Sending electrical sparks through my body.

I tremor his touch.

His kisses leave trails of devastation to the nape of my neck, while his fingers pinched my nipples between his fingers then tug. His voice so ragged, he moans against my skin as I grunt.

I could feel my heat getting wetter as I craved him, more than I should.

"Grayson... please—" I groaned as he looked into my eyes.

"Please what Dove?" He places his hand on my neck, harshly shaking it.

"Please, Prince." I groaned as his eyes narrowed and brows furrowed.

"It's almost like you don't know the way I fuck." He shook my head by my hair again.

He was right. I didn't. I've only heard about it.

All the signs right now... pointed to him being extremely rough...

My heart dropped as he looked back with a smile, "Relax, Dove, it's your first time." I let out a breath.

I didn't question what was about to be done... All I knew was that I was going to enjoy it.

His fingers and warm mouth trailed kisses across my body and tickled across my skin. Warm and gentle, practically teasing the insides of my legs... not rough, deep, or close to where I wanted him to be.

His hands massaged my stomach and hips. He goes back to my thighs as he taunted me with his tongue dancing on my skin. I buck my lips forward in desperation for more touch.

He was waiting.

He looks up at me with greed and his desires for me and sexual gratification.

I feel Grayson's bulge from his pants grow harder as I moan out. I could be dreaming right now.

"Oh, darling..." He whispers in my ear, his fingers making their way to my wet clit, causing me to moan out, craving for more.

"You want to be fucked so badly." A smirk occurred on his face as I closed my eyes hoping he would grant my wishes.

I wanted it. I wanted him to fuck me. Thoroughly. Every muscle in me ached to be filled... slapped and bitten by him.

Grayson inserts two or three fingers inside of me, causing me to whimper, being caught off guard. My core tightened, squeezing his fingers.

I try and force my way down to where his fingers began, but he chuckles and moves his hands away.

"You want me inside of you. My hard cock deep inside of you, pounding in and out..." His voice is raspy and on edge.

Grayson looked into my eyes as they confided in him. I felt both of our hearts in sync as he took a gulp.

He pulled me closer, my body screaming for release.

He grunted into me, both of us shaking. His hands up around me, Grayson pumped his fingers in and out of me at a fast pace as I couldn't help but make incoherent noises.

His lips making their way onto mine as he bites down on my bottom lip, his fingers curling causing me to knock my head back in pleasure.

"Show me how much you want me Grayson." I moaned as he breathed onto my neck.

No words were exchanged.

He started rubbing his thumb on my clit as I let out a loud moan before muffling the noise by shocking my face into his neck.

Grayson's pants were discarded on the floor along with his boxers as he took a deep breath looking at me. He lines his rock-hard dick up with my soaked entrance.

Grayson pulls out a condom from his discarded pants, ripping the wrapper by his teeth, putting the condom on.

He struggled as his dick size was extraordinary.

"Try not to make a sound." He held a wide smile.

"There's people outside." He whispers as I laugh gently.

I pause, my eyes widen, "What?!"

Grayson laughs, "Don't worry we won't do anything that my family would hear."

His voice penetrated through my whole body as he slammed his lengthy dick inside of me, causing me to bite on his shoulder. Grayson starts off slowly moving in and out of me, attempting to tease me.

I moan. My hand slamming on my mouth, "Oh my god, your sister could hear us."

He shakes his head, "She's not going to hear a thing. She's probably blasting Taylor Swift in her eardrums."

My body constricts around him as I nudge towards him making us both groan. I felt every part of him, and he entered in and out of me.

"Harder." I whispered.

He shook his head, "No I'll hurt you."

"Grayson." I moaned in his ear, his pace immediately started thrusting harder and faster, placing one hand on the wall behind me to steady himself. His hip thrusts in and out of me at a steady yet swift pace as he hits deep inside of me.

"Grayson—" He deepens his thrusts, "Fuck, I—."

"I said, don't make a sound." He growled in my ear after feeling myself clench around him already. I bit my lips together as he snapped his hips up into mine, feeling him throb and twitch inside of me.

"Grayson, I'm going to come—," I breathed out as he gave me nothing and went faster. I moan in his neck as he pulls my back and slams his lips onto mine... I kiss him back instantly as his pace starts to falter. My body is sore already but I'm chasing after my orgasm.

"Sluts don't get to come." He addresses me as I look at him with hazy eyes, "And you let him almost fuck you."

I moan as he smirks wickedly.

He ran his hands through my hair, tugging it. Intense pleasure started to wash over me... feeling my stomach tighten. He looks at me with a dangerous gaze.

"What did I say about coming?"

This drives Grayson over the edge as his pace became sloppy, delivering a particularly sharp thrust. In an animalistic pace he pounded on me, so hard I felt him hit my pelvis.

The sharp pain mixed with pleasure became very familiar at that moment. Grayson picked me up, slamming me on the bed.

Spreading my legs wide open, as he slams his dick inside of me once more causing me to moan out.

He adjusts himself to such an angle where he hits the right spot, with full thrusts, and at the same time, he glazes over my clit, sending shivers down my spine.

The rhythmic slapping of his dick going in and out of me turned me on even more.

His voice so raspy and low, he began swearing, halted on

impact within with sharp breath intake when I tried to make out specific sounds and anguished voices within him.

I couldn't take it anymore.

I felt my walls clenching and my stomach starting to loosen, as his dick got even more buried than I would've thought never possible.

Grayson placed his hand on my neck, squeezing as I whimpered and moaned underneath him.

"Fuck. Gray." I warned him as he only quickened his pace.

"I know, Dove." He groaned while placing his other hand on my lower stomach.

"Wh— What are you doing?" I moan out in frustration in the midst of my orgasm.

Grayson lowers his lips onto my ear as he bites my earlobe. "I want to feel myself, going in and out of you... with every thrust, going deeper and deeper."

He pushes his whole length in once more causing me to gasp out, his hand pushing slightly harder on my stomach. Fuck. I felt as though I was in a state of euphoria.

"I want to feel your stomach tighten around me when you come."

"Fuck Grayson—" I knock my head back in frustration and build in pleasure, as I bucked my hips towards him, causing him to grunt out.

He tightened his grip on my neck, as he thrust harder and faster once more.

"Come."

His voice bellowed, causing my back to arch up, my stomach squeezing him, and my walls clenching around his throbbing dick.

"That's it, Adrianna."

He massaged my lower stomach, as I felt myself spill all around him.

I moaned out with pleasure as he pulled me closer with such ease.

"Good girl." He whispered, causing electricity to run up my spine, pulling him in.

I crash our hungry lips on top of each other, I straddle myself on top of him.

He groaned as I was now sitting on top of him, leaning down, his dick not inside of me as it grazes around my folds, causing me to shiver.

I was still majorly sore, and I knew it.

I ran my hands up his chest, as my kisses touched his flex abs, and my hands ran through his silky, blond hair.

I sit up, looking down at him as his eyes roll to the back of his head. I move my hips back and forth, running my fingers down to his dick, adjusting him to push inside of me, as he groaned out.

I threw my hair to the side, so my hair would flip to the side, I stabilized myself from falling by resting my arms on his chest.

I looked at him with a lustful gaze, he looked up at me, as he bit his lip. I took a breath in as I worked my way down on his long, hard, throbbing dick.

Grayson placed his hand on my waist, to slowly guide me down, all the way. I finally make it down as I part my lips in disbelief and pleasure.

I lift my waist up, as I slam back down, causing Grayson to grip on my waist tighter. "Fuck..." He groaned out as I repeated the same motion, only faster and harder. I bounced up and down as he crumbled underneath me. I ran my hands up my breasts as he clenched his jaw.

He sat up wrapping his arms around me, his lips crashing on my nipples as I moaned. I felt his dick twitch as I bounced faster and harder. His breathing ragged and his words became incoherent.

I felt him almost at the edge as he started bucking his hips, at the same rhythm as my bounces, his mouth creeping on my neck as his lips created hickeys.

I bounced faster, feeling his dick throb inside of me, on the edge of his orgasm.

"Come on Grayson, come for me." I groaned while slamming myself back down on his dick even when it hurt like hell.

"It's not about me. Fuck, baby—," I bounced faster, as my moan crept on his neck, my frustrations were high and beyond reach. Grayson bit my neck as I moaned out, feeling his dick still hard inside of me. Without knowing, I orgasmed at the same time as him.

He shudders, as he continues, giving a few more soft thrusts to ride out both of our orgasms. His body wrapped around my tired and weak body. Tears spilled from my face as he kissed them away.

"It's okay, Dove." He whispers, "I'm right here."

CHAPTER 29

ADRIANNA

My whole body felt like it was stomped on by a giant, I could barely move. When I did, Grayson's body embraced mine. I turned to look at him, his face so at peace as he breathed his eyelashes moved.

I took in a breath, my hands grazing his cheek, kissing his forehead, "Even when you're with me, you still want her, don't you?" I whisper.

I heard what Grayson said, but a part of me wasn't naïve. I wanted to save myself.

I didn't want to like Grayson, but we've fought it for so long. It was only a matter of time for us to start falling.

Nothing was wrong with experiencing love for the first and last time since after he gets August back, he would never have to worry about me ever again.

I had only been putting it off because of him.

He might say it wasn't fake, but a pit in my stomach brings my brain back to remembering that he's only with me to make the love of his life jealous.

Don't be fucking stupid Adrianna. He's going to drop you the moment August runs back. I shook my head, pulling myself away from his cold body, heat enveloping mine once more as I got up, walking to his bathroom and took care of my business.

Looking into the mirror my eyes began to turn red, my hands shook as I fisted them up. I opened up a little to Grayson when I showed him my cuts. He didn't pity me. He didn't make me feel fragile. He made me feel equal with him.

I swallow, pulling up the shirt I pulled from his dresser, looking at my scars.

Many told me that I was skinny, but I didn't view it that way, I viewed it in a way that convinced me if I cut myself, I would lose that image that built up in my head.

We match.

My vision dazed as I gripped on the doorknob, my heart racing. It had been a while since I took some medication, I had been distracted by many things the drugs weren't my first priority anymore. It was weird to think that so much had happened and it didn't feel that long from the original deal.

Back when it was strictly just hate, there were no feelings involved, nothing much involved, just our duties.

I had received an email that I had won the presidency, and I felt sort of guilty about winning the title.

I wasn't going to be here to fulfill the work that should be done by a great president. I wasn't planning to make a damn suicide note, but I just wanted it to end soon, and I was prepared.

I do think it's for the best. No one changed my mind.

I walked out of the room, Grayson was still asleep as I smiled, walking closer to his body and then at the clock.

It was 3 A.M.

My house's lights were still on, and it felt like an unfinished puzzle if I didn't go home.

I put my clothes on, taking one look at him, then the ring that still stayed on my finger. I breathe, pulling it out, placing it on his nightstand. I laugh gently.

Running out of his room his kitchen light was dimmed, my

eyes met his sister's, her face beaming. "Adrianna!" She runs to me while holding a cookie.

"Are you supposed to have a cookie right now?" I narrow my eyes.

She hides behind her cookie, "Are you supposed to be sneaking out of my brother's bedroom right now?" She counters with a smirk.

She was her brother's sister.

"Are you guys finally back together?!" She smiled so hard that I was afraid her mouth might stay like that.

"Kind of, yes." I laugh.

"He's such a liar!" She stuffs the rest of the cookie into her mouth, "He said that it was over and that he messed up, but you're back. You love him!"

My eyes widen, "I don't love him yet, Amelia."

"Yet is very promising." She smirks again.

I roll my eyes, "Your brother and I are trying." I reassure her.

She frowns, "I think that he likes the person he is a bit more when he's with you." She backs away, "But you didn't hear that from me."

I laugh, turning her around and pushing her to the stairwell, "Go to bed Amelia."

She continues to walk, still speaking, "Can you call me Lia?" She looks back.

"Why?" I frown.

"I don't like my name."

"I love your name." I say with conviction as she beams again.

"Really?"

"I think your name is beautiful, just like you." Amelia runs back towards me, hugging me tighter than ever, "I'll love it just for you."

I felt my heart swell as she spoke, she pulled away running up to her room. I heard her shut the door before I made an exit to the front door.

As I walk over to my side of the street, I wonder to myself if it was okay if I kept in contact with Amelia when Grayson and I figured out that we were a lost cause. When we find ourselves being together, it's a mistake and something that shouldn't have happened. I find the hidden key, unlocking the gate as I walk in my front door.

My father walks down the stairs, "Where the hell have you been?!" He screamed as I gave a neutral face.

"Out."

"It's fucking three in the damn morning!" He points at the clock as I roll my eyes, I didn't have enough energy for this.

"You're wasted aren't you!" He rams down to me.

I scowl, "No! I'm not wasted I'm fucking tired!"

"Since when have you cursed me?"

Since you've been banging your secretary, I wanted to scream but I didn't.

Instead, I looked at him, "You are out of control! I come home and you're not here." He points at the kitchen, "I expect to come home and have dinner as a family."

"That's funny, considering that every time you want to come home or say you do, you don't" I laugh, "Sorry I wasn't fooled this time."

He shook his head, "You are being disrespectful."

I didn't say anything back as he looked at my shirt. If I had come home in the outfit I wore to the bar, I would've been shipped to a boarding school, I wore Grayson's hockey shirt.

"I told you to stay away from him." He sternly addresses.

"Deal with it, we're dating." I mutter.

He rolled his tongue into his mouth, "You two are a joke together."

"You should be happy. The two richest empires together, it's a golden couple Father."

He paces around my body, and I was starting to show signs of wanting to go into my room and sleep as I yawn, "I'm going out tomorrow too." I informed him.

He laughs, "No you aren't."

"Try and stop me."

"You are making a damn mistake by being with a Prince."

I glower, "I don't tell you who you can and can't date, so why do you think you can tell me?"

"You are my daughter."

I laughed bitterly. No, I was barely an acquaintance.

"Being with Grayson is the happiest I've been in a year, so you either butt out or I will cut you off from my life. Oh wait, you already do that without trying."

My father grows irritated, "Without me, you are nothing."

Precisely.

"Oh right, because you were the one who took me to my mental health checkups and my therapy sessions." I say sarcastically, "I would be so gone without you."

I didn't want to discredit my father, he did make sure I had things I needed, "I paid for that shit!"

I meant... I wanted him by my side, not just paying for it.

"Go to bed." He instructed me as I felt my body weaken from my tiredness.

My father was a lot of things, but a father was not one of them.

CHAPTER 30

GRAYSON

My ear screeching alarm wakes me up. As an attempt to calm down I grab the warm spot on my bed seeing as Adrianna was nowhere to be seen.

I looked around, her clothing and bag were nowhere to be found. I walked over to the balcony seeing her silhouette by her closet, my body relieved to see that she was okay.

I slept so soundly. When the hell did, she sneak out of bed? I laugh to myself, walking over to the bathroom, taking a shower, and getting dressed. I look over to my nightstand picking up my phone when I notice her ring.

Her purity ring, I remembered her saying that she would never willingly give it to me.

But it was mine. Technically, she was mine.

Adrianna Cassian is fucking mine, and this ring on my nightstand proved it to me.

I picked up my phone, looking for her number with a huge smile, I fell back on my bed once again.

I've never been so eager to talk to someone. I felt like I was going ballistic, but it was true.

I wonder if she felt the same. I didn't want to expect her to feel the same about me, not that I never knew what I was feeling.

. . .

> Good morning beautiful ;)

This comes with a good morning text?

> You don't think I'm a monster, do you?

Of course, I do!

Pick me up?

READ 7:11 A.M.

> Be there in a few.

I smile, from ear to ear I run out of my room into Amelia's who was packing up her bag, "You have a necklace chain?" I smile at her while sitting on her bed.

"Why?"

"None of your business."

"Then no. I don't." She sneers at me.

I laugh, "I know you have one Amelia." I look around her room, my eyes narrowing to her jewelry box.

"Don't you dare touch that!"

"You owe me." I say plainly as she rolls her eyes.

"Your fear of butterflies was something that she should've known from the start."

I gave her a look that made him move over to her jewelry box, "You want gold or silver?" She asked as I smiled, thinking of Adrianna's golden skin.

"Gold."

She pulls one away from her drawers full of jewelry. I roll my eyes, "You have about a thousand chains. Why did you feel the need to act like you only had three?"

"Because I think it's funny." She winks at me before I walk out of her room. Before I shut the door she runs towards me, "When can I go and see Finn?"

I smile, "You down to see him after the game? I can ask Adrianna to pick you up."

She nods, "Okay, because I made him a drawing. I hadn't seen him in school much so maybe he might need someone to cheer him up!"

I kneel down to hug her, messing her hair up just a bit before she pulls away, "You didn't have to do that." She pushes me.

I laugh. "Then don't waste my time, next time." She scowls.

"See you tonight!"

"Have a great day at school, darling." I kiss her forehead before picking up my keys and heading out. I turn on my car, backing out of the driveway and pulling on the side of her driveway, I walk over to the front of her house, before I even ring the doorbell, the door opens with Adrianna's father standing by the doorframe.

"You will not be taking my daughter to school." He glares at me.

"Did she say that?" I ask politely as he brushes over my question like it was scrap metal.

"No."

"With all due respect sir, but that is not your decision to make."

"She's my daughter and I am telling you to stay away from her."

I laugh gently looking back at my car, "I think that she can make that decision herself."

"No, she doesn't know what's right for her, she came home at three last night, and I'm guessing that you were the cause of that." He walks closer, "I want you to know that while I might not be able to stop her from dating you, I will try."

I smiled politely knowing that my anger was starting to rise from inside me, "Disrespectfully, Mr. Cassian, you have not been with Adrianna enough to know what's good for her. You don't care about your daughter, but I can assure you, I do."

His face turned stone, and it terrified me a bit, I smiled at the image behind him, Adrianna made her way down the stairs.

Even when we had uniforms on, she never failed to amaze everyone in school.

She looked beautiful.

Though her father does not agree with me looking at her like I was just meeting a goddess, she throws me a warm look.

"Good morning!" She ran past her father, running to my arms.

"Morning, Dove." I wink as her father eyes greeted me with anger and disapproval.

"Come home at a reasonable hour." He demands.

Adrianna looked like she was about to say something but doesn't, "No, I'm good."

I was so wrong about her. I was wrong about everything really. I didn't know anything about her.

She was the first person I ever really had mixed emotions for. I had studied her from afar, but I had misjudged her constantly.

From when she would sneak out of her house, just to feed the stray animals in the neighborhood, I would shake my head on the idea of why anyone would take time out of their day to just *help*.

But when she would read outside her yard, the cats would walks over and keep her company.

She was like an exiled princess in a castle, and I treated her as such.

But she was more than just a pretty face. She was more precious than anything the universe could offer.

I shake my head back to reality, walking her over to my car as her face fell, "I'm so sorry about my dad."

She mutters as I smile, "Now that I have you, no one is coming between us."

Adrianna smiles, looking at me like she was content.

At least I thought so, I never was right when I assumed her emotions but at this moment, we were just happy with each other's company.

"Game today?" She asks as I laugh, driving away from her house on the way to school.

"You actually plan on attending willingly?" I smirked at her.

She shoved me a bit, "No one or anything will ever come between me going to your game. Wouldn't want you to send someone to the emergency room again."

My jaw locks, "Oh?" She halts looking surprised, "Did I hit a nerve?"

I laugh, "Trust me, it depends on how the guys on the ice talk about you I'll keep defending your name even when you aren't there."

I looked over at Adrianna who had a warm smile, my body tensing as she moved closer to me, her hand on mine, "Does this mean no bodyguard will be following me?" She asks.

"Debatable subject."

"Not debatable!" She exclaims, "I paid him five hundred dollars because he helped me one with Brooks..."

I pause, slightly agitated, "What the hell did Brooks do?" I sounded protective. I, of course, didn't mean to sound like I would pound his face with my fist the moment I saw him.

"It doesn't matter."

I didn't want to pry, I could just beat it out of Brooks, I thought in my head. She would never agree with that response, since she believes that I always replied with violence.

I didn't feel like talking to a brick wall. I mean, how the hell did she even date him? He had about two personalities. Sure, he was a ladies man, girls are all over him, but there was nothing special.

Frankly I'm a bit insulted that she dated him. Brooks and I were different. I was rich, and he was a commoner. God forbid his family has asked my parents for loans.

He was a mediocre football player, and I was one of the best hockey players in the damn state. The stats show it. Yes, I could learn modesty, but I like it better when others know I was better than them.

I sigh, letting it go. But as I turn by the school I catch her gaze, "How do you feel, after..."

Adrianna's eyes widened, "I'm sore." She looks down, her face turning red. I parked on my spot; we were a bit early.

I unbuckled my seat belt looking over at her, "Did you enjoy it?" I asked her.

Never in my life have I asked a girl if they enjoyed my sex skills or had a good lay with me, girls would just text me telling me they wanted to see me again, but Adrianna was far different from them.

"I want you right now." She pulls my collar towards herself, gently kissing my lips as I let my hand cup her cheek, her hand gets tangled from my collar, her eyes widening.

Her face turned even redder than I thought was possible, "Oh my god, Grayson that's my purity ring."

I smirk, "I wouldn't call it a ring anymore."

I refer to the way it was dangling on my neck as a necklace, "You gave it to me, right?"

I meant it as literal and not, she laughs, "Yes I gave it to you to keep."

I interrupted her, "And this is me keeping it."

I grab her hand, kissing it. Her face turns to look at the large university. "This is such leverage." She laughs.

I tilt my head, "What do you mean?"

"You were my first, I don't have my virginity anymore." She sighs, "I'm nothing special to you."

"You're my girlfriend." I question as she looks at me with a serious expression.

"You don't mean that." She scoffs.

"Of course, I do. I want to keep seeing you."

"What makes you think I want to see you more than I already do?" She scowls at me.

I smirk, "Well you don't have a choice, you technically are still fake dating me, so you can either accept it or you can fight it, but

I'm warning you right now Dove." I look at her with seriousness, "You'll fall."

Adrianna shakes her head, "I don't like the word falling for us." She grins at herself, "More like drag."

I laugh, "Like dragging each other?"

Adrianna lifts herself up her lips and finds me once again, "I mean, in the future, even when we fight it, we will keep dragging each other in love."

I kissed her, and she kissed me back passionately. I couldn't get enough of her, her smells, her soft skin drove made me absolutely crazy.

The bell had rung which pulled her warm body away from mine, I groaned sadly, "Come on Prince, a day of school is awaiting."

She hops out of the car as I yawn, "I'm too tired to go to anywhere where you aren't all over me." He groans.

Adrianna shot me a look that could kill a dragon, I let my brows furrow rethinking my optimism about going to campus, "We still have time before our classes, I can meet you by the pit."

Looking pleased, she walks away, and I couldn't help but bend my neck over to walk her up the stairs, she looks back at me as I smile, yelling her name, "Dove!"

She looks back with her face concerned, I throw her my jacket, as she shows a broad smile, "My last name looks good on you!" I yell as she looks at my last name imprinted on the back of the jacket, she put over herself.

ADRIANNA

My face warmed as I ran up the stairs to my first class, checking in, I walked directly over to the snake pit, Margo, Verina, and Juliette sat with empty looks on their faces.

"Good morning!" I smiled as they gave me a look, "What's that look for?"

"You are to blame for our hangovers." Verina mutters.

I laugh, "You did that to yourselves, I didn't do anything."

Well, I did something, but they would soon find out, "Where did you even go?" Juliette yawns.

I look behind me as Grayson and his whole team walking up, "I was occupied."

"Occupied?" Margo's eyes narrow to mine.

She takes a look at my hand, seeing that my purity ring was no longer there, her face sunk with surprise.

"Oh my god!" She ran up to me, scooping me around, "Where is it?" She pats down Grayson's jacket, brushing over the fact that it was Grayson's jacket.

"You didn't." Verina's face drops as does Juliette's, "Who's the lucky guy?"

I roll my eyes, "That's what I wanted to tell you guys—" Margo interrupts me, "Is this Prince's jacket?"

I tried to speak again before Grayson and his friends were near our group. I roll my eyes, "Yo Margo, don't crowd her." Grayson sits on top of the table pulling me to sit on his lap.

I could feel his hands, gently on my waist, setting my whole body on fire. I wanted to melt on him.

"That's what I wanted to tell you guys." I muttered again.

Liam's face drops, "Is that Adrianna's ring?" I lift my hands, giving up as Grayson laughs at my irritation.

I look back at him with a scowl, "You want to test me too?"

His face turns serious looking at everyone else, "We have news."

Chris runs up from behind Liam, "I think I missed a chapter or two."

Juliette decides to add on, "We've all missed a chapter or two."

Margo grins, "I didn't."

I groan, "We have news!" I raised my voice as everyone went quiet, even people around us started growing annoyed, "News isn't for you, dip shits." I announce as Grayson laughs.

He bends down next to my ear, whispering, "I almost forgot how tyrannical you are at school." I turn to face him again, "Out of everyone here, I hope to God you don't think I will not flip my shit on you."

Grayson put his hands up in surrender as I rolled my eyes yet again, "Yes, Grayson and I slept together."

I outright said as everyone beamed.

"Yes, Adrianna and I will keep sleeping together." He adds on.

I shoot a look behind me, "Not if you keep this up."

"Are you guys dating, like actually dating?"

I waited for Grayson to answer but he didn't say anything, I shot him another look back, "Well?"

"You literally yelled at me about three times because I kept answering now when I don't answer I get yelled at too?"

I smile at him, "Welcome to a relationship, Prince."

"Wait so you two are in a relationship, like actually?" Verina jumps at the thought.

I sigh, "Well yes, we are."

"We are what you call boyfriend and girlfriend." Grayson adds.

I laugh, "Great job, babe."

"Babe?!" Liam gags, "This is our downfall, you two were each other's nemesis!"

Margo adds, "Are you telling me you two won't argue anymore?"

Neil laughs hysterically, "Now that they are dating, their arguments will skyrocket."

I could agree with that thought point of course, Grayson and I weren't who we were without our arguments.

"Personally, I saw this coming." Liam points out.

Everyone stares at him with a cutthroat expression. "Great job, Einstein."

Margo smiles, "Whenever we find ourselves in these types of conversations, I get reminded that God does have a sense of humor."

Liam flips Margo off as I laugh, "Oh, Margo, you just bring me so much joy when you leave my presence." Liam rebottles.

"I would slap you, but then I remembered that shit splatters!" Margo fires back as Liam gives her a look that could freeze hell.

"I often wonder what life would be like if you hadn't received enough oxygen during birth." Liam pulls down his middle finger as Margo scowls at him, viciously.

"Good thing you know what a middle finger is, you're the reason God fucking made it." Margo seethes as Liam's eyes narrowed.

I felt like they had gone on forever, but they didn't.

Grayson and I found it very entertaining to say the least.

"Can you two please stop? I think I'm losing my will to live just listening to you two go back and forth." Grayson mutters as everyone's head turns toward us.

"You're the one to talk, you and Adrianna never shut the hell up!"

"That's not true!" I defended as they clawed us like birds that were begging for food.

Maybe, it was true, but Grayson and I were just wired that way and obviously now things are different. I mean we don't need to hate everything that the other does. We could just breathe and relax.

Grayson kissed my head, "Speaking of the game, could you maybe pick up Amelia after school and let her sit with you at the rink, Dove?"

I smile, "Of course." I look around to Liam and Margo sending each other murderous looks.

"Margo, you want to come?" I ask as they both break eye contact looking at me.

"No, Ben and I are going out."

I smile at Verina and Juliette, "Yes, I can come but I'm studying for the final." Juliette points out, I nod.

"V?"

She doesn't hide her excitement, "Of course, Chris mind me coming?

Chris frowns, "Uh, you can do whatever you want. Finn will be there; he's been having problems with math, so I need to help him during water breaks."

I never really questioned Chris's personal family life, not that I ever needed to, or even think it was necessary. He was a person that no one could read in just under five seconds, he's been going through many things.

Verina's face drops as she takes a step closer, "Do you need her?" She offers as he smirks.

"Nothing you guys could help with I don't even remember the shit he's learning." He scratches the back of his neck.

"Oh okay." She sheepishly smiles as I thinned my lips, "I'm sure Juliette could help!"

I bump her by the shoulder as she jolts up, "I can?"

"Yes, of course you can, you love math."

"I do?" She questions.

Verina shoots up, "I can help, I promise I'll work really well." She beams, "I love math!"

We all claim the silence and embrace it, "You do?" The bell rings.

Grayson starts to get up walking over to his class, "I'll see you later." He winks as my face heats, bending down to kiss my cheek.

I watch as Grayson and his friends pull away from us, they all had Psychology before all of us, Margo runs up to me, her face beaming. "So how was the sex?"

Verina runs up as well as Juliette, "Yeah. Was it good? Is he good? Or did you enjoy it?"

I roll my eyes, "We are not about to talk about this on college property." I mutter as they roll their eyes in synchronization.

"I think that you enjoyed it. You have the sex glow." Verina jumps up beside me.

I smile, "Yes, of course I enjoyed it. He was perfect in bed; the rumors are true."

Thinking about the idea of Grayson and another girl in bed gives me an urge to throw up, but him being sexually active was known across the university.

Many girls like Kylie, Hannah, Madison, and Lizzy walked up to us, their eyes glazing and burning like they had a reason to be upset with me.

"Kylie." I addressed.

"Adrianna." She counters.

"Margo." Hannah makes notice as Margo smiles with a scornful look.

"Hannah."

"Liz." Verina throws a glare at her as she nods back, "Verina."

Juliette flips off Madison as she ignores her, "Heard you got laid." Kylie interrupts as my face changes.

"Where did you hear that?" Margo walks up closer to Kylie as she backs away, "It's a universal knowledge that your purity ring is no longer on your finger."

I smile, "Glad to know you have eyes."

Hannah walks up to me, her breath smelling like onions, I gag.

"We are just here to let you know that Kylie has called dibs on Grayson since freshman year. You do not get to have him."

I smiled at them, determining whether I wanted to resort to violence like Grayson would, but I decided against it. I wanted to stuff Hannah's face down a garbage shoot. But of course, I didn't.

"Are you in fifth grade?" Verina asked sincerely.

I laughed, "Grayson isn't a damn object, and he can pick who he wants."

Kylie smiles, "He'll pick me."

I stand, my heels clicking on the marble floors of the expensive school, "Let me tell you something sweetheart..." I say with conviction while walking up to her, "You can try and flirt with my boyfriend, but your parents are on the brink of bankruptcy. Trust me, I'm not the one you want to mess with if you still want to keep affording to come here."

Kylie's face morphed to a murderous gaze, "You two aren't dating."

I laugh, "Oh we aren't?" I look around, "Well when you see him, ask about my purity ring that's hanging around his neck, you won't like the response babe."

Kylie's hand shot up, slightly grazing my cheek before I caught it, "You crazy bitch." I whispered before pushing her hand away from me, her body falling on the floor.

"You look angry." I ask as Margo and Verina follow behind me, Lizzy and Hannah helping Kylie out as I yawn from boredom.

"You fucking pushed me!"

I let my eyebrows furrow, "You are fully aware that you had just tried to slap my face."

"You tempted me!" She pointed at me as I gave her a look.

"You can stay away from Grayson, because you calling dibs doesn't matter much now does it?" I tilt my head as she brushes off the dirt that was all over her white buttoned up shirt.

I walked up to her, pulling out a handkerchief and throwing it at her.

It had never occurred to me that the sudden uprising of the women that threw themselves to Grayson on a daily basis was out for my blood. They had every right to be upset, of course, since I never willingly thought about hooking up with Grayson and it becoming a permanent thing.

It wasn't a permanent thing, so other girls could of course still have a chance and I can watch the show from above. Since, I've been informed that committing suicide brings you straight to hell.

I was prepared to go to hell. I was prepared for everything I could just not to feel the ache in my body whenever I hadn't taken a Xanax.

My body shook like it was ready to break down My hands stilled like I couldn't move, and my brain felt like it was being pushed together by my skull changing size.

Instead of spiraling, I paused. I took a breath and went on with my day as eyes stared at me.

Being a Cassian meant that you always have eyes on you, but what shocked me to the core is the fact that sometimes, people's eyes are on you because they admire you and not because they pray for your downfall.

I love it when I defeat and conquer battles. Just because I'm weak internally doesn't mean I have to be on the outside.

CHAPTER 31

ADRIANNA

School had ended and I made a point of going to the mall after school since there was an hour and a half to spare before picking up Amelia. I dragged Verina with me while Juliette stayed behind at a random bookstore.

"What are we exactly doing here?" Verina questions as I give her a look.

"You're seriously questioning why we're here?" She glared at me.

Her eyes widen, "Well, not that I'm complaining about shopping, but there has to be a reason." She mutters placing her hand on her lips like she was on to me.

I smile, walking into Victoria Secret, her eyes widen as I hide my blushed face, "I only have so little of lingerie and since I am finally with someone that isn't ashamed of being with me, I want to make it special."

"Did he ask for you to do this?" She questions while walking over to the mannequin with a beautiful black lingerie set.

"No, of course not," I defended him while walking around casually touching some of the fabrics like silk and cotton.

"Grayson claims he knows me inside and out, and I want him

to not expect something from me, while I might not be sexually experienced as he is..." I take a breath.

"I want to wow him." I nod with confidence as she tilts her head with wonder.

Verina picks up a black thong, my eyes narrow to it, "So you want to seduce him is what you're saying."

"Yes." I sigh, "I don't want to look needy for sex, I just want him to want me."

She laughs, "No offense Anna, but that's the most absurd thing I have ever heard in my life, men are either gay or blind to look at you and not want you."

She looks at me, "My brother is gay, and he still thinks you're hotter than the Sahara Desert!"

My eyes settle on red, sheer stockings that clip to a set of a nice thong and laced see-through bras, my face heating as I envisioned it on my body.

I picked it up, wondering if it was in white as well. I planned on wowing Grayson the next time we have sex, that's if I was good enough the last time and he wasn't repelled away from me.

But he's made it clear that there was nothing I could possibly do to repel him away from me.

Verina winks, "That's definitely it." She eyes up the beautiful red lingerie that I was holding up.

She pauses for a moment, "What does he call you again?"

I roll my eyes, "Dove."

The burden of a nickname that I was sick of hearing, and yet I wouldn't wish it away.

She sighs looking round and tossing me a bra that was laced and had black stitches, "Oh, *Dove* you sure will have the ride of your life."

I laugh at the odd sureness of her jokes. Looking at the bra and placed it in my shopping bag along with a couple of different pieces that I decided that I wanted on my father's card.

As we arrive at the checkout, my eyes lay on Verina.

Verina yawns right before her eyes catch a glimpse of what seemed like none other than Christopher Florence working.

He was working at a cute restaurant across from the store, Verina's eyes shine as I laugh, "You actually like him, don't you?" I ask while the employee takes my items and scans them.

Verina groans, "He's so different."

"Different." I repeat slowly as she nods.

"He doesn't throw himself at me, damn it! No one has seen him with any type of girl!"

I smile, "Maybe he's playing the field, if you know what I mean."

Verina looks at Chris, "Trust me he's not gay." Her eyes were practically glued on him, "Anna if you see the way he looks at me, I know he wants me. I just don't know why he's shoving down his feelings!"

I pondered for a moment before letting out a small giggle, "Well, like you said, he's different."

I swipe my card looking back at Verina, "But in all seriousness V, I don't think that Chris is in a good state." I informed her.

She nods with a look of disappointment, "I just want him to know that he can rely on others." She pauses with a look of continuation of her sentence.

"That he can rely on *me*." She whines.

I pick up the bag being handed to me, walking out as Chris ends his shift running out then spotting us, his face contorting while he pauses, "Girls."

"Chris."

Verina looked concerned and maybe I was looking too into this, but Verina was never concerned for anyone else other than herself and occasionally her friends.

She had never given a second thought to anyone else but as she looked at Chris it looked like she was ready to drop everything in the world for him.

I wasn't going to lie and not think about how Chris looked like a complete mess.

But I wasn't about to tell him that I thought he looked like he hadn't had sleep in weeks, but it was true. He looked downright depressed and tired.

I felt bad, but I don't know what he was obviously going through, I knew it was something serious if he was losing sleep over it.

"Working?" Verina asks.

He looks at us plainly, "I was."

"Fired?" She asked without hesitation.

Chris' face contorted into a smile only meant for her before saying, "Nah, I have hockey."

I nod, "We are on our way over there!" Verina shoots out.

"We actually supposed to pick up Amelia in a couple of minutes," She informs as he nods.

He pauses before answering, "Yeah, Finn wouldn't shut up about her," He grins.

Before a moment of realization his eyes widen, "Shit!" He knocks his head back in annoyance, "I have to pick him up, if I'm late could you tell Grayson?"

Verina halts, "Nonsense! I'll take Finn, he goes to the same school as Amelia, right? Since we are on our way there to pick her up."

Chris looked hesitant, looking like he genuinely was thinking about it.

Verina smiled warmly, "I promise he'll be in great hands!"

Chris takes a breath of acceptance, "Yeah, okay I can't afford being late to the game against Blackwell University anyways."

"Finn isn't that talkative. He's very quiet. Please ask him if he has taken his medicine at the school nurse's office." He rambles.

And right before I think he's done he continues, "And with the math, tell him that I'm going to teach him tonight. I can't afford to lose play time. I might lose my spot on the team."

My brows furrow when he mentions Finn, he had never talked about his little brother, at least to me... I was a bit taken back.

Chris was someone that I never talked to unless I really needed to, it wasn't because I didn't like him, or that I didn't think he was worth talking to, I was always just so hesitant to speak to him.

He was known to be very quiet and kept to himself, Verina never really noticed him before which is partially why he is so hesitant to believe she has good intentions.

There was a spirit in him that I never was brave enough to look into. He always had a certain darkness in his eyes, and it wasn't the darkness that I would see in Grayson's.

Verina places her hand on his shoulder, "I've got this. I promise he'll be safe with me, and I can teach him the math." Chris's face expressed relief as he let out a breath, with a warm smile.

"Thanks, I appreciate this, I promise I'll repay you somehow—"

"—No repaying me!" She exclaims as he simpers.

"I will."

"If you really want to repay me, then I want you to play well during the game and get some good sleep." She suggests.

Chris laughs, shaking his head, "Verina—"

"If you don't get going, you might actually be late." She swats him aways as he stays still.

"Verina. Really, I appreciate this." He looks at her warmly for a moment.

All she could do was smile at him, "I know."

Without another word, he fled, running off to his car.

I look at Verina with a serious expression, "Ver—"

"I know." She interrupts.

"Do you really?"

Verina looks at me with a look I hadn't really seen on her before, "Anna, did you see his tired face?" She said thinly, "I want to help, and I can... I would do anything just to see him smile."

"I've only seen him smile maybe once or twice." She continues, "But when I do see him smile, I'm addicted, and I want to be the reason he does."

I was cautious of my friends; I didn't want them to get hurt. But I knew there was no stopping Verina from her pursuing him.

I always knew people's layers to be either black or white. The saying that "there is no gray" was wrong.

Chris was more gray than black. He had moments when he thought no one was watching and he truly looked at Verina.

Longingly. Like he thinks that having her was straight out of a dream and that there was a pull from him taking her. The worst part was that she wanted to be taken.

She was never a girl that fell easily, men would throw themselves at her, but she wouldn't bat an eye. The moment she realized that Chris couldn't care less, she dug her claws into him.

She craved that attention from men that didn't notice her, but did she notice for one second that maybe Chris couldn't afford to give his attention anywhere else?

I often wonder how much it would take for him to be selfish just this once. He looked like he was going to do whatever it took to fight it.

It was only a matter of time before she realized she loved him. Well, before he would ever let himself start to fall was the most exquisite way of self-destruction.

I picked up Amelia from her school.

Verina and I had separated since she took on the responsibility of taking Finn to the game.

Amelia sat in front, at the passenger seat next to me, staring closely when I finally addressed her staring, "You know your eyes might fall out if you keep staring at me like that." I gave her a very aware expression.

She smiles broadly, "I can't help it, you're so stinking pretty." I smile to myself, admiring her words to me.

She sure is Grayson Prince's sister, isn't she?

"Then I should be staring at you." I counter.

She looks away, "I want to look pretty like you."

"You are pretty like me, even prettier!" I accelerate on the gas; her eyes widen at the sudden speed.

She folds her arms together, "Well, how come the boy I like doesn't notice me?"

"I'm sure they do."

She looked joyful yet again, "I think you're right! I mean you and Grayson absolutely hated each other before falling in love."

I roll my eyes, "We are *not* in love."

"I said falling in love!" She exaggerates as I look at her with a playful expression.

"Grayson and I are a different type of situation, Amelia." I look away, "It wasn't always there," I pause as she leans closer for a better understanding.

"But?" She pleaded for an answer.

I laughed at her hopeless romantic face, "You are so nosey you know that?"

Her full attention to me, "You are the best thing that ever happened to Grayson. I never understood him. He was always grumpy, always out of the house, and hated being around us."

"Grayson loves you guys!" I smile genuinely.

She frowns, looking away "Maybe he doesn't feel like he's a part of the family." I pondered on the statement, Amelia looked bothered, "Since he's our half-brother and all."

My eyes widen as I hit the brakes quickly. I shot eye contact with her as her seatbelt locks to keep her on the seat, "Sorry, I thought there was a squirrel on the road." I say with a shaky voice.

She nods, my face obviously pale as I just swallowed.

Grayson never mentioned— I mean why would he? He didn't owe me an explanation. He looked way too much like his father to have a different one. Then again, he looked similar to his mother, or I guess, stepmother.

I don't know they all had blonde hair, blue eyes, and somehow very gifted genetics.

I take a breath out, "You know Grayson doesn't deal well with emotions, sweetheart." I try to defend him as she smiles warmly.

"But he's been different with you, he actually cares about you, and I know you care about him too." She voices as I nod, parking into my driveway.

"You know, I think you are the best thing that's ever happened to him." She folds her arms with a knowing look.

As she makes the comment, I one hundred percent choose to ignore it.

Amelia beams as I unbuckle her up, "You want me to do your hair before we go to the game?"

She jumps out of the car, "Heck yeah!"

I smile, as she looks at me with a challenging expression, she starts running until we both reach my bedroom, I push her on the bed as she laughs.

As we both got ready, I thought about what Amelia said about Grayson being her half-brother. His family never treated him differently I thought. Without Amelia disclosing this information I would've never guessed.

He's never talked about his real mother, was she dead? Was she involved in his life? I was curious and baffled.

I had put on Grayson's jersey to support him, as well as putting a Hawthorne hockey shirt on Amelia. I had her hair up on French braids, school colors on both of our cheeks. She even helped make a poster with his jersey number, *#22,* to cheer him on.

Amelia sat in front of me as I gathered the poster and my bag, "I have a question."

I look at her, giving her my full attention, "Yes?"

"You and Grayson hated each other. How did you guys get together then?"

I smile, pulling her closer, "You and these questions."

She laughs, "Come on!" She turned just to look at me.

I sigh, kneeling to look at her, "Have you ever seen a painting?"

She nods, as I smile, "Well I love to paint, and every insult your brother has ever given me I bottled up and painted in canvases that I have hidden, but I ripped them up into little pieces. I wish I was honest with myself because everything your brother told me about myself, I knew he was telling the truth."

I swallow, "He ripped my heart apart every time he told the truth. He hurt me, and I smiled through it, I pushed him back, and the recoil hit me like a hurricane. He was there to put me back together." I said thinly.

"Your brother might be a reason for my broken pieces, but he took his time to put me back together every single time, even when he wasn't the reason anymore."

She looked at me longingly, she was enthralled.

"I want someone like that." She makes a point as I squeezed her cheeks.

"You'll find someone when you're older but he's going to have to go through me."

She laughs, wrapping her arms around me.

I picked her up spinning around my room, she whispers in my ear, "You are the most beautiful art piece I've ever seen."

Amelia was precious and I loved her like my sister, nothing was going to change that, I just hoped she would forgive me when I left.

I sigh.

"Let's get to the game."

CHAPTER 32

GRAYSON

"Prince!" Liam screams my name from across the ice rink as I look towards him with a confused expression. Before I knew it, my hockey stick hit the puck that he passed to me.

It almost hit him across the face, but he didn't need to know it wasn't intentional.

"Where's Chris?" Neil asks as I turn to him.

"He said he was working and that he had to pick up Finn, why? You miss your boyfriend?" Liam smirks while skating over to me, pushing me over as I dragged him down with me.

I get up, watching Liam roll around in front of me, I offer him a hand to get up.

The loser he was, he took it, and I took the opportunity to push him over again. As he attempts to look at me, trying to flip me off, I laugh hysterically.

Even Neil couldn't help but laugh.

We hear the door open as we peak. Chris runs in with his uniform and skates on, skating over to us.

Liam began to try and get up before Chris decided to push him down yet again. I laughed even harder. "There you are."

He nods with acknowledgement and says, "I found someone

to take care of Finn." He mentions as we all give him our attention.

"Who?"

"Verina." He mutters as we all pause with wrinkled looks on our faces.

"Verina?" We all say it in unison.

He catches his words, "She insisted, and I couldn't say no; I can't afford to get kicked off the team by being late." He attempts at an excuse.

I knew Chris wouldn't take any favors from just anyone, he would really have to trust someone when it came to Finn.

"I would never turn you in." I said simply.

He looked irritated, "I don't want special treatment, Prince."

I roll my eyes. "You raise your brother, you work three jobs, you go to the smart-ass school we go to, you're a starter on the hockey team, and you fucking have a fight tonight."

Chris goes silent. "Besides, I trust Verina."

Bingo. *No getting close to her my ass.*

"No reason not to trust her." Neil adds in as more players turn up, walking straight to the locker room, knocking my head back.

"Which is why Finn is with her." He says with attitude as Neil looked taken back by the sass from his fellow best friend.

Neil rolls his eyes, changing the subject, "Blackwell is tough. They better have brought their A-game."

Chris looks at the players, he was always good at reading body language, "They did." He gestures at the other team.

Liam skates around me, "No nearly killing someone, today, Prince." He winked as it took courage not to whack him with my hockey stick.

But he pauses, "Wait."

I look around my body, "What's that?" Liam signals to my hockey stick, catching something different.

I had realized that many players had a lucky charm on them every game they've ever played, and it seemed I hadn't. I wanted to change that and what else to use other than one of the people that did change me.

I had written Adrianna's initials with a sharpie on my stick handle, and additionally on the taped blade. I hadn't told her, obviously.

"Adrianna's initials in sharpie." I say with ease as Liam smirks.

"I thought she was just a ploy to get August back?" Chris adds on, as I sigh.

My eyes snapped on his, "And I thought you would never get close to Verina, now she's giving your brother rides?"

Chris backs off, with his hands up in the air as a sign of defeat.

Of course, I saw the teasing coming from them, I would be stupid if I hadn't. A part of me did not consider that if I did get August back, how different things would have gone.

"What can I say?" I look down at the ink, "My girl gives me good luck."

Liam's face turned pleased as he looked at Neil, "You owe me a million dollars." Neil looked at me in annoyance.

"That's so shitty." Neil says as I scowl at him.

"Sorry dude, I'm happy for you but you just made me lose a million dollars."

Neil looked like he just lost a penny. I couldn't help but smile at the fact that Neil was wrong. I wanted to fucking scream from the rooftops that she was my girl.

As my teammates started to gather on the ice, skating laps, a mixture of families and fans started to fill the seats.

I had once again reserved seats for my family and Adrianna, now of course for her sake she better fucking come and sit her ass on one of those chairs or I will shot a puck straight to the damn head of the opposing team captain.

But to my mistake she walks right in with Amelia by her. She had her hair in a messy bun. She was wearing a pair of ripped jeans, with a pair of heels, and the best part about her outfit was my name on her back, she was wearing my hockey jersey.

Amelia had her hair in braids, she had the college-colored

tassels holding them to keep the braids. My family comes right behind them, my stepmother greeting her with a kiss on the cheek.

My father looked the same as usual, he was in his suit and his phone was attached to his ear making business proposals. Amelia held signs, one with my name on it, and one with the whole team's.

I look back at Liam who was going on about his leg feeling swollen.

"You might need to get that checked out." I mention.

"Nah, coach might not let me play. I need to play this game." He made a point.

I skated towards him, "I will not let you play if you are genuinely injured."

Liam pats my back, "I'm fine."

I nod.

I had a weird and unsettling feeling of Liam playing tonight and I wasn't sure if I wanted to be his friend at this very moment or be his captain.

I wasn't sure if it was a choice that I dared to make.

It's the third period.

    We are losing.

    0-1.

My face contorted in pain as Caleb Greenwood rams his body into my torso. I ram him back, but his teammate strikes me.

Liam, of course, skates over to push the guy off me. But to our concern, another guy felt the need to run straight into Liam cross checking him as well, causing him to slam against the hard ice and the guy's body weight rushing him.

The rink went silent as Liam screamed in agony, Chris and

Neil following with anger and rage in their eyes looking for a fight.

The referees pulled them away as I was not restrained. I skated full speed on the opposing team causing them to fall and slam into the boards.

I looked at the crowd, and Adrianna's lost expression on what was going on, and I myself was not sure what really happened.

Medics come to place Liam on a stretcher pulling him out. I skate over to him.

"I shouldn't have let you fucking play." I blamed myself as Liam laughs off the pain.

The crowd got louder, looking back at Chris hooking Holden Kelson. "It's better to be me than anyone else on the team, Prince." He voices.

I shake my head, disagreeing.

"Chris loves this game." He grits out.

"You love it too." I counter as he shakes his head.

Liam continues "Chris loves it, it's the last thing going for him."

I try to speak as he interrupts me, "Neil does it to get away from his parents and fuck— "

Liam doesn't let me get another word in, "This is your whole life if your family doesn't rip it away from you."

"I don't want you doing shit on the ice once you get taken care of." I say sternly as he grins like a Cheshire cat.

"I'm fucking serious."

He shakes his head, "Coach wouldn't let me anyways."

"Is Margo here?" He asks with a simple smile as I look around.

"No, I don't think so, Brookshire."

He shakes his head, laying back down, "With her fiancé, isn't she?"

"I'm not sure."

He sighs, "You don't have to lie to me."

The referee drops the puck on the ice, looking at me warning me to get ready once again. Liam laughs, "I lost my girl."

I tilt my head, "You said you weren't serious with her."

"I was also smoking when I said that, and I was stupid." He lets out.

"Now, she's getting married after graduation and she'll never speak to me again."

"Margo isn't important right now." I said quickly as he rolled his eyes.

Liam looked behind me, "Look at your girl." He gestured over to Adrianna. I try not to move my eyes from the puck and ice.

I hear yells, my eyes find hers, with a bright smile and about six additional posters. She cheers for me.

The medics pull Liam away as he waves me off, the referee losing patience whistling for me to gather in the middle.

I skated over, couldn't help but point my hockey stick at her. "This is for you!" I scream.

Her cheeks are red.

We start the game as the referee drops the puck. The sound of my teammates getting slammed against the boards. I retrieved the puck skating as fast as I could through their defense, yells, and cheers from our side of the rink. My skates dig and slide on the ice with my body and energy releasing as I skate through the defense slamming two of their teammates together. The other players looked terrified of me, the news about Alex Twain's injury has not gone unnoticed.

I take a slap at the goal, the puck passing everybody within two seconds it hits the back of the net. The goal horn goes off, my eyes seeking out Adrianna who was screaming my name. My teammates skated over to me jumping on me and hugging me.

We tied the game as Chris got released out of the box, he skated towards me with a large smile.

Forty-seven seconds left in the game. I wasn't sure if we could make it.

Everyone gathered straight to the center, ready for the next play, Coach Livingston screaming at the team that we could make it.

Chuck skates towards the side and then moves around to look for me. Neil blocked the defenseman who tried to charge.

His movement was choreographed like a dance. He was fast but controlled, I remember when I trained him in his freshman year.

Twenty-one seconds left.

He flashes a smile towards me as he approaches the net. I pass the puck to Andrew, as he passes it straight to Chris who was great with his stick, confusing many other players before he quickly passes it back over to me.

I skate over to the goal line, finding him in the middle, I brush past the defense, passing it to him, before he makes a saucy goal.

The goal horn went off again as I took a breather.

The time runs out as the whole team skates over to us.

2-1.

I couldn't help but look for Adrianna. With a smile on my face, I skated outside the rink, walking towards her, she wraps her arms around me. She seemed to be unsure if we wanted to go absolutely public.

It wasn't for show. It was for us.

I fixed her dilemma, by pulling my helmet off of my head and bending down to kiss her. She puts her hands on either side of my face, it was as if everyone disappeared the moment our lips touched.

I've never gotten lost in a kiss, and I've never understood that saying. Now I understand as my heart skips a beat when she pulls away, I smile.

"You came." I say plainly.

She rolls her eyes playfully, "You are never going to let that go, are you?"

"Never."

A moment of silence falls between us. My smile widens as I took a good look at her, she grimaces, "Take a picture, it would last longer."

I laugh, I didn't care whether it was obvious that I liked looking at her, "And you say I'm the one with the big ego."

"That's because you do." She stresses, matter of a factly.

"You won though which should boost your ego even more!" She exclaimed as I looked at her again.

"Of course, I won." I say with pride, "I had to, I mean I dedicated one goal to you."

Adrianna's face yet again reddens as she pulls me in for the second time, "You are so sweaty."

"Yes, well, skating around for a duration of time will do that to you."

"It's disgusting." She whispers.

I laugh, "You're still hugging me." I whisper.

She hugs me tighter, whispering back, "I know."

CHAPTER 33

ADRIANNA

ne month later.

Officially dating Grayson Prince has been the best ticking time bomb of my life. The eye contact from across a crowded room. The devilish smirk that I grew to love as the month came along. The intimacy of our knowing glances while he was on the ice.

The raised eyebrow and the hysterical laughs when we make stupid jokes because of our complicated banter.

The late-night drives, or when he would pull me down just to sit on his lap whenever a random man approached me at a bar. Our playful teasing, his reserved seat for me at the rink. Falling asleep on his couch with Amelia.

Our nighttime swims out on the lake, he would write me notes and slip them in my notebooks for me to read before my last class.

Grayson Prince has brought me back to life more than any type of drug or proper medication ever has.

I hadn't taken any unprescribed drugs in a month and, I've been regular in taking the medication I need.

I had been attending my therapy normally and helping out Mrs. Prince with the family shelters, donating a gracious amount every Tuesday I came. I had started to paint again, and I've realized that the shelter was a great place to paint.

The families surprised me with a free space with an easel where I can paint any time I desire. It was located in front of the garden, giving me a view of the children playing.

Grayson's stepmother even gifted Margo, Verina, Juliette, and I crochet lessons when they came to see where I went every Tuesday. I had planned to surprise Grayson with a sweater that I tried to make.

Sure, it wasn't perfect, but it was a sweater.

The least I can do since he has provided me with the *best-mind-blowing* sex ever.

It is eight P.M. and I'm at his house, his family was out for dinner, and he couldn't attend because he had hockey practice.

It was surreal to me that I spent more time at his house than mine. My father sent me continuous messages and calls that I continued to ignore.

If all he had to say to me was that I shouldn't be with Grayson, then I didn't need to hear it. He didn't have anything important to say to me.

Grayson's head rested on my lap as I watched *Love Island*. He caved and watched the show with me, of course, I had to watch *Tom and Jerry* with him because it was only fair, he declared.

We found a happy middle, watching *The Harry Potter* movies every time we see fit.

"Why the hell would he do that?!" He yells at the screen.

I roll my eyes, "You know you have to study the plays, right?" I look down at him.

He sits up, "I did memorize some of the plays."

I nod, turning off the television.

"Here, I made something for you!" I launch myself out of the comfortable seat, grabbing the box I placed in the storage room of his house a while ago.

I hand it to him sitting on the floor, hugging my legs towards myself, staring at his eager eyes, "What is it?"

"Why don't you find out?"

"Why did you get me something? It's not my birthday."

I roll my eyes, "That doesn't matter!"

He laughs, obviously I caught on that he only kept talking so that I would get irritated, he opens the box, revealing the hard worked sweater that I had crochet him.

"I made it for you."

He tilts his head, picking it up, "It looks warm."

"You hate it." I get up pulling it away from him and hiding it behind me, "You don't like it."

He laughs, pulling the sweater away from me, "It has my name embroidered on the sleeve."

He looks at me with a grin, "So you would always be on my sleeve?"

I laugh, "Exactly!"

Grayson laughs, attempting to put it on, the sweater stretches, as he put it on. Sure, I hadn't considered measuring Grayson's large muscles when I had begun with this project.

The moment he attempted to breathe out, the back of the sweater rips as I groan.

"I love it!" He exclaims.

I bury my face in my hands, "I worked on that for a month."

Grayson takes it off smiling, "Darling, it's beautiful." He assured as I scowled at him, "Thank you." I sigh as he places the sweater back in the box.

"Grayson." I said with unsureness as he turned to look at me.

"Dove." His lips curving into a golden smile, giving me a small peck, "I love it."

I roll my eyes at him as his grip tightens on me, "Did you just roll your eyes at me?" He asked as I felt my blood pump faster.

Yes, I may possibly have but I stayed silent, feeling the anticipation of him as my body reacts to his. Grayson took a moment to look around the room, it was empty.

He wasn't looking at me, he was casually drinking out of a whiskey glass that he had pulled out earlier. His other hand moved from my waist to my waist band. "Did you just roll your eyes at me?" He asks again as I bit my lips together.

I pursed my lips and gave a small nod; indeed, I looked away quickly as his hand came down my thigh, finally putting the glass down, his touch was full of need but gentle.

His fingers danced like ghosts around my skin as I let out a breath, his fingers finding my zipper, pulling.

My skirt falls down, as his fingers press down even harder on my side. I moan, creating goosebumps all over my body I felt heat rise.

Grayson laughs, "What did I tell you about rolling your eyes?" His hand nearing the insides of my thighs, stroking, his finger lifts higher.

I couldn't help but let my fingers grip his wrist, withering I felt like I was in heaven.

"That I should never do it." I whisper as he bends down to my ear. Oh God... his fingers slipped in the middle of my thighs, feeling his fingers flex to spread me wide.

He was going to—

I bit back my next moan, Grayson's eyes directly over to my throat, throbbing and full of lust. "Don't moan." He whispers while pressing his body on mine, "Hold it in," He continues.

I bit my lip, trying not to swallow and groan. I wanted to moan in his ear badly, his fingers found their way to the apex of my thighs. I held my breath, my heartbeat thumping so fast that it was going to jump out of my body.

I felt Grayson's mouth curve into a smirk as my heartbeat reached my ears, his finger ripping my thong, and on to my pussy.

Oh fuck... Grayson Prince...

I clamp my legs together as his fingers pressed my clit, making me jump. His other fingers find their way to my outer lips, his middle finger circling my clit. I couldn't breathe.

I knock my head back, still holding his wrist as on as his fingers enter me, his thumb stroking my clit.

Pulling out his finger and slamming it back in again made my eyes roll to the back of my head. The next time he pulled out, he added in an additional finger making me close my eyes from the sensation.

"This is the type of eye rolling I want from you." He bites my lobe finally making me moan, "I want you, Adrianna." He said with a need. His eyes on mine, "The feel of your pussy around my dick." I wanted to buck my hips closer to him, fuck I really wanted to.

"Moan, Dove." He groans as I moan, "Good girl, I want to hear you want it baby, I want you to moan my name when I fuck you." He pulls me closer, walking me over to the kitchen.

I breath out. His fingers slamming back again as I groan, gripping his wrist tight. He bends me over the kitchen counter. I feel him level his mouth with my mound.

His breathing labored as I gripped the cold, marble, countertop. He rasps, diving in with his tongue flicking against my clit, making me moan and jolt. Grayson sucked my outer lips, making me bite back a moan. His finger, however, pressed harder onto my clit.

I moan, "That's it, Dove." His fingers fucked me deeper, stronger and with his arm barely moving. He kisses my ass cheek. I couldn't come up with any words, only incoherent moans, "I love how wet you get for me, Dove." He laughs as I spread my legs wider, desperate for release.

I shudder slightly, my body pushing towards him for more friction, "Atta girl." I gulped, his tongue once again on my clit, "So wet baby, gripping me like a damn vice." He whispers in my ear as I bite back a moan.

I shudder slightly shudder, my body feeling closer to release but keeping my breathing controlled, "Good girl." He rasps, praising me.

His lips reach my neck, "I think you deserve a reward for your breathing control." Before I could process what, he said, he moved his fingers inside me, twisting and crooked. I jump, feeling a slight pull on my belly bottom.

I felt flutters in my stomach, his voice low, "That's it Dove. Fuck, I can feel you want to come all over my fingers." He says erratically, I felt like I was trying to catch my heartbeat.

"Can you do that for me, darling?"

I closed my eyes, taking a second to myself to calm down, my hand on my thigh, the other gripping his shirt, I couldn't help knocking my head back, my hand on his erection.

I give him a small squeeze as he continued to pump his fingers into me, flicking my clit, making me shudder as I start to reach my climax. I groan, my body tightening needing to come, needing him to keep going and help me get there.

I begin to moan again as I shut my lips he whispers, "Keep quiet baby." My thighs begin to shake, searching for friction, bucking my hips while angling my body better.

I was close... so close...

"You are doing so good baby," He rubs my clit, "You're almost their baby, come on." He said with a strained voice, my hands still rubbing his cock, causing him to shiver.

"*Oh fuck.*"

I felt myself tighten around his fingers and my thighs began to shake, trying to keep my body still and taking my breath away having the best orgasm of my life.

"Fuck, that's it darling." His fingers slowing around my clit.

I turn around looking at him, his face showed happiness I smile, pushing him to the living room, down on the couch, "You are amazing."

Grayson smirks, "You are fucking perfect." He muttered, I grin, straddling his hips, bending down, and crushing my lips on his while gripping his shirt towards me.

It was like I wanted him to be a part of me, in my fucking bloodstream. Grayson's hands find my hair, he whimpers under my touch, "You said you hate my perfects." I whispered against his lips with a smile.

"I do remember being right about one thing, you are invigorating." He looked pleased.

I begin to sink down to his waist, kissing his tight abs, his head knocking back I let my lips travel to his v line.

He never let go of my hair, only loosened his grip.

I look up at him, his eyes longing, "I've never done this before." I say in a simple whisper as he showed of his dimples by smiling down at me, he brings my face back up to his, placing a kiss on my lips.

"You don't have to do it yet, Dove."

I swallow. I wanted to do this for him. He was perfect and being with him for a little more than a month was the happiest I've ever felt in my lifetime. He hadn't forced me to do anything that I didn't want or wasn't prepared for. He's only made me feel great and I felt like I needed to repay him.

"No." I spoke, "I want to do this for you." I began to travel down to his waist once again, we heard the door lock shake as I bolted up.

"*Fuck.*" He quickly mutters, pulling me up next to him, draping a blanket over his hard rock erection I laugh.

I quickly turn on the television cuddling up on Grayson placing my hand under the blanket his face contorts as I smile, "That's not funny. They always come in such a bad time."

His family walks in with smiling faces, "Good evening, love birds," His stepmother, Sara smiles warmly, "You guys have a great night?"

Amelia, Bentley, Elliot, and Easton ran after their mother, I found myself often wondering whether Grayson did in fact feel as though he isn't part of the family.

"Adrianna!" Amelia runs over to Grayson and me, jumping on top of the couch and laying on top of Grayson and me.

"You're more excited to see her than me?" Grayson drops his jaw, his eyes widen.

"Yes. Well, you live twenty feet across my room." She sneered as Grayson gave a nonchalant expression.

Grayson gets up from the couch, walking over to his brothers, who smile at him, "How's the dating life?" His brother Bentley asks.

I tilt my head, "Don't even try to eavesdrop. They're stupid and everything they talk about is completely nonsense."

I look at Amelia with a smile, "Maybe because what they talk about doesn't relate to a nine-year-old." She places her head on my shoulder.

"I bet what they talk about isn't appealing to twenty-year-old girls." Sara walks over to us, sitting next to me.

Silas walks in after everyone else, his phone against his ear yelling, "Get the damn paperwork signed damn it!" He acknowledges me with scowl.

I sigh, "Will he ever talk to me without a negative comment?"

Sara frowns handing me the cake, "Silas is a really complex man. He wants the best for his family, and our families have always had tension between them that has never been solved."

I read the ingredients as I frown, "I'm so sorry Mrs. Prince, but I'm allergic to kiwi."

She nods understandingly.

"You know... Silas and your father used to be the best of friends. They would conquer the business world by the throat, and no one ever questioned their loyal friendship."

"What really happened?" I asked, quite shocked.

"I'm not really sure, all I know is that it's never been resolved, only got worst and they just stopped contact, where they only make snood remarks about each other whether it is by newspaper and in person."

I nodded, I had never seen my father make decent conversation with anyone, but then again, I have never really seen my father much.

I smile, "About that dinner that never happened." I mention as she nods, "My father was quite busy and I couldn't ask him, but I believe that he hasn't had much work right now."

"Perfect! I'll set up a dinner tomorrow?" She claps, her

husband walking out with a false expression, walking over to Grayson.

I look closely at Grayson, whose face turns annoyed and quite irritated at his conversation with his father. I guess that his father always put him on a pedestal and never once thought about Grayson as his own person.

Sara stands, "Adrianna and her father will be coming over for dinner tomorrow, I expect everyone to be there."

Silas looks over to us with a disgusted face, "I have work."

"You can work from home." She grins at him. He begins to speak before she gives him a look that could kill, he quiets down quickly.

I stand, slowly pulling Amelia in a comfortable position as she slept, walking over to Grayson and his father.

Grayson pauses his conversation with his father, "I'm going to head home." I mutter.

He takes his jacket, "I'll take you home, I don't want you walking by yourself."

"Okay." I smile.

His father looks at me with yet another scowl, "Do you notice that me and my son were having a private conversation?" He says angry, I jolt backwards a bit.

Grayson walks in between us, "Don't talk to my girlfriend like that ever again."

I pull Grayson back, "I didn't mean to interrupt."

Grayson's father rolls his eyes, "We will finish this conversation the moment you get back."

Grayson shrugs off his father as he places his hand on my lower back walking me to the door. He tends to place his hand there on a regular basis now, I hadn't noticed until recently.

"Grayson, you don't have to take me home. Your father and you were having an important conversation. I really didn't mean to interrupt."

"Adrianna, my father, and I only have important conversations. You did not interrupt anything and it's not like my father is upset that you cut his business talk with his least favorite child."

I nod, as he walks me over to my house, "I want him to like me." I mutter.

"I'd be more concerned if my father does like you."

I laugh as Grayson takes a breath, "Are you sure you want our fathers to actually have dinner together?"

I nod, "Yes, and besides I've been figuring out a way to piss off my father and this is the perfect way of doing so. I want him to know that you and I are serious."

Grayson agrees with hesitation, "Is everything okay?" I ask as we reach my front door.

He grins thinly, "Yes, of course, I'll see you tomorrow?"

I get on my tippy toes placing a kiss on his lips, "I hope so."

"I can't wait." I smile as he winks.

"We have forever yet, Dove."

As I walk inside, closing the door, my heart sinks for a moment. I was always great at taking my feelings and bottling it up. In a conflict between what your heart wants versus was your brain wants. You follow your heart.

We have forever yet.

I wasn't strong.

When I looked at Grayson, I felt like my mind was at peace and I couldn't hear the screams in my head. I didn't want to need him. But the moment I was alone with myself, it was suffocating. I couldn't move. I couldn't breathe. I couldn't talk, and my heart stopped.

He restores me to balance. The moments I spent with him oxygen fills my lungs, my heart stops and butterflies flutter inside my stomach, my eyes on his every time to see if he was real.

I wanted him and I think I always will. Even when it kills me to think that our time was limited. It wasn't supposed to be serious, and I cursed myself because I was going to hurt him.

It was killing me.

My body sunk down to the floor. My hands fell on my chest

as I heaved. My hands gripped on the necklace that Grayson had bought me with his initials on it. My heart began racing and my body shook as tears fell down my cheeks. I looked up to see my father staring down at me, I wasn't really sure what to do and neither was he.

A moment passed before he sunk down next to me, his arm wrapping behind me as I let out sobs, "It's okay baby."

I felt guilty despising him for the past months, "I'm so sorry." He shushes me as I lay my head on his shoulder, the same endearment that Amelia had done earlier.

"Don't be sorry, I'm sorry." He whispers as I cried a bit harder. I close my eyes, not really sure if this would turn into a dream. All I knew was that I needed it to be real.

The screams inside my head louder than ever.

I opened my eyes to see no one was next to me. No one was around me. The lights were off, and my house was quiet. I close my eyes feeling my heart breaking a bit more, tears falling on the ground.

I sat there, unable to move, couldn't sleep, and cried a bit harder that night.

CHAPTER 34

GRAYSON

I didn't go home after dropping Adrianna off.
Instead, I took my car and drove over to my mother's house. When I arrived, my mother opened the door. She was hammered. I had noticed that every Tuesday, Adrianna was out so I took the moment to visit my mother and make sure she took her medication.

"Nicholas!" She yells, throwing her arms up with a bottle of Vodka spilling everywhere. I walk in seeing the place a complete mess, I take a breath.

"Where the hell did you get the fucking alcohol?" I pulled it away from her opening up all the cabinets, seeing the shelves that I had emptied to be filled with nothing but booze.

I close my eyes, "Where's the money I gave you last week?"

"I'm glad you're here!" She smiled, but it was a nasty grin, like she was going ballistic.

"I need more." She adds.

I look at the table as cocaine filled the cold counter tops in the kitchen.

I cursed to myself before I scream at my mother, "Mother, where is the money I gave you last week?" I asked politely.

She laughs manically, "You're holding it and looking at the rest of it." She gestures to the cocaine and the bottles of alcohol.

I knock my head forward, "I'm cutting you off," Her body freezes, "I'm not paying you fucking anything. You are not staying here anymore, and you will not come to my family's house for money." I state as her face turned red.

"Oh, so *my family*." She says plainly, "You forget you aren't apart of their family!" She ends up screaming.

"I'm not having this conversation with you," I take a breath to calm myself, "I just came to tell you, you better be out of this house by Friday, or I will make sure you are out." She begins to cry as I roll my tongue in my mouth.

I felt guilty for doing this to my mother, but she wasn't helping herself at all. "What's changed since last week where you just gave me money?" She questions.

I shake my head, "Father found out and he forbade it."

"I never thought you were the following type." She mutters.

"I want you out of the house by Friday."

My mother was capable of terrible things, she wasn't the type to give up, and wasn't the type to make any rational decisions.

"Who was the girl at your game?" She asked.

I holt as I turned to look at her intently. "Don't speak about her." My blood pressure rose as she smiled devilishly.

"Oh, but I would love to speak about my son's love life." She sits on a stool.

I swallow, "She doesn't concern you."

"You concern me." She ponders, her eyes staring.

"Grayson, I hope you remember the type of woman I am and that I will always get whatever I want, whether it hurts others or not. I will go to those lengths." She makes a point as I breath out.

"Do not underestimate me." She continues, "She sounds like a wonderful girl. Very pretty and gentle, but a bold woman, I understand why you have come to liking her. But you should know that women like that don't end up with men like you."

I look down, "They want nothing but the best for themselves, and you Grayson... are nothing but a man who does as he is told, your father has you wrapped around his finger."

"Adrianna is too good for you." She smiles, "If you are too stubborn to believe that she is holding you back to being the man you used to be, I will make sure that she is no longer part of your life."

I slam my palm on the table, making a loud noise, her body jolts as I walk closer, "Are you threatening me?" My body stiff at the thought of any harm that comes to Adrianna has made me lose my damn mind.

"I'm promising you." She stands, "The moment I step out of those doors, is the moment that you will forever worry about her safety."

I pull her back, "If you fucking hurt her, you will be living in jail, and I will make sure you rot in there." I grip her tighter, "I promise you that."

My mother only smiles cracks a small grin back, "I want you to end your sad relationship with her and I will leave, and rest assured that she will not be harmed."

I let her go, "Don't fucking think about coming near her."

he next day.
I had ignored Adrianna all morning, asking Liam to pick her up, I had gone straight to class not meeting in the pit with her I couldn't speak to her after my conversation with my mother last night.

I had felt paranoid, and I didn't want her to get hurt, instead I fucking ignored her. Hell, I even left school early to shoot some pucks in the net before practice.

I even ignored her texts and phone calls; she knew something was wrong. As I skate around the rink, working on some slap shots I hear the door open, August coming in with a frowning face.

"Hey." She asks as I skate towards her, taking off my helmet.

"August." I counter.

She walks over to me, "Didn't see you the rest of school."

I laugh shooting another puck in, "Didn't know you were looking."

"Of course, I am. I care about you, Grayson." She walked up to me, and my heart hurt a bit more.

"Didn't notice." Her hand reaches for mine as she looks down to see Adrianna's initials on my stick she pulls away.

"You never did that when you were with me."

I stayed silent.

August stares, "In the beginning, I thought that you two were only together because you wanted to make me jealous." She swallows, a tear falling down her cheek.

She was correct, of course, but I wasn't about to tell her. "But you really do love her."

"I loved you." I let out as she took a step back, "I loved you and I asked for you back."

"I know." She begins.

I interrupt her, "August you—"

"I want you back Grayson. Call me crazy but I want you back. You've changed. You can handle a real relationship and I want you back. I promise I will never hurt you ever again like I did before."

I was stunned to say the least. "I'm dating Adrianna."

"You don't really want her. You and I have history you and I are meant to happen." She pleads, "I told you that I was going to give you a second chance and I'm handling it to you on a silver platter."

"August, Adrianna makes me really happy." I interrupted her.

Her chest heaves, "I made you really happy too."

"It's different."

"How?"

I couldn't answer the question. I wasn't really sure how to, I always knew the original plan was to get August back and she was back. She wanted me back and it was what I've wanted for a long time.

"I'm asking you to please take me back." She walked closer, her hand on my cheek and I couldn't move. "I know I'm not going to get one hundred percent of you but I'm only asking for fifty right now."

I sigh, "I'll think about it." I mutter. "But I'm not promising anything."

August's face beamed with happiness, leaning close to peck a kiss on my lips, she came in for a longer one as I pulled away, "I'll call you."

She nods, walking away from me. I ran my hands through my hair, throwing my stick to the ground hard, looking up to see Margo staring at me.

I look down once more, as she walks up to me slapping my face hard. I placed my hand on the stinging part of my cheek with shock.

"You dick."

"Margo—," I began as she gave me an irritated look.

She interrupts me, "Adrianna does not need this right now." She says with a tired expression, "She *cannot* afford this right now."

I failed to understand what she was putting down on the table for me, "August and I were just talking, and she kissed me. Nothing is going to happen." I muttered as she gave me a look that told me that she knew I was rambling.

"No." She says, "I want you to think about who you want Grayson."

"Adrianna."

"No. I want you to think about who you want because she does not need to cry over someone who was never hers to begin with. Who does she get to blame when she broke her own heart trusting you?"

I stood, my head and heart full and empty at the same time,

"You look at Adrianna like she's your world and I want to know if it's fake because you can't fake something like that!"

"She is my *everything*."

"Then what are you doing here with August, letting her kiss you and telling her you will think about getting back together with her?"

"It's hard to explain!" I stress, "I don't know if I'm the type of man that Adrianna needs," I let out, "I'm still trying to figure things out for myself, everyone in my damn life seems to want me and her away from each other."

"Do you?" She asks, pure question in her eyes.

"I don't know."

"Then end things with her and stay the fuck away from her." Margo snaps.

I bit my lips together, "Margo."

Margo whips her head back to look at me, "You know the worst part is I thought that you were good for her. I fucking vouched for you to be the one thing in her life that made her want to— "

She cuts off as I swallow.

It was all too much. My psycho mother wanted Adrianna and me to spilt or else she would get hurt. My father hated her and wanted me to end it as well. August coming back to me like I've always wanted.

I always fantasized about having Adrianna the way that I do now, and a part of me feels like I'm still dreaming. Only now, I never thought that I would've wanted her as much as I do now.

I had to do what I thought was right.

"Grayson, I want you to really think about this," She asks as I nod, "If you end up choosing August, I will make sure you never speak to Adrianna ever again."

I nod again. My heart thumping out of control.

"Adrianna is who I want, and August is nothing to me."

L ater that day.
        My family had set up the dinner and we were all
        ready. My father put on a damn suit. I also put one on for
the satisfaction of my mother's happiness.

My sister was in a dress, while my brothers dressed in suits as
well. My mother wanted this to be perfect as she put the
extremely expensive China.

I hear the doorbell ring, opening to see Adrianna looking
lavish and desirable. Her father next to her looking like a stone-
cold vampire.

She beams when she looks at me, with full smiles on her face
she walks up to me, I bend down to kiss her gently.

I paused for a moment remembering Margo and I's conversation about me letting her go, and it was an option I wasn't going
to take lightly.

"You've been ignoring my texts and calls, are you okay?" She
looked at me, of course, she was understanding. She didn't yell,
she didn't curse, she simply wanted to see if I was okay.

"I was just busy, I got sick, and I didn't have it in my system to
go to class." I answer.

She nods, "Oh, well are you better now?"

"Much." I reassured her. Our fathers shake hands as I place
my hand on her lower back, directing her to her seat. Her father
had sat on the other end of the table.

"Grayson, what are your plans for the future?" Her father asks
as everyone settles down to sit together, the housekeeper brings in
food as Adrianna looks down at her dish and scowls.

"Do you not like the food?" I whisper.

She looks up, "No, I'm just not hungry right now." She
answered.

I nod looking at her father, "I'm sorry?"

"Grayson, he is asking what you have planned for your future." My stepmother repeats.

I look at Damon Cassian, "I really enjoy hockey, maybe go pro." I let out.

My father interrupts, "Of course, he isn't sure as he would also like to take on the family business."

Adrianna gives me a wary look, "But you should see him play father. He's a natural. I can't take my eyes off of him." She looked delighted as she placed her hand on my thigh, to calm down my rising stress levels.

"Your father and I used to play hockey." Her father mutters as my eyes reach my father's scowl.

"Silas and Damon," Her father laughs, "The best of the best, we were inseparable in the sport and in business."

I nod, everyone silent as my brother Bentley speaks, "My dad playing hockey?" He laughs, "He never even played one on one with any of us, I understand Grayson because Grayson is a beast on the ice but—"

"While Grayson is great at the sport," My father interrupts again, "He's sloppy with passes, he doesn't communicate well with his teammates, he hogs the puck. He is not a good team leader."

I took a breath as Adrianna's father simply looked happy, "Almost like you?"

My father's eyes froze the whole damn table as I squeezed Adrianna's hand under the table, I wouldn't know what to do without her here.

"With all due respect sir, your son is a great player. If only you took the time to take your eyes off your damn phone for a second during a game, you would see that." Adrianna says with confidence as I look at her.

My father stands, "With all due respect Adrianna, your opinion was not needed. You better keep your mouth shut or you might end up like *your mother.*"

Adrianna froze and so did the rest of the table, it was like a forbidden rule to speak about Mrs. Cassian. I didn't know much about Adrianna's family life only to know now that her father was half present.

Her face falls into a stone expression as I slam my hand on the table, "Adrianna and I are going to get fresh air." I mutter, pulling Adrianna up, walking up the stairs and on the balcony, the dinner table below us.

"Dove," I begin as she shakes her head.

"I don't know my mother. I've never met her, and not one day did I ever think that I had to know who she was."

I place my hands on her cheek, feeling her warmth I could feel her heart pulsing, "I'm sorry."

She laughs, "What are you sorry for? You didn't do anything."

"I don't know why men like my father exist." I mutter as she places her head on my chest.

"If your father didn't exists, you wouldn't exist and, that type of world isn't a place I would like." I shrug as he sent me a look of comfort.

I kiss the top of her head as she looks up, her lips finding mine, "The way you stood up for me got me turned on." I smirked as her eyes flashed with hunger.

"Yeah?" She whispers her hand pressing against my crotch, my eyes widen.

"Oh fuck."

She looked amused, traveling down to her knees I look down at her with greed, "Adrianna." I warn as he hands find their way unzipping my pants, letting them fall midway to my knees.

She licks her lips, greed and lust filled her face, "Baby."

She places her finger in front of her mouth, urging me to be quiet she releases my hard cock out of my boxers, placing sweet kisses around me.

"I thought you said you've never done this." I mutter as she looks up shyly.

"I haven't but I looked up some videos. I want to try it out. I want you to like it."

I smirk, "Dove, I love everything you do to me."

She rolls her eyes at the endearment, "Yes, well I want you to come inside my mouth." Before I say something, her mouth licked the head of my cock, she looks up at me while she does it.

Her hands began to move up and down, I was tense under her touch, she kept sucking my tip. Her eyes kept on my face needing to see me, she loved to look at what she did to me.

She rubbed me harder, while burying her face down until her nose reached my pubic bone. My hand so eager, gripping her hair, my expression twisted, and my thigh muscles contorted.

"If you keep it up, I'm going to come." I rasp as she parts her lips even more, taking in more of my length. She didn't stop. I thrust my lips upwards hitting the back of her throat as I groan.

She pulled away as my chest heaves looking down at her red face. She pulls forward licking the tip of my cock and watched my eyes roll back.

Adrianna flashed me a devious smirk that made my cock twitch and pre-cum gathered at my tip, her fingers never left my hard length. She wrapped me with both hands gingerly. She flexes her movements making me moan at the contact. I look down at her and my large dick made her hand look so small and fragile.

She tugged at the base, "I won't stop until you've come, Grayson, you know how stubborn I can be." She whispers, as her stormy eyes catch mine, a shiver running up my spine.

I couldn't speak, only grunt to respond to her words, her tongue found my aching balls, I almost lost it when she looked back up with a damn smile on her face. She slowly uses her tongue to lick my shaft, a straight line up to the tip and placing a kiss there. Her lips part over the head of my hard dick.

I wasn't quite sure if she was able to completely fit me in her mouth, not many girls did. I didn't care if she did, her mouth was more than a fucking prize.

She swirled her tongue around my tip, my Adams apple bobbing.

"Ugh!" I groan in a whisper, as my whole dick slipped inside of her throat. She put my head into one side of her mouth.

Licking me all around the throbbing shaft, she moaned against me, she sucked and slurped on my head like a dream vacuum.

She pulled me in closer, my dick slipped even deeper into her throat. Did this woman not have a gag reflex?

She had almost taken all of me inside of her mouth, "Shit... Cassian." I hissed, "Always fantasied about this ever since we had classes together, under the fucking table, no one would see."

I look down at her, "The good girl and her mouth around her enemy—Oh fuck!" I moan as her mouth buried deeper, wet, and hard sounds of her slurps around my dick. She cups my balls, while massaging them her throat tightens around my cock, finally she relaxes her throat muscles.

She looks up, like she was asking me pushed in deeper, her mascara dripping and running down her red cheeks. She pulls out, "I want you to fuck my mouth." She whispers as I lick my lips.

"Is that what you want, Dove?" I ask her roughly, my hand still gripping her hair.

She nods, she was my fucking destruction. My large hand gripped her hair even tighter; I wasn't sure if she could breathe, I bend down, "If you want to stop, tap on my ankle twice." She nods, lodging my cock into her mouth, she wanted to go even deeper.

I knock my head back, "Fuck, darling..." I shoved my cock so deep down her throat she started to gag.

She rolls her eyes to the back of her head my deep moans vibrate as her nails gripped on my ass. She held me there as her lips and tongue devoured me, making me groan, I bit my lip, thrusting hard into her mouth.

"Adrianna, fuck—," I look down at her shining eyes, she was ready for it, but was she really? It was her last chance to tap on my ankles I moan, loosening my grip on her hair, one last suck around the head of my cock she sends my eyes rolling back.

"Shit. Adrianna—," I shook, "I'm coming," I spasm under her as she drops her jaw in an awe.

My body freezing without control, "Fuck."

My orgasm took over me like a damn wave of water pulling me into the ocean, black dots swept over my damn vision. My dick still in her throat, she pulls back but not letting me go she bobs her head over and over again which made me throb, euphorically... my knees fucking buckling I came into her mouth.

She sucked all of me until I felt too overwhelmed, she had drained me to the fucking bottom and up. I was mind-blown.

I caught my breath. She pulls me out of her mouth, swallowing all of my come down her throat, I look at her fucking, amazed.

"You are fucking unbelievable." I pulled her up, her lips crashing into mine. She groans into my mouth as I bury my face in the nape of her neck, "You said that was your first time?"

She simply nods as I fix her mascara, patting down her disheveled hair that I pulled, "Damn those fucking videos, you're a natural."

She smiles, "Maybe my mouth is just meant for you." She ponders as I laugh.

"It is, isn't it?" I quickly pull my dick back into my boxers, pulling my pants back up she rearranges her tight dress as I grin at her.

"You better hope you have a fucking hour of free time on what I'm planning for you."

Adrianna's face turns bright red as she swallows, "Maybe we should start heading back."

I pull her back, "No, actually..." I bend her over the balcony.

"If you want to be a part of their conversation, they can hear your moans from over the balcony."

CHAPTER 35

GRAYSON

My heartbeat like a damn drum.

"Grayson, our parents are right below us." I whisper looking behind me.

He smirks, "You didn't seem to care when you blew me." He challenges me as I let my mouth curve into a smile.

He pulls out his dick, gathering my dress up he grips the waist band of my thong, "Mine." He whispers before slapping my ass.

I was fucking lucky that his house was a damn mansion, one fucking moan from me, I would be staring at Silas Prince's face looking up at me.

"One look up and they can see me!" I look behind me at Grayson who ripped a condom wrapper with his mouth, fitting it in his long and thick dick. I pondered on how the fuck I fit all of it in my mouth.

"Then they're going to get a fucking show." He pulls me closer to him, my bare ass flushed against his crotch. He pulls me up against him, popping my boobs out of my dress he pinches both of my nipples making groan.

"Fuck." My gaze darts down underneath us as he sucks on my neck, "Grayson..." I protest as he kisses my lips, silencing me, he smiles against my lips.

He rubs my pussy, and I reward him with a throaty groan, his hands grabbing my handful of boobs. I often wondered if he liked the look of my body, whether I was too small for him, or too big, I was always insecure. But he caressed me, "I love your tits." He kisses my throat.

Without warning, Grayson slides his dick inside me, making me groan and jolt for a moment. He halts mid thrust I panic, "Don't stop please—" I plead as he continues with a slow pace.

My breathy moans and his solid thrusts empty my brain from any problems in the horizon.

He was holding back, and I had no idea why, I fix the problem by thrusting my ass back as he thrust forward, making us both moan in unison, he falls forward. I wanted him balls deep inside me and fucking me mindlessly. I brace my hands on the balcony rail.

He grunts, thrusting himself I moan, "Harder." I instruct as he trusts so hard, I inched forward, "Faster." I add on.

"I hope you feel this for days, Dove." He whispers in my ear as he continues.

I jacked forward and so hard that I almost fell but I caught myself, he was rocking my damn world I was struggling to keep it all in.

My body betrays me by squeezing his dick inside, I was convulsing. My eyes rolling to the back of my damn head. My mouth falls, not really sure if I was dreaming.

He felt so fucking good I wanted him to devour all of me. I looked back at his face which looked like he was lost for words, his heavenly expression made me even wetter if it was possible.

Grayson fucking owned me body and damn soul. But I wasn't mad about it.

"That's it, Dove." He pushes my hair away from my face, tangling his fingers in my locks and pulling back. He kisses me, our tongues dancing around each other.

He moves his mouth from my lips to my damn neck. He's still fucking me with full force and speed. He wasn't getting tired anytime soon. He was hammering me as I was levitating to heaven.

His hand gripping my waist, his fingerprints meant to be permanently there forever. His hand on my hair releases. There he goes again as he lays it flat on my stomach, feeling him with every thrust entering me.

He finds a perfect rhythm, "You feel like heaven." He moans as I only breath out, gripping the railing so hard I was amazed it didn't break. I tried not to come until he was ready.

"Yes! Please Grayson—right there—" I cried out loud, making sure it wasn't so loud that it captures our family's attention.

"Louder baby." He groans.

I knock my head forward, "Fuck Grayson!"

He trusts faster, "That's right baby, I'm the one fucking you."

"Not Brooks."

Thrust.

"Not Anthony."

Thrust.

"Just." He thrust harder and faster I begin to tear up from how good it felt, "Fucking."

"Me."

I moan, my hand over my lips, stopping me from moaning louder than I should.

I couldn't help but moan his name, I could feel juice dripping down my inside thigh.

I felt embarrassed, "Fuck Grayson."

I look back as he smirks, "Good girl, coming hard for me." His hand reaches for my throat, groaning I look forward.

"Grayson, fuck—"

"That's right baby... moan my name, let them know I'm the only one you want to fuck you from behind."

I couldn't take it anymore. I tremble as he rams into me deeper. His balls slap my ass, my tight pussy stretching as his cock molded me inside and out. Tears run down my eyes, as I squeeze him like a damn vice.

Our bodies bang against each other, I felt him everywhere around my body. My senses filled him. I didn't care if we were above my father and his family fucking. He was mine right now and that's all that mattered.

I groan looking back, pure satisfaction in his eyes. I loved Grayson.

I wasn't sure if I was ready for him to know that, even if I knew he saw it in my eyes.

He turns me around, walking closer as my lips envelope in top of his, "That was—" I smile, rubbing my nose on his, "I kind of made a mess." I signal to what was trickling down my leg.

He grins at me, leisurely, "It's normal, Dove."

"Are you sure?" I say with concern as he looks at me kneeling down, taking his tongue, lapping it over my juices that dripped down from my leg. His tongue dragged from the inside of my knees to the inside of my thighs.

The final destination he laps his tongue on my pussy making me knock my head back with a groan.

"Normal." He looks up, meeting my eyes, "And fucking sweet." My cheeks red as I kiss him, flushed cheeks, tousled hair, and heavenly eyes. He looked beautiful. He looked like a damn devil in disguise. He fixes my dress, my hair and my make up once again.

I look at him like I've been deprived of oxygen and inhaled him like he was a source of life.

He leaned in carefully; I didn't feel the need to pull back or take a step back anymore. He breathes and I don't. Though our hearts beat together in unison. I couldn't feel my legs anymore. My fingers felt light and empty.

I always believed it when I heard...

The Devil is real. And he's not a little red man with horns and with a tail. He can be beautiful. Because he's a fallen angel and he used to be God's favorite.

I wasn't claiming that I was God in any way... but Grayson

Prince was my favorite angel that wouldn't change, and I wasn't going to let him fall.

Grayson and I got fixed up quickly walking down the stairs, my father looking at me with question, Grayson's brothers looking at him up and down with smirks in their faces.

I sat down, suddenly famished from the previous sexual activity.

"So, Grayson, are you taking over your father's business then?" My father asks as I look at Grayson's face changed from being neutral to disappointed.

"Yeah, that's the plan." He says plainly while looking over to his father, a first smile that I've ever seen on Silas' face.

He was in a better mood and suddenly I felt as if he was going to ruin everyone else's day, "Yes. The plan is that he drops hockey because he belongs in the business world and have a great wife like his ex-girlfriend that won't betray him." He points out as I jolt in my seat.

"Silas!" Sara yells as Silas smiles at her, "It's the truth, August could be trusted."

"She doesn't have health or mental problems. She won't be able to pass it down to future children."

Grayson's face turned feral, "Please do not speak as if Adrianna is not here." I felt my body freeze and my mind going blank.

How did he know about my health problems or my overdose? "You have no right to speak about my daughter." My dad stands with irritation, I felt tears pool around my sockets.

I didn't need to blink for tears to fall. I wasn't ready to hear out loud that I did have problems, especially from Silas Prince.

I look at Grayson who wasn't really sure what to do. I don't blame him. I, myself, didn't know how to react, I looked at my father for guidance.

I never would.

"I had a private investigator track her every Tuesday." Phillip continued as I felt air leave my body.

"She's with me." Sara answers. It was true but I was with my therapist first.

"She goes to a weekly therapist first which she failed to mention to Grayson, did she?" He stands, "Did you plan on telling my son that you have mental problems?"

I stayed silent. My heart dropping to my damn stomach, "Why did I think coming to this dinner was a good idea?"

He walks up next to me, leading me to get up and walk out of the door, Grayson follows, "Don't fucking expect her to even come back to this house." My father yells as I look down to Amelia's eyes which filled with tears.

She runs over to me, sobbing. She wraps her arms around me, not wanting to let go as her brothers pull her away from me like I was some type of virus.

"You two cannot be together." Phillip yells, "I simply will not allow it."

My father looks at me and Grayson with a restrained face, "Adrianna. I ask you for one fucking thing and that is to never fucking speak to Grayson ever again."

He screams, "I will ship you to Switzerland!"

My tears fall, "She's not going anywhere." Grayson talks back to my father. My father was not a weak man, he worked out every day and was large, sure Grayson was a lot larger, but my father was angrier.

My father stalked up to Grayson, who didn't back down, grabbing his throat and shoving him against the wall. My whole body tensed. "Dad, put Grayson down."

"First, his family disrespects my wife." He urged, "Then disrespects my daughter."

"Dad—"

"Adrianna, stay the hell out of this."

Grayson looks at me, "Baby, it's okay." He muttered as I bit my lip.

My father's eyes deep in Grayson's, "You will not talk to my daughter. You will not touch my daughter. You will keep your damn distance from Adrianna."

"That's not your choice to make!" I yell.

Grayson pulls away, "I won't." His face was red, and his heart was pounding hard.

Silas Prince pulls Grayson over to his side as my father pulls me away from them.

My father looks at me, "Listen to me, for once." He assures as I pull away from him, my head crushing to his chest, I look behind him to see Grayson staring at me.

"How dare you think you can just take Grayson away from me like that?" I screamed at him.

He laughs, "Adrianna, grow up! It's never going to happen. I would ask you to choose either me or his family. But it seems that the head of the household doesn't want you to be a part of their family as well."

He pulls me inside the house, my body trembling as I run up to my room. I could hear my father ordering housekeepers and guards to keep me inside. I cried harder.

I can always run away. He walks into my bedroom, "Give me your damn phone." He instructs as I throw it at him.

"I'm doing this for you." He looks at me, "Grayson does not care about you." I couldn't look at him, "He only wants to defy his family and once he does that, he's done with you. You will thank me."

I pulled my sheets over my body. I wish I could talk to someone. Margo, Verina, and Juliette didn't know what was happening.

I was hoping everything was just a terrible dream, the voices in my head came back screaming more than ever. It was like I was trapped in a dark hole, and I was getting buried alive.

I couldn't ask for help because no one would help me.

No one could.

Chapter 36

Grayson

"You don't belong with someone like that Grayson." My father mutters.

I shake my head, "You had no right."

"I do. I'm your father."

I stand up, thinking about really ramming my fist into his damn throat, "You didn't give her a damn chance."

"I let her stay here." He screams at me, "You are being selfish. You have a damn duty to this family and being with a fucking Cassian is a waste of damn time."

I shake his off, "You tend to forget about our deal." He presses out as I swallow. I did not forget one bit. I thought about it every fucking night.

"The plan was for you to get with her and break her damn heart Grayson." He buried his finger in my chest pushing me, "The plan was for you to break her damn heart, so she has a dramatic episode!" He walks over to me slamming his hand on his office desk.

"You were supposed to have her broken by now." He sneers.

"Things fucking change." I get up pacing around the room.

"Do you want to play hockey Grayson?" He asks me as I pause. It was a sore subject. I wanted to ignore it.

I nod. I didn't want to take over the business that he was shoving down my throat. If I dated Adrianna and broke her heart, he wasn't going to force me to take the business.

"All of this because of a damn girl, Grayson!" He yells even more as I shook my head, "You fell for her."

I look up at him, "This is why I had to do what I did." He mutters.

I stand up, "What did you exactly do?"

He looks over to the floor as I walk up to him full of anger, "What the fuck did you do?"

"I forced August to break up with you." He says plainly as my heart drops. "She needed the money desperately and I had it. My one condition was for her to end your relationship."

I felt my blood pump faster in my veins, "She asked for me back yesterday."

My father simply grumbled, "Yes, I finally allowed her to, she loves you so much."

Guilt. There it was. Fucking guilt.

I fell in love with a different woman when August had only broke up with me because she needed money desperately. I shake my head, wanting everything to make sense.

"She watched you with another woman while she had to feed her whole family knowing that she couldn't have you." My father says thickly as I felt my heart hurt a bit more.

"You owe her yourself, Grayson." He continues as I swallow.

I stand quietly, my heart thumping out of control. "That's not fucking fair." I mutter running my hand through my hair.

He smirks, "Of course it is."

"You loved August before you ever thought about Adrianna."

False. I've loved Adrianna the moment I fucking saw her as much as I hated her.

"You only got with Adrianna because of the deal we made so that you can continue hockey, not to take the business and to make August jealous." He continues as I close my eyes.

"You falling for her was never part of the damn deal Grayson!" He walks up to me, shaking my body as I nod.

I had no excuse. I was a man of my word.

"If you are picking her over your damn dreams of playing hockey, then don't ever ask me why you are miserable with taking over the business."

I licked my lips, as he took a bottle of whiskey, downing it in one sip. "I want to see her heart broken and I want August on your arm at the Winter Charity ball." He instructs as I take a breath.

I look at him with a sneer, "Yes."

"Yes what?" He turns around.

I swallow, "Yes, father."

I look at his picture when he used to play hockey. I never understood why he had such a hate for the sport now. Everyone told me he was a natural.

I had a month before the Winter Charity ball, which meant that I didn't have to end things with Adrianna until then. I reach for my phone looking for her number, she didn't pick up, as it went straight to voicemail.

I had suspected that her father had taken her phone away from her, so I reached plan B.

I called Margo who got Adrianna out of the house I sneak out of the bushes, the thorns prickling me.

Her face beams when she sees me. Margo rolling her eyes, "I'll give you guys five minutes." She whispers while walking away.

"Can I talk to you?" I ask as she looks at me, I lead her to sit on a bench out front.

"Grayson, you don't have to—" She mutters.

I interrupt, "I don't want you to feel like you have to explain anything to me if you're not ready."

She looks at me plainly, I wipe her tears with my finger, "I'm just... I'm so embarrassed." She says as I smile.

"You don't ever have to be embarrassed with me," I sigh looking at her, "You would've made fun of me because of this."

"Sure, I would've." I let on as she stood, "But I hate seeing you cry, Dove."

"My father is an ass." I continue while standing, "You understand I'm never allowed in your house ever again. My father forbids it."

I couldn't help but laugh, "You don't think I have a secondary plan?" I raise my eyebrows, pulling out a pair of keys.

"You bought a car." She asks with a confused face.

"No, a house."

"A house?" Her eyes widen.

I smile, "Yeah, if you can't come to my house, and your father would hate it if I was ever at yours. There's a house that we can both stay at, of course, you would have to agree."

I let my lips quirk up, she's beaming I throw her hands around my shoulders as I pick her up hugging her.

"I told you, no one, *especially* our parents will ever break us apart." I place a kiss on her face, still tasting the salty tears that fell from her eyes prior.

I felt my heart break for Adrianna and me. Our time was limited, and I knew it. She wasn't allowed to know this.

I just wish she would forgive me once it happens. I trace a tiny heart on her back I was going to savor every fucking moment of this.

"You deserve better." I whispered to her.

She shakes her head, "That's where your wrong, Prince. You're all I want." She places her head on my chest.

She felt warm and familiar, so safe like a forbidden home. I wanted to cling onto her for the rest of my life, but it wasn't fair. I swear her whole face lit up like the damn sun when I told her about us staying together.

I just imagined how her golden eyes would look like when I ended stuff.

I was dreading these next few weeks. I was dreading leaving *home.*

ADRIANNA

*O*ne month later.

After school Grayson always had hockey practice or a game, we would then meet up at the cute house that he had purchased for me and him to spend time together.

It was romantic.

Grayson and I were very sexually compatible, the past month there had been nothing but banter, hot sex, and just being with each other.

We had just finished for a third time. My body was relaxed and tired. Grayson's stamina from hockey was something I thanked God every day for. He walks in with a smirk on his face.

I attempt to get up before my knees buckle almost falling to the ground the bed catches me, I sigh.

"My favorite thing to look at is you freshly fucked laying on my bed asking for more."

I looked up at him, he looked majorly unaffected.

"Yes, well, that's the last for today." I laugh.

He crawls on the bed next to me. "I don't really believe in never."

I roll my eyes, "Well, I don't believe in always."

Grayson's body traps me as I smile, his face lowers to kiss my lips gently. "Opposites attract, Dove." He says with a smug face.

I raise an eyebrow, pushing him off me a bit, "Never."

Grayson pull me over on top of himself, I was now straddling his hips, "Always."

He beams as I place my head on his chest, I found that this was my favorite endearment that Grayson and I had done.

"Can you breathe?" I look up at his closed eyes.

"I can't breathe when I'm around you." He mutters as I laugh.

I look outside seeing snow fall on the ground my face beams with happiness as he looks over to the window, "I've always wanted to get kissed in the rain," I smile while still looking out the window.

Grayson looks at me with a dumb expression like I was delusional, "It's snowing."

I roll my eyes, "No shit... but it's different. It makes it more magical... more like us."

I pause, pulling myself and my weak body out of the bed, putting on a jacket, my sweatpants. I pulled Grayson up as he was already dressed for the cold weather; I pulled him outside.

His eyes staring into mine as the snow falls on the tip of my nose, I blow it away. My very own prince charming twirls around me as the snows spirals around us. He places his hands on both my cheeks and pulls me in for a magical kiss.

He bends down, reaching for my butt only to pull me up so that he could carry me. He kisses me like space and time were colliding. Like I was a centimeter off a damn cliff. He pulled me in like he was hanging on to me.

He caressed my face like he was starving, and I was the only meal in the world left. I've never felt this good. I've never felt so damn alive. This is the first time that I've ever felt anything, but hunger and I didn't know what I would do just to keep it that way.

I didn't want Grayson in moderation. I wanted all of him. He kissed me, and all my body ever did was slowed down, like I wasn't running after anything anymore. Every muscle in my body took its time to relax.

He grabs my waist closer to his, with shaking fingers. He wasn't cold, he was in his habitat. He was gentle but rough. I was happy that Grayson treated me like I wasn't some delicate flower, that I could be more than just a fragile vase.

Grayson Prince terrified me because I couldn't imagine what life would've been like if we hadn't taken a chance. He swallows, I look at him, snowflakes rest on his lashes, his chest heaving. He was breathless as he placed his head on mine, and I was in euphoria.

My person. My savior.

He put me down. His lips sinking on mine once more as he looked up at the night sky, it was only us.

And I wish I would stay like this forever, but it didn't. It couldn't, I would have to go home in a couple of minutes and sleep on my bed. I would wake up and go to school ignoring him.

We wished it was different, but it wasn't. We had our own separate lives that we simply had to live without each other.

I thought I could handle it, but nothing in my life could've prepared me from the utter heartbreak that ensued within our story.

Nothing.

F our days later.

He hasn't called me. He hasn't texted me. He hasn't asked me to hang out after his practices.

Ghosting by definition is the practice of ending a personal relationship with someone by suddenly and without explanation withdrawing from all communication.

Grayson Prince has been ignoring me for four days, almost five. No eye contact in the halls, no mischief smirking at me from across the classroom.

I wish I had enough courage to be honest with him and tell him how exactly it rips my heart apart when he ignores me. But I couldn't. I was no strong woman when it came to him. Instead, I stay silent wondering what I've done to deserve it.

But I went to the hockey game, seeing him shine as always, I tried to make sure I wasn't really there. I just came to pick up the jacket that Margo borrowed from me.

I hated being in the hockey arena now, the reminder that Grayson was completely okay with ignoring me. His family in the stands, Amelia wasn't present, and I frowned.

August front row, yelling his name and cheering on the whole team. Of course, my sleeve gets caught on the damn wooden cubby. I pulled it away seeing that my sweater was now ruined.

Margo runs towards me with a wild smile, "Great you're here!" She hugs me as I wrap my arms around her.

"Yes well, I heavily need that jacket."

She rolls her eyes, "I don't know why you don't come to the games anymore. You know your Grayson's lucky charm." She winks.

Margo, of course, doesn't know my issues with Grayson. The only thing she really knows is that publicly we weren't allowed to be together.

And now, I'm guessing privately too.

The buzzer makes a loud noise as the players rush out of the rink to walk into the locker room, I found Grayson's blonde hair. And his eyes couldn't help but find mine as well.

He saw me see him. And I saw him see me.

His eyes retract back on the floor as if I wasn't there. My eyes caught his stick, my initials weren't there anymore, and I felt my heart break.

If I had done something, I wanted to know what. But instead, I stayed thinking that I really hadn't done something to earn his cold shoulder and he just grew to despise me again.

But as I promised myself, I wouldn't give up on Grayson. I certainly wouldn't give up on us. I was lying to myself if I told myself that I didn't want to run into his arms when I saw him for a second.

I frown, Margo's eyes never leaving mine. I couldn't hide it anymore and this proved it. "Did I miss something?" Her voice a bit concerned as I sighed.

"Grayson has been ignoring me." I mutter as her mouth drops.

"Why?" Her eyes widened like she had just seen a ghost.

I shrug, "I don't know."

Margo begins to speak as I block her out, looking around to see Liam walking over with a wide smile. I couldn't help but smile at the stories Margo would tell me about her helping him with his physical therapy.

"Miss Cassian! What are you doing over here?" Liam walks over slowly.

I roll my eyes, "I'm not here long, just to grab my jacket."

Liam frowns, "Not staying for the rest of the game?" He asked sounding quite disappointed.

I look around, "I don't think I'm needed here."

Liam laughs gently, "Nonsense, your Grayson's lucky charm."

My eyebrows furrow at the thought, "I highly doubt that." I laugh.

He shakes his head, "I'm serious!"

Neil walks out with a bottle of water, "You forgot your bottle dipshit." He interrupts as I smile at him.

Neil pauses to catch my gaze, his annoyance to his teammate disappears as he flashes a smile at me.

I nod, to acknowledge him.

Neil nods back, then he tilts his head, "You here for Grayson?"

My eyes widen in fear, "No." I say flatly.

"You know you don't have to be scared of your boyfriend anymore, right?" He comments as I coughed out the lump lodged in my throat.

He nods, looking at me knowingly, "Ohh."

He smiles thinly, "I get it. You and Grayson are going to your small house after the game, and you wanted to let him know that you'll be waiting."

Neil tilts his head with an amused look.

I roll my eyes, "If you know what I mean." He winks annoyingly.

I couldn't help but smile, "Well, if he wouldn't mind, just tell him I'll wait for him?" My jaw hardens as Neil nods, walking back into the locker room.

Acid burns in my throat as I try to swallow it down, I turn sharply to Margo, "I'm going to head out." I say quickly.

She nods, "Call me when you get home!"

I looked down at the floor. I couldn't afford to make eye contact with anyone else, feeling like I was getting judged for being at a damn hockey game.

As soon as I ran outside, I couldn't help but lean against the cold brick wall, looking around to see if anyone else was outside, I closed my eyes.

Quieting down the voice in my head that I hadn't gotten a break from since Grayson's cold shoulder.

Grayson was avoiding me like I was some type of plague. I couldn't help but feel like it was bound to happen. I still didn't want to believe it.

The moment I would accept it was I moment I didn't want to ever imagine.

I took a breath; I could feel my whole throat constrict as I swallow. I suppose I could pretend like everything was okay and it would be. But I wasn't the type to always look at the good parts of life.

I got in my car, driving over to the small house. My bottom lip begins to shake as I kept the tears in from falling. I sigh, frustrated, I pull my body out of the car, taking out my keys.

I open the door, only to throw my bag and jacket on the chair next to the front door. I didn't think about where I wanted to go, only let my legs take me to wherever they thought I should be.

This was my routine. It used to be Grayson and I's routine. But for the past four days, I've come to the house hoping that maybe one day he would come through the front doors with an explanation.

But as I laid on the bed, tears falling from the sides of my eyes,

I lost more hope. I laid there with the lights off, my body heating up the whole bed. I was losing him, and I felt it in my stomach.

The sinking feeling got worse as I laid down for longer. I knew I wasn't going to be okay for a duration of time. I lost him and I didn't even know why.

But I should get used to people I love leaving me without a word, right? It happens over and over again; I should've called it this time. I open my eyes to see the world spinning around quickly.

It got harder and harder to breathe. I couldn't figure out how to breathe like I used to. But I had to get over it.

To get a fucking grip.

I kept going back to the house, hoping that one day he would come. But he didn't, as if he didn't intend to give me any reason or explanation. My heart broke a little more each day I waited.

He was back to being Grayson Prince. Ladies surrounding him, his social media filled with videos and pictures of him, drinking and getting wasted.

I still held hope that he would come back. I arrived at the house every night. Like a damn coward, I kept coming back every damn night.

Whether it was raining.

Snowing.

Sleeting.

I was there because I prayed for him to come back to me. But he never came. I began to tire my hopes, not really sure if I had any more energy to keep waiting for something I knew wasn't going to happen.

So, I stopped coming. I stopped using the keys. I stayed at my home. I went to school, put on the brave face I had before him. I ruled with an iron fist while everyone was more terrified than ever.

And there it was, my body breaking from rhythm. From finally learning how to love myself a bit more every day.

I started to wake up, wishing I hadn't.

Back to square one.

CHAPTER 37

ADRIANNA

"I finally bought my dress for the ball!" Verina's voice was sharper than ever as I looked over to her pulling the dress out of the bag and against her body, twirling.

I smile, "I love yellow on you." I say plainly.

Margo hops out of the bed, "You are going to look so beautiful in that dress, V!"

I look around to look at Juliette who asked Margo and Verina to buy something random for her to wear. She wasn't the type to care about these types of balls.

She thinks it's just a boring tradition that all rich families have to take part in. I simply agreed but, of course, Margo and Verina loved these types of events. Juliette and I couldn't care less.

I yawn, "Tell me how it goes." I start to stand up.

Margo pulls me back, "Why don't you want to attend?" She jumps as I knock my head forward.

"Because I simply think that these balls are for other rich people to judge us because we are the new generation. Why should I care about what they say about me and my goals?"

Margo's eyes looked like thunder striking on an empty field of grass, "These people want you to succeed in life."

I narrow my brows, "They want us to be an ornament to society."

"You're going." She instructs as I laugh.

"Too late. I don't have a dress." I countered as Margo's eyes gleamed with trouble.

I simply regretted my decision to come over, knowing she was just planning to make me go to the Winter Charity Ball.

"Margo..." I warn as Verina runs out of the closet with a long, beautiful, white dress on a hanger.

I grew stunned at the fact that they picked out a dress that I incredibly enjoyed. It was beautiful, and magical. Like it was straight out of a damn fairytale I couldn't keep my eyes away from it.

Margo and Verina nod to each other, "Beautiful, isn't it?" They looked at me as I stood there stunned.

"It's..." I mutter, "perfect."

I take a good look at it, "It's your dress," Margo says in a sing song voice.

I hug her, "I'm not even sure if I want to go."

She looks at me with a sad expression, "But we bought you a dress and everything!"

I pull away, "I can pay you back if you want but I don't think that it's a good idea."

Verina scowls, "The president should be there you know." Margo looks at her with brilliant eyes.

They got me.

"Well, I can be kept updated when other people from the committee tell me how it goes, like you and Juliette."

Juliette grins with a vile look, "Oh, I don't think so."

It turned silent as I sat on the bed, slumping back as my head rested on Juliette's lap. "Let's talk about what this is really about." I close my eyes.

I would rather not but I knew that I needed to talk about it anyways. "This is about Prince." Verina comes over as I open my eyes.

I take a pillow and put it on top of my face with a sorry attempt in trying to suffocate myself. I look at Verina with a frown, "Have any of you talked to him at all?"

They all shake their heads. Margo walks up to me, "I know. It's killing you."

I look at her I wasn't sure if there was much soul left in my eyes, "All parts of me are tired."

She hugs me, "We love you. Never forget that." I smile, Verina and Juliette pile on as I laugh.

"We love you with love that is more than love." Juliette points out, "I read it from Edgar Allan Poe."

And I love my best friends with everything that I have, they have always been there for me whenever I needed them to be.

"You know what!" Verina stands with a finger pointed to me, "Fuck him!"

"He broke your heart. Do you know many men that have broken Adrianna Cassian's heart?" I roll my eyes playfully.

"He didn't break my heart; I didn't tell him I loved him."

She folds her arms together, "But you do love him."

I bit my lip, I couldn't speak it was as if the world got knocked out of me, "We never thought that you and Grayson would be more than just enemies."

I nodded, it was a lot simpler then, wasn't it?

"But you brought Grayson Prince, captain of the hockey team, billionaire, and playboy to his fucking knees Anna."

I look away from her, "You have to let him go and I know it doesn't sound nice to hear, but you have to stop thinking about the way he kissed you, the way he smelled, or the little touches." Margo interrupts, "You have to let him go because he isn't like that anymore. Maybe it was who he was but definitely not who is planning to being."

I close my eyes once more, Margo was right and it was the best decision for me, it only made things simpler to end my life. But my friends have always been a good factor in me waking up in the morning.

I get up, a full rush on energy, "Where are you going?"

They all look at me with concerned faces, "I'm taking all of Grayson's shit and giving it back. He doesn't deserve my tears or any part of me anymore."

I rush out of Margo house, her face looking shocked and Verina's looked flabbergasted.

"You are going to the ball then right!" She screams.

I roll my eyes, "Yes!" I yell back as I hear them celebrate.

I wasn't going to hold myself back from living my life in the remainder of my one week left.

I certainly wasn't going to waste it on Grayson. He didn't deserve my tears or to be in my thoughts.

Verina asked me if I was really in love.

I wouldn't call it love. I call it burning. He burned me with his touch. He burned my heart. The tears that I cried because of him burned the worst.

It burned everywhere.

Did I have any right to drive over to Grayson's house?
No. Absolutely fucking not.
But did I have a good reason to?
Abso-fucking-lutely.

So, I did. I drove to Grayson's house with his fucking sweaters, jackets, his damn necklace, his hockey jersey, and his blankets he left in the house.

I walked slowly to the front door. I was prepared. As much as I wanted to just throw his shit at his face and never converse with him again, I didn't.

Instead, I rang the doorbell and waited. But there it was. Grayson opened the door looking flabbergasted. Seeing him sent me back into a state of feeling that I hated.

Disappointment.

Grayson stood in front of me with a neutral face, it was like he never even touched me. Did it kill him as much as it killed me?

The memories he drew around me were with permanent ink. All I could do was stay right where he left me in the scribbles of a black and white world without him.

I wanted to take all of it back. All the feelings that I spewed, the damn touches, kisses, tears, loyalty, my vulnerability, and my time. I wanted to take everything back when I saw him. I wished that he had never walked into my life.

"Dove." He coughs out hesitantly. I flinched at his words, and he noticed.

"Don't call me that." I say plainly, feeling my words shut to a certain amount.

"Adrianna." He corrects as I look at him,

"Don't call me by my first name." I snapped.

He sighs, "Cassian." He mutters as I look at him blankly.

"I just wanted to return all your things. I don't like seeing them around my room and I don't see why I should." I hand over the box of items to him as he takes it.

I let it hurt.

"Gray, do you want some cookies I baked with Amelia?" I hear a soft voice behind him, my heart dropping to the floor as my eyes reach coral green orbs.

I swallowed. It was like my heart got ripped out of my chest and got stomped on when I saw August Gales behind him, wearing *his* hoodie.

I couldn't find the words to say to him, I only looked in despair and betrayal. I could feel tears building up in my eyes.

"Babe?" She screams as I shook my tears out of my system.

Grayson turns, "Yeah, of course."

August pauses, her eyes meeting mine and I felt the wind knock the air out of me.

She smiles thinly, her eyes never leaving mine, "Evening, Adrianna." I didn't say anything back. I refused to watch him, so I watched her wondering if this was really happening.

My eyes blur and so did the good moments Grayson and I ever had.

"So, you picked her."

Silence.

"I did."

I felt my throat restrict, "Do you regret it?"

"No. We were never real." I felt my heart sting as he kept talking.

"Everything I gave you was real. I'm a fool for believing the same from you."

My heart stung but I smiled at him, he looks at me longingly, "Is that it?" He asked like he was too bothered to ask if I was ever okay.

I only look, my hands shaking, "I just want to know one thing..." I asked as he pulled away from the door, *Why did you do it?"*

Grayson licked his lips, looking like he was trying to find the right words to say. So, I interrupted him, letting a tear fall down my cheek quickly wiping it away, no longer comfortable with Grayson seeing me cry.

"You knew how important you were to me and..."

I look away couldn't bear to look into eyes that I would usually seek comfort in, "...You even knew it was going to hurt me but somehow... someway it didn't stop you?"

The saddest part about being betrayed isn't the betrayal itself but because the people who betray you are the people who shouldn't.

"I'm so sorry," Grayson takes a step closer, but I take a step back.

My heart breaking as if he stepped on it. I held my breath, "Don't come near me."

He closes his eyes, "I wish I can explain."

I look at him again, "Then explain."

He stays silent.

I thought he was healing me, but he broke me even more than

I was before I was with him, "Why did you have to walk into my life when I was perfectly fine?" I say softly as Grayson swallows.

Grayson's silence was so fucking loud it made me irritated, "I didn't mean to hurt you." He speaks.

I gave an irritable laugh, "But you did. You can't take it back because you knew I was going through hell and your fucking solution was to leave?"

I wanted to let all my feelings out for him, taking a step closer, slapping his cheek, I pull away, "You looked me right in the eyes and told me that we still had forever." I start to gather my bag which fell down my arm, "I didn't know that your definition of forever was a thirty-day free trial."

I laugh, walking away, "Rot in hell, Prince."

I walked away from Grayson that day, not planning to ever revisit him. I felt acid in my lungs, and I broke. I felt nothing.

CHAPTER 38

GRAYSON

August is pregnant.

I stood in the middle of the hockey arena, my damn head pounding. I looked in the crowd to look for my lucky charm only to remember that she wasn't there anymore. I wasn't ready to be a father. But I had to be one.

August broke up with me because she believed that I wouldn't take care of the baby with her. She needed money for the basic supplies. She told my father but didn't feel the need to tell me.

After graduation, my father wanted August and I to get married.

He was absolutely fucked in the head for that thought. A baby and a damn wife, I was going to be sick.

I was blindsided. I was distraught and I didn't know how to face Adrianna. I wasn't sure if I could.

Like a coward, I never did.

August came back to finally tell me, thus the reason why she thought that I needed to prove that I could be in a healthy relationship.

For God's sake, we're in our second year of college and she's fucking pregnant. My father did what he did best. He schemed and he threatened. I wasn't exactly sure if the baby was mine. She had told me it was and who was I to doubt her?

I would like to think of her as loyal during our relationship. Nevertheless.

I miss whatever Adrianna and I were. It felt nice forgetting everything for a while, to spend three months being free.

The hardest thing that I have ever fucking done was walk away from Adrianna. I didn't want to, but I had to. We were in too deep. My father started to find out about my meetings with her and hired guards to watch where I went every day after hockey. My father let me play hockey with the rule of breaking her heart and I did.

But I would give it up, I would give up my whole future in hockey if it meant I could be with Adrianna.

But I believed that she was stronger, I believed that my father would get karma slapped on his face when the day comes.

I had to cut off all contact with her because my father would cut me off. I had to provide for a damn baby now. It wasn't enough to stop me, of course, I wanted to see Adrianna and I tried to.

Only to be warned by a sticky note that my mother was also watching my every move.

Nothing broke me more than the empty look Adrianna had given me earlier. I had to tell her, but I didn't know how to. She would hate it. She would hate me.

August going to my father was not a good move.

The puck gets passed to me, my body at rest and slow when I miss it. I bang my stick on the floor as Coach Livingston yells at my laziness.

I wasn't going to lie and say I wasn't slacking. I was, and I wasn't even sorry for it. An hour passed as everyone skated out of the rink and walked into the locker room, Liam and Chris were inside already.

"Get your shit together man!" Neil walks up to me.

I scowl at them, my brain felt fried to have another conversation where I had to stimulate words.

Liam walks up to me with a frown, "Hey Gray, you wanna come with me to the equipment room?" He winks.

I roll my eyes, "How subtle."

He pulls me out of the locker room with a serious face, "That was the worst fucking play I've ever seen." He puts his hand on his hips with a judgmental expression.

"You're Grayson Prince!" He exclaims.

I sigh, "I'm not Grayson Prince without her."

Liam nods, his face a bit concerned as I pull off my skates, "You can't have her, Grayson. You have August."

I sigh again and I made sure that he knew it wasn't a good sigh, "Don't remind me."

"You said you wanted her all along and that Adrianna was just for disposal." He says, my body tensed. I did say that, but inside I knew I was wrong the moment she laid her honey eyes on mine.

"Yes. Well, I'm fucking stupid."

Liam looks at me, "I think what you did was shitty." He makes a point as I nod, I couldn't even be mad at him, Liam's my best friend and I never got mad at him for telling me the truth.

"I wish I could fucking take everything back. If I had to, I wouldn't have gone near Adrianna, knowing how bad it was gonna be."

Liam thinks.

"That statement is improbable. If you had a chance to do it over, you and Adrianna would've still happened not because you are way too selfish to ever give her away just to anyone. You and her are made for each other, and everyone knew it except for you two."

I stayed silent, "I miss her so much, man." I run my fingers through my hair.

Liam quiets down, "I don't think August's kid is yours." He implies.

I look at him, "Oh, you think?"

He waddles over sitting next to me, "I don't think that you guys were involved when the baby was conceived."

"We were dating." I counter as he leans closer, "She could have..."

I look at him with my hand raised, "Are you telling me August possibly cheated on me?"

Liam smugly looks at me, "Yes. That's exactly want I'm saying. August may come off to look perfect in everyone's eyes, but no one is perfect. Everyone has a skeleton in the back of their closet."

I send him a look of worry, "I don't have a skeleton in my closet."

"It's a figure of speech!"

I laugh, "You learned that from Margo, didn't you?"

"Don't change the damn subject, Prince." He breathes out, "This chick is ruining your happy ending with Adrianna. I think that if you find probable evidence that you aren't the father then you're off the hook."

I look at him, "And if she did cheat, how are we going to prove that?" I counter.

He shoots me a scheming look, "Just leave it up to me." He smirks.

I laugh, "I don't think so."

"Do you want Anna back or no?"

I roll my eyes, "Of course, I want her back."

"Then we are going to dig for this information like no one's fucking business."

I get up brushing hm off, "You're crazy."

Liam runs up to me, "You still taking her to the Winter Charity Ball?" He asks.

I groan, "Father's orders."

"I can get some men there to figure it out for me." He gives me a thumbs up.

"You hear if Adrianna is coming?" I pry as he looks over to Margo's office.

"She'll be there."

I couldn't help frowning. She didn't want to talk to me, but I did. So, fucking terribly.

"You do know that she will never talk to you right? I'm pretty sure that she's made a point to ignore you. That's what Margo told me at least."

"I know." I look up at Liam, "She can hate me all she wants. She can fucking curse at me for hours, but I'll get her back," I took off my jersey, "I have to get her back."

I couldn't stop thinking about her. I've been talking to myself for the past week about her and the different ways I could've approached her. But instead, I didn't, I was a damn coward and I fucking couldn't.

She's a once in a lifetime girl and I missed my damn chance. I looked up at Liam once more with a sorrowed expression, "That kid is most definitely not mine."

There had to be something more to it, August was lying to me, and I needed to know why she would.

I picked up my phone looking for her contact, my eyes paused at Adrianna's...

17 MISSED CALLS.
8 MISSED MESSAGES.

I click on August's contact typing...

> Dinner tonight 7?

Sure!

READ 4:22 P.M.

I wasn't sure what my plan exactly was, but all I knew was that I needed to get out of this torment. It's only been a fucking week and I was miserable without Adrianna.

My damn world was crumbling right beneath me, and I couldn't do anything about it. But I had to try. August and I were a closed book never to be opened if this baby wasn't mine... I would leave her instantly.

Margo was right when she said that I was ridden with guilt, it was not love.

"Just because you want to be with them because you made a mistake doesn't mean you loved them at all. It means you're selfish and you want to make yourself feel better."

I plead fucking guilty.

T picked up August and we went to a hibachi restaurant. I got dressed and then picked her up from her house. She was supposed to move in with us, but the problem was that Amelia hated her.

She forced Amelia to bake a batch of cookies yesterday and I've never seen Amelia wanting so badly to lock herself in a damn oven.

"This is nice." She sits on the passenger seat of a brand-new car I bought; I couldn't bring myself to take her on my favorite car. Adrianna's belongings were still there. Untouched.

They will remain there.

I ignore her as she puts her hand on top of mine. I stiffen, pulling away.

"Grayson what's wrong?" She turned to me as I kept my eyes on the road, pulling into the parking lot.

"Don't act like we are on a fucking date August." I sneer as she looks back in front of her.

"I thought it was."

I laugh gently, "I'm taking you because I want fucking answers." I place the car on park, "And I needed to get away from my damn father."

She tenses as we both get out of the car, and get seated her face falls, "Grayson, I don't know what you want from me."

"I want you to be honest with me, damn it." I let out with force as she flinched.

"I have been honest Grayson!"

I breathe out with an annoyed expression, "I don't think you fucking are. August, I'm not really sure what to fucking do if you really are telling me the truth."

She looks at me with a blank expression, "You said you loved me and that you wanted me back."

I shake my head, "Yes, but I didn't mean I wanted to have a fucking child!"

She bends closer, "Well you fucking do, and you have no choice but be there for it because your father said so." She makes a point.

I laugh, "So that's why."

"What?"

"You went to my damn father because you knew he would force me to stay with you." I place my elbows on the table, her eyes searching mine, "What happened from you telling me you would do anything to be with me now?"

I swallowed; I didn't even need to answer the question. She knew exactly what happened. "Adrianna is a high-class bitch."

"Which is what you're going to become when you marry me." I grit out, "And don't ever fucking talk about her."

"I don't know how you could ever like someone like her! You used to make fun of her Grayson, hate whatever she fucking did."

While I do admit that Adrianna and I didn't start off with the best intentions, we built ourselves up to where we wanted to be, and it was perfect for the months it lasted.

"Am I really this child's father August?" I ask kindly.

She looks at me with tears in her eyes, "Yes Grayson, and it hurts me to think I would have cheated on you."

"You fucking dated another guy recently!"

"You think I would have sex with him that easily?" She screams at me as I look around, everyone staring.

"I don't fucking know."

"I can help you provide for the child. Just please tell me if it's really mine."

She sighs, "It's really yours."

I felt my heart drop a second time, my body tense as she looked at me wholeheartedly.

I didn't believe her. "You're getting a paternity test."

Her face held shock, "No!"

My eyes narrow, "You said it's mine so we can make fucking sure of it." I take a look at the waiter; he comes closer for us to order.

As the waiter walks away to get our order in the kitchen, I notice a familiar raven-haired vixen sitting on the other side of the restaurant, only she wasn't alone.

She was with a boy who also looked fucking familiar, and I wasn't about to be happy when I find out who it fucking was.

As August talked, I got up and walked over to Adrianna who simply saw me and never sneaked another glance. Her eyes had never looked so damn dark.

"Cassian." I address her as she only looks up. She was with no one other than Darius fucking Sawyer. The blood in my veins pumped so fucking hard I was ready to throw a damn table at him. But he sat there looking like a damn priest.

Acting like he wasn't only with Adrianna because he wanted to bang her like he fucking told me. "Grayson!" Darius addresses me as I ignore him.

"What the hell is he doing here?" I look at her as she stays silent.

I deserved this. I knew what I was fucking gambling when I broke her heart, but I still did it.

There was nothing I wanted to do more than hold her and tell her I'm sorry for everything, but I couldn't. I had to figure things out first before I told her. I just wish that she'll still be available to speak to me after.

I was fucking wishing to the damn Gods that she would still be on the other side at the end. But it was a risk.

"We are on date." He speaks.

I turn my head to look at him, "I don't think so."

Adrianna finally speaks. It wasn't much but it was something, "We are on a date." She smiles with a distasteful look.

"And it looks like so are you!"

I look back to August who only stared.

"He's fucking using you." I seethe, the words come out of my mouth with such force.

Darius got up from him seat, his eyes blazing on to mine, "Might think about disrespecting me again, Prince."

I laugh, squaring up, I was at least three inches taller than him, "You finally cashing in the ticket that lets me break your other arm?"

I lick my lips as he backs up, "You're lucky I didn't do it last game."

Darius smiles coyly, a malicious one as Adrianna looks at the security.

I'm sure he hadn't forgotten our last interaction.

"Take a punch." I whisper, "I fucking dare you."

His fists form as I smile back, catching his punch before it reached my face, turning his wrist in such an uncomfortable way that I heard it crack.

He takes his other fist and attempting to smashing it against my cheek but misses terribly, I take a punch, hitting him square on the fucking nose.

Adrianna pulls him off as August did the same for me.

"What the fuck is wrong with you? Smashing your fist into my date's face!" She looks at me with utter annoyance, I later notice that I am indeed out of line.

"So, this is how it's gonna be?" She asks.

August stood next to me, "He's fucking using you." I counter again, sounding like a broken record.

"And you weren't?" She lets out as I swallow.

Didn't she remember what I told her about Sawyer? Or was she just trying to piss me off?

I land next to August who I looked at, I hit her belly on accident, "Are you okay?" I spilled out seeing Adrianna's expression.

"Darius didn't fucking do anything to you, you made up lies just for me to not like him Grayson, so please never bother us again." Adrianna said it so vigorously that I backed away.

"Again?" I say quietly, I wasn't sure it projected well at all. My eyes find hers that were now a hue of red. That's when it comes to my head, Adrianna was dating around, and I couldn't stop it this time. I couldn't say much about it because I was the cause of her broken heart.

I was her heartbreak, and I could feel her pull away from me. The feeling in my chest of being stomped on.

"Come on babe, let's go to another place. This one is infested with roaches." I hear August say as I walk over to the table, security staring at me intently. I would love to smash my fist in all of their faces.

August looks at me, full of sorrow, "I'm still willing to take fifty percent of you Grayson."

CHAPTER 39

ADRIANNA

I couldn't breathe.

Here I was again, all alone and in my house, behind locked doors. I thought that I was getting better. I thought I was genuinely getting better. But I'm not.

I'm not anymore. For a month I was happy. For a week I was getting better. For a day I had hope. But in that damn minute I lost it. I've reached my limit.

I feel like I've lost it again. I shouldn't be like this just because of some guy.

But I can't lie to myself and tell myself that I didn't want to become better because of him. I had to get better for myself but what happens when you feel that yourself isn't enough?

I didn't know which was worse.

Days where I feel nothing or the days that I feel everything.

I was drowning beneath large waves and dying from thirst at the same time. I was fucking suffocating.

So here I am again.

On the bathroom floor. With locked doors, I had pills around me, one for me, one for my mind, one for my sanity, one for my heart, one for my head, many for the voices in my damn head.

And I couldn't fucking breathe.

I said sorry for myself too many times, I apologize for saying sorry too much, for everything that went wrong even when it had nothing to do with me. I labeled my fucking forehead a disaster.

It was my fault really; I knew the trouble I was getting into the moment that I agreed to Grayson's stupid terms. He was confused and I shouldn't have fallen into his damn agreement.

I didn't deserve to be a second choice. I didn't deserve to be someone's *maybe* or *what if* or *I'm not sure*. I don't fucking deserve it.

Mixed signals are for assholes. I deserved someone who knew exactly what they wanted.

I looked back at the bottle of pills, still untouched. I paused; it was taking all my might not to pop all of them in my mouth. But I did.

All of the remaining ones. And I lay on the cold floor. My heart thumping inside my chest, I could finally breathe. My head relaxed and the voices disappeared. I finally closed my eyes, feeling the burn in my stomach. The tears in my eyes falling. The drugs weren't enough.

My heart started racing and my hands began to shake. The voices in my head coming back stronger than ever they were fucking screaming at me. Another voice that hates me lives inside my head. My throat began to close up yet again. I always thought that drugs were all I could do to my body. I would lay in bed and hope I would fall asleep before I fall apart.

I got up, tears fell to the floor as I opened all the drawers, my first instinct was for the scissors. But I needed something sharper. Something that cut deeper than I've ever done.

My eyes spotted the knife. And my heart began to race as I grabbed it. It was shiny, the reflection of my red and swollen eyes on the silver.

I felt torn apart, my hands shook as I picked up my phone, my finger hovering on Margo's contact. But I realized that she didn't need this tonight.

So, I put my phone down, sliding down on the floor, the knife near my stomach, my waist, I closed my eyes pain burning as I cut my stomach. I swallowed down the screams, the sobs, the pain as the night went on. I was a drawing board. And blood dripped on the floor.

The emptiness was replaced with the sorrow. All of a sudden, the world began to change color, it was colorless, it was black and white. I felt really tired, like the world has drained me for everything that I gave.

Most nights I've done this, it never went this far. I've never thought the emptiness could've gone this heavy. I was falling apart, and I let the pieces scatter, not letting anyone gather anything because I didn't deserve to be put together.

I would keep it together, gathered, not put back together but *gathered*.

The next day.

I woke up on my bed, getting ready for school. My head was pounding. I had made it a mission not to talk much. Especially to Margo, she would know instantly that something was wrong.

The day was dragging along, as the day ended, I had realized that I left my glasses at the house that Grayson and I stayed at. I drove over after school, only promising that it would take a couple minutes, but it did not.

As I get ready to walk out of the house, the doorbell rings in such a matter than sounded urgent, I run over, opening the door seeing a woman with blonde hair and brown eyes looking at me.

"Hello, do I know you?" I ask kindly as the woman looked at me like I had three heads.

"No, I'm afraid not," She expresses tenderness, placing my hand out for me to shake, "My name is Vivian." I tilted my head, taking her hand and shaking it.

"My name is—"

"—Adrianna." She interrupts.

I nod, "Yes, how do you know that?" I question as she grins from ear to ear.

"I'm Grayson's mother." My face contorts.

"Oh." I didn't know if I hid my shock well.

I didn't really know what to say, only looking at her, she looked like Grayson. I shook my head, "I don't know where he is, I'm so sorry."

She stayed smiling, "Yes, well it seems he's been ignoring me."

My lips thinned, "He has a habit of doing that, doesn't he?"

She scowled, "Has my son done something wrong?" She looked concerned.

"No, he has not, he's just, gone right now and I'm not sure why." I turned away from her.

She smiles, walking closer, she hugs me, "I'm so sorry to hear that."

I wasn't sure why she hugged me, I wasn't the type for physical touch, especially from people that I barely knew. She was odd. I was not about to brush over the fact that she was indeed weird.

I flinch as she pulls away, "Are you okay, love?" She sounded endearing.

I smile softly, "Yes."

She pushes my hair back behind my ear. My face blushed, "Is something wrong?"

I laugh, "I've just never been hugged randomly before." She looks at me with a warm smile. She looked like a damn angel.

"Would you like to have dinner with me?" She asks plainly as I nod, it wasn't like I was doing anything. It wouldn't hurt, would it?

"You're his girlfriend, aren't you?" She asks and before I could counter, she interrupts, "I would love to learn more about my son if that's okay."

I felt bad, Grayson barely talked about his mother. He has barely acknowledged that he really had another family than the one he's with and I couldn't help but feel bad that all she wanted to know how Grayson was.

So, I agreed of course.

I let her enter the house, cooking up something fast like pasta that we could eat together without problems, we sat across from each other.

"Is he doing well?" She asks intrigued.

I smile, "He doing great."

She inches closer, "How did he not mention to me that his girlfriend is so beautiful?" I blushed as I turned away. "Does he have any hobbies other than hockey?"

I laugh, "He lives and breathes hockey, but your son is very great on the ice. He's a super star and he wants to make it big."

Grayson's mother laughs, my smile fading, "Is something wrong?"

She looked at me with a serious expression, "Well, his father forbade it for the longest time." She looked around, "You know I met his father at a hockey game."

My eyes widen, "Really?"

Her eyes sparkled, "He was a superstar alright, I was actually there for the rival team. I was dating the other team's captain at the time, and he was dating Sara Beckham." She coughs, "Well, still dating." She corrects as I frown.

"His father was so in love with the game until he had to pick between the game and his future. I was pregnant with Grayson when he picked the business. I always knew that Grayson would love the sport."

"If you don't mind me asking, why did Mr. Prince pick the business?"

She frowns, "I don't think that I could answer that question my dear." Her lips thinned as I nodded.

"Grayson is a tough spirit. He loves getting everything the way he wants, but that's not always the case. He messes up but trust he will always fix it." She continues, "While Grayson might not want to get to know me, I know he has a good heart."

She mirthlessly grins, "I would love to keep getting to know you since you and Grayson are becoming so close."

I look at Grayson's mother with despair, "Grayson and I are

going through a rough patch." I look away, putting my fork down, "He's dating his ex-girlfriend."

She frowns, "So, if you should be telling anyone that you want to meet their acquaintance or have dinner with them, it's her." I swallow as she looks down. Grayson's mother looked at me with a gloomy face.

"You have any plans tomorrow night?" She asked as I nod,

"I think my friends want me to attend this charity ball,"

She smiles, "What time do you think it will end?"

I think, "Maybe ten."

"I'd like to keep seeing you, if that's okay?" I looked up, confused with her offer. I nod, not really sure why I agreed.

CHAPTER 40

ADRIANNA

It was the day of the ball and I had made sure to wrap myself up before I could come to Margo's house to get ready. The ball was a big deal. It was held to give large sums of money to schools for children in Africa and the Philippines.

I cleaned after myself and stored the pill bottles back to where I found them before the housekeepers came. I had worn something baggy so I wouldn't irritate my wounds.

When I arrived at Margo's house, she was outside in her pajamas, giving a big kiss to Ben who was leaving, looking disheveled. I laugh at the thought that Margo was genuinely engaged.

"Get a room." I approach them as she delivers me a scowl.

She gives him a quick peck. "See you tonight." He says before pulling away and driving off in his fancy car.

"You two make me sick." I gag.

She pushes me playfully, "You and Grayson were like that." I flinch at the thought. Margo understood why I had an odd reaction.

Her face changes, "But that doesn't matter because we are going to have a kick ass night!"

"I'm only going because you three were going to drag me

down there even if I didn't want to go." I look at her with a serious expression.

"Adrianna, you have been wanting to go to this since we were little, and you know you would regret it if you didn't. You are just being stubborn," She leads me inside the house, "You talked to Darius?"

"I did."

"And?"

I roll my eyes, "He'll pick me up at 7."

Margo's eyes gleamed, she shook me, "Yes!"

"This is exactly what you need! Someone who is emotionally available and knows who they want, and he's easy on the eyes." She winks as we enter her dressing room, Verina and Juliette already sat with coffee and croissants.

"You're late." Verina looks at me with a smile.

I sat beside her, "You know I don't have to go to this right?"

Her eyes widen, "You can be as late as you want!" She corrects as I laugh, "You know since you and Grayson are done, we haven't had contact with any of the boys."

Verina and Juliette didn't know any of the details on mine and Grayson's spilt or how we spilt, so I didn't blame them for treating the situation like something I could brush off my shoulder.

"Meaning..."

She frowns, "Well, Chris hasn't texted me or anything."

I nod slowly, "I don't know babe."

"I asked him to come with me to the ball." She let out.

We all looked at her with shock, "You asked Chris?"

"Yes." She looked upset, "But I don't even know if he's coming."

We all quieted, not really knowing how to handle comforting Verina.

"Well, it's not Chris's scene." I say, hoping that it would relieve her a bit.

Juliette gets up she looked hesitant to speak but did anyways, "And why do you keep thinking about this man?"

Juliette takes a look at all of us before continuing, "He's not thinking about you V."

Juliette was always a type to tell the cold hard truth. She never backed down, especially when it came to our feelings. She always told it how it was, and she was right. Chris had made sure to let Verina know he wasn't interested.

"You have plenty of guys who want you Verina, why do you pick him?" Margo pulls out a pair of heels from her closet.

I think that maybe the reason why Verina is having a hard time understanding guys like Chris was solely because she didn't think that others had problems.

And we all kind of had that same mindset, always worrying about ourselves and people we knew, it was a toxic trait for all of us to have but that was just how it was.

"You guys don't know Chris," She looks down as I look at her, examining her body language. She was in deep.

She is most definitely so down bad for Christopher Florence and none of us could save her.

"You're right, we don't. We can only infer from the signs and the way he acts, and he hasn't done much Verina."

She sighs, "He's just shy but we've hung out alone together and he's perfect."

Verina talked about Chris like he was her lost soulmate, and I couldn't help but think she was going crazy. But I guess love makes people sick in many different ways.

I didn't know what happened between Verina and Chris for her to fall for him like she was, but I couldn't judge. At the end of the day, Verina just wanted to be loved like everyone else. She didn't care what it took, but it often made her a playing field for men.

But nonetheless, she believed that there was a man out there who would treat her like the world. Even with her roster of heart-breaks she was still looking.

After all, she believed that with every heartbreak made her closer to the one that keeps her heart together.

W e all put on our dresses, did each other's hair, and put on heels. I could tell this was gonna be a big night and I was going to make sure that I, at least, had a night to remember.

Darius had picked me up in a limo and looked beautiful in his suit. I looked at him in a way that I shouldn't have, I was weak in that moment.

I sat across from him, his eyes linger on my body, and I felt my heart race I smile at him, "Hey, I really appreciate you coming with me."

He nods, "It's a pleasure taking you, darling."

I turn away, as he leans closer, "What happened between you and Grayson?" He pulls away, "If you don't mind me asking."

I shift, "He and I had a falling out and I'm not really sure if we can fix it."

He sighs, "So I'm guessing you aren't in a place where you can give another guy a chance?"

I look at him not really sure what to say, "I'm trying."

He smiles widely, "And I am going to make sure I will not waste it. You are so beautiful that I don't think I can ever look at someone ever again."

I lean closer, suddenly loving the color of his green eyes, staring back at me, "You know you should come to my game on Monday."

I smirk, "You would like that wouldn't you?"

He smirks back, leaning back a little, "I would... you could be my lucky charm." He winks.

I roll my eyes, "I'm no lucky charm, I prefer it if boys do good without my help."

He smiles, his eyes scanning once again, "I'm the best babe. You don't even need to be there, but I think I'll die if I don't see you in the stands."

I lean closer, "Just like I would die right now if you don't kiss me." I felt my heart stop, his hand cupping my face.

"You can stop me at any moment."

I breathe out, "I know."

He leans closer, his lips so close to mine, "Will you?"

"No." I whisper to him as he smashes his lips on top of mine. So eager and willing, he pulled me closer, my dress falling a bit as he pulled me up, his hands on my neck.

I groaned letting my arms fall on his chest, it felt so wrong. It felt like I was cheating on Grayson, but I wasn't. I could do whatever I wanted, and he couldn't do anything about it.

The car stops as I pull away from him, his hands resting on my ass. I smile, "Let's get this party started."

He rolls his eyes, "We can be fashionably late, darling." I laugh, opening the door to see everyone gathered inside.

"But then we would be late."

"That's the point."

I roll my eyes, "Let's go, handsome."

He walks out of the limo, his hand out so that I can hold it, and I do. I had no reason not to.

During the ball, all eyes were on me and him. I couldn't help but think that I was doing something wrong, I was at a party with a man that I was interested in, and I wasn't about to feel sorry for it.

I saw Grayson there, shocker he was with his boyfriends and his one and only girlfriend, I felt a jealous pit in my stomach grow.

They were all in a huddle, I spotted Verina and Margo. Juliette was yet to be seen.

I grow agitated as Grayson's eyes scan my body from head to toe. It was like my body was on a glass case just for his viewing pleasure. And I fucking shouldn't be. He studied me like a damn painting, and I hated being under his gaze.

Darius's hand snaked around my lower back. It was like I got burned. Grayson's eyes, a gaze of red and fury. But he couldn't do anything about it, instead he looked away.

Like I broke his heart. But I did *nothing*.

Darius and I were greeted by rich couples, his family included, I even agreed to donate money for the children. I donated one million dollars originally.

The highest donation being ten million by Grayson Prince himself. I felt cheap, simply changing my donation to fifteen million dollars just to best him and to benefit the children of course.

The hidden gazes between Grayson and I were intoxicating. I felt like he was undressing me, the more he looked at me. As he looked away, I couldn't stop myself from staring.

I refused to look in his way again. I didn't want to feed into whatever game he was playing with me.

"You want something to drink?" Darius looks at me.

I nod, "Whatever you can find." I smile as he nods back.

Liam walks up to me with a smirk, "Sup, Dove."

I sigh with frustration, "Don't call me that, Stink." I smile.

His face alters to annoyance, "Margo told you about that?"

I laugh, "One, you should know that Margo tells me everything. Second, you being called Stink by your mother is cute."

"Yeah, she thought so too."

Liam eyes held a barrel of hatred, "So does Ben, apparently."

I stand a bit more annoyed at him, "Liam."

He sighs, "Yeah, I fucking know I messed up." I look behind him to Margo and Ben looking like they were made for each other.

"I love Margo." I sigh, "And I know you hate showing it, but I know you love her too."

He takes a sip of vodka, "What you did was fucked up." I state.

He nods, "I know and I've never more fucking stupid in my whole life but I'm trying."

I give Liam a really long look, "All of Margo's life, she's always rejected guys who were *only* trying. Her parents would make sure the only guys who courted her were the best of the best. Does it fathom you maybe that when she wanted to be with you, it was because she actually wanted to be with someone who makes her happy without her parents judgement?"

Liam only looked away over to look at Margo once again, "I've never felt this way about a girl." He whispers, then I notice he was a bit drunk.

Liam plucked at the cuff of his shirt, he was sweating, color draining from his face as he watched her with Ben. I, too, was a bit disturbed at the thought of Margo being engaged.

"I've lost her." He grimaced.

"No, you haven't. Margo has you locked in her heart. She has Ben in her front pocket. She's been trying to get your attention since the moment she got back from Greece. You haven't batted a damn eye."

He winced, "Instead you had women on your lap, you enjoyed the women that yelled your name at hockey games, and you didn't like the idea of Margo being there as your girlfriend."

"You deserve this." I continue.

He nods, "I agree."

Liam looked like he had a lump in his throat, having a hard time talking, "We didn't even date. She wasn't my ex-girlfriend. But she was my something." He knocked his head back, "I pushed her away because I was scared of the unknown."

I stayed quiet as he poured more whiskey in his mouth that he shouldn't have possession of, "I didn't know whether she would leave me or not, so I beat her to it. I have issues with trust. She was so fucking loyal, wasn't she? I pushed away the only person who made my fucking days go wild."

I smile, "Have you spoken to her?"

He shook his head, "I wouldn't want to intrude on her new relationship."

I roll my eyes, "You already are. You're on her damn mind every day. She doesn't want to talk about you to manipulate everyone into thinking you two are never going to find each other again, but we both know you will."

Liam smiles confidently, "Damn Anna, I totally understand the words of wisdom thing that Gray would always talk about." My cheeks turned pink, then it changed to a scowl, I straightened.

Liam looks at me with curious look, his head swaying over to Darius, "You and Gray sure do love to rile each other up even when you two are broken up."

I sigh, he swings is head back to look at me, "He's not Grayson Prince without you, you know."

I laugh, "He's been the best version of Grayson Prince without me, Liam."

"I would argue differently." Liam makes a point.

I laugh, "I'm serious Liam, it's over."

"Grayson has been my best friend since I first met him at our first hockey practice ever, and I've never seen that man lose his cool in a game. I've never seen his eyes look away from the puck just to look for a girl in the stands, and I surely have never ever fucking seen him miss a slapshot."

I let my heart fall to the floor, my face feeling like it was hardened, and I was working my best poker face ever. But I felt my emotions slipping.

I swallow, "Does he feel that way about August?" I ask with a dulled expression.

Liam smirks, "I see how he looks at you."

"How does he look at me?" I ask with my face turning scarlet red.

"Like he would love you, even if you were a million light years away."

My composure slips, damn you, William Brookshire. I pick

up my long dress, feeling tears build up in my sockets as I turn my head looking for the nearest bathroom.

Bad news was that these bathrooms were no where to fucking be seen but good news was that they were gender neutral, and I didn't need to find a woman's one.

I rushed into an open room, sitting on the large couch it provided. My tears falling as to took large breaths to calm myself down. I opened my pouch hoping that I was dumb enough to put extra pills in there for my consumption, but I was not. I didn't have anything.

The door opened abruptly as I stood up, Grayson walked in, his eyes darting straight at mine. I felt my heart build and fall at the same time. He did nothing but let the door close behind him.

CHAPTER 41

GRAYSON

I ram the door open abruptly as a golden figure stood up in shock as I walked, annoyance filled all over her face. Her eyes darted straight at mine, and I looked at them, a very striking resemblance to the shining stars.

"What are you doing here?" She asks with an irritated voice as I let the door close behind me.

I sigh, "What do you think my plans are when I walk into a bathroom?"

"I'm using it." She counters.

I narrow my eyes at hers, "It was marked as unoccupied, Do —" I press my lips together remembering that she asked me not to call her by my famous nickname.

"You saw me come in." She picked up her opened bag that made her lipstick fall to the ground.

"Sure, I saw you, but you were taking too damn long."

"That's such shit... I've been here for a minute."

She kneeled down to the floor, picking up her lipstick, her hair falling in front of her face, then the rest of the items in her pouch falling as I watched her face turn red.

I pull her up, "Don't." She looks at me, "I'll pick it up."

I couldn't bear to look at Adrianna kneeling on the floor like she was a housekeeper. She was more than that, she was a fucking princess.

"The only time I want to see you kneeling on the floor is if you're pleasing me."

I smile lazily as I get on the floor gathering her belongings. I looked up to her face, the room was nonexistent as her eyes meet mine once again. They were her weak spot, she loved to ignore them in class.

A silent moment between us passed as I looked away, getting up and handing her purse back, my hand on her waist as hers rested on my chest from the tight room.

I pulled away from her, turning to pull on the handle so that I could leave before I kissed her. But the door didn't budge. I turned the doorknob abruptly as it still wouldn't open.

"Is it locked?" She asked me questions as she rushed me out of the way.

"No, I just fucking like rattling doorknobs."

"Can you manage not being a dick and an asshole for one whole night?" She smiles thickly, "I know it's hard for you to do but please try your hardest." She continues to give me a stone-cold look.

Irritation filled my gut as she stood there. Her eyes diving deep into my soul, hoping to see a crack.

"Do you have a bobby pin?" I asked her.

"Do I look like I fucking had a bobby pin?"

She looked at me as if I didn't see she had her hair down and didn't use a bobby pin, so my luck was out.

"Great. Now, we're stuck." She snarls as I pulled my eyes away from hers.

"Way to state the fucking obvious, Sherlock." I complained.

She walks in the opposite direction to get as far away from me as possible. Sadly, the room was pretty small, so her attempt was funny.

"I can deal with being stuck but being stuck with you, I would rather kill myself." She snapped back as I rolled my eyes.

"Oh please, being stuck with me inside a bathroom with limited space is every girl's dream." I wink, joking with her as she looked away.

It wasn't the same bitterness we had before where she would come at me with a witty response. No, now it was an entirely different kind of bitterness. The kind of bitterness that threatened to suddenly implode and hurt the both of us. I know I was the cause of this bitterness.

I inched closer as I took a closer look at her face. With tears streaming down her cheeks, she looked so incredibly sad. It broke my own heart.

"Then why does it seem like such a nightmare?"

My heart sank down to the pit of my stomach. God, I wanted to tell her everything. Tell her the truth. Tell her that I didn't mean it. Tell her that my situation was fucked up. I wanted to spill it all out.

But I couldn't. Not until I had it figured out.

"Look at me." I walk closer to her.

She avoids my gaze, "I can't look at you or I might lose it, Grayson."

I looked into her eyes as I found myself lost in them once again, "I'm looking at you."

I looked at her as if she were my universe. As if I would promise her anything if only, she would say it. She could do anything to me. I would always try to fight for her.

For us.

She wiped her face quickly giving me another heart wrenching look.

I would often think about the times Adrianna promised she would stay. She was still here, even when I broke her heart and acted like a jerk. She came to the house every night. I didn't show up, but I asked Harvey to watch her.

She would always come, until she didn't.

"What is it?" She asked, "Is there something on my face or are you just gawking?" She turned away as I caressed her cheek.

I swallow, "Just gawking." I answered as she shakes her head with embarrassment.

"Don't roll your eyes at me." I seethed as she scowls back, I couldn't help but want her closer. She couldn't either. My hand gripped her waist tighter as she let out a silent moan, a breath releasing from her mouth.

My breath against her neck. She bit her lips as I licked mine, "Don't fucking do that either." I pushed her slowly against the wall, kissing her neck.

I couldn't help myself and I wish I could, but I couldn't, "Grayson..." She breathed out as I pulled away suddenly remembering our situation.

I closed my eyes, looking at her was too much.

I pull my hand away from her waist suddenly smelling the taint smell of copper, I look down at her delicate and petite figure, "Dove?"

She winced in pain as I looked at my hand, smeared with blood, then looking at her white dressed soaking with a hue or red, "Is that blood?"

She pushes me away with a sour expression, "Don't fucking touch me."

She kept bleeding as I look at her with genuine fear, "Dove."

She turns away embarrassed as I held her hand, "Adrianna, don't be embarrassed." She turned to look at me again, tears falling and this time she didn't care if I saw.

"But I am embarrassed Grayson!" She screams at me and all I can really do is listen. "What do you want me to say?!" She laughs, "We match?" She faces me, "Because we don't. I was so fucking wrong because I thought you understood, but you didn't. You left me when I gave you so much." She poured it all out as I stood there staring at her.

Her eyes were glass. One blink, they would break, "I came to you, with glued together broken parts of me. My wounds still had freshly sewn stitches. But you somehow thought it was okay to mend them and ruin me all over again."

She looked at me with despair.

"*You*. Grayson. *You* were the one who wanted me first. *You* fucking wanted me first and *you* were the one who insisted and reached out. Why am I the one picking up my own damn pieces!" She screamed with hurt and sorrow.

I was speechless, "Why am I the one to feel all the damn pain when *you* were the one who wanted me first?" She calmed down, her face neutral, with her makeup running down her face.

"So don't tell me not to be embarrassed when I trusted you. You embarrassed me. You disappointed me. And I don't know if I could ever forgive you for deceiving me when you knew I didn't deserve it."

She walked closer, tears falling to the ground as my heart felt heavier, "I don't deserve it right?" She asks, "Please tell me I don't deserve it."

I opened my mouth to speak but nothing came out, I wanted nothing more than to tell her that she didn't deserve any of this, that I should've just left the angel in her damn palace.

I couldn't touch her. She would just think I burned her.

I couldn't reassure her. She would just think my words were mocking and condescending.

I couldn't promise her. She would think I'm bluffing.

I couldn't undo my actions knowing they had left visible and bleeding scars on her body. I couldn't say sorry because a mere sorry was not enough to show her how much I regret everything I've fucking done.

I could only stand there where I made no more impact, no more destruction.

Adrianna was the type of girl who wanted to write down her thoughts to remember them, while I looked over them and just ignored them because I hated everything about reminiscing.

She was the type of girl who loved the warmth, where the flowers would grow, while I loved the winter, where everything was dead, and the cold numbed the pain when I played hockey.

She was the type of girl who never wants to forget the great things in life, while I sat there struggling to not want to remember anything.

She wasn't made for me. She was made for someone better. Everything was terrible for her. All I gave her was pain.

I stood and watched her go up in flames. I was a coward because I heard August's yelling from the outside of the bathroom.

"Go." She insists as I closed my eyes, "I don't need you to make me feel better, Prince."

It hurt because I knew she heard August too. I pulled her into an embrace, "I don't want to fucking leave you." I whisper as she sobbed into my chest, "I don't want to ever see you like this, I'm so *so* sorry, Dove."

She quieted; it was serene. Was it worth the three months we were together? I would say yes even if it ended in ruin. Would it be better if I never took her home from that bar?

But then I pondered too much into it and understood the inevitability of destruction. She was hurting, and I couldn't take it.

This is *my* fault.

She looked up, tears had stopped as I kissed the top of her head, "Can you please call Margo?" She swallowed as I nodded, pulling away. I watched her take a seat back on the couch. I pulled out my phone calling Margo's cell as she picked up with a hurried distinct fear asking where Adrianna had gone.

I asked her to come get us at the locked bathroom. She got there in less than a minute. Slamming the door open, she ran straight to Adrianna.

Her eyes remained on me as Margo talked to her. My hand remained on the doorknob, I hesitated to leave, my hand shaking as I turned away from them, unlocking the door from the front.

When I asked Neil to lock Adrianna and I in the bathroom for a short amount of time I didn't think it would slap me in the damn face. I wanted to see if she was okay.

And she wasn't.

CHAPTER 42

ADRIANNA

"Oh, my darling," Margo stresses as she wrapped my waist by ripping a part of her dress.

I swallow, "I'm fine Margo. I just want to get out of here."

"Adrianna, what the hell happened?" She asked while helping me up, "I'll grab my keys." Margo gets up.

I pull her back down, "No, I don't want you coming with me. I want to be by myself for the rest of the night."

She looked guilty, "You aren't saying that just because Ben is here, are you?"

I smile, "I'm saying this to prove a point that I should've just stayed home."

Margo nods, hugging me, "I'm so sorry I should've never ask you to come. This is my fault." She looked at me, cupping my face. "But don't you dare think you aren't talking about cutting yourself on Tuesday at your appointment."

"I'm not going."

"Let's table that conversation." Margo was always adamant about getting me into talking about my problems and I couldn't help but cooperate tonight.

"Grayson and I talked," She gives me a warm smile.

"I know, darling."

I was sober. I hadn't drank but my body felt as though it was hit by a massive truck, "Margo."

I calmly said as she lifts my head up to look at her, "Anna?" She addresses.

I let a tear fall, not minding showing Margo my weaknesses, "I think I'm falling apart again."

She shushes me, "I think you have to realize how far you've come and how strong and magical you are."

"I screamed at him, and he said sorry." I pulled away from her, "I wanted to..."

Margo interrupts me with a gaze of uncertainly, not really wanting to talk about it but knew that we had to, "Anna."

I turn to look at her, "Yes?"

She frowns, scared to ask, "Do you love him?"

The small kisses that we had littered across each other's faces, the kisses that we sent each other from the air, the hungry kisses he would envelope me with when we were alone. My breathy demand of "kiss me" when I was at his games.

Me throwing my arms around his neck, closely hugging him as he kissed the top of my head. Initially, I didn't want to fall in love. Not at all. Falling in love was never in the damn plan for me, I wasn't quite sure how I would handle it.

But at some point, he smiled, and I found my heart being dragged to love him. He came to me with flashing neon lights, red flags, and five billion warnings. But he already had the only living part of me before I could say no.

It wasn't supposed to happen, I wasn't supposed to even like him, but I did.

Damn it. I did.

Margo's face came to my vision once more as I tilted my head. "Yes."

"How much?" She asked with loving filled eyes that I tried to avoid.

"Does it matter?"

"Why does it not?"

I sigh, I didn't mean to fall in love, but I did. He didn't mean to hurt me, but he did. And of course, I knew I loved him, I've been pushing it so deep down that it slipped out without me noticing. I wouldn't have given Grayson the power to destroy me if I didn't love him.

I looked at Margo once more, with a thin smile as she listened, and I knew I wasn't going to get interrupted.

"I gave him every part of me, even the parts that I was ashamed of and yet I still watched him love and choose her at the end of the day. I waited and waited for him to tell me it was a joke, that he would never do that to me."

"But the catch and explanation never happened," I laugh, "The thing is, he told me in the beginning that he wanted her, it was the reason we got together remember?"

"His reason for being with me was always because of her," I swallow, "I was prepared, but it still broke my heart."

Margo kneels in front of me, "I didn't think he hurt you this much." She whispers as I look back at her, not really sure if my soul was still there.

Neither did I.

Margo pushed my hair back as I looked at her with full defeat, "I'd be his if he asked." I mutter.

She closed her eyes and stroked my hair, "I know babe."

Margo sat next to me, it was the first time to ever really see my real and raw emotions, she probably thought she was dreaming, "I hate this. I hate all of this." I let out.

"I can't stop crying like a damn baby. I never cry over a boy, Margo. All I ever do now is think about him and it's making me damn crazy."

She nods, "Anna, you—"

I interrupt her, "He's not coming back, and I know that." I said, "I know he isn't coming back."

"No, you don't." She argues as I turn my head to look at her,

"I never understood why the universe brings two people together only to tear them apart, hoping that maybe they will find a way back to each other. It's a cruel thing. It's a cruel world."

She stands, "But *you*." She signals at me, "You are the hardest thing that Grayson Prince had ever had to walk away from, do you understand me?"

"He walked away from the only thing that ever believed he was more than who he showed. He walked away still being madly falling for you."

I stood up, "Coming here was a mistake and I shouldn't have come. I've embarrassed myself Margo, and I've completely ruined my dress and date."

"You can have my keys, and you can go home if you really want."

I sigh, a breath of relief has finally left my chest, "This wasn't supposed to happen you know, I wasn't supposed to love him like I do."

"I don't think he was supposed to let himself have you in the first place Adrianna."

She hands me her keys, I turn away ignoring her, pulling the keys to myself, "If two people can't seem to stay away from each other, then maybe they shouldn't. "

T took the exit in the back of the ballroom. I didn't want to disturb anyone else's night and I surely didn't want to show the whole guest list my bleeding waist.

I pulled my heels out of my feet so that I could walk through the grass in the gardens faster. My luck was severely terrible as I ran into a certain redhead.

The flowers around me felt like they failed to flourish as soon as our eyes met.

"Fleeing the party?" August looks at me with a bland expression, I ran my hand on the dying rose that had wilted.

I wasn't going to lie, she looked radiant, she always did, she was a natural type of beauty that glows in the sunlight. Grayson and her really did look great together, didn't they?

Maybe that was how it was supposed to be, they were *Romeo and Juliet,* and I was Romeo's bitter ex, Rosaline.

I exhale, "I couldn't stay another minute in there." I answered as she turned her head to look at me.

She leaned against the stone wall looking up as if she was waiting for an angel, "You know, I've been out here for a good forty-five minutes, and Grayson hasn't come to get me once."

Maybe because we were stuck in a damn bathroom.

I swallow, "Maybe because he's looking for you inside."

She wipes the tears away from her cheeks, "He hasn't been looking."

"He's been too busy looking at you." She lets out as I bite my lip, "I don't know why I thought I could replace you; it's always been you."

She laughs, "Grayson and I used to be perfect. There was laughter, so much laughter." She looks at me, "So much love that he would make sure that I would never go unnoticed, he vowed to never let me be alone."

I stood there agape, not really sure on what to say to her, not really sure if there was anything to say, "But I broke his heart, I left him, and he found you." She took a breath in.

"I hated you because you stole the heart of the most unobtainable man in Hawthorne. You took him, and it didn't take long for me to see that Grayson needed you and you needed him. I was so naive because I thought I could replace what you two had."

She glares at me, "I might have him physically, but we both know you will always have his heart at the end of the day."

"August—" I cut her off, my heart breaking. She walks away from the wall, "I'm in no position to give you my opinion of your relationship with Grayson, it's none of my business."

"He picked you and that's all we really needed to know. He wouldn't cheat on you. He would be a faithful man and treat you like you are the world."

"Sure, he can shower me with gifts, but that's where it would end."

"The love that Grayson and I share is different, he would always love me in some way, but it's not the same as the love that he gives you. He gives you soul crushing love and affection."

"I'm so sorry for ruining it." She whispers as I nod.

"He thinks of you every day, I hope you know that even if you two only shared three real months together. You've taken a part of him that I can never get back."

Then she laughs. Hard.

It was like a slap to the damn face, "You are such a fool, falling for my bullshit."

"I grovel for his pieces." She mutters, pulling out her hand. My heart stopped as her ring finger was adorned by a heavy Tiffany ring in 18k yellow gold and a beautiful rock in the middle. My chest stung. My heart felt heavy.

"Grayson bought that for you?" I asked weakly.

She closed her eyes, "Yes."

I turned away my hand on top of my mouth, trying hard not to let out a weak noise of sobs, "It's a promise ring."

"I wanted to show you before you saw it at school. Grayson and I are very much serious, and I want you to know that at the end of the day, I'm the one in his bed,"

"You are the other woman." She stood, "You don't get to have him. And you will stop talking to him." She continues, "There's a reason why Grayson left you high and dry and came back straight to me and it's better for you to know that he's disgusted by you."

My body felt a wave of pain, "You are pathetic. He doesn't want someone that he has to baby, someone who he doesn't have to worry about. He needs someone strong that doesn't need to go to a therapist."

"Did he say that?" I ask, not really sure why I did.

"Yes." She sneered, "The cold hard truth is that you are a huge fucking piece of work. Grayson Prince has no time for your bullshit."

She held a certain look of disdain, "That's why he picked me."

There it was again, the wave of pain that had hit me so damn hard. I didn't even want to try and get up from the pain those words had caused me.

I felt like I was drowning and occasionally swimming up for air, and I couldn't breathe anymore because I was so sick of trying.

"Good for you guys." I smile thickly.

She looks at me, "Now I think that I have a date to get back to." She interjects as I let out a heavy sigh. She let the door close behind her. I let my feet take me to the car, tears yet again falling down my face.

I let all the pinned-up anger that I stored inside me finally release as I slammed my hand on the steering wheel. My eyes shut close as I let my hand clam on the shift.

Blood rushed through my body as it roared in my ears, feeling my heart sprint though it's pulses. My heart rapidly pounding I could barely hear anything.

I was done for. I was absolutely fucking done for. The air around me vibrated as my breath took a hitch.

Then I stopped breathing. On the verge of tears, I felt my whole body breaking and losing life. Just then, there was a crackling sound that filled the whole damn car. I envisioned the glass from the windows, the lights shattering and turning off.

My eyes stayed closed. I only saw pure red. I could only hear my heavy panting and my jaw trembling as I clenched my hands into fists, trying so hard not to scream.

I didn't resist anymore. I screamed so loud that I lost my voice. My heart still squeezing tightly as tears began to stream down my soft and winded cheeks. I always knew that everything in my life was fucked, but it was heartbreaking that I wanted to die. It was one thing I wanted to lose myself. I wanted to just *die*.

So, I checked out every single space where I would leave pills. Sadly, I found some and I took eight of them. My heart slowing down as I close my eyes.

I turn on the car.

CHAPTER 43

GRAYSON

I couldn't think straight after my sad conversation with Adrianna. I felt lost, no words or thoughts could leave my brain. I didn't feel like being here anymore. To be honest, I wanted to stay home.

But I could never go home and rest, knowing the tears and heartache that I had brought to Adrianna. It seemed fucking cruel.

August came towards me with a beaming smile, "Where have you been?" I asked as she crossed her arms in front of her.

"I've been out."

"Out where?"

"Out getting fresh air, Grayson. It's good for the baby." She counters, I suddenly felt no fight in me to argue.

"If there even is a baby." I mutter instead.

She quiets down, "When will you trust me?"

"Never." I plainly say as she swallows, the ballroom quieted down as the violins started to play, the lights dimmed, and the music turned on. She took my hand, and I didn't even really ask for a dance, but I guess she thought that asking was beyond our relationship.

I slithered my hand around her waist, as she dug her nails deep down my back, making me groan as she lifted her head up to look at me. I turn away as she struggles but she pulls me in.

"Stop putting me through this pain, Gray." She snaps, letting her hand travel up and wrap around my tie, pulling my head forward.

"Just be quiet, August." I ask as she latches on my shoulder, as I hiss.

"Please come back to me Grayson."

I push her away, "It's different now, it's different. I used to think you were different, but you lie. You scheme with my damn father. You hurt people and you will do whatever you need to ruin others."

"That doesn't sound far from Adrianna." She snaps back.

I tilt my head with a smirk I pulled my wrist back, "I look at you and you fucking disgust me. I look at you and I think about how I messed everything up with..."

She holds her eyes over mine, almost like she was fighting the tears, "Will I ever be good enough for you again?" She laughs, "It's my fault, how could I possibly think that I could take my place back?"

I said nothing, only stared. "But I had you first." She pleaded, "She's supposed to be the other woman Grayson. I'm supposed to be the one you want." She closed her eyes, I turned away.

"Fucking hell, Grayson I can change! You want me to get plastic surgery for you? I can look like her! God, Grayson it's like she has you on a fucking spell." She lowered her head on my chest, her tears spilling.

"I watch you watch her, and it hurts me because I'm trying to get you back."

Somehow, I felt uncomfortable.

I chased this damn girl's attention for three months, but now I simply didn't care. I was a terrible person, I know that, but my head could not move past the idea of Adrianna going home with Darius Sawyer.

Her gaze moved up to mine, "I'm not her." She swallowed again, "I know I'm not her and I can't replace her."

I swallow hard. She was right. No one could ever replace Adrianna in my life, not a single fucking person or thing could bring the same effect as Adrianna.

She's the only one for me.

Maybe that shit only happens and exist in books, the stories that she would read hours on fucking end. Was I really that naive to think that it would just be me and her?

I face August once more, her eyes widen more as I bend down to kiss her, hoping that there was an ounce of happiness in my body but there was not.

I tasted the salt from her tears as I breathed her in, "I'm sorry August, but no, you can't replace her. I'm with you because of the baby in your stomach and my father's wishes, so please stop playing the fucking girlfriend."

She looks at me dead in the eyes, "If you really loved her, then you wouldn't care. A person that loves you wouldn't leave you. A person that loves you would stick by you, even when you are in your darkest moments. But you don't do that do you? You left her. You left her when you said you wouldn't, right?"

"What does that say about you?" She says as I swallow, "You don't love her Grayson, it's about time you realized it."

I pierce my eyes into hers. "Don't ever fucking mention her again."

Her eyes ran to my silver cold ones.

"I'm not going to sit here and apologize to you because I'm not sorry." She walked backwards slowly as I moved away from her general direction.

"I'm sorry for you because you're ruining yourself because of her." She lets out as I shake my head.

"Adrianna is out of my life understand me?" I glower back. "I'm engaged to you. This is what you wanted remember?"

"She'll never be out of the picture, Prince." She pulls away, slightly. "I want her out of the picture." She continues.

"I'm sorry." She apologizes.

I sigh, "It's my fault for being so irresponsible for getting you pregnant." August turned away, which made me even more suspicious that the child she was carry was not mine. I let my thoughts roam even more, "I wish I could change how things are, but I can't."

"Are you angry with me?" She asked as I said nothing.

I was furious with her. I hated that she pulled me away from Adrianna. I loathed how she was the reason that I couldn't go after Adrianna and kiss her like I fucking meant to.

"Adrianna and I know our relationship can't exceed, so there's no point." I admit as she nods slowly, "It's better for us to part ways and just stick to how it was before we let anything happen."

August smiles, her face red. My whole heart hurt, it felt numb, and it stung the entire time. I thought about the restless nights I've had the past week.

I thought about how she calmed me down with her doe eyes, her hands on mine as she would let me squeeze her hands. She tolerated everything about me that I hated about myself.

I love her for it.

Even with all my damn faults and my fucked head, she craved me like plants craved the sunlight.

I hated Adrianna because she did love me. She didn't have to say it, but the look in her eyes told me the whole story. I hated her because there was nothing, I could do to change her mind.

I had a cowardly plan. I had it planned out that we were supposed to run away together. I would give her the engagement ring. I would tell her to never take it off and she would've promised. I had a plan for us, but it's ruined this time. We had no choice.

"You were willing to give her up for me and the baby?" August started crying, and I just stared at her.

"I know you don't love me anymore Grayson, but I want you to try. I want you to at least remember why you loved me before."

She looks away, "I know you watch her every time she looks away."

I didn't say anything, only waited for the man to stop playing the violin. I didn't love August anymore, I wasn't quite sure if I really did before, besides...

...Everybody knows that it's all about who you look for in a crowded room. That's where your heart belongs.

ADRIANNA

I was upset, of course, I hadn't felt the best. But through my whole life I did know one thing, I knew what it felt like before overdosing and it certainly felt something like this.

First phase of overdosing...

Your heart will start to race. Your heart will feel like a boulder trying to escape from your chest. Fast, furious, and pounding.

Second phase...

You begin sweating. Your hair sticks to your forehead as everything suddenly starts to feel unbearably hot.

Third phase...

You can easily become confused or disoriented. Ultimately, you will lose consciousness. Often blood will appear when you throw up. Everything blends together. You vomit. You're confused. You'll be unresponsive to anything and everyone. You have a slowed breathing pattern, a fleeting heartbeat, causing severe chest pains that will make it seem like someone is stepping on your chest and back at the same time.

I didn't know what to do. I wanted to die. It was the perfect time to die. I did whatever I could. So, I floored on the gas, pressing on the seat as I began to lose vision.

I peered into my side mirror to see if anyone was around me. I twisted the steering wheel, the car shooting out to a corner of a very narrow street I had never seen before.

I didn't want to come home. I wanted to go to a whole different place other than my damn house.

First, I thought that the voices were only with me when I was at home, but I was so wrong. They continued to haunt me while I gripped the steering wheel so hard, I couldn't feel my knuckles.

I closed my eyes for a brief moment, letting the silence take over me as I quieted my head.

Only when I open them, the windshield shatters.

A shower of glass surrounds me like a beautiful thunderstorm of pain.

I clutched the steering wheel as a red car drove itself through the side of my car, wrecking the door even more.

Fear was holding me by the throat as my voice was inaudible. I felt as though I couldn't move. I really couldn't, I could feel something crushing my leg. I could feel my whole life pulling away from me.

I couldn't get out. A fire had terrified me even more as it started on the other end of the car. I turned another corner. I slammed on the door. I shut my eyes as the same red car rams itself through the front of the car.

My body jerked forward, air rushing out of my lungs, my vision turning black, my car finally crashed. The air bags explode in my face, stopping the impact of my face smashing on the wheel. A sharp piece of metal pierces through my leg, straight through my muscle tissue, my heart racing as my vision dazed.

Eventually, I heard the engine die. My ear ringing as my head throbbed. The hood of the car was crushed, as my vision was showered with dots. As soon as I closed my eyes, silence greeted me.

CHAPTER 44

GRAYSON

ater that night.

Everyone was tired, Liam was falling asleep on the couch. Neil never came, but surprisingly, Chris did attend. He danced with Verina and even met her parents. I, on the other hand, was dreading the rest of the night.

August showed off her ring to the elites of society and I sat at the bar tipping the bartender multiple hundred-dollar bills to keep giving me whiskey.

Everyone was getting ready to go. They were packing themselves up to their limos, expensive cars, and making sure they had their affairs in order. I waited for August to get ready. I grabbed my keys from the front, grabbing my coat as well.

I spot Margo looking frantically around as she sat by the sidewalk, Ben was next to her guarding her like a dog.

I walk up to her, her eyes looking at me, pleading with worry and a full horrific expression, "Hamilton, you good?" I asked as she stood up. She shot her panicked eyes at me, her phone besides her ear.

"Have you seen Anna?" She looked terrified.

"She hasn't been answering her phone." She calms down as Ben places his hand on her shoulder.

"What do you mean she hasn't been answering her phone?"

My heart dropped, my throat felt tight and raw, like my lungs were not functioning. I almost couldn't breathe.

"She left early and she's not answering her phone. She always calls me when she gets home safely." Margo stressed as Verina and Juliette came running.

"We checked the bathroom and asked everyone to look but no one has the phone."

I took a deep breath, my heart however wouldn't stop beating harshly, "Why the hell would you let her leave early?" I snapped as Liam walked in front of me, with a warning look to stay calm near his girl.

I bit my lip, pulling it away. I picked up my phone, entering police and 911 on the phone, quickly instructing them to look for Adrianna Cassian, making sure to alert her father and other family members.

I had to agree that it wasn't like Adrianna to take off and not saying anything, especially to Margo.

I had a tight feeling to my stomach, I swallow, "I can help you look." I look around, looking at August, "I can ask Arthur to take you home."

She scowled, "Grayson, I want you to come home with me right now." She instructed as I slammed my fist into the car, making her jump, I wasn't in the mood to deal with her stubbornness or her lack of brain cells.

The only thing that mattered was if Adrianna had gotten home safe, "I can call Neil and ask if he could check her house to see if she got there safe." Chris declares as I nod.

"I'm going to drive around."

Liam looked at me, "I'll come with you."

Juliette pulled out her phone, "I can start filing a missing person report, and Margo, I'm going to drive around by myself." She speaks out and no one felt the need to tell her that she couldn't go out by herself this late at night.

"No one is fucking stopping me," She says with conviction as

I get on my phone, calling more officials to get a search party going.

"Grayson can you try and call her?" Verina asks as I get on my pinned contact list.

"He can't." Margo interrupts, "She has you blocked."

I nodded, understanding completely why she did.

August sat in my car, "I'll stay here and wait for you." She speaks.

I nod, "We're taking Liam's car."

Liam and I strap on our seat belts as Margo gets in her car, telling Ben to keep a search out in the parking lot or the ball just in case.

Verina, Chris, and Juliette all got in a car and started to look in New Crest while we looked elsewhere. She couldn't have gotten far, right?

There is no way that she could've gone more than she could. I prayed to God to tell me she's fucking okay.

I sat next to Liam. I didn't trust myself enough to drive under my stressful conditions. All I could think of was how much I would sacrifice for her.

I was known not to have many weaknesses. I was known to be robust, severe, and borderline fucking reckless, in life and on the ice. I wasn't supposed to care much about people.

It was how my father was. He didn't have a weakness. I still think he doesn't.

I wasn't supposed to have a weakness, but Adrianna Cassian was my weakness, for some twisted reason she managed to squeeze through my barbed wires.

I haven't uttered the famous eight letters, three words to her, and I wasn't quite sure if she would hear it right if I ever did say them out loud, but I knew I meant them… I want to be able to tell her.

But at this very moment I didn't care about anything but her safety. Damn, I didn't care about whether her and I would end up together right now because I just want her fucking safe.

I don't think I would be able to live with myself if she wasn't. I don't think I could ever fathom a life on earth without her.

She was the reason why the earth is so beautiful. Please don't let Adrianna be ripped away from the earth's beauty.

I couldn't stop tapping my knee on Liam's car door, his eyes looking over at me, "She'll be okay." He assures me as I slowly look back at him.

"She better be fucking okay, for everyone's sake." I mutter, quite scornfully. I was sure of my attitude if Adrianna had been harmed in any way.

Liam visibly swallows.

"If she fucking dies, the doctors that tried to help her die."

All hail the wrath of the Prince himself.

L iam and I drove around for *eight* hours.

I felt bad as he started to get droopy, his eyes starting to fall close as I still felt very much awake.

I mean how could I sleep when I knew she was still not fucking found. Neil went to check at her house, anywhere I really thought she would be, but she was nowhere to be found.

It sounded terrible, but I've dreamt about this often. I had nightmares about these types of situations. I would wake up in the middle of the night and I wouldn't be able to go back to bed again.

I couldn't fathom losing her.

I could feel the darker parts of my body devouring me. I'm a damn prisoner in my whole brain. I often found that I waited for her to fall asleep before I could.

I was scared one day maybe she would disappear. God would take away the only angel he sent me because she didn't think I would need saving anymore.

I would watch her breathe, every inhale and exhale until I fell asleep to the sound of her heartbeat. She looked beautiful. If we were in a museum full of exquisite art, my eyes would only remain and be lost in hers.

Her warmth would fill my coldness.

Her brightness lit up the dark and disturbing thoughts that roamed in my head, keeping me up at night.

She was my damn weakness.

But damn, I'm Grayson fucking Prince. I was known to have no weaknesses.

But the moment I saw her, I knew she would be in my fucking blood. I'd live and breathe her.

Both Liam and I jerk, hearing my phone ring. My heart stops, Liam looks at me then back at the road.

I looked down to my phone, seeing Margo's name on the caller ID, I felt my throat tighten. My hand shaking finding it hard to answer, I took a breath before finally picking up.

"Grayson?"

I swallow, closing my eyes, "Margo." I address as I hear heavy sobs on her end of the call.

"I found her." She sniffles as my heart drops to my stomach. Liam hears his girl's sobs, pressing the brakes of the car, giving me look asking if Margo was okay.

"Margo, what's going on? Are you and Adrianna, okay?" I ask, afraid of what the answer might be.

She said nothing and it made my heart pause.

"Where are you guys?" I asked as she sobbed even more.

"She's dying."

She muttered, silence filled the whole car, voices in my head exploding. Margo's voice was flat and voiceless.

"She's dying."

It was the only sentence needed to destroy my whole fucking world in a damn second.

"What are you talking about? Where is she?" I let out, hoping Margo was pulling a damn joke over my fucking head.

"There's so much blood, Grayson." She voiced with a serious and worried expression.

"Is she alive?!" I yell as Liam turned the car around, "Where are you?"

"We are near the abandoned hospital in New Crest, the intersection." She stressed as Liam floors the gas pedal on the car.

"Is there a pulse?" I asked, terrified.

"No." She sobbed, "She was breathing a minute ago, and now she's not." I heard Margo set the phone down, hysterical found itself in her voice as I gripped on my phone scared it might break.

"Margo, do you know how to do CPR?" I ask as she cries even more.

"I'm doing it now." She stresses.

"Call 911." I order as I swallow, "Is she wearing a clock necklace?" I asked, hoping she was.

Margo takes a moment, "Yes."

I breath out, "Press the back." I look at the GPS on my phone, "You just alerted all the hospitals nearby that you need help, and you called 911."

"I'm losing her Grayson." She cries, my heart throbbed as did my temples, my fist building up.

"Don't you dare give up Margo." I demand, my voice losing composure.

"God, please don't give up."

MARGO

My eyes dart to Adrianna's weakened body, she was fail and white as a ghost.

I pushed down her chest.

One. Two. Three. Four. Five. Six. Seven. Eight. Nine. Ten.

Was it my imagination or was this really happening? I stared at the only person I ever really chosen to love. I wanted to die with her, wanting to kill myself for letting her leave the party.

It was all my fault.

"Margo?" Grayson's voice sliced through me like a damn knife. I could hear his voice break; I pressed my hands down against her chest harder, feeling my tears fall.

Eleven. Twelve. Thirteen. Fourteen. Fifteen. Sixteen. Seventeen. Eighteen. Nineteen. Twenty.

Grayson's voice appeared once again. I had forgot he was on the phone; my tears fell on her dress. "Help is coming don't worry, but you have to get her breathing Margo."

He was telling me not to worry?!

I closed my eyes, pressing down on her chest again.

Twenty-one. Twenty-two. Twenty-three. Twenty-four Twenty-five. Twenty-six. Twenty-eight. Twenty-nine. Thirty.

I cupped Adrianna's face, pressing my lips on hers, blowing air into her lungs.

I speed up my compression, breathing into her mouth twice the next time. "Nothing's working!" I yelled, I started to cry even more as I heard the ambulances nearing the road.

"Keep trying Margo." Grayson pleads as I start up my compressions again. My fingers starting to cramp up, they were sticky as her blood seeped through and stained my hands. My eyes blurred with tears I watched my best friend going through death once *again.*

She was my sister, my best friend, my soulmate. Watching my sister not breathing, surrounded by blood mentally drained by brain and my body. I couldn't stop crying, I only pushed harder into her chest, drawing another breath of life into her mouth.

My heart pausing hearing the light breeze of her breath on my cheek. I froze, I had to make sure I didn't imagine it, so I stayed there for another minute, hearing her breathing.

I placed my bloody fingers on her pulse point, her pulse was back, it was weak and fragile, but it was there. My eyes closed in relief, pulling her frail body close to mine, noticing the shard of glass pierced her leg.

I cradled her head into my lap, my hand rested on her chest, hoping it kept rising and falling. I held her tighter, hearing the ambulance approach.

"Margo?" Grayson called out once more, "Hello?"

"Yes. I'm here." I breathe out in relief, "She's breathing."

I could hear Grayson's breath release, a large pause as I look up to the sky thanking God.

"We are near." He notes as I nod, tears shedding more, "I don't think you should come here, it's not a good sight." I pointed out to Grayson as he gave a pause.

"The ambulance is here; you might as well meet us at the hospital." I ramble as he pauses, "No, Liam wants to see if you're okay."

My vision swamped my hazy tears and her complexion against the hue of red. I couldn't even disagree with Grayson. I had no energy to.

The ambulance arrives near us, pulling out the stretcher. The paramedics jumped out of the vehicle, barely sparing me a look or glance. Two men knelt beside us, feeling her heartbeat, giving a quick scan of her injuries.

They started asking me questions, I simply could not answer. I blur them out, clearly in shock as they pulled her away from me.

I felt a hard figure touching my arm, I turned to see Liam's face. He appeared in my field of vision as a lifeline.

I wrap my arms around his neck, sagging against his body, feeling drained. Sobs escape my throat as he brushed my hair away from my face, "Are you hurt?" He asked with concern and full anxiety as I tried to speak but I couldn't.

Grayson rushed next to the stretcher, his hand clamped around Adrianna's as he looked like he was gripping for life, "If she fucking dies, you fucking die." He seethes out like he was spitting venom.

I look at them closely, *Romeo and Juliet*. He looked about

ready to sacrifice himself just to join her on her death bed if she didn't make it.

I would do it for Anna too, she had that effect on people. But right now, I did what I could, I didn't sob anymore. Instead, I cried softly, using as many little tears as possible.

I looked at Adrianna's body as the doors of the ambulance shut. I asked Grayson if I could ride with her to the hospital and he quickly agreed.

Not that his objection would've stopped me, I sat behind the ambulance next to her, her lashes fluttered so beautifully. I felt frantic, like my skull was being cracked open and I was being picked apart as they asked me about Adrianna's medical history.

I held her hand, my limbs were useless, and my heart consistently convulsed in pain. I didn't even want to see want I looked like right now, my eyes were so red, and my lips couldn't stop shaking.

But as the ride quieted and they got her hooked on a machine, my breathing leveled, and my heartbeat calmed. I look at her strong and conquering body.

Oh Anna, there's so much untouched and unfinished in your life that you need to do and see.

CHAPTER 45

GRAYSON

I took over driving to the hospital. I didn't want Liam to go at his slow ass speed. I didn't care if I broke the speed limit, I would pay whatever fucking fine I needed just to get to that damn hospital.

But right when we reached the parking lot, I saw them push Adrianna's stretched in the emergency room. My heart dropped, "Hey, your girlfriend is calling me." Liam said as my eyes shot up at him.

"What does she want?" I said with fully irritated eyes.

"Beats me."

I roll my eyes, taking the phone, "Grayson, I need you home... it's been eight almost nine hours." She insisted as I took a slow breath.

"I can't right now, August." I voiced as she started to sob, like she was losing her life.

"Why?"

August sniffled, "I think something is wrong with the baby." I halt, pausing, looking up to the hospital doors, what type of person would I be if I didn't go to my son or daughter's emergency appointment.

What type of person would Adrianna preserve me as? I could handle the thought of her being mad, she's always been mad about every little thing I've done.

But this moment was a moment I knew I wouldn't forget about all of the rest of my life.

I turn to Liam, huffing, "Take me to August's location." I pulled up the GPS. Liam didn't complain, he simply agreed and started to drive me, "August said it's urgent."

Liam stayed quiet, "She's using you, man."

I stayed quiet.

"And I know you're going to say, she wasn't like that, but people can only change for the better or for worst, Gray. August is not someone I would trust in a million years. "

I sigh, "Until she gives full hard evidence…" I swallow.

Liam looked at me with a face that wouldn't shock others, he was annoyed with my decision of trusting August until proven guilty.

"She would do everything she could just to get you away from Adrianna and you know that." Liam voiced with irritation.

"My mother just texted me." I said as I checked my phone to make sure I wasn't delusional, "They are rushing her to the hospital."

I pressed on the gas, my head started to pound with a force, I wanted to go to Adrianna, but I knew the nurses wouldn't let me see her anyways.

I took a breath, hitching at the far distance of whether I really wanted to care about August.

I didn't give two fucks. But I cared about the type of man my father wants me to be. I know I shouldn't, I don't owe him anything. But the bottom line was, I wanted to be a better man than him.

I wanted to be there for my child, even if it wasn't with the woman I love. I want to be a better man that he will ever be. I wanted to be the best.

For once in my life, I wanted to be number one against him. I wanted to fucking beat him.

Liam knew why I really did it, which made it all the more reason he came with me without fighting me *that* much.

We got to the hospital. I didn't run towards the doors, I walked. It wasn't the type of fear that I felt in my surface of my skin when Adrianna had been discovered.

Liam gets a call from his mother as I walk through the hospital seeing my family there, even my brothers. My mother directed me to August's room. She was laying there looking upset and yet I didn't care enough to ask what the matter was.

Instead, I thought about giving Margo a call to see if Adrianna got to a room safely with a stable heartbeat.

"You're here." She whispers.

I nod, "What happened to the baby?"

She shook her head, "Nothing, it was just a false alarm." She smiled as I felt bile build up in my throat, my fist clamping as anger burst through my veins.

"Are you fucking with me August?!" I sat down frustrated. I looked up at her, tears ran down her face.

"Grayson."

I shook my head, "This cannot be happening."

I stood up running my fingers through my hair, "Was there actually something fucking wrong with the baby in the first place?"

She stays quiet and that was all I needed for her to answer my question. But she sits up, "I want to be everything for you, Gray!"

"I want to be the reason you came here tonight; I want you to tell me I'm the fucking reason you ran through those doors, and not just because of the baby."

She shakes her head, "This isn't fair. I had you before. I had all of you and I don't even know you anymore."

I only looked at her, condescension ran though my head, "I can't give you that August."

She looks down at the ring on her finger, "Nothing." She

seethes. "And I mean *nothing* hurts more than knowing that if everything was dying, I would only want to call you to tell you how much I truly love you, but it would go straight to voice mail because you would be on the phone with *her.*"

I truly didn't know what to tell her, I breath out, I felt bad.

I did but I couldn't force my feelings and if I did, would she want that? Even if she did accept that I would never do that. It wasn't my style, and I would never be able to be the kind of person she wants me to be.

"Did you call your mother?" I asked as she looked away tears spilling. One thing I knew about August was that she was pregnant, ultrasounds showed it, her fatigue and the doctor cleared that up.

I started to walk over to her bag, her eyes widen with fear as I did it, "Don't go through there!"

It was too late for her warning, as I dropped her bag, two phones fell to the ground. I knew and memorized one of them.

It was Adrianna's phone. It was fucking Adrianna's phone.

Blood boiled deep inside of me, as I turn my face to August, "This is a sick joke, right?" I laugh harshly as she stood up from the hospital bed, it took all my might not to fucking scream at her.

"I thought maybe if I took her phone, you guys wouldn't think about why she wasn't answering." She reasons.

I shove her shit on the ground, "Adrianna could've fucking died!"

The water works started spiraling, "She could've fucking died, and you didn't give a damn! You took her phone and you lied to me about you really needing help!"

"You say you want to be better, and you want me to come back to you and yet you do shit like this!"

She sits down, "I'm sorry, Grayson." I laugh, near the door, "Don't say that to me. Don't you dare fucking apologize to me. Apologize to her."

"You and I both know that you couldn't stand up to Adrianna, but if you think it's just because you brought her down. It doesn't mean that Margo, Juliette, and Verina aren't going to make sure you pay for it. You are fucking mistaken."

She swallows, "I'll pay for the babies' expenses don't worry, but only that. I don't want you in my house. I want your shit out of my room, and I want you to make fucking sure never to come close to Adrianna, do I make myself clear?"

She closed her eyes, "Yes."

I breathe out, "Is there something else I need to know?"

She looked at me like she needed to say something, before Liam barged in, locking eye contact with me.

He pulls my brother Elliot in the hospital room, and he had something to say, Liam definitely found out something, *"You* tell him."

Elliot looked at me like he was in physical pain, he looked over behind me to August, her eyes showing me everything I really needed to know. I look down at the floor, shaking my head, laughing at how stupid I've been.

I look back up to Elliot, "Gray, it only happened once." I shook my head at how much of a stupid situation I had been put in.

I look back to August, "Were we together?"

She looks away, "It was why I broke up with you."

My brother and ex-girlfriend fucked behind my back, but that could only mean, "Is the damn baby mine?"

She shook her head, Elliot's eyes sparkling like he had been dreaming for this. It was pissing me off, I walked up to him, "You love her, don't you?" I ask as he pauses then nods his head.

I flash him a smile before ramming my fist into his face. I didn't care that they slept together because the only girl on my mind was Adrianna of course. But it was the fact that they tried to play me like a damn fool believing the baby was mine.

I take a breath, "You two fucking deserve each other." I began to walk out.

Elliot pulls me back, "Father asked for us to do it."

I turn my head back, "Why?!" I laugh, "Does he hate me

playing hockey that much that he was willing to make me believe that baby is mine, so I take over his business.

Elliot shook his head.

"He doesn't want you to make a mistake, Grayson!"

I pulled my shoulder away from his touch, "Doing everything daddy says always right?" I pushed him back, "So help me God Elliot. You are fucking lucky you're my brother, or else your head would be on a damn platter."

"You wouldn't do that to me." He countered as I stepped closer to him, I was taller than Elliot by four inches, I towered over him.

"Wanna bet?"

He stared into my eyes, "Everyone tells me not to make deals with the devil."

I laughed, "Look at the blood that's running down your nose for a reminder."

L iam and I practically flew on the highway to get to Adrianna and the emergency room, my heart ran faster than the time we were traveling.

"How the hell did you find that shit out?" I turn to Liam.

Be smirks, "A magician never tells, Prince."

I roll my eyes at my best friend, "You ran DNA tests on her, and you sampled a bunch?" I questioned.

He laughs, "I hired a bunch of men to collect DNA samples from everyone at the ball and run them over to the lab."

I nod, "Mine wasn't a match?"

He nods, "I checked yours first."

I sigh, feeling relieved that I didn't have to go through leaving Adrianna and again, but did I really deserve her this time?

I've put her in large amounts of pain, and I wasn't sure if I was willing to make her go through it again. I wasn't sure if it was better to live like we did before when we weren't a major part of each other's lives.

It would be difficult, of course, but I wasn't sure if it was the right thing to do.

We rushed into the doors as everyone was seated outside the emergency room. My heart racing as I passed everyone there.

Opening the door of the glass room the separated from the waiting room, only Margo sat in the glass room that separated Adrianna's room.

Margo stands up as she meets my eyes, "How is she?" I asked hurriedly.

She shakes her head with a scowl, "Where were you?"

I sigh, "I had to check up on—" Margo interrupts me.

"Checkup on August?" She narrows her eyes with annoyance in her voice.

"Get out." She says with a flat tone.

I swallow, "Margo."

"She woke up for a second. She asked for you, and you weren't here. You were with August," She walked closer, "That shows where your true intentions lie, Grayson."

"Margo, let me see her." I plead as she looked at me with soulless eyes.

"No."

"Margo." I almost wanted to get on my damn knees to plead for her to let me see her, I didn't want to move her myself, Adrianna wouldn't want it.

"No, Grayson stay away from her!"

"Please, Margo."

She looked at me like she was not going to budge, like a damn statue that wasn't going to move even in the face of a bulldozer.

Margo was someone that Adrianna needed in her life. She was a part of her, and it was something that was never going to change.

"You don't meet a girl like Adrianna twice in a damn lifetime." She says with conviction, "And the worst part is that the only way you'll lose her is if she does die because she will never let you go, not fully."

I swallow, "As her best friend, I break at her sobs in the night. I cry for her, and I wish I can take some of her pain away that not even you could understand, how could you?"

Margo catches her breath, "She's never let anyone else in, but she let you touch her heart even when she barely shows her true feelings to me."

"She saw something in you that was worth her time, and I watched her explore it when knew I shouldn't have."

"But I did."

"She put you on a pedestal that she had been standing on her whole life. She decided that you were the right person to help her step down from it, but you fell, and you dragged her with you."

Margo let out a silent and slow tear, "And yet, she made sure to put cushioned mats and pillows to catch your fall even when she was unprotected."

I stayed quiet, "When I asked you how you felt about her, I saw how you felt in your eyes. Without needing to say it, I knew how much you cared about her." She folded her hands, "So tell me this," She turns to look at the door, "Why should I ever let you walk in there and bring her more pain that she's already in?"

I couldn't say anything one wishing to see Adrianna, "Margo, I'm sorry."

But she cut me off once again.

"My life almost fell apart when Adrianna's heart stopped beating for twenty-two seconds last year."

She sounded voiceless and broken as she let more tears fall down her cheek.

"Margo, please. Adrianna needs me." And she snapped.

"She was finally okay after I helped build her up for the past year. Now she's in that hospital bed because of *you*."

I swallow taking a step back, still staring at the door, terrified of going in now.

"She needs me! She doesn't need you!" Margo screams at me

as I take a step back, closing my eyes as she sits down on the couch, my head spinning.

I sat next to her, her eyes ruby red and her face was flushed with exhaustion. She leaned on the couch's arm rest, closing her eyes as I swallowed, setting my head on the other side of the couch.

T woke up gradually, my senses felt like I couldn't feel the difference between smell and touch. I heard screams and yells coming from the central waiting room, Margo was still sound asleep next to me as I took a sneaky look over to the glass barrier from Adrianna's room.

In the sounds of screams and yells, I hear Liam's voice. My fight or flight has activated, and I spring forward towards the door to see Liam, Neil, Chris, Verina, Juliette, and of course her father. My parents also sat on the other side. My stepmother running to me and pulling me in for an embrace.

I felt shocked waves through my system as I listened to Liam who looked like he just lost his damn mind.

"This was my mistake!" I looked over to Liam's mother, a woman with hazelnut colored hair, eyes that showed of honey, skin tan and sun kissed. She looked exactly like Adrianna.

My eyes turn over to Damon Cassian, his eyes looked tired and stressed, "Don't be so ridiculous, Odessa!"

"No, I should've known! I should've taken both my children with me, knowing you were selfish and irresponsible. I stayed in my damn house the last time she was hospitalized, Damon!"

I turn around shocked, but not more shocked than Liam who stood right behind me.

"Adrianna is fine!" Damon screams back quieting everyone in the room.

She slaps him, "You let her die not once, but fucking twice

Damon!" She runs out of breath, "I cannot stay at home this time knowing my daughter is in there, barely stable!"

My stepmother let go of me as I walked over to Liam. Next to him, I felt my face redden, fire in my eyes as I sought Liam's eyes that were full of confusion.

"Mom." Liam voiced with a concerned expression. His eyes were lost, and his mouth stayed still as a damn rock.

I swallowed, as she faced us with her eyes full of anger and anguish turned into pain and shock.

"Liam?" She questioned.

It was almost like she hadn't noticed that her own son had been sitting there the entire time.

Odessa Brookshire.

Hawthorne's jewel, she runs businesses in transporting jewelry, designing gowns, and overseeing the creation of jewelry. A perfume was named after her and she was the ultimate trophy wife.

She was none other than Liam's mother. She was the fiancé of a very powerful man that was the owner of multiple businesses in Philadelphia.

"What are you doing here?" She asked with concern in her voice.

"I'm here for Adrianna, I don't even know what to ask why you're here." He stared with a lack of emotion as he looked over to his right at Adrianna's father.

It didn't take a rocket scientist to figure out what had just been uncovered.

"Liam, darling..." She starts.

Liam swallows, "This is a sick joke, right?"

Damon only looked at him with a stone-cold expression, "Are you telling me that my father has been in front of my damn face for the past eighteen damn years?"

Odessa's face turned pale, like she had just made the biggest mistake in her entire life.

The whole group knew everything now, Liam's mother and

Adrianna's father couldn't keep it in a capsule for that long. It was bound to come out.

Odessa walks towards Liam, kneeling in front of him, her hands around his face, "Sweetheart, I'm so sorry you had to find out this way. You were..."

Liam interrupts her, "I was never supposed to find out, was I?"

Odessa closes her eyes, "I did it to protect you."

"You make me sound like a damn serial killer Odessa." Mr. Cassian fires back with a scowl.

She casually rolls her eyes.

Liam looks over to Adrianna's father.

"From whom? My father? Damon Cassian? You want to protect me from a man who was basically in front of my damn eyes my whole life?"

"It's a lot more complicated than that." She speaks.

Damon interrupts, "Only that she packed her things, took you and ran to Philadelphia. She left me with your sister. Yes, I tracked her down. I looked for you, but she kept running and running, until she came back and threatened to leave if I even spoke to you personally."

Odessa doesn't waste time to let the tears fall down her face, "It was a mistake I made a long time ago."

"It was a mistake that cost me a father." Liam snapped back, "You know what's even sicker?"

He pauses, "It took Adrianna to face a life-or-death situation for you two to tell one of us the fucking truth."

"I had a sister my whole life and I didn't even know. I had sleepovers with Grayson not knowing that my father lived just in front of his house." Liam stood up.

I heard a door open to see Margo walk out with tears in her eyes like she hadn't registered what she just walked into.

"Where's Liam?" She says in a quiet whisper and her voice breaking.

Liam looks over at her, like he wanted to run up to her and

stay with her for the rest of his life. But he didn't, he only stared as Ben walks up to Margo, "I'm sorry darling, it took me a while to get here."

Her eyes never left Liam's, but a part of Liam knew that he'd lost her. He'd lost his battle trying to win her back. He was defeated.

The doctor walks in the room, everyone silent as he spoke. "Adrianna has suffered a hemorrhage, losing a lot of blood from the accident. She will stay in the hospital for a while and needs a blood transfusion from someone that shares the same blood type."

Odessa stands up, next to Damon with worried eyes, "Of course, we will pay whatever to make sure she's okay."

The doctor pauses, "The money isn't the issue, Mr. Cassian, the issue is that your daughter has a very rare blood type called *Rh-null,* further known as the golden blood." The doctor takes a breath, "Her blood type is so rare. It has no antigens and enormous lifesaving capabilities."

"There are under one hundred people worldwide who have the same blood type as her. Under the small, restricted amount of time we have it will be extremely hard to hunt someone down that can donate."

"She can't receive blood from anyone except for the small amount of people who have the same blood type. This is extremely life threatening."

I felt my heart drop at the thought of Adrianna not making it, and I can feel my body shut down at the thought. Margo's face drops as well as everyone else's.

Liam pulled away from his mother's touch, irritated at mostly everyone. "I'm her brother, I can get tested if I share the same blood type like her."

The doctor shakes his head, "A sibling—"

Liam interrupts again, "I'm her twin brother."

The doctor stops, as he directs the other nurses to take him into the room full of needles. Margo walks over to me, "What is he talking about?" She asks.

I pull away, "It's a long story."

Margo pulls me back, "If it's about Liam then I have a right to know." She seethes, my body felt like stone as I take a breath, "How about you ask him when he comes back?"

"Actually, I don't care." Margo lets me go.

"If you don't care, then tell him, so that he can finally stop making a fool of himself."

She laughs, almost like mocking me right now, "That's the problem with you guys. You think that just because you do a big gesture then every fucking tear just disappears and never happened."

I turn to look at her, finally looking into her eyes, "What happened between Adrianna, and I is completely different."

"Right. Only that you acted like you cared about her then suddenly never talked to her, leaving her alone. She loves you; you know that?"

"And you don't know how much I want to see her wake up so I can say it first." I smile at Margo with venom in my words.

She shakes her head, "You don't deserve her."

I sit back down, "I know I don't but I'm not listening to what anyone says about me and Adrianna."

"All I know is that I need her back. I will blackmail, I will pay, and I will do whatever it fucking takes to make sure that she comes back."

Margo swallows, she looks back to Adrianna's room. There was no doubt that Margo loved Adrianna more than anything, they were platonic soulmates.

"You can either help or you can stand by and watch." I walk towards her, "It's your choice."

Moments later Liam walks out back into the waiting room, his parents stand up as well as everyone else. I look up to his eyes, "I'm a match."

I release a breath, my eyes closing Liam's getting showered by hugs from his mother as his father sat down to get his composure together.

I felt the same way.

Margo had put all the pieces together and understood the situation, except at this very moment, she had forgave him for every tear that left her eyes, for the return of her soulmate.

CHAPTER 46

GRAYSON

It had been a week since the day of the accident.

A week of dread in the halls of Hawthorne University.

A week of no soul left in me. A week of no sunlight.

Liam had been in and out of the hospital giving blood. It was crazy to me that at this second Liam was more involved with Adrianna than I was.

My best friend and my girl shared the same blood, who knew? I wasn't going to lie and say that I was thriving, I was actually failing at everything. Don't even let me get started on hockey.

I've never been bad at the sport; I've always been the best. But the whole team knew I was a wreck, having me on the ice was a liability and I understood why I was benched in the last game.

Everyone knew about Adrianna and the accident. Everyone knew about fucking everything, and it pissed me off because the moment people hear about me being single again, every person interested in me threw themselves at me.

I walk out of my room with my hockey bag, my father stopping me from walking down the steps, "Grayson, I need to speak with you."

I roll my eyes, "I don't want to speak with you, at all." I pass him running down the stairs, my father runs after me.

"Grayson Nicholas Prince." He says with a stern voice as I ignore him, "You are acting like a damn fool over some girl."

I turn around with my fists formed, "Don't fucking talk about her. None of this would've ever happened if you stayed the fuck away from my love life."

"I'm your father. I can be in your life as much as I want to be. The one thing I ask of you is to get your head out of your ass and stop wasting your time on these stupid hockey games."

I smile at him, "You can go to hell."

He pulls me back and my body starts to get irritated, "You're right, I'm sorry. I didn't mean to scold you again. I just think that with her being in the hospital, you should take a break from hockey."

"Dad, cut the bull shit. You don't care about me. You just don't want me to play. Let me make one thing clear, you can start watching your mouth about whatever input you have about my life especially after what you tried to pull with August and Elliot."

I pull my hockey bag over my shoulder, "I don't just forgive and forget. You should know me better than that by now."

I picked up my keys from the table before thinking about making another unnecessary comment but then again, I was never one to thinking about refraining from making a terrible comment when it came to my father.

"Oh, I forgot. You never made an effort to actually know me."

I let out, before walking over to my car I ran over to the other side of the street to Adrianna's house where I rang her doorbell, hoping for anyone to answer.

Unexpectedly her father opens the door, "Mr. Cassian."

"Grayson, what do I owe the pleasure?"

I swallow looking beyond him and the doorway, "I was wondering if I could pick up something from Adrianna's room to bring to the hospital that might make her feel better."

It was true that Adrianna was still not awake, but I would never stop trying.

Damon Cassian only nods, letting me in. It was an odd environment without Adrianna in the house. It just felt like walls surrounding a place.

"It feels empty, doesn't it?" He makes conversation.

I pause, "I—"

"I'm not an idiot Grayson. I know you and my daughter spent countless nights here when I wasn't home."

I nodded as he walked me up the stairs. I wasn't sure what to really say to him. I hadn't really known what to say to anyone these past days.

We approach her bedroom as I walk in, I see the one thing I came for, her stuffed dog that she can't sleep without. I pick *Shovel* up and turn around to meet Mr. Cassian's confused eyes.

"I'm taking it to the hospital, she usually can't sleep without it. It took a while for me to stomach coming into her room after everything."

Adrianna's father was a man with a few words, he didn't say anything, only walking out with a stare that I've had for the past week.

"We actually have a game tonight, sir." I answer as he smiles.

"I didn't know that Liam was into hockey." He looked amused, like he was happy to share an interest with his son.

I let my eyebrows furrow at the confusion that plastered across my face, "Yes, he's getting over an injury right now so he's getting very little play time, but once he's good he'll be back in."

Mr. Cassian nods, leading me to the front door, "I know you think I don't care about my daughter." I didn't say anything, only agreed from the inside my head, "Which is why I think you should understand why I don't want you seeing her anymore."

I turn around, "Sir."

He interrupts me, "I know you're a good kid, but I don't ever want to see my daughter go through the pain that you've caused her the past months."

Yeah, that fucking stung. It was like my stomach had been punched by a WWE wrestler and got jumped by Superman himself. I could have told him he was wrong but there was a huge part of myself that blamed myself for everything that had happened to Adrianna.

"Of course, I'm not going to stop you from being friends with Liam—" He starts as I laugh, "—And you won't."

"And I trust that you will take it in your best interest to agree to my terms."

"Shouldn't that be her choice?" I ask.

He walks closer, "Let's just say that you're lucky that I don't ship her off to another school. She needs a fresh start, and you are not an example of a good start."

What rang through my head was the big speech that Margo had screamed at me. Her best friend and her father have openly told me that they want me nowhere near her. How can I fucking argue when even I believe that she shouldn't be near me?

I sigh, being so sick of everyone telling me that I'm not good enough for her. I was so sick of everyone telling me that she wasn't good enough to be with me.

When were they going to get it through their heads that what they said wasn't necessarily true?

I live and breathe her.

She's in my damn bloodstream. My eyes have memorized her. My ears have her laughs on replay since it's the only thing that calms me down.

And God I wish that she feels the same way about me.

I snap back to reality suddenly remembering that I was in front of Adrianna's father, "I will not repeat myself again Grayson. I hope you understand that this is the best thing to do."

I blankly stare before swallowing a lump in my throat. I only sigh, handing him the stuffed dog. I take a breath as he looks down at the stuffed animal, his face puzzled.

"I think she would appreciate it more if you bring it to her. Whether she's awake or not, all she really wanted was your attention." Without looking back, I left their house.

I sat in the locker room, thirty minutes earlier like usual, feeling antsy and fucking stupid that I hadn't been playing my A-game. I mean no one really had the guts to tell me I'd been playing crappy; they just knew it.

I knew it as well and having Adrianna in the damn hospital was putting me in a fucking wreck, just as bad I was at hockey when we broke up.

I rolled out my leg as I watched Liam walk into the room, his face looked worse than mine.

"How was the hospital?" I ask.

Liam threw his hockey bag on me as I take a sigh, "You're right, I'm sorry I wasn't thinking, I shouldn't have asked... I know you're going through a lot. I'm not my best either obviously."

Liam sits next to me, pulling out his hockey stick, "No one really wants to admit that everyone is going through something right now."

I nod, knocking my head back, "You know your father is out there?"

I laugh, "It doesn't surprise me, he's been drilling me about quitting hockey ever since my breakup with Adrianna."

"You aren't quitting right?" He gave me a concerned look.

I pushed him backwards, "Are you my best friend?"

He flips me off, "Are you really pushing the man that offers pints of rare blood to your girlfriend?"

I pull him forward, dusting off his shoulder, "My apologies."

He stands up, "Technically, you're banging my sister, my twin sister."

I scoff, "It's not technically, I am banging your sister."

"You think I'm older?" He asks.

I pick up my stick from the bench, "You can ask your long-lost father. He told me to tell you that he wanted to have dinner at 7, but I told him we had a game."

Liam nods, with a smile on his face. At a very young age, I always knew that Liam wished for a father figure in his life. His mother was a workaholic, and his stepfather was never afraid to give him a black eye or two when we were growing up.

I always knew about it, and I even offered to call law enforcement, but Liam made me swear to keep quiet.

What he doesn't know was that when Liam and I actually started growing real muscle and I could ram over men I met up with his stepfather, threatening not only his golden boy face but his business that's definitely had its days in the illegal side of the law.

I would do anything for Liam, he was more of my brother than my real ones, Neil and Chris were my family as well, they all were, and it was really clear that we would go through life and death situations with each other.

The rest of the team started pooling in, "I didn't want to tell you this, but maybe it would cheer you up and change the way you've been fucking up your slapshots."

I pick up my hockey stick, "Adrianna woke up this morning during the transfusion." My eyes widen, my heart stops as I whip over to look at him, smacking Chuck on the head, earning a scowl.

"She's awake?"

I felt my body relax and my breath finally unhitching, "She wants to see you."

I finally smiled for the first time in forever, like a big weight had been lifted off my shoulders. She was awake and fucking hell I wanted nothing more than be with her at this very second.

"That definitely just got you on your A game back, didn't it?" He smiles coquettishly.

Liam fucking smiled.

Except I frown, I fucking frowned.

I couldn't see her. I can't see her. I made a promise not to see her. And I promised to leave her alone.

"Hello, did you just hear what I said?" Liam said with a lost expression.

I swallow, "That's great news for you guys."

He laughs, "You're joking right?" He walks in front of me, "That's your girl. You're supposed to blow off this game, run after your girl!"

I shake my head, "No, she's not my girl. And what the hell are you talking about? I would never blow off a game just for a girl, Liam." It stung letting the words just travel out of my mouth like that.

Liam looked like I just stabbed him through his injured leg. I would blow off any game for Adrianna. I'd blow off fucking anything for her.

"Just for a girl?!" He looked aggravated. "You know I'm talking about Adrianna, right?"

I didn't say anything.

"You're making me sick, and I need to get you out of my face." He walks away as I clench my jaw.

I wanted to punch someone. I walked to put a dent on my damn locker, and I wanted to scream in the top of my lungs. But I also knew that Mr. Cassian was right. He couldn't afford the next bad thing that could happen to Adrianna if she ran back to me.

But what hurt more was that I knew she was awake. I knew she wanted to see me, and I knew that I wasn't allowed to.

And to make matters even worse, Liam was pissed at me.

I understood of course, I wouldn't want to talk to me either. Liam never cared much about people, it was really just me and the rest of the boys. But what he had to wrap his head around this past week is that he has new people to care about.

It was hard for him to grasp the content that he cared about Margo more than he really should have to begin with. He cared about Adrianna the more he had to spend time with her.

And now he cared about her the way an older brother would care for a sister. I pick up my stick, taking a breath again as I walk out of the locker room.

My father was in the stand along with my whole family,

including all of my brothers. August was nowhere to be found, rightly so I didn't think I could stomach her being here tonight.

All my teammates started skating out and grabbing pucks as I skate a lap too cool off, they knew that I was in a pissed off mood the way Liam had stormed off the locker room.

They've never seen Liam and I fight. I have never seen Liam and I fight.

I skate over to the middle of the rink with everyone there, I could feel my eyes burning through them, "If I see anything less than what I've seen you do, I will scream at you." I say out loud as everyone nods.

I looked over to the other team, we were playing the Rutherford Ravens, I studied hours of their games. I knew how they planned; I knew how they played, and I knew how they struck.

"They got nothing on your saves, Cole!" I look at him, I turn to Andrew and Chris, "You guys are two of the fastest on this team, show them you can fucking fly."

I turn to Neil, "Keep up the aggression."

I stand, "And just play the game we fucking love, and I promise I'll get my head out of my ass and play like I normally would."

They all laugh, "Good, we miss that guy."

I turn again to look at the other team, Porter Del Monte staring dagger at me. I wink back at him, "I do miss it when others think they're better than me."

I look back at my teammates, Neil rolling his eyes, "It's true, the only thing better than what you're looking at is probably the big man upstairs."

One of my other teammates Jay Villanueva playfully pushes me as my teammates laugh.

My whole world used to revolve around just hockey, that was before I finally admitted to myself that the girl that irritated the living shit out of me took over my mind twenty-four seven.

Now, I forbid myself from having a choice.

It was only hockey.

CHAPTER 47

ADRIANNA

Earlier the same day.
I saw nothing but black. My head felt like a lot of bowling balls were set on my shoulders. My eyes took a moment to focus on other things than just the bright light.

I squint, trying to sit up looking around to see my stuffed animal, Shovel next to me.

"Oh my God, you're awake." I hear a voice; blonde hair surrounded my arm.

It took five seconds for me to see her bright blue ocean eyes. It was Margo, "Anna?" She asked me as I looked back at her, I felt inaudible.

"Nurse?!" She stands up, opening the door as nurses flood the room, putting their hands all over me.

I couldn't breathe, feeling the need to sob as my senses felt filled to the brim.

A hand holds mine; I turn to look at a lady I have never seen in my life. I turned to the right to see my father next to Liam who was hooked on a monitor.

"Grayson?" I force out with a weak voice, "Where's Grayson?" I almost plead.

Unsure of what my need was or why I was in a hospital bed, I felt blood rush through my brain, like I was tender and frail at the same time. A delay of sharp pain shoots up my leg, my mouth opening to a squirm.

"It's okay baby, just relax for the nurses." I heard from an old lady who was taking a needle to my arm.

I hear beeps to my left, my heartbeat at a fast space, "Stop surrounding her!" Margo's voice come to my radar once again, "She's not comfortable with crowds or multiple people at once."

A nurse turns to look at Margo, "Then maybe you and the family members should go."

Margo laughs, folding her arms. "Trust me, out of everyone here, you want me here."

Everything was happening so fast, yet everyone was in slow motion. My body weakened once again. It was like I was sedated.

The nurses pull away, leaving the room in a couple of minutes. Margo rushes over to me with a fast voice, "I'm here." She holds my other hand.

I pulled away from the random lady who had tears streaming down her face. "Dad?" I felt my eyes water at that very moment.

"Oh sweetheart..." He walks closer, the other lady moving out of the way, in the background with Liam.

If Liam was here, Grayson would have to be near, right?

My dad sat next to me, his breathing relaxed and slow. I closed my eyes. The room quieted down as I swallowed.

"Adrianna." My father whispers as he kisses my hand, I didn't say anything, only look at him, "I'm so sorry for everything. I should've been there for you."

I felt my heart ache, tears falling one after the other.

"I'm so sorry, dad..." He shushes me. Margo squeezes my hand with comfort. I missed her so much.

"Where's Juliette and Verina?" I ask, my voice breaking.

"They are coming straight after school."

I look forward, seeing Liam.

"Liam?" I sit up.

"Adrianna."

"What are you doing here? And who's next to you?" She was practically drowning in her own puddle of tears.

"Honey," I looked at my dad suddenly sounding awkward, "That lady, her name is Odessa Brookshire, Liam's mother... and also yours."

I felt a whole wave of shock run through my body, as I stared into her eyes. They shared the same color as mine. Her hair, raven like mine. Even the way her lips pouted was like me replicated.

I swallowed; I didn't know how to react. I didn't think I had enough energy to react in any way shape or form. I was confused and hurt. My own father knew that my mother was still around and didn't feel the need to tell me.

On the contrary Liam looked about as blind-sided as I did. Not only did I gain a mother, but I had gained a brother that I had known distantly for years.

I looked at Liam's arm, it was patched up by cotton and medical tape.

I then realized that I hadn't said anything then, not really sure, I could. It felt like my lips were sewn together. I felt my body freeze.

I did nothing but squeeze Margo's hand who sat there as silent as I was, "Honey?"

I just stared.

"Maybe you should give her some space, Odessa." My father says as I watch their hatred radiate from each other.

"If that's what she wants."

She looks at me like I was her lifeline, but where was that for my whole life? Did she not want to reach out? Did she not want to see me? Or even meet me at all?

I looked away, my father walking closer, "She doesn't have to say anything because I am. I want you to leave the room."

"I'm her mother."

"You may be her mother, but I'm her father legally. I have provided for her and have been with her."

I couldn't take any more of this. I wanted them all out of the room. I wanted Margo by my side, and I wanted my friends on the couch. I want people who actually care about me.

I look at Margo, tears running down my face as she stands, "With all due respect, Mr. Cassian and Mrs. Brookshire, I think you should both leave and let Adrianna take all of this information in without the both of you screaming at each other."

"How dare you!" My mother turns to Margo, her finger raised and her voice moving up an octave. Liam whips in front of her.

"Mother, please."

And our mother backs down, her face hurt and her eyes tortured, "I just want my baby safe." She looks at me again, "Both of my babies."

"They aren't babies anymore, Odessa." My father adds with irritation.

My mother's sad eyes stay on mine, "Yes, well that's the last time I saw them together."

There was a silent moment before Margo walked closer to the door, opening it, hoping my parents would walk through it.

One by one they both walk through. My heart slows down, Margo shuts the door and runs next to me my arms wrapped around hers.

"Thank the fucking lord you're okay." She whispers.

I breath out, "It's okay, I deserved it."

She pulls away, "What?"

I closed my eyes, and I had some time to think about it of course, and it was true. I felt like I deserved every little thing that had happened to me.

It was the second time that my heart had to be revived. Sue me if I'm tired, but I was hoping that the doctors weren't good at their jobs.

It was like all my hopes were being poured into a basin filled with holes, leaking everywhere uncontrollably. For the duration of my lifetime, I have always been told I was a strong girl. A girl who knew exactly what she was doing with her life.

Doctors would tell me the same things every time, that I

would be better off walking away and ignoring the diagnosed signs of my anxiety, depression, and my OCD.

I felt happy when I ignored it, but I felt like I was bottling it up and the accumulated air pressure built up so much to the point of shattering.

I was too embarrassed to talk about it. I was terrified to tell Margo that I had been taking drugs again. That I overdosed again.

I let the tears fall, "I'm so sorry." I sniffled.

My eyes shuttering even harder, "I didn't think it was that bad until it happened. I wasn't thinking and I'm sorry for hiding everything."

Margo pulls away, her eyes still on mine, "Don't ever blame yourself. I didn't know how it feels like to be in your shoes. I wouldn't know how to deal with anything you've dealt with."

No one ever understood me, deeper than the surface of course. No one will ever understand the hell that lived in my head that I never allowed to enter or leave.

I didn't know how to ever respond to it. I was always scared to respond to it. I wondered how it would feel if I ever did.

Margo leans over, "Just because you carry everything so well doesn't mean it isn't heavy."

We both turn our heads to a loud bang of Liam bumping to a random equipment, his face turning bright red.

"Liam!" I sat up, Margo placing her arm in front of me so that I stood back down.

"Adrianna."

I wasn't quite sure how to talk to Liam now, not that we were that close before Grayson, and I got together. A sense of need to speak to him was at play.

"I'm not really sure what to say right now." Margo quickly turned her eyes back to mine, signaling that she was going to leave the room to give Liam and I time to speak to each other.

Liam takes her spot, sitting on the chair next to my bed. "I know this might sound fucking crazy and you don't deserve to find out this way, nor did I." He pauses, "It's just…"

He sighs, like he was embarrassed. I felt my eyes start to water, "I've never really had real family other than my mother—*our* mother... and I don't know how to speak to you as if you're my sister."

Sister. I was a sister.

I smiled; my grin reached the opposing sides of my face. Did he think that this would be easy for me as well? I wasn't stupid, I knew that Liam had donated me the blood I needed to survive.

"Liam, you didn't even know that I was your sister a week ago, but you didn't hesitate to give me blood, I think that actions speak louder than words here."

He looked confused and surprised, "Why are you looking at me like that?" I laugh.

He tilts his head, "How did you know that it was my blood?"

I look at the IV hooked to my hand, the tube travelled to a blood pack which had been hung to administrate blood to my veins, labelled "Liam Brookshire" which also included the date, the same night of the gala.

The same night as the accident.

I look back at him as he nodded, "I don't think I could ever repay you for this, you saved my life."

Liam laughs, "I'm sure you would've done the same if you were in my position." He adds as I thought about it.

And honestly it truly would have depended on whether I was in a fantastic mood or not. Maybe if he wasn't a complete bone-head to Margo, it would've earned him extra points.

I smiled back, "Of course."

Liam nods, "I don't know if you want a relationship with me or our mother, but you don't have to worry if you think mother wouldn't want you. Something tells me that she always thought that she should've took you instead of me a long time ago."

"That's nonsense."

Liam laughs again like I was delusional, "No one has to say it, but I know I'm a screw up Adrianna. I'm a rich kid with daddy and mommy issues that does nothing but slap a puck around every fucking day."

He pauses, "The only person who told me I could be more than that is making it pretty clear that she doesn't think so anymore."

I look back at him, "Liam, no one's perfect. I certainly am not perfect, trust me." He rolls his eyes as I do the same.

"I'm a twenty-year-old girl who's been hospitalized not once, but *twice* because of self-harming, drug abuse, eating disorders, anxiety, and pain killer overdoses."

I look around the hospital room, "I know these doctors, not because I read their name tags but because I've been here so much. I'm practically a regular customer."

We stay quiet. I wasn't sure if he felt the same embarrassment that I had felt, or even a big weight lifted off my shoulders, but he nodded, "We are more alike than I thought. Huh." He makes a point as I agreed with him.

"I have never told anyone about this, only Margo and my father." I add as Liam smiles.

"I don't talk to anyone but Grayson, Neil, and Christopher." He stands up, "I'll bury both our secrets to the grave."

I flinched a second after I heard Grayson's name come out of his mouth. And it was like he knew what the next words to come out of my mouth were going to be.

He interrupts, "He's surviving."

He shakes his head lightly, "He's been a total wreck with you here Adrianna. He's even slacking in hockey." He said it in almost a whisper tone.

My eyes widened, I sat up frantically, "Well, we have to tell him I'm okay, and that we're going to be okay and that everything is going to be just *okay.*"

He pushes me back down gently, "No, you have to stay here and recover. I can tell him before the game today."

I narrowed my eyes, like I would do to people who dare challenge what I ask of them, but I forgot that Liam Brookshire wasn't some student at Hawthorne that was terrified by me.

He was an elite. He wouldn't budge.

"I'm late to the game anyways. I can tell him there." He said as I felt my heart calm down, with a small smile I closed my eyes.

"Can you tell him to come by?" I say slowly.

He shakes his head with a small laugh, "Nothing is going to stop that man from running over to you the moment he hears your awake."

I couldn't help but feel like the world was collapsing and reassembling itself over and over again.

It was like I was finally on my final mile of the marathon, and I can feel the finish line so close, and I've never felt better.

Liam soon left which made me excited to finally hear Grayson's voice again, or even just see him.

I looked over to my side, seeing my stuffed animal cuddled up next to me. Only he knew that I couldn't sleep without the damn dog.

I sat there rethinking every possible thing I could say to him, did I tell him I miss him first or that I was happy to see him?

Should I stand and hug him? No, that would be terrible if I could trip and fall. Should I express that I couldn't imagine a world where we don't work out?

That was it. That's what I was going to tell him, so I sat and waited.

Except I sat there for hours and hours. It was now midnight.

I had no calls.

No visit from him.

And no hope that he cared.

CHAPTER 48

GRAYSON

It was a good win. The team skated out of the rink with beaming smiles on all their faces. I felt like I've never played harder than that game. My heart thumped like a damn drum.

But at this very moment, I sat outside the hospital bench. I couldn't go in to see Adrianna. I knew that by the looks that the guards had sent me guarding the waiting room.

But I sat there, nevertheless. The worst part of my damn day was getting into an unnecessary fight with Liam.

My phone rings as I answer it with a bit of hesitation of saying something right ahead.

"Hello?" The voice was scarce. I thinned my lips together gathering the flowers I had bought and walked towards my car.

"Do I know you?"

"Grayson, it's your mother."

I let my deep breath out, rolling my eyes. "Do you need anything mother?"

"I need to see you." She muttered quickly, I wanted to ignore her requests. But she was still my mother, I cared for her.

"New Crest." I said plainly, hanging up the phone immediately.

I walked out of the car as she was perched up against the willow tree that I would lay against whenever I threw a tantrum.

"You have to make this quick. I have to get home to help Amelia with her algebra homework." I look over to her as she stands guarded.

"Okay." She paused.

"I need money." I smile as she walks closer, of course what fucking else could it have been about. Why else would she need me to meet up with her?

"For what?"

She pauses again, "I need money to take care of myself Grayson."

"It looks like you're doing just fine without me, mother." I replied to her as she sent me a scorned look, like she was ready to slap me.

"I miss you." She instead changed her face to a look that make could fool and old man. But never me. I knew for a fact that she was just playing me which was awful because no mother should have bad intentions to her son that she claimed she loved and cared for.

But here we are yet again.

I turn around to ignore her comment.

"Do you know me mother?" I asked plainly with a false smile on my face yes again. I faked it so much that it came easy.

"Well, of course. You are my son."

"Then what is my favorite color?" I turned around.

"Have I ever been in love? Do I prefer cats or dogs? What's my dream? What type of food do I enjoy? Who's my favorite artist? Do I enjoy playing the piano?" I looked at her face that was beyond terrified to answer.

"You don't know me." I kept my eyes on hers.

"I've lived with my stepmother for most of my life giving her the silent treatment, giving her shit, always taking her for granted because I thought that I owe it to you not to love her too. I didn't want to be guilty by making you upset that I picked her over you like father did."

Her head lowered to the ground, "Grayson."

I cut her off again, "But I shouldn't have ever felt that way. I should've loved her sooner because she knew my favorite snack before a hockey game, she knows my favorite pieces to play on the piano, she knows that I got a dog bite when I was seven that sent me to the ER."

I laughed sarcastically, "And yet I tried to defend you. I was shitty to her because I was upset that she got the number one spot in fathers life, when it truly was because she deserved it. You are nothing but a person who needs money for her own gain."

"That money is for me to get better."

"Bullshit!" I walked closer to her, closing my eyes, "You smell like a damn Brooklyn back street."

"You don't know what I've been through." She explains as I ignore her once again.

"Nice car." I let out, scanning her car that was parked on the curb.

"You like it?" She walked towards it with a smile, "I stole it."

My eyes widen, "You what?"

She laughs, "I'm joking, you never joke with your mother anymore."

I take a labored breath, "You need some work on the paint job though, its scratched up at the front. I like this red paint on it though."

She then turns silent.

I turn back around to her, "I'm not giving you money so you can buy drugs." I stare.

She shakes her head, "And here I thought you cared about me."

"I do, which is why I'm not giving you the damn money." I

walk over to my car, "I want you to get some help and if I would ever actually donate you money then it would be for that exact reason."

I take a labored breath, "And the reason I'm doing this is because I cared about you mother." She looked back to see police car alarms and her face gave the response of panic.

She looked completely and utterly guilty.

"I looked back on the damn house tapes as soon as Adrianna was in that hospital. Did you seriously think that I wouldn't check up on my girl every day when we were broken up?"

I shake my head as the police started pulling in, "I saw you meet up with August. Don't worry, I won't let you go lonely in the jail cell. As for the baby, Elliot will be getting full custody and you are never to see Adrianna or me every again."

Two police officers pull her arms behind her back cuffing her; I felt an uneasy feeling run through my damn veins. Seeing my mother being placed in the back of a police car wasn't my ideal way of feeling happiness and relief but it gave me ten percent of it.

"For as smart at you claimed to be, you should know that a billionaire's daughter's car has a camera installed which could clearly see what car rammed into her."

My mother couldn't say anything. Only look at me like I completely betrayed her. My heart broke but not as much as it would've if I let her get away with something like this.

There was no going back, and I knew that.

Still, there was a part of me that wished that she was a better mother for me to be able to defend.

It had been weeks since my mother's arrest. I had ordered the arrest to be kept on the low and for Adrianna not to be alerted and it had seem that she didn't want to remember anything from the crash anyways.

Liam was still ignoring me, making it difficult to be on the same damn hockey team with him, I walked the hallways of Hawthorne University sneaking a peak at Adrianna who hadn't spared me a glimpse.

I didn't blame her. I wouldn't be a good fan of me either after I didn't show up to her hospital room to see her, or remotely even say anything to her.

I want her back. I want my girl back and it was killing me inside that she wasn't next to me, that I wasn't near her. I knew she was in obvious pain; she still had a brace on.

I wanted to come to her, I really did, but the image of her being killed rotted inside my brain. The illustration imbedded into my conscience when she started bleeding in front of me when I touched her.

It was only a damn sign that she didn't belong with me and the only thing I gave her was a faith close to death.

But we had debate class, and it's the one class we had to talk to each other. For the first time since the accident. For the first time since everything.

We had been separated into rows on opposite sides she was on the other, with Liam, while Margo and I sat on the same side she hated me as well.

Mr. Kingston stood in front of everyone introducing today's topic of *Loyalty versus Love.*

I was told to defend *Love* while she defended *Loyalty.*

"Who would like to begin?" Mr. Kingston asked as I looked at Adrianna's face. She stood up quickly, her eyes remained everywhere but mine. I wished to have seen them again.

"Mr. Kingston, I would rather have loyalty than love. It's difficult to find someone that really only has their eyes set on yours from the beginning. Anyone can love you and say they love you yet still harbor hatred and hurt for you even if their feelings are true."

I stood quickly, her eyes still not on mine yet everyone else's is, "While I admire loyalty, it isn't true in all ways. Some people aren't loyal to the bone and are only loyal to you when they also need something tom you. Once those needs have conjured a different route, so does their loyalty. But love is a true way of expressing a feeling that cannot be replicated or bought. Loyalty is prone to blindness against a person's actions. Loving someone is a gift that is offered to the other person with no expectations of returning love."

"Not all love stories end in happily-ever-afters." She fires back.

I swallowed the lump that got stuck in the back of my throat, she began to speak again. "Love means nothing without loyalty, many would define acts of love as sacrifices such as jumping off a burning bridge or dying for someone. But those are acts of loyalty. Not love."

I stepped in again, "I wouldn't want loyalty, it sounds forced. Many people have been in love with each other, and their souls stay in love. But when they meet different people, their loyalty will obviously change.

Adrianna's eyes finally met with mine, her body facing my way, in front of the whole class, "Love is nothing without the trust you put on your partner every day to just be there. Having the trust that they will be there when needed and the understanding that no matter what happens you don't have to worry if they will come back or not."

I felt the room quiet, "How about a child and a parent?" I look at her as she folds her arms, "A mother or father can love their child as much as the universe can let them, but doesn't loyalty go both ways?"

"If a mother and father love a child, then shouldn't that child show loyalty? Shouldn't they automatically have that tested the moment the child was born or could the first look that the father and mother give that child be the look of love?"

I didn't want to make it personal, so I steered the different direction, "Children deserve great parents, but not every parent deserves children."

Adrianna and I quieted looking around the class now understanding that it was out of the line to be arguing without letting others talk.

The professor looked at both of us with a thinned smile. "You two may take a seat." Adrianna sat down gracefully as I flopped down on my seat, irritation rippled through my whole body.

I wonder if she ever thought about why I didn't come to see her, but then again it was selfish of me to wish she did when I know damn well that she had to get over me somehow.

I would think about it for hours and hours, convincing myself that I made the right decision.

But it didn't matter what I thought. Deep down I knew it was the right thing.

CHAPTER 49

GRAYSON

"What stores do you like to shop in?" I listened to her talk as my eyes steered to look at Liam's face.

His eyes widened towards me as if he didn't know what to say. I particularly didn't know what to say either.

He had been hanging around his random girl that goes to Maxwell University that's been all over him. Don't get anything twisted, he and I are not back to being "buddy buddy." We just didn't want Chris or Neil to feel that they had to pick sides.

We booked one of our traditional private tables at the Lavo club, Chris and Neil were out meeting girls. Liam looked like he was having fun and I looked absolutely fucking miserable.

I sat across from Liam and his girl of the week, taking out my phone and clicked on my contact list. Adrianna's contact came up and I paused, clicking to our messages.

The old-time stamps felt like a knife to my heart. I felt my face drain color, but the lighting saved my ass from looking worse than I did.

I felt like a coward.

The texts I didn't respond to, where I could practically feel her heart break through the screen.

What did I do?

Grayson, please I want to talk.

It's getting late, are you still coming?

You changed your mind?

READ 12:48 P.M.

My thumb hovered over the call button. Genuinely thinking to click the button. I knew I never would actually do it; I was too much of a coward.

"Don't even think about it." I hear Liam's voice intrude my thoughts.

I roll my eyes at my former best friend, "Are you tired of being a dick now?"

Liam stood up walking towards me, his girl walking away to flirt with a random guy at the bar, "I will always be a dick, but I just mean I know that look in your face. It has Adrianna all over it."

I say nothing.

"Don't even act like you don't know what I'm fucking talking about. I'm not mad at you." He sighs.

"I was mad at the fact that you felt the need to lie to me when I know whenever you lie. I knew everything you were telling me was bullshit, but what I couldn't wrap my head around was why you lied."

He passed me a drink, as I poured it into my mouth. I shook my head, looking over at him, "Tell me honestly Liam…"

I sigh, "Do you think that everything that has happened didn't happen because it was a sign for us not to be together?" I chuckle, a bit irritated.

"I can't put her through that heartbreak again, that risk, I can't put myself through seeing her almost die and not being able to do anything about it again."

I take another needed drink, "We fall apart when we're together."

Liam shakes his head in disagreement, "What if it falls together perfectly Gray?"

"It doesn't matter because she hates me now. And I don't blame her, I've put her through some shit." I drink once more, "I'm not enough for her. I know she deserves better, and I will try to be better for the one woman I've really truly wanted."

Liam looked forward to the bar like I was, still I knew he was listening.

"Before we got in the argument, your father told me to stay away. It's the least I could do after what I put her through, I can't be selfish with her Liam, I can't."

Liam laughs, almost mockingly I turn to him with confusion, "You think this is funny? I'm actually thinking about jumping off a cliff man."

His voice was lowered, "I've watched you deprive yourself from Adrianna from the day you first saw her. I've watched you two argue, flirt, fight, look at each other from a distance, and sacrifice for each other. For the three months you two were "together" I watched you be happiest you've ever been."

I stayed quiet, "I wish you could've seen yourselves. I've watch the apparent hatred between the both of you reveal into you being in love with her." He hands me a half-filled bottle of whiskey, "You've loved my sister since we were three, even if you both try, that doesn't just go away."

"Your sister huh?" I laughed at the change of term.

He throws me a death stare, "Don't change the subject."

I place the bottle down, "We shouldn't be drinking tonight. We have a game tomorrow." I picked up my phone to check the time. "I'm heading home." I stood up while picking up my hockey Leather-man jacket.

Liam sat up, "Always so responsible."

"To take my mind off of things, I might do some shooting drills and work out." I smile.

Liam's girl came back, "Baby did you get me a flower for Valentine's Day?"

Liam quickly checked the time, figuring out that it was two minutes past midnight, making it actually Valentine's Day.

"Happy Valentine's Day Liam." I toss the bottle of whiskey at him.

He laughs while catching it, smiling at me, "Happy Birthday, Gray."

ADRIANNA

It was 1 A.M. and I couldn't sleep. I laid in the dark with a pounding feeling in my chest, stretching my arm to grab my phone from my nightstand.

It was Valentine's Day.

I closed my eyes with a wrenched feeling tugging my stomach. This couldn't be it.

I was ultimately ruined for other men. I can't look at even one person without thinking or comparing them to Grayson.

I felt miserable and weak that I still thought of him as the one I was supposed to be with, but I'm here to accept to break that stereotype that I can just "get over him" or "you deserve better." I was so sick of it.

My mind and heart never agreed on anything. Always trying to prove the other wrong and it made me overthink every little thing in my life.

It gave me anxiety and it only made the cement walls that surrounded me feel even taller.

But this time, my mind and heart were calling his name. I pulled up his contact on my phone resisting the urge to call him.

I didn't want to crawl back. I didn't want him to know that he was still in my mind. I tossed my body to lay on the other side, only for my eyes to be struck to his car pulling up his driveway.

He looked like he had a fun night. I knew Liam, Chris and

Neil were out clubbing because Verina was stalking them and kept us updated on her quest to make Chris fall for her.

Margo has been unreachable lately; I knew something was going on with her family, especially with her new fiancé.

Juliette always had her nose stuffed in books and kept herself busy with volunteering projects. My father has been home lately, I think he's scared of leaving the house now.

It saddened me that it took me almost dying for him to stay.

I sat up to see Grayson in his room, pulling off his shirt and throwing it in the hamper, laying down on his bed with his hands covering his face.

For a moment I thought about walking over to my balcony to watch him, but I resisted. He stands up, picking up one of his many hockey sticks.

He didn't have a good day.

He always let's steam off by playing hockey. I couldn't help but think if it was because of me.

They have a game tomorrow that I have to attend. My father wanted to watch Liam play the game they both love.

He shuts off the lights, who am I kidding?

If he wanted me, he should've came. But he didn't. He left. He gave up.

I should too.

"You guys made it!" Liam smiles at my father and I as he directed his way to us.

"We wouldn't miss it for the world." My father says as Liam opened his arms up for a hug.

"I saved you guys a seat next to my mom; it should be near the front." He pulls away giving me a side hug.

Chris and Neil walk out of the locker room with gloomy faces, "What's wrong with you two?" I ask.

They shook their heads, "Team Captain is in a prissy mood, he's asking for Liam."

I bit my bottom lip, Liam looking at me apologetically, "I'm sorry I have to go. Duty calls." Liam ran in the locker room the next second.

Chris looks around, "Is Verina here?"

I look around, "I'm sure she's roaming off somewhere with Juliette."

He nods, looking slightly eased.

I hear my voice being called loudly in a far distance. I turn my face to look at the direction of the yells, my eyes focus on a little girl with blonde hair, beaming eyes and a huge smile running towards me.

"Anna!" She yells as I get on my knees with open arms for her to come crashing into an embrace.

"Amelia!" I felt my heart race as she buries her head deep in my hug.

"I'm so glad you're okay, I was so worried for you." She pulls her head away to speak, "I couldn't sleep, Grayson couldn't sleep, I wanted to see you, but I couldn't." She rambled on as I smiled.

"I'm okay now, it's okay."

She takes a moment to look around, "Are you ever going to come back to our house?"

She didn't understand anything, and I felt like I was stabbing her relentlessly when I say, "I don't think that's the best idea right now, darling."

"Whatever Grayson did, he can fix it." Her voice was pleading, it was a bittersweet feeling.

She was right, he could fix it. But he didn't.

I knew he cared about me. I could see it in his eyes, and I could feel it, but I also knew that he didn't care enough to tell me why he couldn't be with me.

"I don't know about that." I smiled thinly as her smile disappeared into a rare frown.

"Amelia!" Her head turns to look at one of her brothers

calling her name. My arms loosened for her to leave, but she stayed for a second, a sense of rebellion deep in her eyes to stay.

"You should go." I grinned, forcefully, thinking about how letting Amelia go was possibly the last thing that I had to let go of Grayson's life in mine.

She slowly left my embrace, walking towards her family.

My father directed us to our seats, the game was about to begin. I waited for Margo to arrive as the team warmed up. She walked in with Ben, running next to me.

I wasn't a big fan of hockey, and I knew that, but I slowly developed a love for it through the past year because of Grayson dragging me to the games, except he didn't have to drag me to the last ones I attended. I was happy to be there.

I understood why he craved it so much, the rush, the screaming, the support, and the love. It was a part of him that no one could compete with.

He would pick hockey over anything; it was the only place he knew people wouldn't judge him. Ironically, all people do behind these boards is judge him. But as I watched him play the game, his soul wasn't in the game anymore.

He wasn't skating to the best of his ability. He wasn't celebrating his scores. He was ramming people over just because. And the more it happened, the more people talked around me commenting about how he was "crashing and burning" or that he was a "one hit wonder" or even "it was too good to last." My heart sank to the core when it hit for the third period.

Liam looked exhausted and upset. The whole team did.

"I have to use the bathroom." I whispered to my father as he nodded his head for me to leave, I quickly ran down to the front of the locker room.

Resisting the urge to ask about Grayson, to see if he was okay.

But I didn't care at this moment, swallowing my pride. I was never that strong anyways when it came to him. I was mad at myself as I kept walking over to the lockers.

Until I stopped, Liam looking at me like I was his last breath, "What's wrong?" I asked as he looked panicked.

"Grayson's gone."

GRAYSON

I felt like I was suffocating in that rink. My head was pounding the entire time as if my skull was about to break. My hands turned crimson, and my knuckles started to break from gripping my stick.

I was one game short from having a break down. I shifted uncomfortably.

I saw Adrianna inside, and I felt like my chest was ready to just break. I turned my head to face the ground, sweat dripping down to the tip of my nose.

How could a simple concert floor fucking merge into me seeing Adrianna's face. Maybe I was going crazy. No, I already knew I was crazy.

I miss her, and I wasn't even going to lie about it anymore. I would scream it on the top of the rooftops if I could.

Everything was driving me mad. I thought about her infamous sideways half smile that I can't get out of my head every fucking morning and even at night.

I missed kissing her, smelling that signature scent of her hair that she managed to embed into my damn mind. I missed every way she looked at me whilst she was thinking about something.

Her hands running smoothly though my hair, her amusing ass smirk that drove me nuts. I even missed her stupid stuffed dog that would have more bed privileges than I did.

I fucking missed the way she would look, right when she was about to kiss me.

I missed knowing the fact that at any minute, she would look up and find my eyes settling on hers from across the room, now I was sure that she did everything in her power to avoid me.

I missed her fiercely, painfully, and atrociously. So much so that if I had any questions before everything went to shit, I would be willing to take any torture, just to ask her right now.

And maybe that was childish of me, but I didn't care because, *I just fucking miss her.*

As I sat on the curb outside the hockey rink. I take a long hard look at my car, genuinely debating whether I should drive off and never come back.

But I would never do that because I would have to leave her.

I threw my hockey stick on the floor. I wasn't planning on going back in. I wasn't planning on ever playing hockey again.

I was ready to give all of it up. Fuck it.

I heard a voice from a distance, yelling at a phone but I knew the voice from anywhere, I heard it all my life. That same tone. That same voice laced with disappointment.

He turned the corner, my father's eyes stared directly at mine. He hangs up the phone immediately, "Why aren't you in there?"

I laugh, shrugging, "It's not like you want me in there anyways."

He holts, "Since when did you care whether or not I like you doing anything? You've been dating a Cassian and never once asked me how I felt about it."

I felt my hand form a fist as he sat next to me, "Calm down, it was a joke." He grumbles, "I know I've made it clear that I hate that you have put your body and soul into hockey. But I want you to talk to me."

I felt a discomfort churn in my stomach as he shook his head, "What's going on in there?" He asks.

Genuinely.

"You've lost a couple of games, and you would've never let that happen."

"I know I suck at hockey right now." I yell.

He looks at me harshly, "Grayson what is going on with you?"

I wanted to punch him for even asking me that question.

I sigh, "We are number two in the damn state," His eyebrows raise in question, "I can't be number one without her. Without her by my side, I lose sight of the game. I've been making mistakes that I never should have made. I'm letting the fucking team down."

"Grayson, I know you have had this issue and need to always be number one." He breathes heavily, "And I get it, but you need to be strong Grayson." He pauses, "This isn't the son that I raised."

I shake my head, "You don't get shit! Do you even know the reason I have tendencies to always want to be number one?" I stress, "About fucking anything?"

My father could only stare.

I knock my head back, "It's because of you damn it!" I slam my hand on ground as my father flinches.

"Me?" He questions as I stare up at him.

"Number one gets the best." I let out, "Number two gets whatever is left over. I'm not Sara's kid and that makes me number two in your eyes." I say plainly as he swallows.

Before he could say anything, I beat him to it, "I might look like you guys, but I'm a fraud, the triplets look like Sara, Rhylee looks exactly like Sara. But I just try and blend in but I'm the black sheep of the family." I disclose.

"I'm not a part of the family because you aren't even on my birth certificate as my father, you haven't even adopted me, you have made it seem like I'm just an instrument in your world." I make a point.

My father looked like he had just been hit by a bullet, "So I try to make up for it, by being number one in school, hockey, society, even sacrifice my happiness so that I could take over the business and many for the first time I would be number one in your eyes."

I shake my head, feeling like an idiot, "Adrianna was the only one who was brave enough to tell me that it gets lonely being first all the time. So, she fought me for days and nights for the spot. And I realized, it's not worth it."

I could feel my chest constrict as well as my jaw clench, "I've treated Sara like shit when she's been fucking wonderful, I guess I'm just bitter because at the end of the day, my mother was just a secret mistress, and you've always looked at me like I was the consequence that you have to live with the rest of your life."

I draw an irritable breath while I stand, "So forgive me that if I can't be number one anymore, I don't want to play hockey."

"Grayson." He walks closer as I shake him off, "I'm so sorry I've made you feel that way all this time. I never meant to make you feel like I loved you any less because you aren't Sara's." He consoled.

"You might not be hers, but you are fully mine and I love you. But I got to tell you I'm trying my hardest, and I know I've done a shitty job at showing you I love you, but that doesn't mean I don't."

He laughs somberly, "Your girlfriend practically showed me how much of an asshole I am." He referred to Adrianna, who brought a smile to my face.

"She's the only one who truly makes you smile." He scratches the back of his neck as I truly was lost for words.

But then he draws back a confused look almost like he didn't believe what I had just said, "But quitting hockey?" He looked exasperated. "Are you kidding me?" He retorts.

"Father, I don't care whether you approve or not because I think I'm dying every single day when I'm not with her. I don't care whether I have to forcefully take care of the business. Sure, I've played hockey forever and I love it. But I can't love it when I feel like I'm suffocating." I blurted out.

He takes a moment to understand what I was saying, and he pauses to look at me, "Do you know why I quit hockey?"

The forbidden question.

"I fell in love with your mother, and she was pregnant with

you. I couldn't love anything else but her and you. You weren't even born yet." He continues.

"And as you grew up, I had to give up something I loved for love. I gave up hockey." He continues, "I also messed up the day I left your mother because she wasn't the woman I fell in love with. I met Sara and I think she changed my whole life because she was pregnant with your brothers."

I took a breath.

"I loved your mother, yes, but I wouldn't change anything that happened. I took my father's business to provide for our family. And I've never regretted it." He sighs, "When August came into my doorstep, I couldn't help but think that maybe you were meant to have the same life I did."

I set my jaw, "We aren't the same person." I mutter.

He nods, "I know."

It was like he couldn't wrap his head around it, "This is a girl that you've hated since you met her, you complained about her, you would've rather jump off a cliff before having to converse with her."

Then he smirks.

"But then again it never passed me by that your eyes always sparkled when she was near."

"I didn't get an option when I had to pick between hockey and my love for your mother and you, but I'm giving you an option now."

"But we had a deal." I let out a bit of a laugh. "It was either hockey or Adrianna with the business."

He smiles looking up to the sky. "Yes, but when it comes to you, I tend to always change my morals don't I?" He laughed gently as I felt the smile from my lips appear.

"I am now aware that I haven't always been fair to you so, I'm asking you now." He breathes out a labored breath, "Do you really want to give up hockey because of her?"

I stayed silent for a second, "I would do anything for her."

He nods, "If you were ready to give up hockey for her then I have an incredible feeling that maybe she means more to you than you let on. Besides, I think your sister will skin me alive if she finds out the reason why Adrianna doesn't come by the house anymore."

I laughed once more, like everything was falling into place, my father stood up, picking up my hockey stick and handing it back to me.

"They're looking for you in there." He mutters, "And go get your girl."

CHAPTER 50

ADRIANNA

"I can't help you Liam." I mutter, "I'm so sorry but..." He interrupts me.

"Adrianna, you helping me doesn't mean that you have to get back together with Grayson or that nothing the past month has happened, because it did and I'm sorry for that." He pants.

I didn't think people really understood the part of me that wanted to finally get over Grayson.

"You and Grayson weren't together that night of the accident, but that didn't stop him from checking every damn street of the city. He didn't sleep. He couldn't come home. We practically had to force him to come home."

I frown, "I didn't ask him to do that."

Liam looked at me like I had officially lost my mind.

Except I felt like I was about to lose my mind, the idea of going through the heartbreak over and over again. I was always stuck at the same square in this game, and I was tired of losing myself over it.

"I can't help you Liam, I'm sorry." I turned around to make eye contact with my father.

As I begin to walk away from him, Liam pulls me back, "Our father told Grayson to stay away from you." He reveals.

"And I get it because I was pissed off at him first, but Grayson is terrified of losing you again, and not in a breakup way. I'm talking about a you-not-breathing type of way." I swallowed a lump in my throat, terrified that maybe it as painful for him as much as it was painful for me.

"Liam, I just need time to process things." I felt my hands shake, "I know that you are just being Grayson's wing man like always but as your sister... you are put in a different position now."

My eyes stay on Liam who takes a breath, "I get it." He grins thinly as I nod my head, my eyes straighten to Grayson who walked from the back doors.

The whole team calms down with one look at Grayson. His mouth opens as he approaches me with a tense look in his eyes.

"Adrianna..." He almost whispers like my name was a forbidden word.

My eyes directed away from his, "Looks like your problem is solved." I swallow, backing up closer to the seats.

"Anna." He repeats.

I turn around, "Good luck." My shoulders tensed as he walked closer. I quickly moved so he couldn't reach me.

"Grayson!" Liam yells for him to join the team back on the ice. For a moment, I hear his steps get closer to me, but as I turn around, I see his skates walking over to the ice.

I walk slowly back to my seat, Margo's eyes set on mine, "Are you okay?"

"No." I murmur as she hesitated to talk, but Ben interrupts her. The game began with the teams crashing into each other.

But I couldn't pay attention. My father makes eye contact with me. "Please tell me you didn't go and look for Grayson." My face cringed, disgusted at the thought of my father stopping me from speaking to Grayson.

"That does not concern you."

He smiles aggressively, forcefully, "You are my daughter and I forbid you from ever talking to him."

I turn to his face, "Liam and Grayson are best friends. Liam is your son. Does that mean he is not allowed to talk to Grayson?" I laugh harshly, "I would love to see how that ends."

I turn back to the game, "But then again, it would most definitely end your relationship with Liam."

My father didn't say another word. I only stayed quiet in my own thoughts.

As the game went on, my head was all over the place. The sounds of skates against the ice, the screaming audience, the horrible noises that babbling children made the pressured tormenting in my head worse.

"I hope you don't think that I will treat Liam differently than you." My father adds as I felt irritation bubble inside me.

I turn to him with anger written in my eyes, "Are you serious?" I harshly let out.

He looked confused, "What?"

"You have known me as your daughter throughout my whole life. But you have never once showed up for any of my debates, my speeches, and my award ceremonies. Instead, it was Helen and Ellen who showed up." I spoke freely not caring if anyone really heard.

He looked speechless.

"But the moment you hear that your proclaimed son has a hockey game, you drop *everything* to be here. In front row."

I look forward, he says nothing.

"It takes me almost dying a *second* time. *A second time.* For you to show up to one of my... *things.*" I scoff, "How do you think that makes me feel?"

I focus my eyes on Grayson, "And you have the audacity to tell me who I can and can't see. You have the nerve to tell me that you weren't 'treating Liam differently.'" I quoted him in anger.

He begins to speak as I cut him off, "Did you tell Grayson to stay away from me?" I finally turned to him. My gaze hardened on his shocked face.

"You're acting crazy." My father laughs gently, almost unbelieving of my outburst.

It was like he didn't even take my feelings into consideration. He once again puts my thoughts and feelings as a second priority. I felt like screaming. I was ready to throw a damn hockey puck at him.

"Stop." I almost scream at him with my voice breaking.

"Stop lying to me. Please, I am not a little girl anymore." I push my words towards him as he shuffles in his seat, clearly looking uncomfortable.

"Adrianna, you are acting very childish. If you had a problem today, then you should've stayed home." He looks at his watch, as my hands shook.

I squeezed my hands tighter to settle, "Are you fucking serious?" I laughed harshly, remembering that we were still around many people.

"Just answer the question." I ask with conviction.

He reluctantly nods, "I did it for your own good. He's not right for you."

"You told Grayson, the one person I asked for when I woke up from my coma to stay away from me?" I ask him, my voice breaks once again.

"I did it for your own good. He's not good enough for you." I felt tears building up in my eyes. Little by little, I felt them trickle down my cheek.

"You don't know what's good for me." I voice.

"I am your father. You are not to going to disrespect me." He mutters as the whole crowd goes silent.

For a moment my eyes direct themselves over to the game, the center of the ice. Grayson's body was on the floor, not moving. As soon as my eyes hit the scene, I felt my blood go cold, shock coming through my veins. My body froze as I looked at Margo who stood up to get a better look.

My tears fall uncontrollably at the sight of Grayson.

But I look at my father, and I look at Grayson's body. My heart dropped. I stood up, my hands gripping the handrail to run down. My father's hand catches mine from leaving his side, "Adrianna."

I whip my hand away from his, "You are not stopping me from going after him. I will always go after him. You can either try to stop me and fail. Or you can let go of my hand and be there for me like a father." I whisper viciously.

His eyes grip on mine. Like I would disappear if he blinked.

"Please." I plead as it took one more second for him to let go of my hand. I ran down to the floor, looking for Liam and the opening to get to Grayson as soon as possible.

Paramedics and players tried to get in my way, but I avoided them like a plague. I began to shiver from the coldness of the rink, pushing everyone away from him.

My hand is instantly on his cheek, "Grayson?" I say softly, fog emerges from my hot breath.

I look around, "Is he okay?" I ask around, no one answers me. I could see his family running up by the boards.

"Oh my God." I felt my tears fall on to his uniform, his eyes fluttering I paused, his mouth quivering trying hard not to laugh.

I felt fury in my veins as I push him off, "Oh my God, you jerk!"

I stood up to walk off as he pulled me back in, "Adrianna. Please, this was the only way I could've gotten you to talk to me."

I roll my eyes, "How are you so sure that I would've—" I cut myself off to see how many eyes were on us.

"That doesn't matter. You're such a jerk." I scowl at him harshly as he stands up, skating in front of me.

"Adrianna please just wait and give me a moment of your time, please." He stresses as I fold my arms.

"I love you." He pants out. His eyes on me begging for me to stay, "I'm so in love with you. You are it for me." He continues, my eyes locking on his.

"You are the love of my damn life." He said it strongly, with reassurance. "I am so completely and utterly enraptured by you. I can't think, I can't breathe. I suffocate without you." His words grit out between his teeth.

He pulls off his helmet, throwing it on the ice, cold, floor, "Grayson, we're... we—" I couldn't finish my sentence.

"We aren't over. We can never really be over because I could never get you out of my head. You live there. You own me. I am yours." His eyes softened. He was hoping, *wishing* for me to accept his apology, his confession.

"You know I don't believe in many things, but I believe in us. The moment I saw you, I was in love. Your smile, your laugh, especially when you tell me how much of a jerk I am. Every moment with you makes me believe in love. You take my breath away. You leave me defenseless."

I hadn't realized how much I needed to be near him and just *him* until now.

"I hate waking up and knowing it's another day where I don't get to piss you off. I would rather see you and have you hate me than to never be able to be near you again." He was beginning to run out of breath, which was weird when he could run laps easily.

"I never thought I could feel this way about someone, but here I am in the middle of this hockey arena." He looked around, his face turning red.

I begin to cry a little harder with a smile on my face, "You might change your mind again." I whisper.

He shakes his head, denying my sentence, like he wouldn't accept it. "My mind never changed."

"No girl could ever make me watch *Love Island* for hours straight. No girl could ever make me wake up in the middle of the night and kidnap their stuffed dog, just because they couldn't sleep." He makes a point as I stood there just staring.

"I know I've made mistakes in the past, but I have never changed in the way I live and breathe you. I can't take this agony any longer, Dove. I look like a damn fool in front of everyone, even you and I know that, but you don't have to say anything."

"I know I will never deserve you and I know that I've put you through shit, but I will spend the rest of my life making sure you know just how much you mean to me." Grayson trembled, staring into my eyes.

He looks around, talking a moment to swallow his pride, he curses under his breathe, "Fuck it." Then he begins to get on his knees with his hands out like he was worshiping me.

"Adrianna Elaine Cassian, please forgive me. Please take me back, I will spend the rest of my existence to show you how much you mean to me." I could see his eyes swell.

"God, I am so sorry for everything. I'm sorry for the pain I have caused you, I am sorry for making your life a living hell, I am sorry for not telling you that I have loved you the moment I set my eyes on you." He looks over at Liam who gave him two thumbs up.

"I'm sorry for not seeing that you were it for me all along." He sniffles as I let my lips curve into a warm smile.

"And... I'm sorry for accidentally ripping the sweater you made for me." He laughs through his weak voice.

I began to fall in front of him, inside his arms, laughing and crying together, *this* was it.

If I tried to push him away, I would be lying to myself. Grayson was the only one that would ever make my heart beat wild and fast.

I close my eyes, buried deep into his embrace, "I hate you." I shudder in his arms.

He laughs, "I don't care about what your father says. I don't care about what anyone says. I *want* to be selfish." He whispers, before kissing me.

I pull away, "You've owned me since we were three." I whisper, "You've been my desire ever since that day, always on my vision board." I muttered as he opened his mouth to say something.

"You are my vision board, Dove." He lets out.

His lips envelopes mine. I completely surrendered to him. Letting his tongue slick over my bottom lip, his hands dig possessively into my waist, and his arms warm up my whole body from the cold and freezing ice.

As he starts to pull away, I panic. My body pulls him in tighter. A helpless sensation rams through me as I tangle my hands into his hair. I could hear the crowd roar with applause and cheers.

I smile against his lips, before looking around at everyone's supportive, beaming faces. Margo was now near the glass with tears running down her eyes. She waves at me while I wave back, she whistles loud as our biggest supporter.

Grayson's teammates were creating chants. I looked up to my father, who was clapping his hands steadily. And my mother who was also clapping along while chanting.

Some poems don't intend on rhyming.

Some stories start in the end.

Sometimes it rains when it's not supposed to.

My life was filled with flowering and endless disasters.

Even after disaster, there is a chance to regrow. After all, a flower only grows stronger with weathering and time.

My therapist has always told me not to strive for perfection, but there was one thing close to it. At the end of the day, I am not perfect, no one really is.

But at this very moment with him, I think I've found the closest thing to near perfect.

Epilogue

GRAYSON

"Ouch!" She grips my arm as I laugh.

"You said you would be fine!"

Pain flashed through Adrianna's eyes as she lifted her hips from the tattoo bed, "I am fine!" She voices.

I roll my eyes at her obvious lies, "How's it looking over there Neil?"

Neil looks up, "Stop bothering me, Prince. Then, maybe we can finally get this done."

I bend over Adrianna's bed, so she could look at me upside down, "You look gorgeous, Dove." I let a kiss fall on her forehead as she closed her eyes.

"You guys are fucking crazy." Neil says as my eyes turn to his.

"You made sure it's mine?" I ask with a crinkled eyebrow.

"I'm pretty sure when you asked me to get your fingerprints tattooed on your girlfriend's waist, I would make sure I wouldn't mess that up."

I walk up next to him, "You better not have."

He pushes me off playfully as the whole group walks in the room, "How's she doing?" Margo asks with her fiancé's arm wrapped around her shoulder.

"Adrianna has a strict no talking rule when she's on the bed." I say as Margo nods towards me.

"She's dying, isn't she?" Verina adds as we all turn to Adrianna pulling up her middle finger to all of us.

Liam walks in, taking off his jacket, "Only you two would ever get tattoos as crazy as these." He points to my chest, the part right above my heart laid a tattoo of Adrianna's lipstick kiss stain.

"Isn't your dove tattoo and her crown tattoo good enough to show that you two are in love?" Liam adds.

I smile, "She's mine," I shrug playfully, "What can I say?"

Adrianna crossed her arms in front of her, knowing full well that she would be receiving a full punishment for that later.

"How much is this again Neil?" I asked him.

He thinks for a minute, "Two grand." He said with no emotion as I nodded, looking for my wallet.

Liam spots it on the table, my eyes widen as he picks it up, "No worries. I found it. Two grand he said?"

"Liam don't—" I warn him before he shuts the wallet with a disgusting face, throwing it at me, whilst covering his eyes.

"Oh my god! You are sick sick SICK individuals." He yells as Margo laughs.

"What is it?" She asks as Liam takes a seat, making Juliette move away from her seat.

"You don't want to know." Liam says.

I take my wallet, "My wallet has a picture of my girlfriend in her lingerie on display for my pleasure." I say as Adrianna laughs at her brother's bad luck.

"Maybe that's a sign to never touch my wallet, you wing nut." I voice as Chris walks in with a big brown bag of take out.

"I got the food!" He places it down on the table only to be greeted by Liam's shamed face.

"What happened?" He asks as everyone laughs, "Grayson and my *sister's* awful relationship that's what happened."

I roll my eyes at him, "You don't even know the half of it."

His eyes widen, hands covering his eyes, screaming.

Margo laughs, "He doesn't know about the ring attached to your necklace, does he?" She smirks cheekily as I shake my head.

Neil's buzzing ends as Adrianna sits up with a bandage on her waist, I look over to her angelic figure and stunning eyes.

"You good, Dove?"

"Better than Liam will ever be after that disaster." She laughs at the group, as Liam takes his hands off his ears.

Neil walks over to the small, short table, setting all the food out for the group to devour.

Everyone gathered around to eat, while Margo's fiancé had to leave for a business meeting as she sat next to Liam who looked at her longingly.

Chris sat across from Verina who by the looks of it would not give up until she captured his attention. But every time her eyes would steer away from him, his were always on her.

Neil sat away from Juliette who set her book down to enjoy with a lunch.

And I sat next to Adrianna whose face lit up when she saw a cereal box with the maze on the back. She makes a remark, "You know, not one cereal cartoon is a girl."

We all looked around to each other, thinking about a rebuttal or even another argument to refute her statement but evidently, she was correct.

"How about the pebble ones?" Chris asks.

She shakes her head, "No, he was a man."

"We should create our own cereal brand." I add as she smiles at me.

"And make a cartoon woman as the mascot?"

I make a confused ridden face, "Why would I do that? If it isn't broke, don't fix it." I laugh as she pushes me to fall over, only I took her down with me.

"Go to hell." She whispers, pinching me slightly.

"Are you asking me on a date? Because if you are, I would only say no in a country where there's a cereal cartoon mascot who's a girl." I wrap my arms around her, as her hand rests on my cheek.

She tries not to laugh and opts to kiss me instead.

Liam audibly gags again as I take my other arm away from Adrianna to flip him off.

With all the people who surrounded me, I was in a state of equilibrium. I wasn't home, but it certainly felt like it.

THE END.
Thank you for reading!

About the Author

LIANA TIAMZON IS A YOUNG UPCOMING AUTHOR WHO WRITES ABOUT A BEAUTIFUL TOWN FILLED WITH AMAZING CHARACTERS. SHE CREATES LOVE STORIES FULL OF HEARTBREAK AND PLOT TWISTS WHETHER THEY BE PLATONIC OR ROMANTIC. SHE GREW UP IN THE PHILIPPINES BUT CURRENTLY LIVES IN PENNSYLVANIA. SHE ENJOYS LISTENING TO MUSIC, WATCHING ROMANTIC MOVIES, AND READING ABOUT ROMANCE. SHE LOVES FINDING NEW FRIENDS AND INDULGING THEM IN HER NEW ROMANTIC FICTION STORIES.

Made in the USA
Las Vegas, NV
02 May 2024

89414154R00284